THE LAST JEDI

DATE DUE			
414069			
1621179			
1945779			

STAR WARS

THE LAST JEDI

MICHAEL REAVES
MAYA KAATHRYN BOHNHOFF

BALLANTINE BOOKS • NEW YORK

Star Wars: The Last Jedi is a work of fiction. Names, places, and incidents either are products of the author's imagination or are used fictitiously.

2013 Ballantine Books Mass Market Edition

Copyright © 2013 by Lucasfilm Ltd. & ® or ™ where indicated.
Excerpt from *Star Wars: Dawn of the Jedi: Into the Void* copyright © 2013 by Lucasfilm Ltd. & ® or ™ where indicated.

All Rights Reserved. Used Under Authorization.

Published in the United States by Del Rey, an imprint of The Random House Publishing Group, a division of Random House, Inc., New York.

DEL REY is a registered trademark and the Del Rey colophon is a trademark of Random House, Inc.

This book contains an excerpt from *Star Wars: Dawn of the Jedi: Into the Void* by Tim Lebbon. This excerpt has been set for this edition only and may not reflect the final content of the forthcoming edition.

ISBN 978-0-345-51140-9
eBook ISBN 978-0-345-53896-3

Printed in the United States of America

www.starwars.com
www.delreybooks.com
facebook.com/starwarsbooks

9 8 7 6 5 4 3 2 1

Ballantine mass market edition: March 2013

To my family, for not minding all the times
I blathered on about droids, lightsabers,
and Force-adepts. And for reminding me
that even Jedi have to eat, sleep, and do the laundry.
—MKB

This one is for Grant Fairbanks—JMR

THE STAR WARS NOVELS TIMELINE

**BEFORE THE REPUBLIC
37,000-25,000 YEARS BEFORE
STAR WARS: A New Hope**

c. 25,793 YEARS BEFORE STAR WARS: A New Hope

Dawn of the Jedi: Into the Void**

**OLD REPUBLIC
5000-67 YEARS BEFORE
STAR WARS: A New Hope**

Lost Tribe of the Sith†
Precipice
Skyborn
Paragon
Savior
Purgatory
Sentinel

3954 YEARS BEFORE STAR WARS: A New Hope

The Old Republic: Revan

3650 YEARS BEFORE STAR WARS: A New Hope

The Old Republic: Deceived

Lost Tribe of the Sith†
Pantheon
Secrets

Red Harvest
The Old Republic: Fatal Alliance
The Old Republic: Annihilation

2975 YEARS BEFORE STAR WARS: A New Hope

Lost Tribe of the Sith†
Pandemonium

1032 YEARS BEFORE STAR WARS: A New Hope

Knight Errant

Darth Bane: Path of Destruction
Darth Bane: Rule of Two
Darth Bane: Dynasty of Evil

**RISE OF THE EMPIRE
67-0 YEARS BEFORE
STAR WARS: A New Hope**

67 YEARS BEFORE STAR WARS: A New Hope

Darth Plagueis

33 YEARS BEFORE STAR WARS: A New Hope

Darth Maul: Saboteur*
Cloak of Deception
Darth Maul: Shadow Hunter

32 YEARS BEFORE STAR WARS: A New Hope

**STAR WARS: EPISODE I
THE PHANTOM MENACE**

Rogue Planet
Outbound Flight
The Approaching Storm

22 YEARS BEFORE STAR WARS: A New Hope

**STAR WARS: EPISODE II
ATTACK OF THE CLONES**

22-19 YEARS BEFORE STAR WARS: A New Hope

The Clone Wars
The Clone Wars: Wild Space
The Clone Wars: No Prisoners

Clone Wars Gambit
Stealth
Siege

Republic Commando
Hard Contact
Triple Zero
True Colors
Order 66

Shatterpoint
The Cestus Deception
The Hive*
MedStar I: Battle Surgeons
MedStar II: Jedi Healer
Jedi Trial
Yoda: Dark Rendezvous
Labyrinth of Evil

19 YEARS BEFORE STAR WARS: A New Hope

**STAR WARS: EPISODE III
REVENGE OF THE SITH**

Dark Lord: The Rise of Darth Vader

Imperial Commando
501st

Coruscant Nights
Jedi Twilight
Street of Shadows
Patterns of Force

The Last Jedi**

*An eBook novella
**Forthcoming
† Lost Tribe of the Sith: The
  Collected Stories

19 YEARS BEFORE STAR WARS: A New Hope

The Han Solo Trilogy
  The Paradise Snare
  The Hutt Gambit
  Rebel Dawn

The Adventures of Lando Calrissian
The Force Unleashed
The Han Solo Adventures
Death Troopers
The Force Unleashed II

**REBELLION
0–5 YEARS AFTER
STAR WARS: A New Hope**

Death Star
Shadow Games

0

**STAR WARS: EPISODE IV
A NEW HOPE**

Tales from the Mos Eisley Cantina
Tales from the Empire
Tales from the New Republic
Winner Lose All*
Scoundrels
Allegiance
Choices of One
Galaxies: The Ruins of Dantooine
Splinter of the Mind's Eye

3 YEARS AFTER STAR WARS: A New Hope

**STAR WARS: EPISODE V
THE EMPIRE STRIKES BACK**

Tales of the Bounty Hunters
Shadows of the Empire

4 YEARS AFTER STAR WARS: A New Hope

**STAR WARS: EPISODE VI
THE RETURN OF THE JEDI**

Tales from Jabba's Palace

The Bounty Hunter Wars
  The Mandalorian Armor
  Slave Ship
  Hard Merchandise

The Truce at Bakura
Luke Skywalker and the Shadows of
Mindor

**NEW REPUBLIC
5–25 YEARS AFTER
STAR WARS: A New Hope**

X-Wing
  Rogue Squadron
  Wedge's Gamble
  The Krytos Trap
  The Bacta War
  Wraith Squadron
  Iron Fist
  Solo Command

The Courtship of Princess Leia
A Forest Apart*
Tatooine Ghost

The Thrawn Trilogy
  Heir to the Empire
  Dark Force Rising
  The Last Command

X-Wing: Isard's Revenge

The Jedi Academy Trilogy
  Jedi Search
  Dark Apprentice
  Champions of the Force

I, Jedi
Children of the Jedi
Darksaber
Planet of Twilight
X-Wing: Starfighters of Adumar
The Crystal Star

The Black Fleet Crisis Trilogy
  Before the Storm
  Shield of Lies
  Tyrant's Test

The New Rebellion

The Corellian Trilogy
  Ambush at Corellia
  Assault at Selonia
  Showdown at Centerpoint

The Hand of Thrawn Duology
  Specter of the Past
  Vision of the Future

Scourge
Fool's Bargain*
Survivor's Quest

*An eBook novella

THE STAR WARS NOVELS TIMELINE

NEW JEDI ORDER
25–40 YEARS AFTER
STAR WARS: A New Hope

Boba Fett: A Practical Man*

The New Jedi Order
Vector Prime
Dark Tide I: Onslaught
Dark Tide II: Ruin
Agents of Chaos I: Hero's Trial
Agents of Chaos II: Jedi Eclipse
Balance Point
Recovery*
Edge of Victory I: Conquest
Edge of Victory II: Rebirth
Star by Star
Dark Journey
Enemy Lines I: Rebel Dream
Enemy Lines II: Rebel Stand
Traitor
Destiny's Way
Ylesia*
Force Heretic I: Remnant
Force Heretic II: Refugee
Force Heretic III: Reunion
The Final Prophecy
The Unifying Force

35 | YEARS AFTER STAR WARS: A New Hope

The Dark Nest Trilogy
The Joiner King
The Unseen Queen
The Swarm War

LEGACY
40+ YEARS AFTER
STAR WARS: A New Hope

Legacy of the Force
Betrayal
Bloodlines
Tempest
Exile
Sacrifice
Inferno
Fury
Revelation
Invincible

Crosscurrent

Riptide

Millennium Falcon

43 | YEARS AFTER STAR WARS: A New Hope

Fate of the Jedi
Outcast
Omen
Abyss
Backlash
Allies
Vortex
Conviction
Ascension
Apocalypse

X-Wing: Mercy Kill

45 | YEARS AFTER STAR WARS: A New Hope

Crucible**

*An eBook novella
**Forthcoming

Dramatis Personae

Aren Folee; Antarian Ranger (human female)
Darth Vader; Sith Lord and Emperor Palpatine's enforcer (human male)
Degan Cor; Toprawan resistance leader (human male)
Den Dhur; former journalist (Sullustan male)
Geri; resistance mech-tech (teenaged Rodian male)
I-Five; sentient protocol droid
Jax Pavan; Jedi Knight (human male)
Laranth Tarak; Gray Paladin (Twi'lek female)
Magash Drashi; Dathomiri Witch of the Singing Mountain Clan (Zabrak-human female)
Pol Haus; sector police prefect (Zabrak male)
Prince Xizor; Black Sun Vigo (Faleen male)
Probus Tesla; Inquisitor (human male)
Sacha Swiftbird; Antarian Ranger (human female)
Sheel Mafeen; poetess (Togruta female)
Thi Xon Yimmon; Whiplash leader (Cerean male)
Tuden Sal; Whiplash operative (Sakiyan male)
Tyno Fabris; Black Sun lieutenant (Arkanian male)

A long time ago in a galaxy far, far away. . . .

"The Jedi are extinct; their fire has gone out in the universe."

—GRAND MOFF TARKIN

PART ONE

VASTER THAN EMPIRES

one

"Sakiyan freighter *Far Ranger* requesting clearance for departure."

I-Five's mimicry of Tuden Sal's gruff voice was flawless. No one listening—or, more to the point, no vocal analyzer scanning—would know that, in reality, the Sakiyan merchant was sitting in a safe house somewhere in the twilight warren near the Westport, plotting infamy against the Empire. No one, that was, except for the *Far Ranger*'s crew and her lone passenger.

Jax Pavan, his hands on the *Far Ranger*'s steering yoke, realized he was holding his breath as he waited for the Westport flight dispatcher to approve their departure plan. He let his tension go with a soft rush of air and ignored the urge to reach out with the Force to give the dispatcher a nudge. It was tempting, but best not to take the chance. Even something as minor as that could alert Darth Vader to their movements . . . if Vader was, against all odds, still alive.

Jax believed that he was. Even though he hadn't sensed the Dark Lord's uniquely powerful indentation in the fabric of the Force lately, it was difficult to conceive of such power, such concentrated evil, being gone, being over, being *done*. And until he gazed upon Vader's corpse with his own eyes, until he could reach out and touch him with the tendrils that constituted his own connection with the living Force and sense no reciprocation . . .

Well, until that came to pass, Jax knew he couldn't be too careful.

And speaking of erring on the side of caution . . . was the silence on the comlink just a little too long? Had someone suspicious of the freighter's relatively new Sakiyan registry connected the ship to Jax Pavan?

Am I overthinking this?

"*Far Ranger,* your ascent plan is approved. Your departure window is . . ."

There was a pause, and Jax held his breath again. I-Five glanced at him and let two pearls of luminescence migrate, left to right, along the top outside rims of his photoreceptors—the droid's equivalent of rolling his eyes.

"Ten standard minutes—on my mark."

"Aye," said I-Five.

"Mark."

"Beginning ascent." I-Five cut the comlink and turned to Jax. "She's all yours. And not a single battle cruiser on our tail, that I can see."

Jax ignored the droid's sarcasm. His left hand eased forward on the thruster control as his right pulled up and back on the steering yoke. The ship, a modified Corellian Action VI transport, lifted from the spaceport docking bay into the night sky, which, even at this elevation, was a blaze of ambient light. Jax felt the vibration of the ship through the yoke, felt it merge with his desire to be away from Coruscant until it seemed to him that *Far Ranger* itself yearned above all things to leap into hyperspace before even clearing the atmosphere.

The sky changed. It warmed to twilight, to daybreak, to full day, then cycled back again through dusk and twilight as they soared, finally, into the flat black of space. They saw no stars; the glorious blaze of the city-planet's night side was enough to drown out even the nearby nebulae of the Core completely.

I-Five sent a last message back to Flight Control in Tuden Sal's gravelly tones: "*Far Ranger* away."

"Aye. Clear skies."

The droid shut down the comlink and Jax navigated above the orbital plane, adjusted course, and set the autopilot to their first jump coordinates. Then he sat back to clear his head.

He felt a touch—in his mind and on his arm. Laranth. He turned his head to look up at her. She was grinning at him—or at least, she was doing something that was as close to grinning as she was likely to get. One whole corner of her mouth had curled upward by at least a millimeter.

"Nervous, are we?" she asked. "I could feel you angsting all the way up in the weaponry bay."

"What were you doing up there?"

"Getting the feel of the new triggering mechanism."

"Nervous, are we?" Jax mimicked, smiling.

"Being proactive." She gave his arm a squeeze and glanced out the viewport. "I'll be glad to be out of this gravity well. Too much traffic here by half. Any one of those ships—" She nodded toward their closest companions in flight: a Toydarian grain transport, another Corellian freighter, a private yacht. "—could be targeting us right now."

"You're being paranoid," Jax assured her. "If Vader were watching us, I'd know. *We'd* know."

"Vader watching us—now, *there's* a cheery thought." Den Dhur stepped onto the bridge and slid into the jump seat behind Jax. "I'm hoping he's watching us from beyond the crematorium."

"Paranoia," I-Five said. "Another human emotion I just don't get. The list of things both animate and in-

animate in this galaxy that are capable of utterly anni-
hilating you is longer than a superstring . . . yet real
danger evidently isn't enough: you organics aren't happy
without making up a bevy of bogeymen to scare you
even more."

Jax said nothing. In the months since their last confrontation with the Dark Lord—a confrontation in
which one of their Whiplash team had betrayed them
and another self-immolated trying to assassinate Vader—
they had heard not even a whisper about either his
whereabouts or his condition. There had been no re-
ports on the HoloNet, no rumors from highly placed
officials, no speculation or stories by various life-forms
in places like the Blackpit Slums or the Southern Underground. It was as if the very concept of Vader had vanished along with his corporeal form.

And yet Jax still couldn't believe that his nemesis was
dead, as much as he wanted to. The entire scenario had
been *too* perfect. In the thrall of a potent drug that enhanced Force abilities in unpredictable ways, Vader had
lashed out wildly, trying to fend off his would-be assassin. The release of energy had been enough to vaporize
the unfortunate Haninum Tyk Rhinann, who'd pushed
Vader over the edge—in more ways than one. Both of
them had fallen a great distance. Rhinann had died.

Vader had vanished.

If Darth Vader had been a normal human being—or
even a normal Jedi—Jax could assume he was dead, as
well. But he was neither of those things. He was at once
less and more than human. At once less and more than
a Jedi. He was a powerful merger of the human and the
inhuman. He was a Sith . . . who had once called Jax
friend. For Jax suspected—no, *more* than suspected,
knew—that Darth Vader had somehow once been Anakin Skywalker. He had sensed it through the Force, and

in their last encounter Vader had confirmed it with a slip of the tongue that might well have been intentional.

The man who wouldn't die.

"You going to share that load with us, Jax?" Den was looking at him with eyes that only seemed lazy. "Have you sensed anything about Vader since . . ." The Sullustan made a *boom* gesture with both stubby-fingered hands.

Jax shook his head. "Nothing. But Den, if he'd died, I think I'd know that. There would have been a huge shift in the Force if a being of that much focused power was destroyed."

"I saw the flaming backwash from ground zero," Den objected. "That wasn't a shift?"

"No, that was a light show. Mostly flash, with a little substance. It was enough to kill Rhinann. But I don't think it killed Vader."

The Sullustan looked to Laranth. "No joy from you, either?"

"Sorry, Den. I'm of the same opinion. He might be severely injured and in a bacta tank somewhere, but he's not dead. The most we can hope for is that he'll be out of commission long enough for us to get Yimmon to safety."

"You just came from Yimmon, didn't you?" Jax asked Den, and at the Sullustan's nod, he added, "How does he seem?"

Den shrugged. "About like you'd expect a guy to seem who's been nearly dead four times in the last three weeks."

Jax took a deep breath and let it out slowly. Those near-hits were why they were removing Thi Xon Yimmon from Coruscant. The leader of the anti-Imperial resistance cell known locally as Whiplash had been targeted a number of times in the past weeks by Imperial forces. In two cases, only the fact that Jax and his team had a friend on the police force—a Zabrak prefect named Pol Haus—had tipped them to the threat in time to avoid it.

In a twisted way, the Imperial attention to Whiplash—and Yimmon in particular—was flattering. It meant they had risen from mere annoyances to serious threats. Perhaps the Empire had even made the connection between the local resistance on Imperial Center and the broader movement that was springing up on a growing number of far-flung worlds. In practical terms, this meant that—over the last several months—the Imperial orders had gone from "shoot 'em if they get in the way" to "ferret them out, track them down, and destroy them."

The Emperor had also changed tactics. Absent from these recent attempts at annihilation were the Force-sniffing, raptorlike Inquisitors. Now the attacks came from Force-insensitive bounty hunters and battle droids. It was as if, having failed to turn the gifts of the Force against Yimmon and his cohort, the Emperor was simply throwing every mundane weapon in his arsenal at them.

Jax wanted to believe that these were the acts of a desperate tyrant who had just lost his most potent weapon. He wanted to believe it as much as he wanted to believe that Vader was gone. But . . .

The man who wouldn't die.

He shook himself, realizing he had come to think of Darth Vader as inevitable . . . and immortal.

Whatever hideous truth lay behind that feeling, Jax could not let it distract him from the hard reality that the Empire wanted Whiplash dead and buried. The Empire, being the hierarchical beast that it was, figured this was best done by destroying the brains of the organization. But Yimmon—with his dual cortex and a personal cell of operatives that included a Jedi, a Gray Paladin, and a sentient droid—was a hard man to kill or capture. Still, the last attempt had come close. Too close. *Way* too close. It had taken out several storefronts and more than a dozen innocent citizens who happened to be too near a tavern that the Whiplash had used to pass messages.

Jax couldn't shake the memory of the street in the aftermath of that attack. The bodies littering the walkway, the sharp smell of ozone in the heavy air, the photonic imprints of people on the walls of the buildings, reverse shadows caught at the instant of death. The hushed sense that the entire neighborhood was holding its breath, readying a roar of outrage . . . a roar that would fall on deaf ears.

Outrage against the Empire seemed futile; Jax had to believe it was not.

The decision to move the resistance leader from Imperial Center had been almost unanimous. The sole dissenting voice had belonged to Yimmon himself. Only a great deal of convincing had finally gotten him to agree that relocating their base of operations to Dantooine was the wisest move.

And none too soon.

Jax shook off the feeling of dread that threatened to settle over him. For the hundredth time that day, he opened his mouth to tell Laranth about the "summons" he'd gotten three days earlier from a Cephalon Whiplash informant. But caution and Den's presence kept the words from his tongue.

"I'm going to go back and talk to Yimmon," he said, rising. "Take the helm?"

Laranth nodded and slid into his seat. Jax turned to I-Five. "Ping me when we're about to jump to hyperspace, okay?"

"You don't trust us to enter the corridor correctly?" asked the droid.

Laranth merely looked at Jax through her large, peridot-colored eyes.

"Of *course* I trust you. I just need a front-row seat for the jump. Yeah, I know it's not rational," he added when I-Five made a testy clicking sound. "I just need to see the stars change. That all right with you?"

"As you wish," droid and Twi'lek said in eerie unison.

Jax thought he heard Den Dhur chuckle softly.

He found Thi Xon Yimmon sitting at a duraplast table fashioned to look like wood. It looked like wood for no other reason than that Jax liked wood. On extended missions in space—which seemed to happen increasingly as resistance activity picked up and spread—he wanted to be reminded that somewhere there were worlds with forests alive and growing.

He had a real tree in his quarters—a tiny thing in a ceramic pot. It was a gift from Laranth and was many hundreds of years old, though it remained tiny. I-Five had shown Jax how the masters of an ancient art form called miisai trimmed and guided the branches. Jax had learned to do it using delicate tendrils of the Force. The practice had become a meditation. So, too, had going through the forms of lightsaber combat with his new weapon—a lightsaber he and Laranth had constructed using a crystal that had come to him from an unexpected source. The weapon's weight was a comforting presence against his hip; no less comforting than being able to stow the Sith blade he'd been using.

He'd had no time to meditate in the last two days. He'd told himself it was because of their aggressive time line for moving Yimmon offworld. He knew better. It was because meditating led to thinking about the message the Cephalon had given him.

*   *   *

Time, for a Cephalon, was a somewhat malleable substance. "Plastic," a philosopher or physicist might have said. Den called it "squishy." Whatever modifier seemed most appropriate, it all came down to the same thing: Cephalons "saw" time as other sentients saw spatial relationships. Something might be before you or behind you or beside you, but if you turned your head to look, it was visible. If you walked around an object, you could see different sides of it—gain different perspectives. A crude analogy, but approximate to the way Cephalons saw time. A moment might be before them or behind them or on top of them—future or past or present—yet they could but turn their immensely complex minds and perceive it, move around it, and view it from different points.

This perception might—or might not—have had something to do with the fact that Cephalons had what was known variously as augmented or punctuated intelligence. This meant that they had, in addition to one big brain, several "sub-brains"—ganglionic nodes, really—that took care of more atavistic body functions and left the big brain free to do . . . well, whatever it did.

Through his connection to the Force, Jax had occasionally come close to grasping the reality of this, but even a Jedi couldn't fathom the precise nature of the Cephalons' relationship to time. And, alas, what Cephalons could *not* do terribly well was communicate what they perceived. Tenses were lost on them. What happened the previous day or last century was as "present" as something that would happen the next day or a century in the future. And since they were linked to one another through the Force, a Cephalon might very well be able to "see" something that hadn't happened or would not happen in its own lifetime.

Which was why receiving a message from a Cephalon Whiplash operative before a major mission was, to Jax

Pavan, a severe test of his Jedi patience. He often sent the more dispassionate I-Five to interview Cephalons, but this time that hadn't been an option. When Jax had received this message, I-Five had been off with Den Dhur and Tuden Sal, securing a series of bogus ship's ident codes that might be needed for their journey to Dantooine. So he'd gone by himself back into their old neighborhood near Ploughtekal Market to meet with a Cephalon who'd installed itself in a residence that catered to non-oxygen-breathing life-forms. Cephalons preferred methane and liked their atmosphere a little on, as Den put it, the "chewy" side.

Jax had arrived at the Cephalon's address in heavy disguise. To outsiders he appeared to be an Elomin diplomat—just the sort of visitor a Cephalon might be expected to have. Diplomats and politicians were always looking for an edge when it came to future—or past—events. The Cephalons had no scruples about divulging information. They merely were incapable of communicating it clearly.

Jax found the alien in a loft that was considered grand by Cephalon standards. Within the methane-infused habitat, it kept a variety of kinetic fountains, sculptures, and art wall displays. The Cephalons liked movement. The huge being—whose designation, Aoloiloa, loosely meant "the one before Lo and after Il"—lived behind a huge glass-walled barrier in which it floated in its soup of methane like a gigantic, mottled gray melon. It ate and communicated via a baleen that strained nutrients from the methane soup and vibrated to give form to thoughts that were displayed on a panel in an antechamber outside its inner sanctum. The name, Jax knew, was for the benefit of other sentients the Cephalons interacted with—a means for those temporally challenged souls to distinguish between individuals. Presumably the Cephalons had their own mysterious way of doing that.

Jax had announced himself using the translation device next to the Cephalon's display panel.

"I, being Jax Pavan, come as bidden." *Now warn me of an Imperial plot.*

The Cephalon, of course, did nothing of the kind. Instead, it asked a question: *Depart you (have/will)?*

Jax blinked. Clearly a question about a future event. "Yes."

—*Crux.* The word typed itself onto the display panel.

"Crux?" repeated Jax. "What kind of crux?"

—*Nexus,* said Aoloiloa. *Locus. Dark crosses/has crossed/will cross light.*

"Yes, I know what a crux is. What does it mean—in this case?"

—*At crux: Choice is/has been/will be loss. Indecision is/has been/will be all loss.*

Jax waited, but the Cephalon did not elaborate.

"What does that mean: 'Choice is loss. Indecision is all loss'?"

—*It means what it means. Everything.*

Jax kept his thoughts composed with effort. *Listen,* he told himself. *Listen.* "Whose choice?" he asked. "Whose indecision? Mine?"

—*Choice upon choice. Decision upon decision. Indecision is/was/will be cumulative.*

"Indecision over a period of time? Or the cumulative indecision of a number of people?"

The Cephalon bobbed up and down slowly, then turned away from the transparisteel barrier that protected it from the oxygen-nitrogen atmosphere of Coruscant.

So, silently, Jax had been dismissed. He'd walked back to the art gallery and event center that served as

Whiplash headquarters pondering the Cephalon's words: *Choice is loss; indecision is all loss.*

Any way he interpreted that, it did not sound good.

Jax stopped in the hatchway of the *Far Ranger*'s crew's commons, studying the Whiplash leader where he sat at the faux-wood table. "You're still not resigned to this, are you?" he asked finally.

"Would you be, if you were being asked to relocate and leave the heart of your operations? The only reason I agreed to this is that if the Emperor suspects I've moved, he may focus his efforts on finding me and give the network on Coruscant some relief."

"The attack near Sil's Place was too close, Yimmon. And the loss of innocent life involved . . ."

The Cerean nodded wearily. "Yes. That, too. That bloodbath was . . . unforgivable. That he would send battle droids, have them kill indiscriminately and widely . . ."

"Apparently, they knew we were in the area, but their information wasn't precise enough to target effectively. Photonic charges gave them a shot at killing some of us without extreme damage to the infrastructure." Jax couldn't quite keep the sarcasm out of his voice.

"Maybe. And maybe . . ."

"What?"

The Cerean shook his immense head. "You said it yourself once: It felt as if the Emperor was desperate. If Vader is out of the way for a while and the Inquisitors can't track us without you sensing them, that makes some sense, but . . ."

Jax felt a niggle of unease but shook it off. He'd understood the Cephalon's warning, he told himself, and heeded it.

"Are you suggesting the Emperor might not be as desperate as he seems?" Jax asked Yimmon.

The Cerean sighed, his breath rumbling deep in his

broad, muscular chest. "Let us just say that I have never known Emperor Palpatine to be prone to panic. But—as I said—with his champion out of the way . . ."

"Any more intel from our informants?"

"None. No one has seen Vader or heard so much as a rumor about his condition since your last meeting."

Their last meeting—in which Vader had tried to punish Jax for still being Jedi, in which he had cultivated a traitor within Jax's team, in which he had tried to make use of a rare biological agent to enhance his own connection to the Force. Jax found it ironic that, in his unenhanced state, Vader might have succeeded in capturing or killing him . . . along with all his companions. But the Dark Lord had overreached and defeated himself. There was a lesson in that about hubris and impatience. Jax wondered if Anakin Skywalker—imprisoned in that towering black survival suit, held together by cybernetic implants—would recognize it.

"Then this is a window of opportunity," said Jax. "To be timid now . . ."

"Timid?" Yimmon laughed. "Am I not showing timidity by running?"

"No. You're showing wisdom. Whiplash needs you. The growing resistance needs you. The Emperor's flailing around almost got you killed."

Thi Xon Yimmon looked up at Jax with steady eyes the color of old bronze. "What if he is not flailing around, Jax? What if there *is* a method to these attacks?"

Jax pushed away the cold that tried to invade his core. "Then we'll remove ourselves from harm's way. Look, Yimmon, if he'd known Sil's Place was the pass-through for our operatives, he would have simply taken it off the map. If he'd known where our base of operations was, he would have sent his bounty hunters and his battle droids and his Inquisitors there and killed us in our sleep. What could he possibly have to gain by plunging randomly around like a rancor in bloodlust?"

"Perhaps what he *has* gained—my leaving Coruscant. My disconnecting myself from the battle long enough to relocate and regroup. Long enough for *him* to regroup. This may be a window of opportunity for the Emperor, too."

Jax levered himself away from the hatch frame. "I've told you, if you want my team to stay with you on Dantooine—"

The Whiplash leader shook his head wearily. "No. Tuden Sal needs you on Coruscant. He's unhappy enough that you're the one serving as my nursemaid on this voyage. He's right. I'd talk you out of this if I could. I'd like to have our best near Palpatine . . . and Vader, if he re-emerges."

If? No, not *if*. Jax knew it was really only a matter of when.

two

Their route to Dantooine had been decided in a heated consultation during which Laranth and I-Five argued for a direct shot into Wild Space and from there into Myto's Arrow, while Tuden Sal and Thi Xon Yimmon counseled that they take a more mundane approach along a heavily traveled trade lane.

Myto's Arrow was a narrow corridor that would take them from the fringes of the galaxy directly to Dantooine through a patch of unstable space stressed by the gravitational tides of a particularly violent binary star system most pilots called simply the Twins. Its saving virtue was that the heavily fluctuating magnetic fields around the binary pair cloaked any attitude changes a ship made as it passed by. Theoretically, a master pilot with an enemy in hot pursuit could flee into the binary's gravity coil, drop out of hyperspace just long enough to make a radical course change, then leap again in a completely different direction while the pursuer tried to figure out which way he'd gone.

The mere mention of Myto's Arrow made Tuden Sal's face pucker. His recommendation that they make port on Bandomeer made Laranth's eyes roll.

"There's still a pronounced Imperial presence on Bandomeer, Sal," she had objected. "After Vader crushed the miners' revolt last year, the Emperor has kept a watchful eye on things."

"Which is why no one would expect a ship full of subversives to make port there," Sal argued. "You would be just one more cargo ship doing its mundane business in an Imperial port."

Ultimately, Thi Xon Yimmon had made the call. "What's less remarkable than a freighter stopping at regular ports of call? I think Sal's right. If anyone does suspect *Far Ranger* of being anything more than what she seems, they may well have lost interest when all we do is drop into a series of ports to off-load and take on cargo."

And so they had ended up here, on the well-plied Hydian Way, headed out toward the Corporate Sector . . . except that they had no intention of going that far. They would make port on Bandomeer, communicate briefly with the nascent resistance cell there, then move on, stopping sequentially at Botajef, Celanon, Feriae Junction, and Toprawa, where they would contact the remnant of the Antarian Rangers.

The Rangers—little less reviled by the Emperor than the Jedi—had disappeared from the Empire's scanners, but they were far from dead. There was, in Jax Pavan's heart, a deep but fragile hope that perhaps the same was true of the Jedi. That perhaps he was not, as he often suspected, the last one.

At Bandomeer there was, indeed, an Imperial presence. There were also one or two Inquisitors, which meant that Jax and Laranth remained aboard *Far Ranger* in a state of dormancy. I-Five and Den carried out the playacting necessary to barter for ionite—which also resulted in contact and an exchange of information with members of the Bandomeer version of Whiplash.

Ionite was a substance of extraordinary properties— it canceled out whatever charge it was presented with, be it negative or positive—which made it ideal for defeating such devices as shield generators and communications grids. It had also proved an effective component in weaponry, which made it valuable to the resistance.

Cargo holds full of ore and ingots, *Far Ranger* lifted again and continued her sojourn, making several ports of call along the Hydian Way and navigating the final leg with an amount of ionite sufficient to the needs of their allies on Toprawa.

They made Toprawa ten days after leaving Coruscant—their plan: to pause there before backtracking slightly to pick up the Thesme Trace toward Dantooine. Toprawa was a world whose temperate zones were covered with lush forests that encroached on every port and outpost. The small spaceport they called at was on the outskirts of Big Woolly township in the cool northern reaches of a major landmass. "Big Woolly," Jax had learned, was a reference to the appearance of the nearby mountain range, with its fleece of native conifers. They elected to berth away from the main docking complex on an open landing pad, intending to call as little attention to themselves as possible.

It was near sunset when Jax debarked from *Far Ranger* to find himself surrounded by massive conifers whose sweet, tangy perfume overwhelmed the mechanical scents of the spaceport. He was overwhelmed, as well, by the sheer vividness and vitality of the forest. It was neither as lofty as the growth on the Wookiee homeworld, Kashyyyk, nor as lush as the rain forests of Rodia, but it wrapped the constructed artifacts of the spaceport with teeming life. It was exhilarating and soothing at once, and Jax wished, for a moment, that they could simply stay here—all of them—and make Toprawa their new headquarters.

"Majestic, aren't they?" Yimmon was at his elbow, gazing across the durasteel landing pad at the sentinel spikes of ruddy bark and blue-green foliage, now tinged with gold from the planet's lowering sun. "And amazing how something as massive and enduring as those trees should also be flexible enough to bend to the wind."

Jax took in that feature of the surrounding giants. Deeply rooted, ancient, strong, and connected to the larger force of nature, yet they bowed and shifted at the invisible promptings of wind and weather. He supposed there was a lesson of some sort there.

"I envy the Rangers their capital." Yimmon sighed. "Though Dantooine is not unpleasant."

Jax smiled. "Does this remind you of home?"

The Cerean nodded. "Still, I've rarely seen trees this tall on my homeworld. There is a vibrancy here that is . . . intoxicating."

Jax had to agree. The cool, moist air was heady. He breathed deeply of it. It reminded him of the scent given off by his tiny miisai tree when he caressed its branches with his fingers . . . or with the Force.

"They say," Yimmon said, "that the Force flows in the sap of forests like these."

"Who says?" Laranth came out onto the landing ramp to survey the Toprawan landscape.

"Ki-Adi-Mundi, for one," said Yimmon. A member of the Jedi High Council, Ki-Adi—a Cerean—had led the Grand Army of the Republic through several key battles, only to die in the violence and treachery of Order 66. He was a particular hero of Thi Xon Yimmon.

Laranth smiled. Jax knew what she was thinking—how bemusing that a man of Yimmon's heroic stature should have heroes of his own.

"Well, then," she said, "if General Ki-Adi said it, it must be so." She stretched out a hand toward the trees and closed her eyes as if testing the truth of her own hero's words.

Curious, Jax reached out as well with tendrils of the

Force, probing the fringes of the forest, caressing the branches and boughs, feeling the texture of bark and needle, tasting the life force of the sap.

Yes. It was there—a silken fabric of Force energy. Like a murmur of sound, an undercurrent of vibration, an ambient throb of light. It was lovely. Cool and deep as the shadows . . .

Shadows.

His thoughts eddied. Had there been a flicker—the merest shiver—of something not of the forest?

Jax blinked and glanced about the landing pad. Another vessel—meters away—had just drawn in its landing ramp and was revving up its engines. Perhaps the ripple in the energy of Toprawa's verdure had come from there.

"Are we going to stand here all night admiring the scenery?" I-Five exited the ship with a whisper of servos. "I had thought we were supposed to make contact with an important customer?"

"Yeah, the sun's going down," said Den. "Aren't we supposed to see a lady about some ore?"

Jax nodded. He thought about the fleeting extrasensory impression that he'd just encountered, and decided it must have been some eddy or backwash. "Right. Laranth and I will make contact. I-Five, if you could get the cargo ready to off-load . . ."

"Consider it done."

Disguised, Jax and Laranth made their way to Big Woolly. The small city had grown up around the spaceport—a crescent of tightly clustered businesses and homes that fanned out from the port facility, roughly five kilometers across at its widest point. The inn at which they were to meet their contact was at the northern tip of the crescent along a curving avenue whose businesses catered largely to merchants. It was a respectable meeting place for successful shipowners and merchants. Hence, the disguises that Jax and Laranth had adopted allowed them to fit into the clientele.

Jax, in a tailored synthsilk suit and gleaming black boots, looked the part of a successful freighter captain. Laranth, ostensibly his business partner, wore the flowing, diaphanous robes that declared her a member of a merchant clan. She'd also affected a pair of vivid orange, silky, bell-trimmed mantles over her lekku, thus effectively concealing both her truncated left lekku and her emotions. The damaged lekku was an old injury Laranth had received in a firefight; it was also an identifying feature that she usually declined to mask. Now, though, it was critical to conceal both identity and telltale changes in hue. Her blasters were concealed; Jax had left his lightsaber with I-Five. This was not the sort of place one advertised the bearing of arms, and he wanted no one to suspect that he was a Jedi.

As part of her headgear, Laranth also wore a medallion that, like the lekku mantles it adorned, was more than just stage dressing. It was a sigil that was meaningful only to its intended target—an Antarian Ranger.

They entered the large main room of the Mossy Glen Inn and looked around. Jax smiled. How different this was from entering Sil's Place, where everyone contrived to look at you without seeming to look at you—or the Twilight Taverna off Ploughtekal Market, where everyone in the room turned to assess each newcomer's potential to be exploited in some fashion. Here, they drew only the most casual of glances. Jax sensed momentary admiration of their physical appearance, but no clandestine regard.

The variety of sentients was not remarkable in any way—there were life-forms from a dozen worlds, though human colonists seemed the best-represented group. All were well dressed and well curried—to their species' standards—and all seemed to be enjoying a good meal, a good drink, a good laugh, or a good haggle.

Laranth looked around the room with a brisk, businesslike gaze, then led the way to a staircase that rose upward into the softly lit reaches of a second floor. It was quieter up here, and duskier. Little lamps flickered on the tables, and a huge fireplace at the far end of the room sent light and shadow dancing over every surface. The shadows would not stand still and be recognized as one thing or another.

Ambiguity. Jax found it suddenly discomfiting, for reasons he had no time to contemplate. He felt a subtle shift in Laranth's energies—a sharpening of her regard. She strode down the length of the room to a semicircular booth at the right flank of the great hearth. Jax followed.

A woman sat at the booth. She was dressed in a sleek cutaway coat with synthfur collar and cuffs. Her hair was drawn back in a tight coil at the nape of her neck, and her gray eyes were bright and assessing. Jax suspected that the skirt of her coat concealed a number of weapons.

Laranth inclined her head. "Greetings. Do I have the pleasure of addressing Aren Folee?"

"You do," replied the other woman, dipping her own head minutely. "And you are . . ."

"Pala D'ukal," said Laranth. "This is my partner, Corran Vigil."

Folee nodded in greeting. Her expression was one of polite interest, no more.

"We bring a message from a common friend. A Cerean gentleman of your acquaintance, recently from Imperial Center."

Folee's eyes lit. "How is he?"

"He is well. He speaks highly of you and recommends that we do business."

Folee indicated the seats opposite her. "Please."

They slid into the booth.

"How confidential are our dealings?" Jax asked, glancing around the subtly lit room.

Folee didn't answer right away. Instead, she reached up and palmed a medallion she wore around her neck on a thick metal torque. "Very confidential now," she said. "If anyone's snooping, they're getting only the most deadly boring of trade talks fabricated from our actual conversation. So we ought to discuss a bit of trade to give the dialogue generator some fuel."

Jax was intrigued. He'd heard rumors about the sort of antisurveillance device they were apparently now being screened by. Its ionite circuitry didn't so much jam snoop signals as feed them cobbled-together dialogues that made use of the raw material of actual conversation. It required only that the speakers clutter their verbal trail with just enough innocuous debris to fool potential eavesdroppers. The device screened out programmed "hot" words and phrases but, as far as any surveillance systems were concerned, no jamming was taking place.

"Nothing could be easier," said Laranth. "As it happens, we've got a cargo hold that contains enough ionite to gum up a whole shipload of surveillance snoops."

"And in return?"

"One of those lovely medallions you're wearing, for one thing," said Laranth. "We could really use that tech at home."

"And information," Jax said, "about the Imperial presence in the sector."

Folee grimaced. "Well, there is a presence, or at least the dregs of one. Messed up my last big mission really good. Killed a lot of resources—both material and personal."

"Understood," Jax said. "We've sustained our own

losses . . . which is, frankly, the reason our mutual friend is moving his base of operations."

"To?"

"As any pilot would say: to the point." Jax drew on the tabletop with one fingertip. A long diagonal line. He dotted the end of it with a sharp tap.

Folee frowned, then nodded in comprehension. "Any pilot" would know that the planet at the "point" of Myto's Arrow was Dantooine. She glanced up, caught the attention of a serving droid, and ordered drinks and a plate of finger food—necessary items for serious and amicable negotiations.

When the droid had trundled off with their order, the Ranger leaned toward Jax and Laranth, looking from one face to the other. "Does this move mean that we are close to incorporating our efforts and moving against our competitors together?"

The question was earnest and had behind it the weight of deep and visceral disappointment and loss. Aren Folee may have spoken casually of the killing of resources, but her feelings about it were far from casual.

Jax exchanged a glance with Laranth. "Closer, perhaps. Very close to orchestrating those efforts more effectively, at least. That was one of the incentives our friend had in relocating. Where he *was* based . . ."

"Was increasingly bad for his health," Laranth finished. "Communication with satellite organizations was difficult at times. Though there is something to be said for hiding in plain sight—"

"Or getting lost in a crowd," added Jax. "Unfortunately, our . . . competitors are making it hard to stay lost."

Folee nodded thoughtfully. "Communication is not an issue here. We have a most effective network that gets to the point quite efficiently. But about the, um, competition in the area—it is, at times, most fierce. Recently, for example, the trade route between here and the Telos system was overrun with our competitor's ships. They're big boys, too. Far outweigh anything we lowly little Rangers can put in the space lanes. So, if your cargo holds are modest . . ."

"They are," Laranth and Jax said in unison.

Folee smiled. "Then I'd advise against even bothering going any farther up the Hydian Way. This is as good a place as any to replot your course."

Their food and drink arrived and they made a show of imbibing before they settled into conversation once more, setting up an arrangement for the off-loading of as much of the ionite as their allies on Toprawa could make use of.

"Coming back this way?" Ranger Folee asked as they concluded their arrangements.

Jax looked up and met Laranth's eyes briefly before saying, "We hadn't planned on it. We figured to take a more direct route back to Imperial Center."

Folee's gray eyes widened. "You're going back to Imperial Center? Why?"

"We have . . . interests there, as you might expect," Jax explained. "Business to see to—"

"And people counting on us," added Laranth.

"You could have that here, too, you know," Folee said. "I could really use a couple of associates with your . . . talents."

She had Jax's attention. "Our talents?"

"Clearly you both have a connection to the Force. I'd heard that our friend was working with a couple of especially talented individuals. Individuals whom the Emperor found of particular interest. I suspect he meant you two."

Jax looked at Laranth. Was Aren Folee a Force-sensitive? He considered briefly trying to probe her mind, decided against it; if she were sharp enough in the ways of the Force to be either a benison or a menace, she'd notice his efforts. If she wasn't, there was no point to it anyway. "What makes you say that?" he asked.

"I'd heard one of these special operatives was a Twi'lek, for one thing."

"And the other?"

Folee laughed. "Subtext. Half of what you say to each other is unspoken, and you complete each other's sentences." She sobered quickly and leaned toward them again. "I'm serious. We could really use you here. This is the best of all worlds—literally. We're on a main trade route, so there's a lot of covering traffic for our ships and special cargo, but we're far enough from the center of the galaxy that the Empire doesn't normally pay us much attention. We're just an outlying trade center. But I can safely say there's a lot more going on here than meets the Imperial eye. We have an extensive underground—and I do mean underground—network." She glanced down toward the floorboards, then back up. "Sound appealing?"

Laranth sat back in her seat. "Of course it does. But . . ."

"But," concluded Jax, "with our friend offworld, someone needs to run the business on Imperial Center."

"Does it have to be you?"

Did it? Jax had to admit he'd asked himself that question a number of times in recent weeks. He also had to admit that Toprawa had strong appeal. He shot a glance sideways at Laranth. She was sitting stiffly erect behind a wall of reserve. He couldn't, for once, tell what she was thinking, but he suspected she was a bit outraged by the thought that she and Jax might abandon their operations on Coruscant.

He looked back at Folee, smiled regretfully. "I'm afraid it does," he said.

*   *   *

"So . . . we finish each other's sentences." Laranth strolled beside Jax as they made their leisurely way back to the ship.

He smiled. "Apparently."

"Next we'll be eating off each other's plates."

They walked on in silence until they came within sight of the spaceport. Then Laranth said, "What do you think about what Folee proposed?"

"About basing ourselves here?" He shrugged. "I don't see how we can. Whiplash needs us on Coruscant."

"Does it?" She swung around to face him. "Might we not serve the cause better out here, where our forces are building? It seems to me that this is where the front is. *This* is where the resistance will become a real force in the galaxy."

Jax was stunned. This wasn't the Laranth Tarak he knew. Laranth, the fiercely loyal, the champion of honor and duty. He laughed uncertainly. "Who are you and what did you do with Laranth?"

She made an impatient gesture. "Not joking, Jax. On Coruscant, it feels like the walls are closing in. They're learning to read us. Learning to know what sort of situations we involve ourselves in. What sort of people we'll risk our lives to help. On Coruscant, they're learning how to bait us—how to get to us . . ."

Jax raised his eyes to the dark wall of trees that embraced the spaceport. Uncomplicated. Natural. Real ground beneath his feet, the scent of grass and tree needles, the simple susurration of wind. Coruscant, with its barrage of sounds and energies—its clutter of angles and jagged, chaotic patterns of light and shadow—seemed suddenly suffocating. It was like living in a hive. There was no distance between you and the next person . . . and the next person could be an Imperial operative with instructions to capture or kill you. If you didn't have your Force sense tuned to danger level every minute of every day, you could be caught off guard.

Come back to Toprawa and work with the Antarian Rangers? Maybe use it as a base to find other Jedi—if there *were* any other Jedi—and build a new Order? Come back to Toprawa . . . with Laranth?

He brought his eyes back to her face. In the moment their gazes locked, to do that—to return here with her and blend into the underground network—was something he wanted beyond reason. The desire rose up in him and almost swamped him.

Almost.

He took a deep breath, and let the desire out.

"We can't just leave Coruscant, Laranth."

"Tuden Sal has turned out to be a real asset," she argued. "He's smart, politically savvy, driven . . ."

"And still thinks it would be a good idea to assassinate Palpatine."

That stopped her. "Yes. True. All right. But Pol Haus can balance that out, don't you think?"

"Pol Haus isn't, strictly speaking, a member of Whiplash. He's an ally, certainly, but . . ." Yimmon had assured them that the Imperial Sector Police prefect could be trusted, but Jax didn't know how much influence Haus held over Tuden Sal.

"Wouldn't you rather be out here?" she asked pointedly. She tilted her head back and looked up at the night sky. It glittered with a million stars, the broad swath of pale radiance that was the Galactic Core gleaming like a river of light.

"It's . . ." Jax's voice caught in his throat. "It's not about what *we* want, Laranth. It's about what the galaxy *needs*. It needs to be free of darkness."

She shivered visibly. "Will that ever really happen, do you think?"

He stepped toward her. Put his hands on her shoulders. "Laranth, is something wrong?"

She shrugged free angrily. "By the Goddess, Jax! Tell me one thing that's *right*!"

"You? Me? Our connection to the Force?" He smiled—or at least tried to. "The fact that we complete each other's sentences?"

She took a deep breath, exhaled, and shook her head, making the row of tiny bells that edged her lekku mantle sing. "Sorry. It's just . . . going back to Coruscant feels like going back into a trap." She turned her head toward the landing field, started walking. "Let's go make sure the ionite is ready for our customer."

"Sure." Jax fell into stride with her.

Maybe it *was* time for them to consider a new base of operations.

The *Far Ranger* left Toprawa with her nose set toward Ciutric. They would arrive at Dantooine after a series of careful intermediate jumps. Jax piloted the ship as far as the Ciutric system, then adjusted course and relinquished the helm to I-Five to retire to his private quarters.

The miisai tree sat atop a column, beneath a wash of light. His meditation mat sat before it, and it was there he went now, sitting cross-legged on the floor. He took a deep breath, focused on the tree, following the contours of its elegantly turned trunk and branches with his eyes. When he closed his eyes, the image of the tree remained—the spiraling trunk, the uplifted branches, the bristling energy of the needles. He saw it as a figure of pale green light—a ghost image imprinted on his retinas.

There is no emotion; there is peace.

Peace. He had to dig for that just now, delving beneath the slurry of emotions that he'd been managing

since they'd made the decision to move Yimmon away
from Coruscant. Jax realized, for the first time, that he
had taken it as a sign of failure. It felt, sometimes, as if
they were in constant retreat—running from the Emperor. Running from Vader.

Running from themselves . . .

There is no ignorance; there is knowledge.

No. He knew they weren't running. It was a tribute to
their success that the Empire had increased its pressure
on them. And from his new headquarters, Thi Xon
Yimmon would be far freer to organize a resistance
worthy of the name. Out here, Jax told himself, there
would be far more opportunities to network with other
resistance cells like the one on Toprawa.

There is no passion; there is serenity.

Toprawa.

Aren Folee's world had seemed the seat of serenity,
and her offer for them to stay there and work with the
Antarian Rangers was, he had to admit, appealing.
No—more than appealing—seductive.

There is no chaos; there is harmony.

Jax reined in his thoughts. The Whiplash needed to
be on Coruscant and—right now, at least—he and
Laranth needed to be there, too. Maybe later. Maybe if
he and Laranth and the others could raise up replace-
ments. Maybe when battles had been won and some
balance returned to the Force.

There is no death; there is the Force.

The image of the miisai still burned behind his closed
eyelids. It struck him as paradoxical that this tiny specimen, with its fragile sprigs, was a close relation to the
towering columns of wood around Big Woolly's spaceport. Both drew life from soil and sun. Both pulsed
with life force. Both were at once strong and flexible.

There was, indeed, a lesson in that, he realized, and it
turned his thoughts toward the way he had experienced

the Force, standing amid the trees of Toprawa. It had been different from his normal perception of it. He had always "seen" it as a web of energies in which he existed. When he used those energies, he saw them as tendrils or ribbons that reached out from his core to interact with the material universe.

But on Toprawa, he had experienced the Force as something that flowed up from the heart of a world, through the arteries of every forest giant and into the atmosphere with the oxygen. In his mind's eye, he saw the trees—the great, monumental trees—roots in the ground, reaching into the skies, simultaneously moving and still.

It was suddenly very still inside Jax Pavan. He opened his Force sense to the miisai where it sat in its pot of soil. He could see it, then; he could *feel* it—the Force originating in some infinite well, flowing up through the slender trunk and gracefully turned branches, breathing out into the ether.

He drew in a deep breath, his mind hovering on the verge of epiphany. He felt an echo from that moment of ineffable peace when, months earlier, he had for a brief flash touched the hem of the Cosmic Force. He felt the stirring in his veins and arteries and, wanting it desperately, reached for the realization that was just beyond his grasp . . .

And touched the black heart of vacuum.

Vader!

Jax recoiled, literally thrusting himself backward and inward, away from that chill connection. He wanted to believe it had been merely a manifestation of his own apprehension, but he knew it was not. He had felt Darth Vader's touch as surely as he felt the deck of the *Far Ranger* beneath him.

He flung himself up from the meditation mat and out

into the passageway. No more than a couple of steps down the curved corridor, he came face-to-face with Laranth. Her eyes were storm-dark, her expression grim. He needed no verbal confirmation from her; neither did she need it from him. They had both sensed it.

They turned as one and ran for the bridge.

three

Den Dhur stared out through the viewport and considered whether the relief from boredom offered by challenging Thi Xon Yimmon to a game of dejarik was worth the extreme humiliation that would inevitably follow. So far he had been unable to last more than ten minutes against the Cerean. Yimmon had an unfair advantage, of course, given his dual cortices. Den had considered asking if he could possibly turn one of them off, or distract it with the calculation of pi to several thousand places, or some other engrossing pursuit, but that would be whining. He hated whining. Especially if it issued from his own lips.

He stretched, yawned, and glanced over at I-Five, who was piloting. "Are we there yet?" he mumbled.

The droid turned his head, fixing his companion with both optics. "Obviously, we are not there yet, or we would . . . be there. We are scheduled to drop out of hyperspace in exactly twenty minutes, thirty-three seconds."

"Just making conversation."

"Why? Oh, wait—let me guess—you're bored."

"Aren't you?"

"I don't get bored. It is one of the advantages of having a machine intelligence as opposed to an organic one. You biologicals are plagued by the sense of time passing. I have no such issues."

Den sat up straight in his seat, staring curiously at the droid. "How *do* you experience the passage of time?"

Five turned his optics back to the viewport. "Which kind? Universal time, as in Tiran's theory? Or hyper-time?"

"Uhh . . ." Den had only vaguely heard of the great Drall physicist Tiran's unification of sublight time and space, and he'd never heard of hypertime. Blasted if he'd let I-Five know that, however. "Not like the Cephalons, right? You don't experience time that way. I mean, the way you described it to me once—like objects in space."

"Ah, yes. I do recall that conversation. I suggested there was a trash bin in your future. You assured me of your ultimate optimism."

"Yeah. But do you—experience time like the Cephalons do?"

"I rather think no one experiences it quite like that. The difference between the way you and I experience time is a function of the way our memories work. Your memory is volatile. Mine . . ."

Den gave the droid a sharp glance. Why the hesitation?

"Mine is not," the droid finished blandly. "Unless someone wipes my memory core—"

"Which has happened."

"Which has happened," agreed I-Five. "But if no one meddles with it, it remains intact."

Mercilessly intact, Den knew. Though they had been wiped some twenty years ago, I-Five's memories of the death of his human friend Lorn Pavan—Jax's father—had been restored in vivid and complete detail. As had the droid's betrayal at the hands of Tuden Sal. Den often wondered how Five could bring himself to work with the Sakiyan in Whiplash. He doubted *he* could be so sanguine about it—despite the fact that Tuden Sal had lost all of his business holdings, had been blacklisted by the Empire, and had had to relocate his family to a frontier planet where their lives went on without him.

"The memory of an organic life-form," I-Five said, "is manipulated by the emotional current that goes along with the events *in* memory. They change, expand, contract, assume epic proportions, or become submerged in those currents. It is at once a great strength and a great weakness."

Den had opened his mouth to reply when Jax and Laranth exploded onto the bridge.

"Drop out of hyperspace and ping the escort," Jax said tersely. "Vader's after us."

The words were no more than out of his mouth when the *Far Ranger* seemed to hesitate like a dancer pausing in mid-step, then dropped back into normal space, her automatic systems taking over to make certain she didn't collide with anything solid or get dragged into a gravity well.

Den scrambled out of the copilot's seat, allowing Jax to slide into place at the console and activate the heads-up display.

I-Five swiveled his head to look at the Jedi. "I didn't do that, Jax. I hadn't time. We were just pulled back into normal space."

"Where?" asked Laranth.

"Apparently, right where someone wants us," said I-Five.

Den saw what he meant. Other ships were popping into normal space all around them. While millions of kilometers distant, the Twins still set the void ablaze with their deadly display. His throat clamped shut and his extremities felt as if his temperature had dropped by twenty degrees. There were so many of them! They formed a rough half sphere around *Far Ranger* and were moving toward them, seeking to cut off retreat.

"Jax . . ." Den forced the name between his arid lips. "Jax, tell me you have a plan."

"Are they Imperial?" asked Laranth, though she surely knew the answer.

Jax didn't answer either question. "I make twenty of them."

Twenty! Twenty Imperial ships for *them*? For one tiny rogue freighter?

"He knows we're aboard," Jax murmured. "He *knows*."

Laranth made a noise that was half growl, half moan. "How can he even *be* here?"

"I don't know. He just is." Jax turned to look at her. "Man the dorsal weapons. Den, you take the keel battery—but first, get Yimmon into a life pod."

"You know what he'll say—"

"*Get him into a pod.*"

"What are you going to do?" Den asked. Out of the corner of his eye, he saw Laranth wheel around and disappear into the main passageway.

"We're going to try to squeeze between the Twins."

Den closed his eyes. "I didn't need to know that." Then he fled the bridge, on his way to Thi Xon Yimmon.

"You're serious?" said I-Five. "You really mean to dive between two disintegrating stars?"

Jax's fingers flew over the navigational console, correcting course, setting speed. "Not exactly. Just close enough to two disintegrating stars to mask our signature. Then reorient and shoot off toward Dathomir."

"Dathomir?"

"Can't take a chance on leading him to Dantooine. Too risky."

"And by 'shoot off,' I assume you mean leap to hyper-

space. In the gravity eddies between a white dwarf and
a blue giant."

"Yes."

"Which is immeasurably risky."

Jax paused to throw his metallic friend a tight smile.
"Didn't say it wasn't risky, Five. Just preferable to the
alternative." He put his hands on the copilot's steering
yoke. "Transfer the controls to my station."

"Transfer, copy."

Jax saw the status light at his station go green and
punched the ion drive hard. They leapt forward right
into the brilliant, spangled veil of matter and energy
that stretched between the two stars. Behind them
now—and above, below, and flanking—the Imperial
vessels pursued, closing the net.

Jax had a magnified visual of the closest vessels that
confirmed his suspicions: this was a large contingent of
the Dark Lord's 501st attack fleet, known as Vader's
Fist.

Which one? Jax wondered. Which ship was Vader
on? He had no intention of reaching out to know for
certain. Somewhere in the phalanx there was a flagship,
of that he was certain. Possibly even that big cruiser
that was now hanging back behind the smaller vessels—
the ship whose gravity generators had no doubt sucked
them out of hyperspace. It was the only ship of real size
in the formation; the rest were frigates and attack cor-
vettes with a few TIE fighters thrown in for good mea-
sure.

"You're aware that this is suicide," I-Five said.

"We don't have a choice. Well, yes, we do—give up or
fight. Neither decision is likely to result in any of us living to a ripe old age. Maybe we should have stayed on
Toprawa."

"Maybe we should have."

Closer loomed the blue-white river of stellar matter.

Closer drew the individual fingers of Vader's Fist. *Far Ranger* bucked, then suddenly seemed to be flying through taffy. The thought was almost funny—the flow of substance between the stars was something in the nature of a cosmic taffy pull. And they might just end up as a small, crunchy bite amid the creamy starstuff.

Jax tilted the ship's bow down and to port very slightly, skimming the shores of the stream. The ship fought him, trying to sail straight to the heart of the white dwarf. He held on, shooting between the dwarf and the giant, through the hurricane of hot plasma being siphoned off by the smaller, denser star.

It was like stepping into chaos. *Far Ranger* was buffeted by a howling inferno; the hull temperature spiked.

"Exterior temperature registering five thousand degrees," I-Five reported.

Jax closed his eyes, letting the Force take him, imagining it as a web of freezing energy around the little freighter. He experienced something he had never felt before: as if the currents and eddies of energy between the two stars were linked through him like reins in his hands. He felt the currents, gently manipulated the reins, navigated the eddies.

"We'll be out the other side in ten seconds," I-Five informed him.

"Course is set. Go to hyperdrive on my mark."

"Copy."

Jax looked up at the chron in the heads-up display. "Mark in five, four, three, two, one—"

"Belay that!" I-Five said.

Jax felt it before he saw it. They came out of the binary storm into a pocket formed by another contingent of ships.

Proximity alarms screamed and Jax did the only thing he could do. He flipped *Far Ranger* end over end, intending to flee back the way they'd come. They'd have to leap from the matter stream. But the flaw in that plan became immediately apparent as a formation of five ships emerged from the Twins' torrent.

Jax knew without probing that the one at the center of the formation carried Vader.

He hit the comlink. "We're surrounded! Fire at will! Everything we've got!"

The response from Laranth and Den was immediate— laser and charged particle beams sprayed from the *Far Ranger*'s batteries. The barrage from the dorsal battery concentrated on the central ship in the enemy formation. Laranth knew who was on that ship and knew, also, that under no circumstances could they let him board.

They had one chance and one chance only, and that was to break the Imperial formation, get back into the tidal flow between the stars, and leap to hyperspace from there. It was beyond suicidal, but there was no choice—they *could not* let Vader board and take Yimmon.

Jax drove *Far Ranger* right at Vader's flagship and felt a sick wash of dark amusement sweep over him just before the enemy opened fire. The first shots were a warning, missing the ship by kilometers, but they swiftly drew closer. In seconds, they'd be raining on the *Far Ranger*'s shields—shields that, even with the previous owner's augmentation, could not come close to withstanding more than a few seconds of concentrated Imperial firepower. They would buckle, collapse, and then . . .

There was a ping and a pop of ambient light from the communications panel. I-Five reacted instantaneously, returning the ping. "Our escort has found us," he said.

"Which means we can find them," Jax said. "Feed the coordinates to the life pods, then go to Yimmon."

"You're not going to abandon ship—"

"Only if we have to. Go!"

The droid sent the coordinates of their escort's telltale and hastened from the bridge.

Jax looked up through the viewport. They were bearing down on Vader's ships fast, and the four big fighters flanking him were tightening their formation. A blast of Imperial fire shook the little freighter, glancing off her shields. They were targeting the ion drive. Jax waited for a second shot to hit, then yanked the yoke hard over, sending *Far Ranger* into a tight spiral. If he'd timed it right, they'd fly—belly up—right beneath the flagship, slicing between it and its nearest neighbor.

If . . .

The barrage of fire from the gun batteries continued as they spun. To Vader it probably looked as if one of his shots had found its mark and sent the Whiplash ship out of control. If he wanted them, he'd have to reverse course and follow them back into the matter stream. If the Force was with them, he'd be too late.

Two klicks from Vader's ship, Jax dropped *Far Ranger*'s bow a fraction more and dived toward the brilliant light. He reached for the hyperdrive controls.

And time stood still.

Jax felt as if he were diving into water. In one instant momentum was exchanged for a floating free fall.

They'd entered a stasis field.

Jax's mind grappled with the idea. A large ship of the line could generate such a field, but for something as small as Vader's cruiser to produce one was flatly impossible. His thoughts laboriously parsed the situation, aware of and frustrated by the field's slowing of his neurons. Fortunately, his Jedi training helped him resist it—otherwise, he would simply have been frozen, in body and brain, and his next conscious awareness would have likely been seeing Vader looming over him.

Jax tried to focus. In order to escape the situation he

first had to understand it. The explanation struck him as the ship's spiral slowed further, and he studied the representative dots of the 501st's ships arranged on the heads-up display. It came to him, then; the answer lay in their dispersement pattern. The stasis field was being generated by the five ships *as a unit*—spun among them like a spider's web, each ship generating a section of the invisible strands as they flew in a pattern that was flawless and exact. That was likely attributable to the presence of Darth Vader—likely with a select group of his Inquisitors.

Jax threw the ship into reverse; the movement seemed to take forever. The hull groaned and shimmied, but they were held fast . . . and being drawn up toward the flagship. He'd figured it out, but too late to implement an escape.

Suddenly he could move again—subjective time was back to normal. He didn't need the pinging instrumentation to tell him what had happened: the Dark Lord had abandoned the stasis field in favor of a more effective tractor beam. A mistake on his part that Jax would take full advantage of.

Jax triggered the comlink. "Abandon ship. All hands, *abandon ship*!" He activated the escape klaxon, scrambled out of the pilot's seat, and headed aft.

The call to abandon ship echoed from Den Dhur's headset. He was so focused on reorienting himself after the sudden cessation of their plummet toward ultimate doom that the sound of Jax's voice shocked him. He tumbled out of the weapons station and onto the platform beneath the gimbaled chair.

The ventral battery was just below the forward cargo bay. Through the cowling, bursts of laserfire illuminated the keel with flashes of bright coherent light.

First a stasis field, then a tractor beam, he thought. *Why, oh, why didn't we keep some of the ionite?*

Den hauled himself up the ladder, out of the battery, and into the cargo hold. He paused to orient himself. Jax had said to get to the life pods, but they'd be stuck in the tractor field just as effectively as the ship was . . . well, until Vader docked with them for boarding.

The thought galvanized him. When Vader docked, the Imperials would have to lower their shields *and* force *Far Ranger* to lower hers, *and* they'd have to turn off their field for a moment. That would be all the time available in which to get the pods away and out of the tractor field.

I have *to get aft.*

Den's thoughts imploded as the ship was rocked again by an external force. The bump was followed by the groaning of the hull. All the blood fled from Den's brain. Instinct took over. He scrambled for the cargo bay hatch. He'd just reached it when there was a sound like the firing of a thousand thrusters. The lights flickered, then failed completely. The engines fell silent.

So did Laranth's laser cannon.

It only now struck him that he'd been hearing her continued firing from the time he'd left his own post—until now. That was good, Den thought. Now the Twi'lek madwoman would *have* to abandon the kriffing ship. They were dead in space, no engines, no weapons, no life support—

He skidded to a halt as the realization hit him. *No life support!*

Den swallowed his fear, drew his blaster, and started cautiously down the long fore-and-aft passageway. He'd taken the precaution earlier of fastening his comlink to the collar of his jacket; now he thumbed it to I-Five's frequency.

"Five? Den here. Come in."

Silence . . . then, just when Den thought he might weep: "I-Five here. Where are you?"

"Just abaft the forward hold. You?"

"Amidships, lower deck, heading up. We're being boarded. Port side, through the cargo bay."

Den's knees quaked. "On my way to you." He turned and bolted for the nearest ladder.

He'd just stepped out onto the upper deck when the sound of groaning metal came again from his right. He choked back a yelp of sheer terror and took off toward the stern as fast as his short legs would carry him.

Jax had felt the tremors running through the ship as the Imperial stormtroopers worked at boarding her. He had assiduously *not* tried to locate Vader. He was working to keep his Force signature damped down. The weight of his lightsaber at his hip was some comfort, but he hoped he wouldn't need it. If it came to using his lightsaber, that would mean he'd allowed Vader to get too close.

He sped aft in the suffocating gloom, slowing as he reached amidships. Was Laranth still up in the dorsal battery? Surely not. Surely she had abandoned her post on his order.

Or not. Laranth could be stubborn. He hesitated, peering into the gloom of the transverse passage.

But without power, he argued, and with the ship caught in the tractor beam like an insect in amber, she could no longer fire her weapon. She would have opted to protect Yimmon. She would have gone for the life pods. He moved forward again.

He caught up with I-Five as he stepped out of a stairwell onto the upper deck.

"Where are Den and Laranth?" he asked.

"Den is on his way," said the droid. "And until they

knocked out our systems, Laranth was still firing at the Imperials. I assume she's been forced to flee."

Jax frowned. Under normal circumstances, he would have simply reached out and found her through the Force, but he couldn't chance that now, only comfort himself that she had not reached out for *him*. He looked forward along the starboard passageway. There was nothing to see. He turned his attention aft. "She's probably already at the pods. Let's go."

There were five life pods in *Far Ranger*'s complement—two in the stern on each of her two decks, port and starboard—and one just abaft the bridge. Each was equipped to hold four people comfortably, five only if they were on very good terms. All of them now held the coordinates of the Antarian escort, but they wouldn't by the time they were all finally deployed. Only the one Jax and his companions took—the one in which Thi Xon Yimmon awaited them—would rendezvous with their backup. He thanked the Force for Aren Folee.

They reached the aft transverse passageway and made their way along it to the first of the life pods. The locking mechanism glowed green—occupied. I-Five pinged Yimmon, who popped the hatch.

Yimmon was alone in the pod. No Laranth.

Jax tried his comlink. She didn't answer. Which might mean nothing . . . or it might mean . . .

A slow creeping dread enveloped him. If he could only reach out. Just a tendril of thought. The merest thread . . . He closed his eyes, extended his feelings . . .

"Jax?" I-Five put a metal hand on his shoulder just firmly enough to arrest his attempt to reach Laranth. "What now? Do we wait or split up?"

Den was about amidships, nearing the intersection with the transverse passageway, when two things hap-

pened almost simultaneously: the emergency lights began
to flicker on and off, and he stepped into a sudden pall of
acrid smoke. He stopped, heart pounding, and peered
into billowing clouds luridly lit by golden light and flickers of brighter incandescence from some point roughly at
the center of the transverse passageway.

He choked—less on the smoke and more on the sudden realization of where it must come from—the dorsal
weapons bay. He put himself in motion again, forcing
himself to move through the smoke and intermittent
light. He could hear the pop and hiss of fried circuitry,
the ticking of cooling metal.

*Please, Triakk, let her have gotten out. Merciful War-
ren Mother of all Sullust, I beg you!*

He hurried toward the confluence of the transverse
and fore-and-aft passages. As he'd feared, the source of
the smoke was the weapons battery. It was also the
source of a string of what could have been either curses
or prayers delivered in a husky female voice. The litany
ended with, "That's it! Come on—come on—come *on*!"

Laranth!

Den reached the spot below the battery and peered
up. The retractable ladder was halfway down, but
Laranth was still up in the bay, working over a control
panel that looked as if it had imploded. Her face was
crisscrossed with cuts; her bare shoulders and lekku
bled from numerous wounds.

"What're you doing?" he demanded. "Get out of
there!"

"Not yet. Not until I send Lord Vader one last message." She was reaching for the firing mechanism—or
what was left of it.

Peering up through the transparisteel cowl over her
head, Den realized what she meant to do. The dorsal
turbolaser cannon was aimed right into the belly of Vader's ship at point-blank range.

"Laranth, *no!*"

But she was already committed. The emergency lights brightened as power surged; she fired.

The backlash was so intense it swept Den off his feet and tossed him down the fore-and-aft passage as if he were a leaf in the wind.

In the flutter of amber from the emergency lights, Jax surveyed the life pods. There was one to either side of an access tube that ran from where they stood down to the cargo deck and up to a scanner array. He considered sending I-Five and Yimmon off in the port pod, but if they split up it would severely complicate their escape plans. He'd opened his mouth to tell I-Five to join Yimmon in the pod when an explosion lit up the fore-and-aft passage. The ship bucked fiercely, throwing Jax to the deck. Rising, he felt sudden cold. It was as if someone had siphoned the freezing void of space into his soul.

He scrambled to his feet, peering forward along the fore-and-aft corridor. An acrid odor reached him, breathed out by the ship's sputtering emergency life-support system. Through the flickering light, Jax realized his view of the forward section of the ship was obscured by smoke.

No.

Jax ran, vaguely hearing I-Five call his name.

The ship felt wrong beneath Den's booted feet as he dragged himself upright in the choking swirl of smoke. It was bobbing like a cork, which made no sense. The A-grav field was either on or off. If it was on, the boson field generated mass and stability; if it was off . . .

He staggered back to the weapons battery and was scared witless when a large, solid figure flew out of the gloom, nearly knocking him down again. It took him a moment to realize that it was Jax. The Jedi reached up into the battery and hauled on the half-deployed ladder. The warped scrap of metal fought his attempt to pull it down fully.

Den heaved himself upward. He was just able to grasp the bottom-most rungs of the ladder and add his weight to it. He heard the sharp, guttural rasp of labored breathing but had no idea if it was Laranth's or Jax's or his own. He choked on the acrid vapors, blinked as dying circuitry spat sparks at him.

The ladder jerked downward and Laranth fell from the battery into Jax's arms, her bones shattered, her life force flickering like the emergency lights that lit her ravaged face. Her left lekku was nearly severed, and a piece of shrapnel had pierced her neck, just beneath her jawline, nearly severing a cortical artery.

Den could only cling to the ladder and watch. He pulled his gaze from Laranth's face and to Jax's. That was far worse. He had to look away.

He turned his eyes aft and his breath stopped in his throat. I-Five had started toward them from the stern. Yimmon had left the safety of the life pod. Behind them, just climbing out of the stairwell . . .

"*Jax.*" Den's voice was a raw whisper.

He looked back at Jax and Laranth, and caught the moment in which Laranth breathed something into Jax's ear and then gave her soul back to the Force. It felt as if the entire universe paused to observe the moment before moving forward again.

Jax didn't need to be told what Den had seen in the aft passage. Den could see that he knew. The knowledge was written in the sudden stiffening of his body, in the hard remoteness of his eyes as he laid Laranth's broken shell gently on the deck and rose.

His lightsaber hummed to life, lighting the dim corridor with blue-green ambience. Jax stepped aft, the smoke eddying around him. Den watched, helpless, as the Jedi approached I-Five and Yimmon. The Whiplash leader and his droid protector were blocked from escape by a towering black figure flanked by a quartet of stormtroopers.

Darth Vader drew his lightsaber, as well, and took one long step toward Jax and his companions. His weapon thrummed to life, its blood-red radiance spilling up the bulkheads. The ship shifted again, the A-grav field flickering like the lights. One of the stormtroopers hastened to Vader's side and spoke to him, gesturing upward, his voice too low to hear.

In answer, Vader made a sharp motion with one hand and the stormtroopers turned as one, leveling their weapons at Jax.

"Your dead comrade," said Vader, his dark voice betraying no emotion, "disabled our stasis field—an act for which she has paid with her life. This ship is drifting into the matter stream between the stars, so you will forfeit that, as well. I have but one more thing to take from you."

"My life?" Jax asked, his voice harsh and raw.

"No. That would be too easy, wouldn't it?"

The stormtrooper nearest him turned his helmeted head. "But Lord Vader, the Emperor's orders—"

Vader raised a gloved hand, fisted, and the trooper fell silent. "I am well aware of the Emperor's orders. I execute them in my own fashion. What I take from you, Jax Pavan, is the very thing you have been so jealously guarding these many months."

He turned his masked face toward Yimmon. The Cerean's eyes rolled back in his head and he slumped against the bulkhead behind him. Vader reached out with his free hand and made a grasping motion that arrested Yimmon's slide. Two of the stormtroopers moved quickly to grab his arms and lift him up.

Jax and I-Five leapt in unison, Jax's lightsaber spinning. The stormtroopers fired and a burst of hard, particulate light flooded the passageway.

Den had no time to cover his eyes. He was blinded, utterly. When he was able to see again, Jax stood in the center of the passageway, his lightsaber raised defensively. The corridor was littered with debris. Vader and his troopers were gone, and with them, Thi Xon Yimmon.

The ship was dead in space, drifting toward oblivion. Laranth's body lay broken on the deck. And I-Five . . .

Den tried to move and nearly tripped over something at his feet. He looked down. I-Five's head, battered and blackened, lay on the decking before him.

four

They had to leave now or they never would. He knew that Laranth's body was just an empty shell.

He knew that. He was, after all, a Jedi. Death was no stranger to him.

And yet he wanted to linger within one broken vessel, cradling the other in his arms. Or, barring that, to take Laranth's body with him into a life pod.

He shut the urges down.

There is no death; there is the Force.

Her last words.

He looked around for Den. The Sullustan was still alive, quivering against the bulkhead with I-Five's head in his arms. Jax had to get Den off *Far Ranger*. And to do so, he had to leave Laranth behind.

He forced himself to move. He deactivated his lightsaber and put a hand on the Sullustan's shoulder.

"Get to the life pod. The one to starboard."

Den looked up at him through haunted eyes; Jax saw his own reflection in them. "Not . . . not without you."

"Wait for me. Give me a minute—that's all I'll need. If I'm not there in a minute, take off."

He sprinted for his cabin then—*their* cabin—trusting that Den wouldn't try to follow him. It took him only seconds to dart in and get the miisai tree—all of Laranth that was left to him. He spent another second considering the idea of not joining Den in the life pod.

He shook his head. *Stupid*. He was being stupid and tragic. This was not the time to make life decisions.

Carrying the tree, he raced aft again, pausing only to sweep up one of Laranth's blasters—the only one still in one piece—and to touch her ruined face. Her flesh was cold. Her house was empty.

The ship shuddered again, reminding him that he had limited time—not that he expected Den to leave him behind. Not really. He reached the life pod and swung inside, sealing the door behind him. Den was sitting in the copilot's seat, working on I-Five's head, reconnecting a few of the myriad wires that straggled from the droid's neck. Jax thought he saw the droid's optics flicker briefly, but the effect was too ephemeral for him to be sure.

He slid into the pilot's seat—not that he'd be doing much piloting—strapped in, and hit the launch mechanism. Seconds later they were flying through the Twins' tidal bore.

It took long, agonizing moments to win clear of the stars' gravity, but they did at last. In the relative silence of the capsule, Jax swiveled his seat to look at Den. The Sullustan stared back, I-Five's head pressed between his hands. His gaze was on the tree in Jax's lap.

"She . . . um . . . she gave you that?" Den asked.

Den's voice was so soft, Jax barely heard him. He nodded. "Stupid, I suppose, but . . ."

"No. Not stupid. Not at all."

"You waited more than a minute."

"You *took* more than a minute."

"I ordered you to go."

"*He* ordered me to stay." Den hefted the droid's head.

"Den . . ."

"I *did* order him to stay," said I-Five succinctly. His optics flickered, unmistakably this time. "I've lost enough today, as it is. We all have. Losing you . . . *not* in my plans."

Jax felt as if his bones were melting. His hands shook. He grasped the arms of the pilot's chair to stop them—grasped them until his knuckles turned white.

"Choice is loss; indecision is all loss," he murmured. "I choose Yimmon—I lose Laranth. I choose Laranth—I lose Yimmon. I hesitate—I lose both . . . and the ship *and* you."

"Except that I'm still here," I-Five said emphatically. "Though admittedly, I've lost a bit of weight." After a pause, the droid added, "In some sense, Laranth is still here, as well. Remember your training, Jax. There is no death; there is the Force."

Jax stared out the viewport at the void of space, aware that, behind them, the *Far Ranger* with her lonely cargo was diving into the starstuff—returning to the primal forge. It was easier to meditate on those words than understand what they meant. He'd lost his Master and understood them, he thought. He'd lost Nick Rostu and thought he'd understood them. But this—losing the woman who'd been his most intimate companion, the person who completed his sentences—this was not like those losses. He felt as if a piece of his own soul had been ripped away.

The piece that gave it light.

He wanted, desperately, to reach out through the Force and feel her there—to make certain the Jedi man-tra was truth. He told himself he did not only because it would betray his continued existence to Vader.

But Vader knew. He had taken the Whiplash leader, almost casually blasted I-Five to bits when the droid had tried to stop him, and just as casually caused Jax's muscles to lock in titanic spasm. Then he had turned and left with his troops.

A loud ping sounded in the silence. A light flashed in his eyes. He looked through the tiny porthole, saw a ship hovering perhaps half a klick away. It was their Ranger escort, come to rescue them.

Or what was left, he thought. Two broken men and a broken droid.

five

The Rangers' small stealthy vessels—which they called darts—scooped up the life pod carrying Jax and his companions at the fringes of the Twins' gravity well, docked with it, transferred them to Aren Folee's ship, and carried them back to Toprawa.

Jax spent the entire journey in a state of mental lockdown. After that last explosion of anguish, he was a pit. A hole. A yawning gravity well into which light fell without effect. He watched the mouth of the abyss from a high, detached point within his mind—the invisible seethe of emotions at the bottom could not be allowed to rise to the surface, or to leak out.

Vader would believe him dead, broken down into free ions by the Twins' plasmatic inferno, and he feared that even a whimper in the darkness of his soul would expose him.

He felt Den's gaze on him, and Aren Folee's when she turned from the ship's helm. He could even feel I-Five's regard. He still hadn't gotten used to that.

He relaxed his guard a bit when they reached Toprawa, even noticed when the ship dived straight at a rocky cliff and—at the point of impact—simply slipped through the holographic disguise and into a great, hollow cavern that was not entirely natural.

There were over half a dozen ships of various sizes ahead on the cavern floor. Overhead, the roof of the mountain disappeared into darkness punctuated by pale yellow lights. They twinkled in the mist of a waterfall that plunged like a ribbon of crystal from an unseen source down hundreds of feet to the cavern floor. Jax followed its silver path with his eyes—the group of ships ahead were on an island in the middle of a small lake.

"This is amazing," said Den quietly. Then to Jax, "When you said they had an underground, I didn't think you meant it literally."

"Welcome to Mountain Home," Aren told them.

She guided her dart expertly to the island and set down in the lee of a larger vessel that Jax recognized as a *Helix*-class interceptor. The small, armed freighters had been outlawed by the Empire because of their speed, maneuverability, and firepower. The first ships off the Arakyd assembly line had barely reached their new owners when the Emperor had commanded them to either strip the vessels down or get rid of them. Most had obeyed—apparently, some hadn't.

This interceptor was fully armed and seemed to be undergoing repair.

As Aren Folee settled the dart to the sand, Jax emerged from dormancy enough to examine the other ships nearby. He recognized several: A Kuat Systems Cloak-Shape fighter that was in the process of being fitted with new missile launchers, a Cutlass patrol fighter, and a third ship that couldn't be what it appeared to be.

Jax took a deep breath. "Is that a Delta-7?"

Aren shut down the engines. "It is. Want a look?"

Want. That was an alien idea. He nodded anyway. They disembarked—Jax still carrying the miisai tree, Den carrying I-Five's head—and the Ranger led them over to the sleek, wedge-shaped vessel. It was damaged— so badly scorched that the original color of the ship was almost obliterated. It had been red, which meant it had belonged to a specific Jedi. The Delta-7s—officially, the *Aethersprite* series—had been used by the Jedi so extensively most people had simply called them Jedi starfighters. Jax had never had the opportunity to pilot one.

He moved around it, beneath its sharply pointed bow, feeling as if he'd entered a shrine. He put a hand up to touch the port wing, noticing as he did that the droid socket was empty.

"Whose was it? Do you know?" he asked the silent Ranger behind him. He could feel her gaze on him as he moved aft under the wing.

"No. When it was found, it was drifting, empty. The astromech was gone."

Jax turned to look at her. "At Geonosis?"

"After. But it had drifted so far out into space, no one has any idea how or even when it got there. The navcom had been wiped clean."

Jax touched the vessel again, trying to glean from it any sort of energy signature he might recognize—something that might suggest to him which of his fellow Jedi might have piloted the vessel. There was nothing identifiable, only a diffuse imprint. He took his hand away, wiped his palm on his tunic.

Aren stepped over to him and laid a hand on his arm. "We should go. You'll want to contact your people on Dantooine and Coruscant."

He pulled away from the Jedi vessel. "Where are we going?"

"Foothill. That's where our headquarters is."

"Foothill, Mountain Home—code names?" asked Den, who'd trailed them at a short distance.

"More like generic descriptors. There's a network of subterranean passages that run under the spaceport and right up to the edge of town. We give them street names. It makes you seem a bit less shadowy when you can walk and talk openly in daylight about your supersecret underground township. People just think you're talking about locations in Big Woolly."

I-Five made a clicking sound. "Township?"

Aren looked at the droid remnant and smiled, as if talking to a bodiless machine was something she did every day. "You'll see." She turned and led them toward where the waterfall met the cavern lake, sending up plumes of mist.

"How was this all made?" Den asked.

Aren shook her head. "The big vault—we honestly don't know. It was something we stumbled across at the beginning of the war. Most of the townward part we carved out of the rock and soil."

She led them past work crews and pilots, who watched and sometimes waved. They crossed a wooden bridge that seemed to end at a ragged pile of boulders. Beyond those, screened from the cavern itself, was a pathway that ran around the perimeter of the cave on the outer shore of the lake. Aren turned left and led them right up to the waterfall. The pathway ran behind it and into a tunnel wide enough for the three of them to walk abreast.

Perhaps calling the Ranger outpost a "township" was too grand, but it was more than a mere bunker. There were branching corridors, storage rooms, living quarters, a dispensary/infirmary, a meditation chapel, and a small cantina of the type you might find aboard a space station.

The place was populated, if sparsely, with sentients from a number of worlds, though most seemed to be human. All found Jax and his companions of interest; all clearly knew Aren Folee well.

"Where are you taking us?" Jax asked as they reached an intersection with a second tunnel.

"That depends on you," Aren said. "On how you feel. I can take you to quarters. You could rest—sleep for a while—"

"No," said Jax, more sharply than he meant to. "I don't want to sleep."

"Eat, then?"

When Jax didn't answer, Den said, "I don't think either of us is hungry right now. What's option number three?"

"I take you to Degan."

"Degan?" I-Five repeated.

"Degan Cor. He and I share leadership here. I represent the Rangers. He represents other interested groups. Are you—that is, do you want to meet him now? I could at least show you to some quarters so you have a place to put your . . . your tree?" Her voice lifted questioningly.

Jax glanced down at the miisai—the only thing in his possession he needed a place for. Besides the clothing he wore, he now had exactly four other belongings: two lightsabers—the Sith blade an anonymous someone had given him and the new one he and Laranth had made— the pyronium that Anakin had given him long ago "for safekeeping," and the Sith holocron his father had bequeathed to him. These he carried on his person.

"I'll keep it, thanks."

She nodded, though she radiated bemusement.

"I'll keep this, too, thanks," said Den, lifting I-Five's head. The wide corners of his mouth turned up in a smile, but the expression didn't reach his eyes.

Jax realized, suddenly, that he wasn't alone in his grief. How could he have felt that he was? He turned to Aren Folee. "We'll need a droid tech, if you can spare one—to help us with I-Five."

She gave the droid's head a long look. "I thought that looked like an I-5YQ unit. It seems unusually . . . curious."

"Long story," Jax told her. "But Five is . . . more than

just a droid. He's been my companion and friend for—" He found himself unable to finish the sentence.

"I understand," said Aren.

Though she couldn't possibly have understood the relationship between man and machine, Jax knew she understood grief and loss. She had no doubt experienced it herself in recent years, given that the Empire took as dim a view of the Rangers as they did of the Jedi and had tried to wipe them out, as well.

"Follow me." She turned left into the intersecting tunnel, which was even wider than the first and better lit. The floor underfoot was a polished, pale gray stone with streaks of green.

"It so happens that Degan Cor is a mechanical genius," Folee went on. "He's retrofitted most of the systems on the vessels that have come through Mountain Home. He's not an expert on service and human adjunct droids like your YQ unit, but he knows a lot about artificial intelligence in general. He runs a vessel and vehicle repair facility up top." She glanced up at the rocky roof overhead. "Has a reputation as the go-to guy for broken hyperdrives. I don't know if we have any parts lying around for an I-Five, but I'm sure he can do something to help you out."

Degan Cor was a tall, lanky man in his prime with dark eyes of indeterminate color and hair so black it seemed to absorb light. He wore a mech-tech's coverall beneath a long vest of many pockets whose contents were a mystery. Den would not have pegged him for a resistance leader in a million years—which was probably part of what made him an effective resistance leader.

He had no parts for an I-5YQ lying around, but he did offer Den access to his workshops and an assistant of sorts to help patch together a body for the shattered droid. Den was grateful for anything he could get. Repairing I-Five dominated his thoughts, and he let it. It was vastly better than what strove to push his constructive agenda aside. There was an image in the back of his mind: a dark passageway clogged with smoke and fitful light, a twisted ladder, a broken body . . .

Den shook himself and tried to focus on what the Toprawan resistance leader was saying. Something about their loss.

Yes, *their* loss. Jax's loss. Whiplash's loss.

Den was overwhelmed for a moment by the sheer magnitude of it: Laranth gone, Yimmon taken, the ship gone, and Five . . . He gripped the droid's head more tightly and realized he was shaking.

"Do you mind?" a scratchy voice said from beneath his arm. "You're covering my audio inputs."

Den laughed reflexively and set I-Five's head on the low table in front of the hassock on which he sat. He didn't take his hands off it, though. He had a horrible feeling he'd collapse if he did that. Glancing at Jax, he wondered if the Jedi didn't feel the same way about the little tree that sat between his booted feet and that he caressed with his fingertips.

Degan Cor handed Jax, then Den, a cup of steaming amber liquid. Aren Folee served herself from the carafe on the table as her co-leader folded himself into a chair diagonally to Jax and across from Den.

"It's *shig*." Degan nodded at the cups. "We grow the *behot* for it locally. I find it bracing. Figured you might need bracing after what you've been through."

What we've been through. Den found himself back in the smoky passageway again. He dragged himself out. He figured he'd be doing this for a while, and he also had the feeling it wasn't going to get any easier as time went on.

"Thanks," Jax said, and sipped the beverage.

Den sniffed at his. Citrus-y. He sipped it, feeling it

burn its way down to his empty belly. It really did feel bracing. He closed his eyes. It was dark behind his eyes.

Dark in the passageway.

He opened his eyes and inhaled again the perfume of the *shig*. How long would it be before he could close his eyes and not go back to the *Far Ranger's* last moments . . . Laranth's last moments?

Degan Cor was watching Jax soberly. "I took the liberty of alerting your people on Dantooine that something had happened—that there had been a problem. I thought maybe I should let you tell them the details. Unless, you'd rather I—"

"No." Jax shook his head. "No, I need to do that. And I'll need to get through to the Whiplash on Coruscant, too."

And tell them what? Den wondered.

"Of course," said Degan. "What *did* happen? How did Vader know where you'd be?"

"I don't know. I wish I did. I hate to think it was simply that he's now able to sense me."

"Simply?" repeated Aren, and Degan's dark eyes widened.

"At our last encounter he ingested a powerful biotic agent that . . . I think it opened the floodgates on his Force perception and overwhelmed him. Initially, anyway. Like trying to put that waterfall out there through a small tube. Or passing all the power from a hyperdrive through a single bus. There's no way to be sure what effect that may have had on his Force sense. Although I wouldn't have bet that it would have become *more* sensitive as a result."

Degan was nodding. "Right. Usually if you overload a sense, it's deadened for at least a while after. Although, it can also become hypersensitive—or even both in turns. It's equally likely there's a mole in your organization."

He grinned mirthlessly. "Not sure which is worse—a hypersensitive Sith or a spy."

"I'll take the spy," I-Five said. "I think we may have a chance of discovering who that is."

The two Toprawans blinked at him in surprise.

"It almost had to be someone in the room when we made the plans to go to Dantooine," I-Five continued. His voice was thin and reedy without the resonating chamber his torso afforded. "Or someone in the *Far Ranger*'s prep crew."

Jax shook his head. "Could have been someone at Westport Control. We did file an itinerary."

"Yes, but the Twins weren't on it. Only Whiplash operatives knew at what point we were going to depart from the itinerary. As did a handful of people here."

Jax glanced up at Degan Cor, who shrugged.

"The droid is right, Jax. And that's something . . . we'll have to consider." He exchanged glances with Aren Folee.

"What will you do now?" Aren asked. "Go on to Dantooine?"

"No reason. We'll go back to Coruscant. Regroup. Figure out how we can get Yimmon back."

Degan and Aren exchanged glances again. Then the lanky mech-tech leaned forward in his chair, elbows on his knees. "You could work out of Toprawa, Jax. You're not only welcome here, you're needed. This is where the battle will be won. Out here, where the Empire has to spread itself thin. A number of the squadrons out here are for show. They don't do anything but maintain a strategic presence—unnerve the locals. We let them think they're doing that while we build a fleet right under their noses. You could be part of that—command your own wing of fighters."

Den held his breath, watching Jax's expressionless face intently.

"Why me in particular?" Jax asked finally.

"Aren and I both know you're Jedi, though no one else here does . . . or at least, they're not supposed to. Your talents could be very useful out here. And you could have a ship. Any ship you wanted—even that old Jedi starfighter. More than that, though—there are pockets of resistance to the Empire that are working independently. Sometimes we get in each other's way. Sometimes we end up working at cross purposes. One group of rebels wants to go for blood, another wants to play a waiting game. With you in the vanguard, I'm convinced we could bring all of them together under one mandate. Get them working in concert with us instead of at odds. You could unify this effort, Jax. They'd rally behind a Jedi. You'd be a miracle to them, because right now they think the whole Order's dead."

Jax's face grew even paler. He reached down and brushed the boughs of the tree with the tips of his fingers. He shook his head. "I have to find Yimmon and free him."

"Understood. But—"

"Vader could have killed him, but he didn't." Jax's gaze moved from Aren to Degan. "After months of trying to assassinate him—striking blindly, wildly—suddenly they spring a well-set trap and capture him. Yimmon said something before we left Coruscant that I should have listened to. He said it felt as if we were being herded. Encouraged to do just what we did—leave Coruscant. I don't suppose it matters at this point whether the whole thing was a plot or whether they just got lucky at the end. The result was that they have the one man whose knowledge about Whiplash could completely destroy it. If we don't get Yimmon away from Vader before he gets that information, Whiplash is dead—and any other parts of the resistance Yimmon has knowledge of."

Degan Cor shook his head. "Jax, what makes you think Vader doesn't already have that information?"

Den found it suddenly hard to breathe. In all the craziness, he hadn't even considered that. From the grim expressions on Aren Folee's and Degan Cor's faces, he could see that they had.

"Thi Xon Yimmon is the undisputed leader of Whiplash," Jax said doggedly. "He was leader of Whiplash from the beginning and had at least one Jedi Master who was content to be one of his operatives. There was a reason for that. Yimmon has more mental discipline than some Jedi I knew. He's exceptional, even for a Cerean. And none of us, except maybe Laranth—" He stopped, licked his lips. "I'm not sure even Laranth knew how sensitive he was to the Force."

"Still . . ."

"And there's something else," Jax said. "On the ship, when Vader reached out to control him, Yimmon seemed to lose consciousness. Or rather, to give it up. To me, it felt as if he just disappeared or—or shut off before Vader could control him. For a moment, I thought Vader had done it, but it seemed to surprise him. He had to react quickly to keep Yimmon from collapsing. If Yimmon has some way of suppressing his consciousness or denying Vader access to it, he may at least be able to buy some time. But I have no way of knowing how long he can hold out."

"What do you intend to do?" Degan asked.

"First, we've got to warn Whiplash. Tuden Sal needs to know what's happened, because chances are he's going to have to dismantle and rebuild the entire network and that's going to take time—time he may not have. Then we need to find Yimmon."

The resistance leader nodded. "We can give you a secure relay to your contacts on Coruscant. But what if you can't find Yimmon?"

"I can't think that way," Jax told him. "I have to believe that I *can* find him. That I *will* find him. And soon. You said I could have a ship. I'm going to need one to get back to Coruscant. Unless we find out otherwise, I have to assume that's where Vader will take Yimmon."

Degan nodded.

"How close is that old interceptor to being repaired?"

"A couple of days."

"Can I—"

"Of course," said Aren. "With one stipulation—that you'll seriously consider coming back to Toprawa and joining the Rangers . . . whatever happens with Thi Xon Yimmon."

Den took a deep breath in unison with Jax. The Jedi nodded. "I'll consider it. Seriously. Right now, I need to use your hypercomm to see if I can get a message to Whiplash."

six

He had to eat. He did it without half tasting what he put in his mouth. He drank copious amounts of the hot *shig* because it fooled him into thinking his mind was alert and working properly. He had to sleep, too, though he put it off for as long as he could. When he noticed that Den was doing the same thing, he opened his mouth to lecture, then closed it. Who was he to talk?

The tired mind wanders. If there is an unpleasant place for it to go, it will go there. Right now his was wandering down an avenue of thought that was all too disturbing. He had sent a terse, encrypted message to Tuden Sal on Coruscant, but as yet, there had been no reply. Jax didn't know whether Sal had gotten it or not—or if he was even alive to get it.

Conjecture was futile. Jax decided to try meditation as an antidote. In the small but cozy quarters Aren had given him next to Den's, he sat before the miisai tree, following its feathery boughs as if he were navigating a city canyon on Coruscant.

Following the flow of the Force.

There is no emotion; there is peace.

He'd thought exhaustion would be a form of peace. But Jax now realized the folly of eschewing sleep for the past thirty hours. He needed his mind to be clear and steady. If he was going to find Yimmon, he needed every faculty and power he possessed at his command—faculties that were presently shutting down.

There is no ignorance; there is knowledge.

He not only needed knowledge, he needed to be able to marshal it, recall it, use it. He was far from that—far from even knowing where to begin his quest for Yimmon.

There is no passion; there is serenity.

But he *wasn't* serene. Passion roiled just below the surface—passion that had no practical outlet. What he wanted—to go back in time, to rewrite the last two days—he could not do. He tried to haul the burst of energy under control, to redirect it back to the path—to the tree. But his mind rebelled, urging him to *do* when there was no clear thing to be done.

There is no chaos; there is harmony.

There was nothing *but* chaos. Nothing. Jax Pavan, Jedi, was empty of anything but disorder and turmoil.

There is no death; there is the Force.

As a Jedi he had been taught that, at death, an individual became one with the Force. If that were true, might he not be able to feel Laranth through the Force in some small way? Again, he felt the urge to reach out in the hope that Laranth would reach back. He repressed the compulsion, fought it down. And he could no longer pretend that Darth Vader was the reason for his reluctance.

He felt the tears on his cheeks, warm and wet, just before the sobs racked him.

The "assistant" that Degan Cor gave Den was a kid. A Rodian kid. An orphan. Which meant that, as much as Den felt like refusing the offer, he didn't.

Really, how did you say no to an orphan?

The kid had a droid that he'd built himself. He called it Candy because it was a "sweet tin can." It had once been an old P2 unit but bore little resemblance to one now. The kid—his name was Geri—had replaced the P2's turret with the head of an RX series pilot droid. Den thought "Bug-Eyes" was a far better name for the thing than "Candy," but he wasn't about to say anything out loud. He hardly had room to comment about the size of anyone else's eyeballs—besides, it might hurt the Rodian boy's feelings.

If the assistant wasn't exactly impressive at first glance, the workshop he ushered Den into surely was. It was thirty meters long and roughly half as wide. The equipment and tools—though clearly scavenged from a variety of sources—were mostly state-of-the-art with a lot of upgrades and modifications, some of which would have been mind boggling even if Den hadn't been nursing a sleep-deprivation headache that was unimpressed with the four hours of shut-eye he'd managed to get over the past two days.

The droid diagnostic station was extraordinary. It had not one but three artificial intelligence modules daisy-chained together in such a way that the operator could assess and repair a droid's neural pathways in less than half the time it would take with one.

"That's amazing," said Den. "Degan put that together?"

"No. I did," Geri said. There was no boastfulness in the simple admission. The kid grinned in that queerly Rodian way, the corners of his mouth turning up as the tip of his protuberant muzzle turned down. "Degan says I have a knack for machines."

Hero worship. As Den recalled from somewhere in his misty past, it felt good to have heroes.

"Then we've come to the right place," said I-Five from under Den's arm.

The Sullustan jumped. He'd forgotten the droid was there.

Geri's grin curled farther up at the corners. "Got that right! Wait'll you see the inventory."

He crossed to a pair of metal doors at one end of the workshop and pushed them open, then beckoned to Den.

The kid was right. The "inventory" was incredible—droids and bots and parts thereof lined the walls of a room not much smaller than the workshop itself. Den had expected a mad jumble, but the parts were arranged neatly, if randomly. Heads and turrets, treads, legs, and arms were racked in a celebration of orderliness, but . . .

"Okay, I can see you've got a system," Den said, "but I don't quite—"

"They're in Rodian alphabetical order," Five said testily. "May we get on with finding me an appropriate vehicle?"

"Yeah," Den said. He asked Geri, "Got anything in an I-5YQ?"

Proboscis wrinkling and head swiveling, Geri surveyed his inventory. "We don't get much call for protocol droids here. Mostly I repair tech-bots. I have a 9T and a couple of 5Ys." He pointed at a peculiar, stumpy-legged droid with long, slender arms and no exoskeleton.

"I'd look like a garbage snipe. Don't you have anything more closely approximating my original body?"

"I have part of an LE-BO2D9. But only the torso, arms, and head. Mostly we've got arms and cortices. Those are the parts we use most."

"Do you have the rest of that RX unit you used for your little friend there?"

Candy, who'd been sitting silently in the doorway behind them, let out a bleep of outrage at the adjective.

"Pardon," said I-Five. "I meant no disrespect."

Candy accepted the apology with a single chirp.

Geri was shaking his head. "Sorry. The head was all we salvaged."

"I can empathize," I-Five told the RX-P2 hybrid. It uttered a muted trill.

"What are your top three desired features?" Geri asked, sounding like a used-droid salesman.

"Strength, maneuverability, and modifiability."

Geri considered this, then began prowling through the neat racks of bots and parts, muttering to himself.

Den, bored and bone-tired, glanced around the workshop. He found his gaze returning again and again to a shadowy corner of the room in which he could just make out someone standing and staring at him.

"Uh, Geri—who's that?"

The boy looked up and followed his gaze into the shadows. He laughed. "That's not a who. That's a what. It's a BB-4000."

"A what?"

"Let me see it," said I-Five.

Den picked up the droid's head and carried it back into the corner.

Gazing at what stood there, Den frowned. It looked like a man in close-fitting dark blue coveralls. But it wasn't a man. It wasn't moving. Not a muscle. Not a breath. Not an eye flutter beneath the closed lids. It was weird.

He realized, belatedly, that it was standing in an open crate. A neatly printed label along one side read: BB-4000.

"This is a droid?"

Geri didn't bother to look up from his rummaging. "It's a Bobbie-Bot, an HRD—human replicant droid."

"How," asked I-Five, "in the seven hells of Frolix did you manage to get one of these?"

"We've got two. You've heard of LeisureMech."

"Even *I've* heard of LeisureMech," said Den. "They

risked everything on the success of their human replicant series. Customers didn't take to them, and LeisureMech went under."

"Yeah, well, when they went under they sold off all
their remaining stock. Degan got ours for a song. I
think they're pretty cool, even with—y'know—that
whole weirdness about him being too human to feel like
a droid and too inhuman to seem like a real person."

"He is, indeed, pretty cool," said I-Five. "Is he func-
tional?"

"Nah. One of the reasons Degan got them so cheap
was the lack of working processor units. They're wired
for brains—all the relays are in place to the frame and
musculature—but there's nothing in there."

"Interesting," I-Five said in a tone of voice that Den
found far too thoughtful.

"Five, you don't want one. They *melt*. Don't you remember? Kaird told us he'd seen one melt." Den shuddered at the memory. "In the Factory District, just
before we—well, *you*, actually—blew the place up real
good."

"Good times," I-Five said softly. Then he continued:
"Anyway, those were 3000-series droids. This is the
next generation; a different design than the previous
models. They gave up on genomic/algorithmic programming and cloning organs from synthflesh, and
concentrated on neural net parallel processing, which
greatly increased neural interaction and downgraded
the development of killer memes. The downside was
that it took longer and cost more—"

"But no disgusting puddles to get out of your carpet,"
Geri finished. "Except it wasn't the melting that killed
LeisureMech. It was the ECD."

Den shook his head. "The what?"

"Eerie Coulee Disorder," said I-Five. "It refers to a
pronounced sense of unease experienced by most hu-

mans and humanoids when they encounter a droid that appears almost, but not quite, human. Most humanoids are genetically programmed toward pareidolia, which is the ability to extrapolate complex images or sounds from simple stimuli; seeing a face in the clouds, for example. The Witch Nebula is a classic interpolation of—"

"He'll go on like this for hours if you let him," Den remarked.

"It's kinda interesting," Geri said. "But," he continued, addressing the droid, "what's your point?"

"My point is that the problem is easy to fix. It's a simple matter of shade-shifting in subtle skin tones. The droid looks weird to sentients because his skin is too uniform a shade."

Geri stared at him. "Huh. Y'know, that makes a lot of sense. Too bad you weren't working for LM back then. Wonder why none of their engineers ever thought of it."

"Probably," said I-Five, "because they never asked a droid."

"May I remind you," said Den, "that your master power switch is still operational, and ever so much easier for me to reach?"

The droid uttered a mechanical snort, then asked Geri, "Did you find anything useful?"

"What? Oh, yeah. What about this?"

He lifted something out onto the floor. It was a ridiculously compact collection of metal rods and joints surmounted by what looked like a shallow soup kettle or an AT-AT pilot's helmet. It barely came up to Den's kneecaps.

"Uh," Den said, "isn't that a little . . . small?"

"Oh, sorry. Here." Geri tapped the bot on the top of its helmeted head and it unfolded itself, popping up to become recognizable as a diminutive but immensely strong DUM pit droid. Not much over a meter in height, the DUMs were used to repair aircars and Podracers . . . which Den suspected must be vanishingly rare on this densely forested part of Toprawa.

"How'd that get here?" Den asked.

"One of the Rangers used to be a champion Podracer down south. It's a lot drier and desertier there," Geri said. "Anyway, she was a race driver until she wiped out about two years ago. Lost an eye. She's got an implant now, of course, but she gave up racing. This little guy—" He indicated the pit droid. "—got his neural net scragged in the same accident. One of the drivers came into the pit too hot."

"So," I-Five said, "it has no brain."

"Yeah. Just the basic reflexes. I can fold him up and unfold him, order him to walk around, but that's about it."

"Strong, maneuverable, and modifiable," mused I-Five. "And great manual dexterity—a plus if I'm going to self-modify. I'd say it will do just fine. Will my cortex fit under the helm?"

Geri considered this. "With some modifications. Of course, I could just mount your head on the chassis."

Den stifled a chuckle. "That would be . . . interesting."

"Yes," agreed I-Five. "It would. And I don't want to be interesting. I want to be invisible. Where we're going, invisibility is a definite asset."

"Well, great," Geri enthused, rubbing his hands together. "Ready for a little science experiment?"

Den took a deep breath. "Look, Five. This is great for now, but . . . but you don't want to—y'know—*stay* that way, right?" He inclined his head toward the little pit droid.

"Eventually, I should like to find my way back into a YQ chassis or something equivalent. But for now, this will do. Although I'd also like to take along some spare parts, Geri, if you don't mind."

Geri's muzzle contorted into a grin. "Freezin'," he said. "Let's do it."

"I'm surprised you didn't consider the Jedi starfighter," said Degan. His voice was muffled and tinny due to the fact that he was lying inside the interceptor's ion-exhaust manifold, aligning the baffles.

"Too small," said Jax automatically. "It's made to hold only a pilot and a droid."

"I could mod it for you. We could make room for your Sullustan friend."

This came from the engineer assisting Degan with the refit. Her name was Sacha Swiftbird. Swiftbird had been her alias during her Podracing days, and she'd kept it even after coming to the Rangers.

That puzzled Jax. She couldn't have been much older than he was and had been forced into early retirement by a horrific accident—which she hinted had been no accident at all, but the vicious revenge of a losing driver—during a race. It had left her with a cybernetic implant where her left eye had been, and a silvery fila-ment of scarring across her upper and lower eyelids. Right now both were covered by a thick lock of black hair. It was hard to understand why she'd want to keep the name that went with that dead life. Jax didn't ask why. In fact, he found it hard to meet her pale gray gaze. Her scars reminded him of Laranth's. The Gray Pala-din, too, had been left with scar tissue—her personal souvenirs of Order 66 and Flame Night.

Jax shook his head, his gaze on the drive manifold. "I'm not really ready to advertise to the galaxy that I'm Jedi. And I don't need fighting capability. What I need is stealth with speed and muscle. This is perfect."

He could feel the woman's regard for a moment more,

before she shrugged and knelt to rummage in her tool-kit. "Your call. But if I were you, I'd jump at a chance to fly that baby."

"You're not me," Jax murmured, regretting the words the moment they left his mouth. Fortunately, Swiftbird didn't seem to hear him—or if she did, she chose to ignore the jibe.

"Well, this may not be as sleek and piratical as the starfighter," Degan said, pulling himself out of the interceptor's manifold. "But it'll hold your crew with room to spare, that's for sure. And cargo as well, if you need it."

"Yeah," added Sacha. "And it'll surprise the pants off anybody who mistakes it for a stock freighter."

That it would, Jax suspected. "Are you sure you don't need the ship more than we do?" Jax asked for the tenth time.

Degan paused in the act of wiping his hands on a towel, glanced at Sacha, then gave Jax a look that neatly penetrated tissue and bone and drilled straight into his soul.

"We're all *we*, Jax. We're all Whiplash, whatever we choose to call ourselves. Rangers, resistance, freedom fighters . . . It doesn't really matter. We're all on the same side. If you need the ship, you get the ship."

Jax smiled his thanks, wishing that the expression were more than just a physical tugging of his lips.

"What are you going to call her?" Sacha asked.

Laranth. The name leapt to Jax's mind so quickly, he almost spoke it aloud. "I . . . hadn't really thought. I suppose I'll let Den pick something."

"Laranth." Den said the name immediately when Jax asked him, later that day.

He stood with Jax, Degan, and Sacha on the landing pad beneath the soaring vault of Mountain Home, looking up at the interceptor. Seeing the sudden shuttering of Jax's face—the cold remoteness of his eyes—he winced. "I-I mean, it seems like we ought to do *something*—"

Jax cut off a flare of sudden anger—at what or whom, he was uncertain. Maybe he was angry at the universe, or at the gods, or at the Force for abandoning them. For abandoning *her*. For putting Yimmon in the hands of Darth Vader and the Emperor.

Den started again. "I want to remember her, Jax. I want to honor her. I want—"

"You want her to still be here. So do I. But she's not." Jax closed his eyes, then added, "Laranth . . . is a good name."

"I agree," said a voice practically in Jax's ear, "that a battle-ready, stealthy vessel such as this one would be a fitting recipient of Laranth's name."

Jax swung around. *"Five?"*

The little pit droid with I-Five's voice had stalked across the landing pad with Geri following triumphantly in his wake. The odd-looking droid turned its single, oversized "eye" to the vessel, giving her a sweeping once-over. "She looks quite fit."

"So do you," Degan said tentatively. "A bit, um, different than the last time I saw you."

"Think of me as a work in progress."

Sacha gave him a wry once-over. "You're a bit more outspoken than Ducky was, too."

"Ducky," I-Five repeated.

"My pit droid. You're wearing him." She gestured at I-Five's new armature.

"I hope it doesn't distress you."

"Nah. In fact, I'm happy to see his pitiful remains have been put to good use."

Something in the tone of her voice and the tilt of her head made Den suspect the ex-racer wasn't nearly so blasé as the remark implied. He crossed gazes with Geri over the top of I-Five's new head—now level with his own. He'd left the little Rodian in the workshop supposedly working on some logistical problems caused by I-Five's large cortex. Problems that—to the exhausted, emotionally drained Sullustan—had seemed insurmountable.

"I see you solved the braincase problem."

The Rodian shrugged. "Yeah . . . well . . ."

"Geri," said I-Five, "is a resourceful and creative young sentient."

Geri grinned and ran a hand along I-Five's carefully handcrafted braincase. He had created a sort of sagittal crest that ran from the front of the helm to the back in an elegant and gleaming ridge. "It's got all sorts of shielding up in there, too, and a special shock mount. Not to mention that the crest is reinforced with tri-clad durasteel. If all else fails, he can serve as a battering ram."

Geri's ubiquitous droid, which had rolled up behind him on the platform, uttered a trill of what sounded to Den like mechanical laughter. I-Five swiveled his head to regard the other droid. "I fail to see the humor."

"You would," Den muttered.

Jax shook his head. "I don't know if I'll ever get used to your voice coming out of that . . ."

"Don't get used to it," I-Five advised him. "I've no intention of staying like this."

He advanced toward the interceptor with a delicate whir of servos. Geri had certainly done a nice job on the mechanics.

"Correct me if I'm wrong," I-Five said, addressing Degan, "but doesn't the Helix-class freighter have an LBE flight computer?"

The mech-tech nodded. "Enhanced, of course."

"Of course. Can you enhance it further to allow for direct interface with a second artificial intelligence?"

"Meaning you?"

"Meaning me," I-Five said. "At least in my present incarnation."

"It's got a mount for an auxiliary R2 unit, but—"

"That should do nicely, I think."

"But you're not an R2 unit."

"Not at the moment, no." I-Five turned to Geri, gesturing toward the tunnels that led back to the underground facility. "I have an idea. Are you ready for some more science experiments?"

Geri's face lit up and his eyes seemed to grow bigger— if that were possible. "Freezin'!" he enthused, and loped off toward his workshop with both droids in tow.

Jax watched them with an uneasy expression on his face. "Den, would you go make sure they don't do anything that . . . can't be undone?"

Den nodded, getting it. Things were changing a bit too fast for him, too. He followed his "assistant" and the droids from the cavern.

"So, what's this plan of yours?" Den asked I-Five when they'd reconvened in the workshop.

"It is easier to show you than to tell you," I-Five said, and reached up to release a catch on the underside of his helm. It flipped up to reveal a steel mounting cage suspended in a well behind the little droid's optics. "Geri and I were able to place my synaptic grid cortex into this case, which will allow it to be moved more easily from one receptacle to another."

Den just blinked at him. "That's . . . um. Wow. So when you were talking about the R2 . . ." He trailed off as Geri steered just such a unit out into the center of the workshop under the bright lights of his operating theater. "You intend to interface directly with the ship through the astromech."

"Isn't that just freezin'?" Geri asked enthusiastically. "Man, I wish I had a droid who could think like this one."

Candy's bleat eloquently conveyed complete outrage.

"Freezin'," Den muttered, and dived back into the work. Keeping his hands and mind busy distracted him from the hard reality of what it meant to return to Coruscant under their present circumstances.

seven

Jax was letting nothing distract him from their return to Coruscant. He had wasted a day and a half. It was enough. He had a deadline now—a window of opportunity in which to try to track Vader's movements since the ambush. The interceptor would be ready for her shakedown in two days' time. He needed to bring something back to Coruscant with him besides loss and grief. He needed to return with some sort of lead on Thi Xon Yimmon and Darth Vader.

To that end, he'd broached the subject with Aren Folee as they sat together in the mess hall of the subterranean complex.

"All I've got," he told her, "is data from the escape pod. If I could get data from any ships or observation posts you have in the sector . . ."

"No sooner asked than done," she said. "We've been working on that angle already."

"Any conclusions?"

"About where he went? No. But at first blush it looks as if he used the gravimetric distortions around the Twins to disguise his movements. Clearly, they had to have jumped into the area, then used ion propulsion to position their forces."

"Which would have left a trail."

"Exactly. So if you want to come to the command center—"

He really didn't want to be in the command center. He'd already noted that his presence had attracted much attention—and speculation—about who he was and where he'd come from. "Is there any way I could work on this from some other, more private location?"

Aren nodded. "Sure. There's a workstation-slash-conference-room right next to the communications bay. I can have any data you want routed there. Do you want my help in going over it?"

"No," he said more sharply than he meant to. "I . . . might need the tracking data from your ship, though. You might have picked up something . . ."

Something I failed to notice, he finished silently.

She looked as if she were going to reply, but didn't. She just nodded and went to make arrangements for the data transfer.

Jax was in the workstation when Den came looking for him about an hour later.

"They said I'd find you here. What are you doing?"

Jax looked up from the sim he was constructing from the several data streams he'd sampled from tracking stations and ships that fed the resistance telemetry. The work was slow and piecemeal, even with the help of the station AI.

"Trying to figure out where Vader came from and where he went."

Den's face brightened. "Looks like I got here just in time, then. I've got just the thing to make the work go faster—a hot-rod pit droid with all sorts of bells and whistles. Weaponry, force shields, redundant core mechanisms, and a through-put of a gazillion teraflops per second. The downside is that it comes with I-Five's acerbic personality. Couldn't get Geri to program that out of him."

Jax took a deep breath and let it out. He wasn't sure

he was ready for levity yet. "Are you sure he's up to this? Have you run diagnostics on him?"

"Up to it? Sure we've run diagnostics. He's fine. Well, okay—apart from having been blown to bits. Whatever reinforcements your dad put in Five's braincase saved his life . . . or facsimile thereof. He can do this. Better than you can. He doesn't have to wait for the data to be visible before he decodes and understands what it means."

Jax glanced down at the flat-screen display he'd been studying. He wanted the data to be visible—*needed* it to be visible—with an intensity he didn't understand. Somewhere in that data was the answer to a question, the question to which Jax Pavan really wanted—*needed*—an answer.

Why? *Why* had Laranth died . . . and was there a scenario in which she *didn't* die?

"If I-Five parses all of this, I might as well go climb a tree, Den."

"With all due respect, if we don't let him parse it, we might miss something."

"You mean *I* might miss something."

Den opened his mouth, closed it, then opened it again and said, "Yeah. That is what I mean."

He was right. Jax knew he was right. The Jedi fought with himself over it momentarily, recognized both the futility and stupidity of the fight, and nodded. "Right. You're right. I'm not thinking clearly. Let's bring I-Five in."

It was the right decision. As wrong as it felt.

Within five minutes of putting I-Five in charge of the data streams Jax realized another reason he'd been avoiding this collaboration. It reminded him forcibly that Laranth was gone. As long as he existed on his own, her specter agreed to stay at bay. When Den and I-Five weren't there, working as a team to remind him of her absence, he could pretend it was temporary. With the familiar voices in his ears, he knew it was not.

He shook himself. He had to get used to this. There was no other option.

I-Five's new chassis lent the proceedings an air of considerable surrealism. The pint-sized droid eschewed a chair and seated himself on the workstation desktop, from which he manipulated the data by plugging a much-enhanced digit directly into a port.

Jax shared what he'd been thinking about the ion trail and the need the 501st had to maneuver into the vicinity of the Twins at subluminal speeds. I-Five confirmed the appropriateness of the approach immediately and within minutes had constructed a sim of the ambush from the cobbled-together output of a host of sources—including his own data from the *Far Ranger*. He displayed his sim via a holographic projection pod that Geri had installed behind his optics.

It showed the moment of their emergence from the Twins' fractious gravitational fields into the "free" space beyond, and the speedy approach of their reception committee. The *Far Ranger* was a bright point of blue light; the Imperial ships were red. Other traffic in the area was rendered in a muted green.

Jax felt as if had a lead weight in his chest—heavy and poisonous. The Moment, frozen in time . . .

"There," said Den. "Ion trails."

There were indeed ion trails. They ran like fine filaments of crimson thread away from the Twins toward the Galactic Core; they ended at the point the ships entered local space just outside the Twins' gravity well.

"That's where they came from," said I-Five. "Let's see if that's also where they went."

He ran the sim forward in time, past the moment in which Jax had hesitated between ensuring Laranth's safety and Yimmon's, past the moment in which Laranth drew her last breath and said her last whispered words, past the moment when I-Five was blown apart, past the moment in which Thi Xon Yimmon was lost to the Dark Lord, past the moment in which the *Far Ranger* was shredded by the forces of the twin suns . . . and finally, past the moment when the blood-bright shards streaked away and disappeared into hyperspace.

Den let out a low chuffing sound that—for a Sullustan—functioned like a whistle. "They're *not* all headed back to the Core. Some of them are outward-bound."

But Jax had noticed something else in the sim—several separate patterns of green signatures that had also left threads exiting local space within the same short time period. Some were oriented in the same direction as the red signatures, while others seemed to have been heading for the Core Worlds when they jumped.

"What are these?" He indicated each of four separate patterns.

I-Five shifted the display to show the new pattern of points and trails in yellow. "I would say those were formations of vessels in the vicinity of the Twins that headed out at approximately the same time Vader's squadron did."

"When did they enter?"

I-Five ran the sim backward again to the point at which Vader's Fist appeared from hyperspace. The pattern of crimson dots that represented Vader's 501st was augmented by a sun-bright scattering of yellow ones.

"They all came here together, apparently," said I-Five. "And look at this . . ." He ran the sim forward in time again. One of the red points of light seemed to be headed off in company with a set of the yellow ones.

Jax watched as the ships separated into five groupings and moved toward the Twins. Then the lone red light changed course, rejoining its fellows and moving toward the Moment.

"Obviously," said Den quietly, "those were all Imperial squadrons. I'm honored to have required so much firepower."

Jax rocked back in his seat. *Vader*. Vader had been in that lone ship—the one that had altered course. He had brought that many ships and assigned them different positions because he'd had only a general idea about where the *Far Ranger* might be. Something had changed his mind about that. Maybe he'd just picked up their signature or maybe they'd done something to betray themselves. Jax supposed he might never know. But he did know the general direction Vader and his forces had taken entering and leaving the area. Some of the ships had returned to the Core, apparently, while others had gone elsewhere.

That was all the tactical display revealed—two groups of ships that jumped to hyperspace with different orientations. The question was: which group was Vader's command ship with—and was Yimmon aboard?

Den had tried a number of times to draw Jax into the modifications that he, Geri, and I-Five were making to the droid. Modifications that, under any other circumstances, Jax would have taken a keen interest and even had a hand in. But Den found the Jedi was focused with laser sharpness on one thing and one thing only— tracking Vader's ship. He had searched myriad hyper- comm messages looking for mention of a fleet of Imperial vessels or, barring that, a group of starfighters with an Imperial cruiser acting as a mother ship.

There was one vague report of an unexpected and brief Imperial presence on Mandalore, several others— less vague—of a large contingent of Imperial fighters moving through the Galactic Core. A decision had to be made, then, about which route they would try to trace, and there was no exact information on which to base that decision. Which meant that Jax Pavan must feel as impotent as Den Dhur did. Of course, Jax had the Force to fall back on, so Den asked what he'd gleaned from that resource.

Nothing, he'd said. But there was something about the way he'd said it that left Den with a cold, clammy sensation in the pit of his stomach. *Did you even check?* he wanted to ask, but didn't. Instead he merely asked, "Where are we going, then?"

"Coruscant. It makes the most sense that Vader's gone there, where the Emperor can oversee the interrogation and where he's got the best security apparatus in place."

Where the Emperor can oversee the interrogation. Now, *there* was a phrase that sent a vacuum-level chill through the bone.

eight

The night before the *Laranth*'s shakedown, Jax couldn't sleep. Couldn't meditate. Could barely think straight at times, though he knew that for the sake of his companions and the resistance he had to pretend that he could. So in the middle of the night, he decided he might as well move his few belongings onto the ship and get used to her "feel."

The interceptor was much smaller than the *Far Ranger*, and Jax found that though the captain's quarters reflected the size differential, they were comfortable enough. He located a place for the miisai tree on a tray that pulled out from the wall next to the bunk. The little "smart pot" the miisai now nestled in was equipped with a set of contacts on the base that allowed it to sync with the ship's power grid. It used a delicate sensor array to monitor the plant's nutrient supply and liquid and kept it watered by pulling the needed moisture from the air. A soft yellow light glowed on the front of the shallow pot when the nutrient reservoir became depleted, and a proximity alarm sounded a gentle tone if it sensed movement in the vicinity of the hungry tree—a mechanical means for the miisai to ask for food. Jax swore he would never have occasion to see the light or hear the tone.

Now he filled the reservoir with some crumbled bits of a protein bar that the smart pot would break down into its component parts. Then he sat cross-legged on the floor of the cabin and tried to clear his mind. He focused on his breathing—on visualizing the Force as ribbons of healing energy that wrapped themselves around him.

As before, when he opened his eyes, he saw the energy pulsing and flowing up through the little tree—root to trunk to delicate branch. It danced among the needles and sent filaments out toward him to entwine with the Force ribbons he was generating.

This was a new experience. He was surprised at the sense of warmth and serenity he felt watching the energy strands from the miisai mingle with his own. His meditative state deepened and, at last, he was able to invoke the Jedi mantra.

There is no emotion; there is peace.
There is no ignorance; there is knowledge.
There is no passion; there is serenity.
There is no chaos; there is harmony.
There is no death; there is the Force.

He turned the words in his mind without delving too deeply into their meaning. The rhythm of them was what he craved.

Yes, *craved*. That was the word. He'd spent days in turmoil; this softly eddying tranquillity was balm.

He savored it momentarily, then turned his thoughts to Thi Xon Yimmon . . . and to Darth Vader. There was a trembling in his concentration when he did that, but he held his thoughts steady. If he was to use the Force to help him find the Whiplash leader, he must be steady. He pictured I-Five's holographic tracers of the Imperial ships as if they floated in the warp and woof of the Force energies around him. He reached into and through the image, groping for the darkness that would be in Vader's wake.

In a split second he was back in the dim smoky corridor on the *Far Ranger*, face-to-face-mask with the Dark Lord.

"I have one more thing to take from you," Vader had said.

Jax cringed away from the reality.

Anakin Skywalker had said that.

Anakin had taken Laranth from him—Yimmon, too. And more. How much more, Jax was only just beginning to realize.

Why? Why was the Dark Lord toying with him as a predator toys with its prey? What possible benefit did the Empire derive from that?

The answer came in an epiphany. This wasn't about the Empire or the Emperor. Vader had said it himself: he obeyed the Emperor *in his own way*. This was about *Vader's* choices, not Palpatine's.

What was it the Cephalon had said? *Choice is loss; indecision is all loss.*

Had that been as true for Anakin Skywalker as it was for Jax Pavan? Had there been a moment in which the Dark Lord might have engaged him in battle—perhaps killed or captured him—and had the man behind the mask missed that opportunity in his own moment of indecision?

"Why do you hate me?" Jax murmured. "What have I done?"

The answer came to him as strongly as if it had been spoken aloud: He had *survived*. He had survived Order 66 and he existed to this day as a reminder of . . . what—of failure? Was Jax merely the one who got away—or was there more to it than that?

When he looks at me . . . does he see what he might have been?

Jax's memory provided him with a startlingly vivid image of sparring with Anakin at a time when he had assumed he and his friend might both someday achieve the station of Jedi Master. That had been *his* aim, anyway, though he had often been struck with the uneasy sense that Anakin was not content with that.

He reached into the small pocket in the sash of his tunic that housed the pyronium Anakin had given into his care. It gleamed on his palm—a gem the size of a small egg, iridescent and otherworldly. It was an unknown quantity, alleged to be a source of unimaginable power. A power that was—also allegedly—to be called forth *if* one only knew the secret. And that, Jax had been led to believe, was revealed on the Sith holocron he had received from Haninum Tyk Rhinann. The holocron that his father, Lorn Pavan, had once tried to acquire.

Another unknown quantity. Jax still had the holocron, but he had never attempted to access the knowledge it contained. Sith holocrons were rare, powerful, and reputed to be deeply disturbing to the Force and seductive to Jedi who interacted with them unprepared for the assault that deep a store of dark knowledge could make on reason. The holocron created a slight disturbance in the Force through its very existence—at least Jax could feel its subtle pull when he was near it—and he had not wanted to risk attempting to activate it.

Truthfully, he doubted he had the capacity to do that now. His fractured concentration rendered his unease with the Sith artifact irrelevant.

Jax glanced up at the shelf the miisai sat upon. The holocron was tucked into a small trove in the rear wall of the niche created when the shelf was extended from the bulkhead. He was sometimes tempted to lose both the pyronium and the holocron by entombing them somewhere so he'd never have to think of either again, but he hadn't followed through on the impulse. The thought of having them fall into the hands of Darth Vader was blood chilling. So he kept them close, reasoning that someday he might find a legitimate use for them.

Certainly, neither had pleasant memories attached. By the time Anakin had given him the pyronium—to keep for him, he'd said—Jax had already had concerns about his friend. He remembered the first time he had glimpsed Anakin in a moment of anger, radiating tendrils of blackest night—whipcords of darkness that had writhed about him, straining outward.

They had been sparring with their lightsabers, and *something*—to this day, Jax wasn't sure what—had transformed the other Jedi from an amicable, if distracted, sparring partner into a driven foe. He had suddenly launched himself at Jax like a berserker, forcing him to parry a swift series of blows that might easily have killed him.

Jax had seen darkness in auras before, but never like that and never in a fellow Padawan. Anakin had appeared—in that moment—to stand at the nexus of a whorl of rage and frustration. He was a black hole—sucking light and color from anything or anyone in his gravitational field.

That moment had passed so swiftly that Jax thought he'd imagined it. He'd been left reeling and confused—and embarrassed when Anakin had broken off the attack, grinned at him, slapped his shoulder, and asked, "What's the matter, Jax? Am I too much for you?"

Later, he'd been on the verge of telling his Master what he'd sensed, but the fact that even Anakin's own Master, Obi-Wan Kenobi, watching from the sidelines, seemed not to have noticed anything had silenced him.

If Jax had spoken of what he'd felt then, would things

have been different? Had that been yet another moment in which choice was loss and indecision deadly?

He drew in a sharp breath and tried to marshal his thoughts, slipping the pyronium back into his sash pocket. The tendrils of darkness that he had once thought imaginary he now knew were the threads of Darth Vader's immense potential power. He thrust down images of the Jedi Temple, the sparring circle, the memories of Flame Night that threatened, suddenly, to intrude. He called back the mental image of I-Five's tactical display, then reached into it—toward that one, bright spot of crimson—seeking the darkness that always eddied in Darth Vader's wake.

No.

The uneasiness stopped him just short of putting his "hand" on the trailing edge of that darkness.

He'll sense you. He'll know you seek him.

(The *Far Ranger,* filled with smoke and the smell of burnt flesh, emergency lights flickering, Laranth lying dead behind him on the deck . . .)

He thrust the memory down and reached again.

Leave it for now. Let him think you might be dead.

Jax hesitated in the act of touching the darkness, wary of his own uncertainty.

(Vader standing in the smoky corridor, coldly taunting.)

Jax opened his eyes and flung himself to his feet, panting. Was there no situation that did not require choice? Was there nothing he might do without indecision?

He looked around him at the snug cabin, laid a hand on the metal bulkhead. It was neither warm nor cool to the touch. The ship was silent. Not even the ventilation system was audible as it breathed warm air into the compartment. He imagined the vessel was waiting for him to do something—to *decide* something.

He did. He decided to leave the ship and return to his quarters in the underground complex. He left his belongings and the miisai tree behind.

The shakedown cruise went off without a snag. I-Five's brain was successfully paired with an R2 unit that Geri had scavenged from storage and fitted neatly into the ship's astrogation system. The setup gave the interceptor the reflexes of a bat-falcon—as swiftly as I-Five could conceive of a maneuver, the ship could execute it. If they found themselves in a battle situation, that ability to make seamless, split-second decisions could mean the difference between success and failure—or life and death.

The shakedown completed, the ship refueled and laden with a couple of crates of I-Five's "spare parts," Jax, Den, and I-Five stood on the landing pad in Mountain Home with their hosts. Besides Degan Cor and Aren Folee, there were a handful of others, including Sacha Swiftbird and Geri.

Degan had offered to send Sacha along with Jax to facilitate any necessary repairs on the ship and to serve as emissary from the Toprawan resistance. Jax had declined the offer.

"I don't know what sort of situation we're going to be confronting on Coruscant," he'd explained. "Whiplash is in the process of reorganizing itself; the Imperials may be in a state of heightened security or even heightened aggression. Vader has very likely taken Yimmon there to interrogate him. I don't want to put anyone else's life in danger unnecessarily."

He didn't add that the presence of a woman on the ship would only underscore Laranth's absence.

"Put *my* life in danger?" Sacha objected. "I'd be there to protect *you*, Pavan, not the other way around."

"I'm not doubting your capabilities . . ." He'd started

to hedge, but she fixed him with that too-direct gaze and he'd swallowed the words.

"I know what you're doing. You're not comfortable with me. I get that. I wouldn't let it push me into stupid decisions if I were you."

He'd opened his mouth to respond, and she'd stopped him. "Yeah, yeah, I know—I'm *not* you."

"I was just going to say, I don't think the decision is stupid. You could be of help, yes. You could also be out of your element. Aren says you've rarely been off Toprawa and that you've never been to Imperial Center. It's a . . . a different sort of place."

She gave him a lopsided grin. "You mean I'd be in the way and possibly call unwelcome attention to myself by gawping at everything."

"Something like that."

She'd shrugged and dropped the subject. Neither she nor Degan brought it up again.

Their farewells were brief, and their hold was full of useful items for the Whiplash, including some of the ionite and a selection of droid parts for I-Five and Den to experiment with. They lifted off in the dead of night without running lights, piloted by the droid's R2 persona. Once in hyperspace, I-Five completed integrating the vessel's false identity into its every virtual nook and cranny. For obvious reasons, it could not be the *Laranth* in galactic records. People who knew of Jax Pavan might associate that name with him.

He hadn't cared what she was called when it came down to it. She was just a ship. Den rechristened her *Corsair,* and so it was *Corsair* that bore Jax and his companions back to Coruscant.

nine

The *Corsair*—a small, independent freighter registered to a tiny consortium on Toprawa—landed at a satellite docking facility of the Westport that was geared to
handle vessels of diminutive size. She nestled in among a
dozen or so ships of the same tonnage on a landing platform and disgorged her crew—a human male with dark,
unkempt hair, a Sullustan mechanic, and a pit droid
that had been tasked with carrying their belongings.

To the casual observer the ship and her complement
were ordinary and unworthy of any particular attention, but to those who had been keeping an eye out for
just such an occurrence—the landing of a small ship out
of Toprawa with a shiny new registry, for all that it
seemed to have been buried in the system for five
years—the event signaled the need for quick action.

And so, when "Corran Vigil" and his crew stepped
into the terminal building with the intent of taking a turbolift to the deep sublevels, they met with an escort. A
Zabrak official wearing a worn, dark long-coat and ac-
companied by two uniformed officers flashed credentials
at them. Jax Pavan didn't need to see the credentials. He
knew whom he was dealing with.

"Corran Vigil? I need to take you in for questioning,
if you don't mind. Actually, even if you do mind."

Jax stared at the other man. "May I ask what this is
about?"

"There's a little problem with the registration on your ship and a certain connection to someone who's gone missing."

Jax nodded, shifting his weight from one foot to the other.

The Zabrak regarded him with wry amusement. "I do hope you're not going to do anything rash, like try to run off on me. I assure you my associates here are used to that sort of thing. They rather enjoy a good run, in fact."

Jax sighed. "Look, Prefect, I don't know what this is about, but—"

"Come with me and you'll find out."

"Come where?"

"Imperial Security Bureau."

Den Dhur let out a hiss of breath. "Great Mother of all . . ."

The prefect pointed a long grayish finger at him. "Language."

He herded them into a lift and they shot down into the bowels of the terminal, exiting into a cavernous parking area. A pair of police speeders were drawn up to the curbing in front of the terminal's transparisteel doors.

The two uniforms prodded the prisoners into the backseat of one of the vehicles, carefully locking the hatches from the outside. Then they saluted the prefect smartly, went to their own vehicle, and sped off. The prefect watched them go, then slid into the front seat of the aircar, started it, and took to the lanes.

He said nothing as he drove his passengers deeper and deeper into the duracrete canyons.

Finally, Jax spoke. "Prefect Haus, we're clearly not going to the ISB. Where are you taking us?"

Pol Haus looked up into the monitor that gave him a clear view of the vehicle's backseat. "Of course we're not going to the ISB. What the hell would I be taking you to the ISB for? As for where we *are* going—we're there."

Even as he spoke, Haus pulled in behind an old police barrier and brought the aircar to a stop. Before them was a disreputable-looking building with a blackened façade and street-facing windows that looked like blank eyes. The prefect popped the locks on the doors of the police speeder. They opened with a hiss of hydraulics.

"Everybody out."

Den's heart was hammering in his throat as he climbed out of the police aircar and looked around. Haus had brought them to an abandoned transit terminal—some long-dead remnant of the planet-city's maglev system. There wasn't another sentient in sight—which did nothing to calm Den's nerves.

"Is this the part where you pull out a blaster and frag all of us?"

Haus turned and looked down at him with an air of exasperated bemusement. "No. This is where I deliver you to interested parties." He started walking in the direction of the ancient building, his coat fluttering around him like the wings of a hawk-bat.

Den looked up at Jax, who took a deep breath and strode after the police prefect.

"I-Five?" Jax murmured. "Keep a laser eye on him, okay?"

"Done," said the droid, and Den knew he would be doing exactly that. One of the modifications he had made to his DUM chassis was to replace the light emitter next to his optic unit with a weapons-grade laser.

Pol Haus had sought their help a number of times in the past, and he had helped them in turn, drawing closer and closer to an alliance with Whiplash. But things were inside out now, and for all they knew Haus could be in the service of the enemy—might somehow even be the mole that had leaked their plans to move Thi Xon Yimmon. This fact was not lost on Den.

Jax's mind was apparently moving along the same avenues, for once they were inside the abandoned terminal he asked the prefect, "What do you know about . . . the situation?"

"More than you're probably comfortable with me knowing. This way."

Haus led on past several long, deserted concierge counters and down a darkened concourse to what was clearly the entrance to a maglev embarkation platform. Den peered into the gloom of the tube. The walls were no longer gleaming and smooth, but neither did they look as derelict as he'd expected.

Haus pulled out a comlink and spoke into it. "I have a delivery for immediate pickup."

There was a curt answer from the other end of the link.

Haus pocketed the device and turned to Jax and Den. "They'll be here in a few moments. I just wanted to say . . ." He hesitated, and Den realized he'd never seen Haus show this level of diffidence—feigned cluelessness, irascibility, surliness even, but not hesitance. "I was sorry to hear about Laranth. Yimmon, too, of course, but . . ." He shook his shaggy head. "I'm just sorry. I know what it's like to lose someone that close."

Jax was regarding the prefect with solemn intensity. He held his gaze for a moment, then nodded. "Thank you."

"You lost your smart-mouthed droid, too, did you?"

"He did not," I-Five said crisply, "lose his smart-mouthed droid."

The Zabrak stared at the little pit droid, then uttered a bark of laughter. "Glad to hear it."

With a bow wave of cold, oily air and a soft whisper

of brakes, a hovertrain glided out of the darkness of the tunnel and stopped at the platform. A door hissed open in the first car.

Pol Haus tilted his head at it. "All aboard."

Den gawped. "We're going to HQ on an old maglev?"

"Not exactly." Haus herded them onto the train.

The interior of the vehicle had been stripped of its original passenger seating and now looked more like a vestibule in someone's corporate offices. Before they could ask whom they were going to see, the door to the next car opened and Tuden Sal appeared.

The Sakiyan's smile came nowhere near inhabiting his eyes. "Hello Jax, Den—I-Five?"

The droid inclined his head with a click.

"I wish we were reuniting under less . . ." Sal seemed at a loss for words. "Under less dire circumstances," he finished, then gestured to the car behind him. "Welcome to Whiplash HQ. Come on in."

Even as Sal led them into the second car, the train closed its doors and left the station. Den was surprised at that, but even more surprised that Pol Haus came with them into the inner sanctum.

They sat around a low table in the second car—Tuden Sal, Jax, Den, Pol Haus, and four Whiplash captains—a Togruta poetess named Sheel Mafeen, the Amanin owner of Sil's Place, Fars Sil-at, a Devaronian songstress named Dyat Agni, and a human black-market trader named Acer Ash. I-Five stood between Jax and Den; Pol Haus had taken a seat to Jax's right—the place Laranth usually occupied.

How long, Jax wondered, would it be before he stopped reminding himself of where Laranth would be or what she'd be doing if she were here?

"Do you have a sense," Tuden Sal was asking him, "of how Vader might have known where you were?"

Jax shook his head. "None. Maybe they . . . Maybe it was the ship. She might have been compromised in some way. Maybe there's a mole—"

"There were only six of us in the room when we made those plans. We swept the safe house for surveillance equipment before we pulled out. There was none."

"None of us," Fars Sil-at said, tipping his large head to indicate his fellow captains, "was aware of how Yimmon was getting offworld or when. And clearly the ISB had no idea where our previous headquarters was, else they'd have just come in and wiped us out. They're not subtle that way."

"What about your contacts on Toprawa?" Sal asked. "The Rangers. Could one of them or their associates have turned traitor?"

It was a horrific possibility, but a real one—and it made Jax shudder.

"Ostensibly," he said slowly, "only a handful of people in the Toprawan operation knew about the move: Degan Cor, Aren Folee, a mech-tech named Sacha Swiftbird."

"Folee could be the spy," the Sakiyan mused. "She had a mission go belly-up on her last year. Her two accomplices were caught. She wasn't."

A chilling thought, but if the Ranger had betrayed them, wouldn't Jax have sensed something in her bearing—even as he was now sensing the waves of tension and fear washing out from Tuden Sal and his confederates? Maybe not. Maybe not, given the emotional state he'd been in at the time.

"If one of them was a betrayer," Sheel Mafeen suggested, "certainly Jax or Laranth would have sensed it."

A wave of relief rolled over Jax. Both he and Laranth had met with Aren *before* their disastrous mission. Neither of them had sensed anything off about her then. If there was a spy, it was not the Antarian Ranger . . . or at least not *that* Antarian Ranger. There was still Sacha Swiftbird. She hadn't been with the Rangers for that long, and she had tried to make a case for him bringing her back to Coruscant with him . . .

He looked into the faces of these comrades-in-arms and realized that this rampant distrust was, in part, his doing. It could paralyze them if they let it. They couldn't let it.

"We have to trust someone, Sal," Jax said. "If we're going to get Yimmon back, we have to trust our allies because we're going to need them . . . and they're going to need us. There is . . . one member of Aren Folee's group who might bear watching. I'll make sure Aren is aware of it."

"*If*," the Devaronian repeated gruffly. "*If* we get Yimmon back. One must wonder what the odds of such a thing are."

"You've chosen an interim leader, I assume," I-Five said, calling abrupt attention to his diminutive presence.

Sal shook his head. "We have determined that we must have not one leader, but many. Each with different spheres of responsibility. Pol Haus, for example, is chiefly responsible for intelligence and security."

Jax turned to the police prefect. "He is?"

"It seemed to make the most sense," said Sal. "He has insider knowledge of the workings of the ISB. And he knows how to keep us well hidden. This—" He gestured around them at the hovertrain. "—was his doing."

Jax stifled a twinge of distrust. Pol Haus had been in a position to give them up repeatedly and hadn't. He'd run interference for them, made sure the Imperial Security Bureau was looking the other way, hidden Whiplash operatives, and been in close contact with Jax and

Yimmon. He'd had every opportunity to kill or capture them and hadn't.

Still . . .

"So, you're in all the way now?" he asked the prefect.

Haus nodded. "I'm in."

"If this has proved one thing to us," Sal said, "it's that having all our credits in one bank doesn't make sense. Our leadership needs to be redundant, and yet each of us requires a certain autonomy and a certain amount of overlap."

Pol Haus was watching Jax intently. "Of course, now that *you're* here, I, for one am perfectly willing to relinquish—"

Jax shook his head adamantly. "No. I can't lead you. I can't take Yimmon's place. It's because of me that we're having to replace him. It's up to me to get him back."

"Is that even possible?" Sal asked. "As strong a mind as Thi Xon Yimmon has, Vader will eventually break him."

"Yimmon wouldn't betray the resistance," Jax murmured.

"No," Den said quietly. "But what if he doesn't have a choice? Do we know what tech the Emperor's got up his bloody sleeves? Do we even know what Vader is capable of?"

No, Jax didn't know what Darth Vader was capable of. Aboard the dying *Far Ranger* he thought he had seen him fail to manipulate Thi Xon Yimmon's mind and have to settle, instead, for manipulating gravity. Still . . .

"I've never known a Force-user as powerful as Vader," he admitted. "Which only makes it more critical that we rescue Yimmon."

Pol Haus slouched back in his chair. "How do you propose we do that? At the moment, we have no idea where they might have taken him. He could be here on Coruscant, or he could be at any Imperial stronghold. And if we do determine where he is, how do you propose we rescue him? There's every chance that Vader will only use him as a trap to catch you. You're the real prize, Pavan, and I think you know it."

Jax was shaking his head. "No. He could have gotten me at the same time he got Yimmon. If he'd really wanted me—"

"You're not thinking clearly, Jax," said Den. "Laranth had just blown a hole in Vader's vessel and shut down his tractor beam. He was out of time. He thought we were, too. He thought the interstellar flux would take us out. It's only thanks to Aren Folee and her crew that it didn't."

Den was right. Jax stared at his friend without seeing him. *He didn't have to kill me. He'd already done worse.*

"Whatever Vader's reasoning," Sal said sharply, "we have work to do. We are in the process of scrapping our network and starting fresh. We have abandoned every safe house, every drop point, every pass-through, every escape corridor, because Thi Xon Yimmon could jeopardize every one of them."

Anger flared in Jax's heart. "He'd die first."

"I hope you're right."

Jax stood as if the padded seat had shocked him. "Yimmon is your friend!"

The Sakiyan looked up at him wearily. "Yimmon *was* our captain. Our counselor. Our leader. We have to go on as if he is gone for good. He'd expect it of us, don't you think?"

Jax started to protest.

"Let me put it another way," Sal said. "Do you think Thi Xon Yimmon would want us to jeopardize the entire organization to locate and rescue him? Sacrificing all other priorities?"

From the reactions of Pol Haus and the other operatives, Jax could tell this was not the first time they'd had this argument. There was anger at this nexus— contention. Haus was staring at something invisible on the curving wall of the train car, his horned brow creased in a scowl. Fars, Acer, and Dyat were nodding grimly; Sheel was looking down at her clasped hands.

Jax looked to Pol Haus. "You agree that we should . . . give up on Yimmon?"

"*I* do not," murmured Sheel beneath her breath.

Haus put his hand over the Togruta's to silence her as he met Jax's eyes. "I think it's safe to say that Yimmon would have argued that Whiplash needs to regroup, retool, and rethink its strategy—and do it quickly. We're in the process of that now. And when that's done—"

"When that's done," Sal said, his voice tight, "we need to strike at the Empire while they suppose us to be reeling from loss. This is a tragedy only if we allow it to be. If we view it instead as an opportunity to act in ways the Emperor would never expect us to, it will remain but a personal loss, not a loss for the resistance. They suppose us to be a headless creature. But, as Pol Haus has suggested, we have six or seven heads where before we had only one. And each head is capable of directing the efforts of the body."

"Strike," Jax repeated. "Strike how?"

Sal's gaze touched briefly on the faces of his cohorts. "That hasn't been decided yet. But it must be decisive and devastating."

Jax spread his hands in a gesture of entreaty. "What would be more devastating than snatching Yimmon out of the Emperor's grasp?"

Tuden Sal grimaced. "Perhaps if we had even a glimmering of where he is—"

"We have a glimmering," said I-Five.

The assertion brought a sudden silence.

"Go on," said Pol Haus.

"I traced the route Vader's forces took to get in and out of the area they trapped us in. We're fairly certain that some of the vessels—possibly even Vader's—made a call on Mandalore, then went on from there toward the Mid Rim."

"*Some* of the vessels?"

"The larger part of the legion came back to the Core. Yimmon may even be here on Coruscant at this very moment. If we put our forces into finding him—"

"We cannot," the Devaronian growled, "throw everything into finding Yimmon. You are not even certain of his whereabouts. In truth, he may already be dead. And even if he is not, every resource we dedicate to finding him is a resource we do not have for other, larger tasks." She ended her statement with her gleaming red eyes focused on Tuden Sal. "Is that not right?"

Sal shifted in apparent discomfort. "Dyat is correct. In your absence, Jax, we have . . . moved forward on plans to strengthen our contacts within the Imperial Security Bureau. If we have to curtail those efforts, we will lose any ground we have gained."

"You have been gone," Dyat told Jax, "for over a month. That is long enough to have thrown this entire organization into a turmoil from which we have only recently emerged. Consider the consequences, Jax Pavan, if Darth Vader has done this with the full expectation that we will, as you suggest, pour all our resources into retrieving our stolen leader."

The words hit Jax like a physical blow. He sat down, feeling as if his legs had been swept out from under him.

"You're right." He leaned against the back of the seat, closing his eyes. "We can't bend all our resources to finding Yimmon." *But without those resources, we'll never get him back.*

"Jax looks like he could use some downtime," Pol Haus said brusquely.

"Of course," said Sal. "If you don't mind . . ."

Jax felt a touch on his arm and opened his eyes to find Pol Haus standing next to him. "Why don't I show you and your team to your new quarters?"

Jax nodded silently and rose to follow the prefect into the next car. Den and I-Five brought up the rear. Haus led them through a lounge car that offered an open common area replete with food service machines and various seating areas. The car behind that was a sleeper with two private compartments accessed from a left-hand corridor.

"This one is Sal's," Haus nodded toward the first door on the right. "The next is one I use on occasion."

They proceeded through the next car to a door near the far end. "Will that do for you, Den?"

The Sullustan shrugged and started to move in that direction. He hesitated and looked back over one shoulder. "Five? You coming with me, or . . ."

"I believe I will remain with Jax for the time being."

Den glanced at Jax and nodded. "Good idea."

When Den had closed his door, Pol Haus ushered Jax into his guest quarters. They were more than adequate, being about twice the size of the captain's cabin aboard the *Laranth*. There was a bed that lowered from the wall, a seating area, even a small bar at which one might eat with a guest. I-Five entered first, checked the place over, and stationed himself by the door.

Jax just stood in the middle of the floor, feeling momentarily directionless.

"Not everyone agrees that we should write Yimmon off as lost," Pol Haus said. "At least Sheel and I aren't on board with the idea."

"Factions?" I-Five asked.

Haus turned to look at the droid. "I wouldn't go that

far. Just . . . uncertainties. They're not used to operating without strong leadership, but at the same time, they're a bit leery of electing a single strong leader again."

"The Empire seems to function with a single strong leader," I-Five observed. "An absolute ruler, in fact."

"The Empire's leadership is in a position of power. The Emperor rules through secrecy and fear, while he has only one thing to fear himself . . . well, that is if he's smart enough to fear it."

"Vader." The word dropped from Jax's lips like a stone.

"Yeah. Vader. Am I right?"

Vader—the random element. "I'd like to give the Emperor more to fear," Jax murmured.

Haus's lips curled wryly. "Then you and Sal should be on the same wavelength."

Jax roused himself and turned to regard the police prefect. "Should I be? Should I just leave Yimmon in Vader's hands? Just move on?"

"What does that Force sense of yours tell you?"

"That I should not."

"Can't argue with the Force." Haus sketched a salute and left the compartment.

Jax stared after him, aware that there was a wealth of subtext there that he was too weary to grasp.

"Lie down, Jax," said I-Five, "before you fall down."

He did, but just barely.

ten

Sleep had come with difficulty. Jax's emotions were still clouding things, and his mind seemed determined to take dark paths his soul did not wish to tread. He slept restlessly, pulling himself out of turbid dreams before they could take hold. In the most benign of these dreams, he saw I-Five's tactical display of Vader's Fist as it intercepted the *Far Ranger*, took the ship, and fled with Yimmon.

In dreams he saw what he had not allowed himself to witness in the tactical display: that moment when the blue light that was *Far Ranger* winked out of existence, torn apart by the competing gravitational forces of the Twins.

As much as he wanted to wake then, he didn't. He couldn't. Instead, he watched the fleet of bright dots speed away and slip into hyperspace, to emerge near Mandalore. In his dream, he saw that emergence, too, and woke wondering again why Vader would make a stop on Mandalore. Did it have anything to do with his prisoner?

When he finally gave up on sleep, Jax meditated, but he found it hard to concentrate without the miisai to serve as point of focus. It did not help that the seemingly dormant pit droid had stationed himself in one corner of the room.

Jax returned to his bed and slept, but fitfully. When

he woke, I-Five was gone. Jax emerged from his quarters feeling only half awake, his mind wanting to dart here and there. He went in search of something to eat.

The lounge was empty. He availed himself of the food and drink dispensers. He looked out the long horizontal slits that served as windows. Not much to see—just flickers of light as they moved through the maglev tunnels. They were in motion now, but Jax knew they'd stopped during the night. Where, he had no idea. He had to admit it was brilliant of Pol Haus to have come up with this way of protecting the Whiplash leadership: by using the Underground Maglev literally, rather than as metaphor.

Jax turned at the sound of a door opening and closing to see that Den and I-Five had entered the car. Den didn't look as if he'd slept well. His oversized eyes were bloodshot, and his eyelids drooped.

"You look like I feel," Jax told him.

"My condolences," the Sullustan said, and went to get a steaming cup of caf and a protein cake.

I-Five—though Jax still had trouble thinking of this pint-sized droid as I-Five—moved gracefully to the table where Jax was sitting and surveyed the Jedi with his single oculus.

"Condolences, indeed," said the droid. "You did not sleep more than two, perhaps three, hours last night—and most of that in short naps. After your first wakeful period, you got hardly any REM sleep, which means you're not dreaming."

"I thought you were in regen. And I'd rather not dream, if it's all the same to you."

"It is not all the same to me. REM sleep is necessary to most sentients' well-being. If you don't get the required amount there could be repercussions, ranging from depression, exhaustion, and hallucinations all the way to a possible psychotic break."

"Yes. All right. I know."

"I may have to medicate you. I considered doing it last night, but reasoned that you'd be displeased if I did it without permission."

Den snorted volubly and set his caf down on the table. "I'm sure *displeased* doesn't begin to cover it."

"I don't want to be medicated," Jax said quietly. Even as he spoke the words, he knew a niggle of guilt: it seemed somehow wrong to shut the dreams out. *She* inhabited them still. He thought longingly of the miisai tree, still in his quarters aboard the ship.

We won't be here that long, he told himself.

"So, what's on the agenda for today?" Den asked.

I-Five uttered a muted beep. "*Must* there be something on the agenda? Perhaps you two should take this chance to rest and restore yourselves."

"We're going to do reconnaissance work today," Jax said. "I-Five, I need you to sniff around Space Traffic Control. Talk to the AI, if you can. See if there's been any unusual activity."

"Such as incoming vessels from the Five-Oh-First?"

"Exactly. I'm going to find Pol Haus and see if he's heard anything interesting out of the ISB. We need to locate Vader."

Den looked at him shrewdly. "You're not going to let this go, are you?"

"Are you ready to let it go? To let Yimmon go?"

They locked gazes for a long moment, then Den sighed deeply and shook his head again. "May the Warren Mother help me, no. No, I'm not ready."

"It might be wise, however," I-Five said, "to let Tuden Sal believe that we are, for the time being."

Jax nodded and took another sip of the steaming caf. He hated being anything less than completely honest with his comrades-in-arms, but dissension in the steering group was the last thing they needed. As far as

Tuden Sal and the others would know, Jax Pavan was grabbing some much-needed downtime. Only Pol Haus would be privileged to know how far that was from the truth.

Disguised as an Ubese merchant, Jax appeared at Pol Haus's headquarters, presumably to lodge a complaint against a Sullustan trading partner. He blustered his way in to the prefect's office and, once in Haus's presence, paced the floor until he had located any surveillance devices, then placed himself so that his gloved hands were visible to none of them.

"May I ask," Haus said, eyes narrowed, "why one of my lieutenants couldn't help you?"

Jax struck a belligerent pose and asked, in the mechanically amplified croak common to the Ubese, "Speak you Ubeninal?"

Haus's gaze dropped to his own hands. "Yes. But I am not as good at signing it as I am reading—"

"Then I shall speak and you shall listen. A creature of Sullust has stolen my favored pit droid. I demand that you come with me at once and confront him." That was what Jax said aloud—what he signed in the Ubese nonverbal lingo was something entirely different.

"Your . . . pit droid?" Haus repeated, scratching around the base of his left horn. He glanced from Jax's hands to his eyes, hidden behind the lenses of the face mask Ubese wore when among alien races. "I could have one of my associates—"

"Not good enough. This Sullustan creature will not respect your associates. He believes himself above the law. I suspect he is aligned with Black Sun."

"Really?" Haus watched Jax sign his real intent, then nodded. "Black Sun, you say? Imagine that."

"He is a thief. He is more than a thief. I have proof. You come."

Pol Haus rose from his formchair and moved to snag his disreputable coat from a hook by the door. "If you can prove what you say, sir, I will be happy to accompany you."

They descended to the constabulary's vehicle park and took Pol Haus's speeder out into the gray canyons.

"Where are we going?" Haus asked.

"Ploughtekal Market."

They reached that spot in silence. Haus parked the speeder and they got out by mutual consent, losing themselves in the noise and activity of the bazaar. It was the same as always—a barrage of sound and movement, an explosion of vivid colors overlaid on the cold and dark grime of Coruscant's substructure. Jax heard the chatter of a dozen worlds—Basic being spoken in another two dozen accents. Laughter. Argument.

In short, life going on.

Jax shook himself, uttered a rasping sigh.

Haus glanced sidewise at him. "What do you need?"

Jax shut off the voice amplifier and spoke normally, his head tilted toward Haus's so only the prefect would hear. "Information. I need to know if there's any unusual activity going on inside the ISB."

"What am I looking for?"

"An Inquisitor presence or a heightened security level in the detention areas, maybe."

"As if they had a special prisoner?"

"Yes. And . . . if Vader's back."

"That, I can tell you right now, because I've always got feelers out for Vader. He's on Coruscant—I got confirmation just before you showed up in my office. And according to my sources, most of his legion returned with him. Which kind of makes you wonder where the other ships went—and why."

It did make Jax wonder, but he was momentarily consumed by the idea that he and Vader were sharing a planet. Warring impulses raced through him—to find Vader and confront him, or to get as far away from him as possible. Could the Dark Lord feel his presence here? Did he know he had not killed Jax Pavan? Was Jax endangering Whiplash by his mere presence?

Haus stopped walking and turned to face Jax. "Does Sal know you're still thinking about going after Vader?"

"I'm not thinking about going after Vader. I'm thinking about going after Yimmon. And no, Sal doesn't know. Are you going to tell him?"

"Do you intend to interfere with his plans for Whiplash?"

"Of course not."

"Then I have no reason to tell him, do I? I want Yimmon back, too." The prefect turned and started walking again.

"Why doesn't Sal?"

The Zabrak made an impatient sound. "I think you're reading him wrong. I think he wants Yimmon back. He just believes—for the reasons he cited—it's dangerous to dedicate all of the organization's resources to it."

"But?"

A sidewise glance. "Who said there was a 'but'?"

"Give me some credit, Haus. I haven't lost my Force sense. I can read your ambivalence, and I'm aware that Sal's reluctance is soul-deep."

The prefect laughed, though Jax detected no humor in him. "*But*—I think he could afford to dedicate *some* resources to finding Yimmon. To give him his due, I think he probably doesn't want you to be among them. At least, if I were in his position, *I* wouldn't want to lose you to a quest."

"But?" Jax prodded again.

"*But* I'd also understand that if you don't give your all trying to get Yimmon back, you might as well be off-world. Sal needs you—Whiplash needs you. But it needs you with your head on straight, your heart in one piece, and your soul not stretched like a superstring between here and Wild Space. It needs you doing what you do best—furthering the resistance."

Jax stopped and regarded the police prefect with wry appreciation, meeting his deceptively lazy amber eyes. "You don't miss much, do you?"

"Give me some credit, Pavan. I don't miss *anything*."

Jax parted company from Haus in the heart of the marketplace. As he walked, he felt a strange combination of restlessness, impatience, and exhaustion. He chafed at having to wait for information; he wanted something to act upon—some certainty of direction. Was Yimmon here or somewhere else? If he wasn't on Coruscant—then why was Vader here?

Deep in thought, Jax lost track of where he was until he looked up and recognized the neighborhood. The Cephalon who had summoned him before they'd left Coruscant on their failed mission lived only meters from the corner where he stood. He stopped and gazed down the plaza to the entry of the Cephalon's building.

Why here? What did he imagine Aoloiloa might tell him if he showed up on its doorstep? What did he *want* it to tell him?

Here's what you did wrong, you ridiculous human. Why didn't you listen to me? Are you deaf? Blind? Insensate? All of the above?

He meant to turn around and retrace his steps to the market, but didn't. Instead he let his feet carry him to the Cephalon's tower. He signaled his desire to come up—to be granted an interview.

Maybe he'll just tell me to go away.

But the Cephalon didn't tell him to go away. And so, committed, Jax entered, arriving in the antechamber to find that Aoloiloa had acquired a couple of new sculptures since his last visit. It seemed, in fact, to be admiring them when Jax stepped up to the window and greeted it, removing his Ubese face mask and voice amplifier.

Aoloiloa turned slowly and bobbed over to the window.

—*You have/will return(ed).*

The words scrolled across the communications display in the anteroom.

"I return. And I regret to tell you that I . . . experienced the truth of your words: *Choice is loss; indecision is all loss.* I failed to make a choice and lost all."

—*You wish/wished/will wish?*

"I . . ." He stalled. What did he wish? What did he expect the Cephalon would or could tell him? What he might have done differently or better? He already knew that, didn't he?

"I wish to know . . . if there was anything I might have done to . . . to produce a different result."

—*To not lose all?*

"Yes. To not lose all."

—*That is/was/will be a different path. Every choice makes/has made/will make its own path. Many trails lead/have led/will lead to crux.*

"Crux—yes, you said that before. You said: *Locus. Dark crosses light.*"

Or dark *will* cross light, or dark *has* crossed light, or . . .

—*Yes. Locus. Nexus. Crux. Dark and light cross/ crossed/will cross.*

"You mean that *wasn't* it? It hasn't happened yet? Or do you mean that it *did* cross and that I made the wrong choice; went down the wrong path; whatever."

The Cephalon bobbed silently for a long moment, then said:—*Listen.*

Listen? Jax couldn't recall a time when he had heard

a Cephalon say anything that carried even that hint of urgency or command.

"I'm listening."

—*Yimmon's separation destroys/has destroyed/will destroy us.*

Jax's hair stood on end. That was the most intensely personal message he'd ever received from one of these ethereal sentients. "Us? You mean the Cephalons? Or Whiplash? Or—"

—*All of us.*

The words on the display looked the same as every other trail of letters and syllables, yet Jax's Force sense— completely focused on the Cephalon—told him that it was *not* the same. Aoloiloa was disturbed by the words— perhaps even afraid.

"You mean he . . . he's going to betray the resistance?"

—*Your truth: Choice is loss; indecision is all loss. Dark crosses/has crossed/will cross light.*

"And makes gray?" Jax asked reflexively.

—*Eclipse,* said the Cephalon.

eleven

Eclipse.

Dark crosses light, blotting it out. Darkness reigns.

But only for a time, Jax argued as he made his way back toward Ploughtekal Market. Then the light returns.

But how long a time? Was that what the Cephalon was trying tell him? That Yimmon's separation—his capture by Vader—could bring about the eclipse of the resistance, of what little freedom and hope existed because of it?

Certainly, the Jedi Order had already been eclipsed; for all Jax knew he was the last living Jedi Knight. He had begun the training of only one Padawan, but Vader had seen to it that Kaj Savaros had been compromised— nearly destroyed, in fact.

There was a part of Jax that saw that as a mercy. Kajin Savaros had possessed a sensitive nature, too much raw talent, little training, and even less self-control. The result could well have been even more catastrophic. Jax hated to think what Kaj—with his wounded soul—would have made of the loss of both Laranth Tarak and Thi Xon Yimmon. The youth was at least safe where he was—spirited away to Shili and into the care of The Silent, those most mysterious, veiled healers.

Jax felt a slight flutter among the muted streamers of

the Force that floated around him in the crowded marketplace. All sentient beings had some Force signature. In most, it was faded, almost transparent. To a trained Force-user like Jax, these muted signatures provided only a subtle background weave against which a more pronounced Force signature was like a bump or loop in the stream of the ordinary.

He was experiencing such a bump now—a familiar one. He followed his sense and was not surprised when he found himself in front of Honest Yarg's Droid Emporium (all sales guaranteed!). The heads-up banner floating above the tawdry shop also promised new and used / complete and parts / trade-ins welcome! The words were punctuated with the smiling effigy of Yarg himself. Yarg was a Gran. A happy Gran, if the holographic portrait of the waving sentient was any indication. Beneath his three half-open eyes, his bovine mouth affected as close to a human grin as possible for one of his species.

Trust me, it said.

Jax entered the emporium and glanced around. There were half a dozen patrons from a variety of worlds browsing through the inventory of complete and disassembled droids. The source of the Force signature was in the far right-hand corner of the warehouse. Even from this distance, Jax could tell that I-Five was bristling with very undroidlike umbrage while Den Dhur—hands gesturing for calm—tried to communicate with the third figure in the tableau: the proprietor, Yarg.

Jax approached the group, making sure his vocal filters had been switched back on. He picked up the gist of the animated conversation immediately.

"He does not wish to sell me," I-Five was telling Yarg emphatically. "He has said this repeatedly. With as many sensory organs as you possess, how can you not have understood this point? Least of all," the droid continued, ignoring Den's attempts to butt in, "does he wish to sell me for *scrap*. The point of this visit is to purchase a complete—or even partial—protocol unit. Preferably an I-5YQ."

"And I have told you," the Gran replied mildly, gazing down at the little droid, "why it is that I have no I-5YQ models at this time. They have—as I have also told you—become quite rare, being antiques. Why, just last week, one of my buyers found one on Alderaan priced at—"

"Antiques?" bleated I-Five, on the verge of overtaxing his vocalizer. "They are *not* antiques. They are vintage devices of—"

"What is this?" The grating tones of Jax's Ubese voice box cut across the droid's objections.

Six eyes turned to look at him.

"I send you to find a protocol droid and you fall into dispute with this kind and patient proprietor? Please, finish your business without delay."

Den's eyes widened, and for a moment Jax wondered if he'd forgotten what disguise the Jedi had adopted that morning. Then he bowed—bobbing obsequiously several times—and apologized both to Jax and to Honest Yarg.

"Is something amiss, sir?" Den asked Jax, concern creeping into his expression. "Is there . . . some emergency?"

"No emergency. I merely wish to be gone from this pestiferous planet as soon as possible. Have you business you must make with this sentient?" He nodded his head toward Yarg.

"Actually, yes, I do. But our pit droid seems to have shorted a circuit or three. If you could take him outside . . ."

"I see no reason—" I-Five began.

Jax silenced him with a gesture. "Come, machine. We will let my associate haggle in peace."

Outside, Jax moved to lean against the face of the building. After a moment of hesitation, I-Five moved to fold himself practically in half at the Jedi's feet.

"What was *that* all about?" Jax asked quietly in his natural voice.

"The Gran," I-Five said, "are a particularly frustrating species. They are careful to a fault, friendly—also to a fault—and they love to tell long-winded, multigenerational stories. In fact, I believe they make them up on the fly as a matter of strategy, figuring that you will buy the first thing that comes to hand just to get them to stop talking."

"Are you all right?"

"Am *I* all right?" repeated the droid. He swiveled his single oculus to peer up into Jax's face—as if he could read its expression behind the Ubese mask. "What makes you ask?"

"You're usually so careful about staying inside your droid persona. Pretending to be . . . less than you are."

I-Five looked away. "I'm . . . not used to the limitations of this chassis."

Jax crouched next to him, bringing his goggled eyes on a level with the droid's single optic. "You are not just a machine. If I needed anything else to remind me of that, I got it just now. I followed your Force signature here, Five. You're not even supposed to *have* a Force signature."

"Your point?"

"My point is that I haven't thought about how you . . ." He hesitated, tried again. "It had not occurred to me to consider how what we've been through has affected you. Until this moment. I forget, sometimes, what you are."

"And what is that?"

"My friend. My father's friend. *Laranth's* friend."

The single oculus focused on Jax's face. "I am all of those things. I am even Den's friend . . . inexplicably."

Jax smiled behind his face mask. "Do you . . . Does this . . ."

"Yes," the droid said simply. "I do. It does. Perhaps I do not experience attachment or loss as you do, or as Den does, but I do experience it. . . . Are you perhaps suggesting that I am compromised by this?"

"I don't know. I just know that, under normal circumstances, it would be unusual for me to find you arguing with a sentient about the virtues of your previous chassis. And it's just occurred to me that you might be missing that, too."

The metal helm tilted sideways. "Interesting. I hadn't thought of that possibility. You may be right."

"Happens once in a while."

Den came out of the shop, trailing a small antigrav pallet piled with containers.

"You met with Haus, right?" he asked Jax. "What's happened? What's wrong?"

"Vader's here on Coruscant—that's what's wrong. We need to move."

Jax was back. At least that's what it looked like from where Den Dhur stood. He felt an overwhelming sense of relief to see the Jedi motivated and moving. Planning. He wasn't thrilled about the prospect of snooping around the ISB and trying to track down Vader, but he recognized that it was their only way of finding Thi Xon Yimmon.

I-Five had been using his time to interface with any city subsystems that would allow him access. He'd had limited success—with the exception of something he stumbled across in the Empire's financial systems: a large amount of credits had flowed recently from Imperial coffers to several accounts on Mandalore. The Emperor was buying up someone's services, although with the identity of the account holders carefully hidden, it was hard to tell whose.

Bounty hunters—that's what Den thought. Jax and I-Five agreed. But for what purpose? To hunt down Jedi? If so, that was one of those good news/bad news scenarios. Bad news—Vader was stalking Jedi. Good news—Vader believed there were still Jedi to stalk.

They were in the throes of packing up their practically brand-new belongings when Pol Haus turned up at one of the Whiplash's rotating stops and boarded. He came directly back to Jax's quarters and dropped a sealed packet onto his bunk.

"What's that?" Jax asked him.

"A Coruscant police uniform and lieutenant's pips. I brought them for you to use the next time you need to pay me a visit at HQ. I can't have random characters cluttering up my office on a regular basis; it's too amusing to my staff. I have the feeling you're not going to get to use it, though."

"Why not?" Jax asked him. "What's going on?"

"Something I don't understand. Vader is here. He's been seen in ISB headquarters and he's reportedly met with Palpatine. *But*, there's none of the sort of activity I'd expect to see if he'd brought a high-level prisoner with him. No reassignment of guards, no concentration of Inquisitors. In fact—and this is the really peculiar thing—the Inquisitors have been dispatched offworld. Or at least the cream of their crop has been."

Jax set his shiny new pack down by the door of his compartment and gave the prefect his entire attention.

"Tesla?" he asked.

Haus nodded. "Apparently he and a number of the senior members of the group were shipped out of here yesterday."

"Shipped where?"

"That is not a matter of record, even in the ISB. Vader gave the word, and they took off directly from the bureau's landing platform. Took an Imperial transport with an unregistered itinerary. Which brings me to my other piece of news: Vader's long-range shuttle is sitting on the pad at the ISB right now, running preflight procedures."

"Where's it going?"

"No clue. No itinerary. And I'm not in a position to ask."

"Any idea when it might lift off?"

The prefect shook his head.

"We need to get to the spaceport," Jax said tersely. "*Now*."

While Jax and Den moved their meager belongings to the *Laranth/Corsair* and picked up the droid parts they'd bought at Yarg's Emporium, I-Five ran preflight procedures and tried to ferret information about Vader's vessel out of the streams of data. With the cargo in the small hold, Jax went to the cockpit where I-Five was hunkered in front of the communications console.

"Anything?"

"Actually, I was just about to hail you. It seems Darth Vader's ship is holding until fourteen hundred hours. Or so the captain told the flight controller at Eastport."

Den came in out of the corridor to lean against the hatch frame. "Why would he announce that to the flight controller at Eastport?"

"Eastport is close enough to the Senate, Palace, and Security Bureau that any special traffic from those facilities changes the flight patterns for civilian craft. I thought perhaps monitoring Eastport's communications—and any changes to their inbound and outbound traffic—would prove enlightening."

"Good call," Jax said. "Did the captain say why he's holding?"

"No. Just that he's holding."

Jax checked his chrono. Five hours. He made a quick decision. "I'm going up to the Palace District to see if I can get close to Vader's ship."

I-Five went so still that Jax thought for a moment the droid's joints had frozen. "Why?"

"If he's brought Yimmon to Coruscant, he may be moving him to wherever he's sent the Inquisitors."

"Or he might have sent Yimmon on ahead with those other ships."

"But if he's *here*, Five, I might be able to get to him."

Den stepped fully onto the bridge. "Yeah, and it might be a trap."

"A trap? How? As far as he knows, I'm dead."

"When it comes to Vader," Den said, "all bets are off. The Force only knows what Vader thinks. We should lie low here and be ready to shadow him when he takes off."

"I, too, would advise against closer inspection," I-Five agreed.

Jax shook his head, frustration bubbling just under the surface of his calm. "I can't pass up an opportunity like this. If we wait until he lifts off, our chances of being able to trace him aren't all that good. We'd still be taking a shot in the dark."

"And if you get too close to him on the ground, you'll be taking a chance that he'll sense you—if he hasn't already," argued I-Five. "Better a shot in the dark than a shot in the head."

"If he'd sensed me he'd have come after me. This landing zone would be crawling with Inquisitors. But he's sent his most effective Inquisitors offworld. I need to know where they've gone." Jax eyed Den, who was still standing in front of the hatchway, blocking his path. "Are you going to let me out?"

"I shouldn't," growled the Sullustan. "I think this is a crazy idea."

"I'll be in disguise. No one's going to suspect a police officer of being Jedi."

"Nobody but Darth Vader, maybe," Den said.

Jax laid a hand on his shoulder and met his worried gaze. "I'll be careful. Trust me. Okay?"

"You, I trust. I'm not sure about anyone else. What if that uniform Haus gave you is a flag? What if it's been wired or chipped?"

"I checked for chips."

"What if Vader knew you'd do something like this and had Haus give you a uniform you thought would give you safe passage? What if—"

Jax squeezed the Sullustan's shoulder and shook him gently. "Den, we can't distrust everyone. If Haus were a double agent, he'd have brought Whiplash down by now. He's had repeated opportunities to do so. I trust him. You should, too."

Den exhaled, nodded, and stepped aside. "All right," he said. "But I'd like to go on record as saying that I've got a bad—"

"Noted and logged." Jax went to his quarters and changed into the uniform. A few minutes later, Lieutenant Pel Kwinn left the ship and headed for the Palace District, a large diplomatic pouch slung over one shoulder.

twelve

The Imperial Palace grew up out of the crust of Coruscant like a malignant coral reef, a mountain of native stone, duracrete, and transparisteel with a crown of spires that reached greedily into the sky. The Senate District, Security Bureau, and Eastport were mere satellites of the massive structure, and existed in its shadow.

Though many kilometers away from the Palace itself, Jax still felt it as if the ISB sat atop the world and watched.

Shaking off the sensation, he looked away from the Palace and turned his attention to the forecourt of the Imperial Security Bureau. Guards were plentiful. Fortunately, they were all Imperial Guards, and all human, with not a Force-sensitive among them. Farther in, with Darth Vader in residence, there would be stormtroopers . . . and Inquisitors.

Jax was prepared for that.

He crossed the broad plaza without hesitation and approached the first checkpoint that would require him to present identification. He offered his identichip, keeping the Force tightly coiled within him. He'd added blond hair and blue eyes to his disguise—his own Master wouldn't have recognized him.

The guard—a human—scanned the identichip, obviously bored. Boredom was good.

"Lieutenant Kwinn?"

"That's right."

The guard raised an eyebrow. "From the Zi-Kree Sector? I don't think I've seen you before. Where's the usual courier—Sergeant . . . what's his name?"

Jax met the question with the most subtle tendril of the Force possible.

"I've been on this duty for months. I carry the most important dispatches. You've seen me here before."

The man looked up into Jax's eyes and frowned. "Wait, I know you. I've seen you here before." He glanced at the diplomatic pouch. "That must be quite important. Not something a prefect would task a sergeant with."

Jax smiled and stepped through the checkpoint. "Exactly."

"So, what is it, Lieutenant? What's in the pouch?"

His core suddenly twenty degrees colder, Jax turned on his heel, a plastic smile on his face. "You know what? I have no idea. They hand me a bag and they say, 'Take this to Security.'" He shrugged. "It's all *need to know*. And I don't. Just a beast of burden, I guess."

The guard laughed. "Aren't we all?"

Jax moved across the broad permacrete courtyard, feeling the tiniest wriggle of concern that perhaps Vader was strong enough to sense even that infinitesimal use of the Force. He hoped not. If there were any Inquisitors about, their emanations would surely mask it. On the other hand, if he met one of them . . . well, he'd just have to think fast.

He knew that the ISB's internal landing platforms were fairly deep within the complex. He also knew that security would be much tighter there. It was a chance he'd have to take. He kept his head up and his steps confident.

What he wanted was a vantage point from which he could see Vader's transport clearly. A vantage point like the one offered by the high walkway that ran between the control tower and the hangar bays that housed the bureau's contingent of stealth fighters. The only problem was that, to reach it, he'd have to pass through the offices of Airspace Control.

He'd planned for that.

Jax made his way to the interior of the bureau, presenting his "credentials" to a series of guards. When he was confronted with his first stormtroopers, he knew he was getting close to the goal.

He strode briskly up to the checkpoint and presented his identichip.

The stormtrooper's assessment of Jax's ID was perfunctory, at best. He barely glanced at the data scrolling across the screen of his reader. He didn't cross-check it with security files—which would have revealed that Lieutenant Pel Kwinn had retired over a year ago and moved home to Corellia. Stifling a yawn, he handed the identichip back to Jax, who received it with what he hoped was a commensurate amount of boredom and moved on.

Almost too easy, he thought; then, just beyond the stormtroopers' checkpoint, he was confronted with a whole set of choices: left, right, and straight on. A short flight of natural stone steps led down into a broad, high-ceilinged gallery that was different from what had come before. This was the oldest section of the ISB complex, and also the most secure. The ribs of the gallery's vaulted expanse were durasteel and clearly intended to withstand a major assault. A sign at the far end of the corridor proclaimed this area to be ISB AIRSPACE CONTROL.

Jax glanced left. An armored archway led to the offices of Airspace Security. To the right, a set of thick doors led out into a manicured garden courtyard that flanked the gallery. He could see the full length of it through the transparisteel windows that ran down the right-hand side of the hallway, admitting a shimmering wash of natural light.

The garden contained sculpted foliage, walkways, and benches placed so the visitor could admire the statues and moving holographic images of Imperial heroes. Jax recognized an alumabronze sculpture of Palpatine in his Senate robes, as well as one of Phow Ji, the hero of the Drongaran occupation. No doubt there was an effigy of the Emperor in one of his guises in every display of statuary in the complex.

Jax started down the steps, head high, stride certain—the model of a policeman and official courier. He'd gone only a few steps when he felt a ripple in the Force. A moment later, the doors of the control center glided open and a hooded figure stepped out across the threshold.

An Inquisitor.

For Jax, time slowed to an impossible crawl, though his feet still moved him forward. He could not pass the Inquisitor in such close quarters. A particularly adept one would almost certainly sense that there was something different about this particular policeman, and while Vader had ostensibly sent his best and brightest offworld, all Inquisitors were, by virtue of their station, high-level adepts.

Jax stopped. With a feigned air of annoyance, he produced his comlink and pretended to be speaking to someone. As the Inquisitor moved toward him down the long gallery, Jax turned and exited through the right-hand doors into the courtyard, continuing to ask questions of a pretend superior on the other end of the link. He kept walking until he had put the statue of Palpatine between himself and the Inquisitor.

He could see through the arched windows along this side of the corridor that the other Force-user did not hesitate, but exited the hall without even a nod at the troopers guarding it.

Jax sat on a bench in the lee of the statue, still pretending to be in conversation with someone, and scanned the garden courtyard. There was another door at the far end, diagonal to the Flight Control entrance. That was the only other access. He had no doubt that there were cams everywhere in this restricted area. Under normal circumstances they wouldn't be a problem—he could make them see what he wanted them to see—but with Vader so near . . .

Jax wished, for the hundredth time, that he had some idea what long-term effects the bota had had on Vader's Force abilities. Not being able to gauge an adversary's resources accurately was nerve-racking. Jax got up and paced around the statue of Palpatine, his eyes taking in the surveillance cams. Drawing on the merest breath of the Force, he calculated what was perhaps the only blind spot in the area and made for it, his steps meandering as if he were more intent on his feigned dialogue than where he was putting his feet.

If he'd had more time, he would have tried to procure some taozin scales to mask his Force signature—but he should have thought of that back at the market. He had what he had—his own native intelligence and creativity, the Force, and the fact that there were other Force-users in the complex whose presence would offer some camouflage.

Between two holograms of some long-dead Imperial luminaries, which screened him from two holocams, and blocked from a third by a bronze free-form sculpture with some iconic meaning he couldn't begin to guess at, Jax pocketed his comlink and pulled a long, hooded robe out of the diplomatic pouch. It took him mere seconds to draw the robe on over his uniform and pull the cowl down over his face. Pel Kwinn, police lieu-

tenant, disappeared; it was an Inquisitor who stepped
out from between the holograms and reentered the gallery at the far end, the diplomatic pouch hidden beneath
his robe.

The doors to Flight Control slid open, and he strode
inside.

Jax took a moment to orient himself. Before him was
a pristine room filled with ISB functionaries. Beyond
them, a huge expanse of transparisteel looked down on
the landing stages. He could see the shaft of the control
tower at the far right, the walkway stretching from it
to the hangar bays. Straight ahead, the wing tips of a
Lambda-class long-range shuttle peeked above the rail-
ing of the walkway.

He might, he realized, actually be able to see the
landing platform from the windows right here in the
offices. But Inquisitors didn't, as a rule, tend to loiter
around staring out windows. He turned right and made
his way to a set of doors that would take him outside
and allow him access to the base of the control tower.

There were two more stormtroopers stationed at the
tower entry. They didn't even look at him as he passed
by. In fact, both averted their gazes.

But once inside the tower, he realized his dilemma: A
Jedi could manipulate a sentient being. But he could not
control a turbolift AI that was asking for his security
clearance before allowing him to ascend.

Jax considered going back outside and Force-jumping
to the walkway, then discarded that as too great a
risk—the area was too open, the guards would have to
be distracted. There must be emergency stairs . . .

He had turned to look for those when the turbolift
behind him was activated from above. The lift was
going up! Jax moved swiftly to the doors and pried
them open. High above his head the lift continued to
ascend the fifty or so floors toward the top.

The walkway access was half that distance.

Jax swung himself into the lift tube and Force-jumped. He'd no more than left the ground when he realized the lift had stopped short of the top and was descending again. Swiftly.

Time slowed to a crawl for the second time that day. Jax's gaze sought the doorway to the level he needed to reach. He would get there at approximately the same time the lift would.

There was no escape that way.

Nine or ten meters from the first floor, he reached out both hands and called the Force to his fingertips—just enough to buffer his impact with the descending lift. It was still a bone-jarring jolt, one he was sure the occupants of the lift car felt. Grasping the undercarriage, Jax let momentum carry his body into contact with the steel box. His feet found purchase on a crossbar that ran along one edge.

Air rushed by him, roaring in his ears as the lift descended. The long robe he'd affected was molded to his body, the hood obscuring his vision. He shook his head, and the hood lifted away—he almost wished he hadn't bothered. Now he could see the floor of the turbolift shaft rushing up to meet him.

It'd be all right, he reminded himself, as long as the carriage didn't use the entire depth of the shaft to halt before bobbing back up to its stop. Of course, if he was really lucky, it would stop on the second level.

He wasn't that lucky. The turbolift shot down to the premier level, and its antigravity cushion engaged. Jax, caught in the field, was suddenly weightless. The cloak billowed. He held on with his entire will, knowing that gravity would return with a vengeance when they reached bottom.

The car dived below the first-level exit, the ground floor rushing up to meet it. Jax coiled the Force within him, knowing that if he had to use it to save himself he would very likely give himself away.

The lift stopped and gravity reasserted itself. Jax felt at once the pull of the planet and the light pressure of a padded crossbeam against his back before the car bobbed lightly back up to the exit portal. It vibrated as its doors opened and its occupants exited.

Now, would it just sit here until someone else called for it, or . . .

The lift hummed. In moments, it was ascending again with Jax still clinging to its underside. He watched the portals for each level as they slid by. He wanted Level Nine . . . and there it was.

He swung his legs down and let go of the lift's undercarriage, then used the Force—gently, oh so gently—to slide down the curving wall of the shaft to the Level Nine portal. There was just enough room for him to stand on the lip of the entry. He applied the minimum amount of effort to opening the doors and all but fell through them out onto the high walkway.

In the lee of the tower, he adjusted his cloak and hood, then slid slowly down the sparkling length of permacrete until he could see the target.

Vader's shuttle sat in the center of the largest landing stage, dwarfing the smaller vessels close to it. The *Lambda*-class shuttle, its wings folded, tips pointing skyward, was well armed and well guarded. Stormtroopers— no doubt members of Vader's Fist—stood at intervals, facing outward as if to accost anyone who might approach the ship.

Standard procedure? Or evidence that there was a special passenger on this trip?

Jax felt a chill down his spine. He'd been sweating during his encounter with the turbolift, but now he was freezing cold. Did that shuttle contain Thi Xon Yim-

mon? Was there any way he could find out without revealing himself?

He'd been moving more and more slowly along the
walkway, his head tilted as minimally as possible
toward the shuttle. His spirit was not quiet. He wanted
to fling himself over the parapet, rush to the ship, and
tear it open to reveal what—or who—was inside. He
willed himself to calmness, to dispassion.

Impossible. He settled for focus.

He had come here at great risk and could not go back
without knowing *something*. Gritting his teeth, he
reached questing tendrils of Force sense toward the vessel, seeking Yimmon. He applied himself to the bow of
the ship first, reasoning that a prisoner of such importance would be kept in or near the detachable forward
section of the vessel in case an emergency forced them
to separate the bridge from the cargo and passenger sec-
tions.

His steps slowed further as he concentrated. There
were people aboard the vessel, but their similar energies
told him most were the cloned soldiers of Vader's guard.

But here was a different signature . . . and there.

He withdrew slightly. That, surely, was the taozin-
blurred energy of an Inquisitor. He moved on, feeling
every inch of the vessel as if it were a model he held in
his hands.

He finished with a deep sense of disappointment.
Maybe Yimmon was in the building beneath Jax's feet.
Maybe he simply hadn't been put aboard yet. Jax
wanted Yimmon to be here. Desperately, he now realized. He wanted . . .

He had no further opportunity to consider what he
wanted. The ramp of the ship was extending from the
port side of the vessel. Two Imperial officers descended
to stand at the lower end.

Jax stopped walking and turned to face the ship.

Below him, someone moved from the shadow of the walkway and strode toward the vessel in a swirl of black robes.

Every hair on Jax's body stood on end.

Vader.

I should keep walking, Jax told himself. He should seem to be just one more Inquisitor going about his mysterious duties. He tried to make his feet move, but his gaze refused to let go of Vader.

He had left his lightsaber aboard the *Laranth* and now regretted it. He could still throw himself over onto the landing platform. He didn't need the weapon to use the Force effectively—something Laranth had always been at pains to remind him. She thought the Jedi were too obsessed with uniformity as opposed to unity. You could have one without the other, she had argued. A Jedi shouldn't limit him- or herself to a particular weapon or even to a particular way of doing things. Successful life-forms were also adaptable life-forms. But Laranth was dead and the man responsible for her death was, even now, crossing the duracrete surface of the landing stage.

Or . . . was the man responsible standing atop this walkway, looking down at his nemesis?

The thought struck Jax hard enough to make him take a step backward. Below, on the sun-washed plat-form, Darth Vader had paused to speak to the officers awaiting him at the bottom of the ramp. The conversation was brief and one-sided. At its conclusion, the Dark Lord took a step onto the landing ramp.

Then he hesitated, and turned to look up at the man on the walkway.

One's face was obscured by a mask, the other's by the shadows of an Inquisitor's hood, yet still Jax felt naked before the touch of Vader's regard.

Do you know who I am?

It took the full force of Jax Pavan's will to bow his

hooded head deeply to the Dark Lord, then turn and resume his slow, gliding walk. He entered the Flight Control facility on the opposite side of the walkway. Only once inside did he quicken his pace.

He passed one or two Inquisitors on his way out of the building. He did not acknowledge them in any way, nor they him. He passed through checkpoint after checkpoint, glad that the Inquisitorius inspired such fear that the guards were reluctant to even look at him.

When he left the bureau complex and recrossed the broad plaza, the space between his shoulder blades itched. In his mind's eye he saw that masked face with its obsidian goggles turned up toward him, stripping away layers of skin and bone to ultimately bare his identity.

Or so it had felt.

But . . .

He didn't know me, Jax told himself. *If he'd known me, he would have challenged me. He would never have let me walk out of there alive. If he'd known me, I would have felt it.*

Still in Inquisitor's guise, Jax returned to the Westport, hoping that by the time he got there he would have stopped shaking.

At the point Den realized he was checking the chrono every five minutes, he stopped glancing at it. Jax had been gone for over two hours without a word, and the Sullustan wished desperately—not for the first time in his life—that he wasn't stone deaf when it came to the Force. At least then, he told himself, he'd know if Jax was all right or if he'd been discovered . . . or worse.

"Why didn't he take us with him, Five?"

The question had been revolving in his mind since Jax had set off for the Palace District. It was driving him crazy. He turned his gaze from the landing pad to look at the droid, who was tinkering with a new chassis design through his onboard holodisplay.

"I mean, if Yimmon *was* there, and Jax had any hope of rescuing him, he'd need backup, right?"

I-Five swiveled his head so that the oculus was aimed at Den. "Jax may have reasoned that a lone Jedi would have a better chance of rescuing Yimmon than a Jedi encumbered with a couple of miniature sidekicks."

"Okay, I can see why he might not take me. I'm frankly not that quick or stealthy or impressive. But you? You're not a liability by any stretch of the imagination. Especially since we got those laser units installed. You can do just about anything but fly."

The droid's monocular optic spun as if in contemplation. "Antigravity generators come in fairly small packages these days. With perhaps a repulsor unit for swift ascensions—"

"Stop it!" Den exclaimed. "You're trying to distract me."

"What makes you think that?"

"I *know* you, Tin Man," Den said, pointing a stubby digit at I-Five's lens. "You've been wondering the same thing, haven't you? Why would Jax leave *you* behind?"

"I can't say that I have." Five shut off the holoimage of a souped-up I-5YQ unit. "What I have been doing is sorting through possible reasons why he may have done this. The most obvious one is that he's afraid of putting us in harm's way."

"That's not his decision to make, blast it! It's *ours*."

"It could be reasonably argued that someone had to stay with the ship, keep it liftoff-ready."

"Like I said, I could have seen him leaving *me* here, but not you. He needs you, Five. Probably more now than—" Den broke off when a flicker of movement at the periphery of the landing platform tugged at his eye. "What was that?"

I-Five turned his gaze to the exterior view. "I saw nothing—which, given my monocular vision, is unsurprising."

Den half rose from the copilot's chair. "It was there. Over there by that fuel port." He pointed at the bright yellow housing of a robotic unit that dispensed liquid metal fuel.

I-Five tapped the control panel and brought up the displays showing views starboard, port, and aft. Den flicked his gaze from one screen to the next.

"Are you sure—" I-Five began.

"Yes, I'm sure. I'm—there! Right *there*!"

A cloaked figure flitted from shadow to shadow, passing from the fuel port to a stairwell on the port side of the landing pad.

Den felt as if every drop of blood in his body had congealed.

"An Inquisitor," I-Five said with irritating calm. "Perhaps we should let him know he's been seen."

Den shook his head. "No. Let's just . . . keep an eye on him . . . or three. Let's not tempt fate, okay?"

"What if Jax returns while he's out there?"

Mother of Sullust, he has to ask?

Den licked his lips. "We should ping Jax."

"And if he's doing something stealthy at the moment we ping him? We were instructed to keep radio silence."

"I hate this," Den said. "A *lot*."

They watched for several minutes as the Inquisitor made a circuit of the ship—once, then twice.

"I don't get it," said Den. "What's he doing?"

"Sniffing, perhaps? Trying to see if he can 'smell' a Jedi."

That made sense. And it meant that if Jax returned while Vader's little Force hound was out there . . .

Den got up and slipped into the short corridor that connected the tiny bridge to the body of the ship. He popped open the weapons locker and took a blaster from the rack.

"What are you doing?" I-Five was standing in the hatchway.

"I'm gonna go chase him away."

"No, you're not. I am."

The droid scuttled past Den and made for the air lock. He had let down the loading ramp before Den could get to him. With Den standing in the hatch, his heart beating hard enough to sway him back and forth, I-Five stalked down to the bottom of the ramp and looked around.

"Thieves!" he squeaked in a high, tinny voice. "I saw thieves, Captain Vigil!"

His head performed almost a 360-degree swivel before swinging back in the opposite direction. When his oculus was pointed away from the Inquisitor's last known position, he raised a slender arm, pointed a finger 180 degrees away from where he was looking, and fired a bolt of blue energy from his fingertip. It struck the housing of the umbilical cabling—now retracted— that had powered the ship's systems while she was docked.

There was a sudden flurry of sound and movement and then . . . nothing. Or at least as much nothing as there could be on a landing stage at a busy spaceport. Den held his breath, blaster in hand, and tried to listen—to *sense*—the shadowy presence of the Inquisitor. It was a vain attempt. When it came to the Force, Den Dhur was an inert lump of protoplasm.

I-Five moved into the shadow of the ship's keel. "Perhaps, Captain," the droid said, "you should go monitor the pad from the bridge. I'll stay down here. Just in case."

"Uh, copy that." Den swallowed, then hastened back to his seat in the cockpit. He turned his eyes to one display after another: bow, port, starboard, aft. The shadows of the dockside equipment seemed almost solid in the glare of Coruscant's sun. He scanned every one of them, repeating the process—once, twice, three times—before his heart rate began to assume a more normal rhythm.

At the end of his third cycle, he closed his eyes and took a deep breath, wishing Jax would return. Praying to the Great Mother that he would return with Yimmon and this nightmare would simply be over.

"I'm coming back aboard, Captain."

I-Five's voice came to him through the droid's comlink. Den took a breath of relief.

"Okay. Okay. Great."

He opened his eyes to watch the little droid climb back up the landing ramp and saw the Inquisitor step out of the shadows of the spaceport directly behind him.

"Five! Your back!" Den yelled, but I-Five couldn't hear him—in his panic, Den hadn't activated the comm.

Still, the droid turned to face the Sith operative. Den saw the light on the laser port built into his oculus flash red as it charged up.

The Inquisitor stopped, raised his hands as if to forestall attack, then put back his hood.

Den all but melted into a puddle on the deck of the bridge. He was still lounging limply in his seat when I-Five and Jax entered. Jax had removed the Inquisitor's cloak and looked more or less as he had when he'd left earlier.

"Why did you *do* that?" asked Den.

Jax frowned. "Do what?"

"The . . ." Words failing him, Den briefly pantomimed a hunched-over sinister form, large eyes narrowed to slits, finger crooked, clawlike.

"Oh. A precaution. Vader and his lackeys expect

Force signatures from Inquisitors, not members of the local constabulary."

"Okay. I get that, but why all the skulking around the ship? You afraid we might have picked up a bug or a bomb or something? I mean, you scared the mopak out of us. Or, well, out of *me,* anyway."

Jax's frown deepened. "What skulking?"

I-Five made a soft bleep. "We've been monitoring an Inquisitor for the last fifteen minutes or so making a circuit of the ship. I thought I'd just driven him off. We assumed . . ."

Jax's face had paled above his uniform. "That wasn't me. I just got here."

PART TWO

FLIGHT AND PURSUIT

thirteen

Jax's hands flew over the *Laranth*'s controls, seeming to go in two directions at once. Den felt as if his mind echoed the movements. The difference being that Jax's hands were sure, methodical, swift; Den's thoughts were frantic, chaotic, and just plain scared.

Did the Inquisitor's presence mean that Darth Vader knew Jax Pavan was alive and on Coruscant? Knew what ship he flew? Knew, even, that he had paid a visit to the Security Bureau? Or was the Inquisitor merely on patrol, groping after Force adepts as Inquisitors always did, and had been drawn to Westport by Jax's residual signature?

If Vader had known Jax was alive on Coruscant, Den told himself for the twentieth time, he would have done something. Maybe he still didn't know . . . yet. But what would he make of his Inquisitor's report that he had been fired at on Landing Stage 184Z at Westport? I-Five's bit of playacting notwithstanding, anyone who fired at an Inquisitor was going to draw swift attention from the Imperials.

And so they fled . . . in a legal, orderly fashion so as not to draw further attention. Any thought of waiting out Vader's departure was forgotten.

Den could see the agony of that decision on Jax's tense face as they lifted off and executed a series of course adjustments that put them on a heading for the Hydian

Way with an alleged cargo of machine parts. Moments ticked by as they sped out of the Coruscant system, their sensors sweeping surrounding space for pursuers, or an ambush, or anything out of the norm.

We're just a tiny little freighter from Toprawa, Den thought, as if his brooding could have any possible effect on reality in their pocket of the galaxy. *We're not worth investigating.* He kept repeating that in his mind like a sort of mantra, seeking to squeeze whatever comfort he could from the words.

Which wasn't much . . .

They reached the threshold of the system's gravity well without mishap, which—as much of a relief as it was to still be alive—left Den feeling limp with exhaustion. He looked at the star charts on the navcom display, swallowed hard, and asked, "Where to, Jax?"

When the Jedi didn't answer, I-Five prodded him. "Toprawa?"

"That's my vote," Den said. "We've got allies there, after all. A place to park and regroup, anyway."

"That makes sense," Jax agreed. "Except that it might make sense to Vader, too."

"Really?" I-Five split his concentration between copiloting the ship and determining its course. "Do you think he has any idea that we're still around? I rather imagine that his overweening self-assurance predisposes him toward believing we're all dead. So much so, in fact, that I doubt he'd recognize evidence to the contrary."

Jax turned and stared at the droid for a moment, as if examining the concept in his head.

"Y'know," Den piped up, "I'll bet Five's right. Otherwise, he'd've been all over us. In fact, if he'd sent that Inquisitor after us, we wouldn't be in space right now."

"We need a course before we enter hyperspace, Jax," I-Five pressed. "Is it Toprawa?"

"Have you forgotten that we might have a betrayer there?"

"I haven't forgotten," I-Five said after a moment. "In point of fact, I never forget anything. And I suspect Den hasn't forgotten, either, in this particular case, though his hippocampus is somewhat inferior to my memory chip."

"Thanks a lot," said Den.

I-Five ignored him. "Neither of us is denying the possibility that someone in Aren Folee's organization might have leaked our course to Vader. But what else might we do? We've lost any chance of monitoring Vader's shuttle as it leaves the system."

Jax took his hands from the controls. "Because of me," he murmured.

"Pardon?" The low, curving helm tilted askance and the oculus cycled as if to focus more tightly on the Jedi's face.

"We're unable to monitor Vader's movements because of me," Jax repeated. "Because I acted precipitously . . ."

"What else could you have done? It made sense that Vader would bring Yimmon back to Coruscant."

Jax shook his head. "I don't sense he was ever here. I think he was sent wherever that other contingent of ships was sent. Though I wonder why Vader came back here without him. Not that I'm complaining—it bought us more time."

"Maybe," Den said reluctantly, "he came back here because he's already gotten the information he needed to bring down Whiplash."

"No. He would oversee that himself. We'd be seeing an explosion of activity around his headquarters. But it's quiet as can be, and he's leaving again."

"Then perhaps our logical next move," the droid suggested, "would be to head for Mandalore."

"Mandalore," Den repeated, his eyes widening. "You don't think they'll still be there?"

"No," Jax said thoughtfully, "but I'm hopeful we might find out where they were going."

"How? Are we just going to hang out in taverns and ask everyone we meet if they happen to know where the Imperials went? Rumor is rampant that Mandalore is a divided society these days. If that's the case, whom do we go to for intel?"

"Whoever seems in the best position to have it."

"On what excuse? We start asking questions all over the place, and any hope of keeping a low profile—"

"I seem to recall," said I-Five, "that you used to be a journalist. One of the perks of having a memory chip," he added drily. "Perhaps that would provide a suitable cover and a reason for asking questions all over the place."

Den felt as if he'd just awakened from a deep sleep. A spark of something like hope—or at least *not* like panic—curled around his heart. "I . . . well, yeah. I guess that could be a good cover."

"Indeed," I-Five agreed. "And though it galls me to contemplate it, I can be your indispensable metal side-kick. Jax, meanwhile, can employ subtler methods of fact-finding."

"Or," Jax said, "we could just be pirates."

Den grinned. He liked the idea of being a pirate. Pirates ostensibly did much business on and around Mandalore's ill-named moon, Concordia. And pirates would have every reason to be interested in the movement of Imperial ships and troops.

"All *right*. I like this plan. We can hit arms dealers, public houses and cantinas, ship repair yards—people in those places *always* have their eyes open for Imperial activity. What do you think, Jax?"

But Jax had risen and was on his way aft.

"Jax?"

"Sounds good, Den." He turned. "I-Five, since you've already filed a flight plan for the Hydian Way, why don't we make a quick jump in that direction, then adjust course? I'm going to change out of these clothes."

"Consider it done."

"Don't you want to be up here to see the stars blur?" Den asked.

"No." Jax disappeared into the fore-and-aft corridor.

Den stared after him for a moment. "I'm a little worried about him."

"Only a little?"

He looked at I-Five. "He's blaming himself for everything that's happened—you realize that, right?"

"Yes."

"I know that's not justified, but . . ."

"But?"

"It struck me just now . . . what if that whole thing with Vader's shuttle *was* a trap? A ploy to get Jax to reveal himself?"

"If it were, do you honestly think he'd have gotten out of the ISB unscathed? Or that this ship would still be in one piece?"

"Well, no. Unless Vader has some ulterior motive."

"Vader has faced off against Jax often enough, with results disastrous enough, that I expect he would want to make certain of Jax's destruction if he even half suspected he was still alive. He would hardly let him slip through his fingers again. Jax could easily just sail off into Wild Space or the Unknown Regions and never come back."

"Yeah, he *could*. But he wouldn't. And I'm pretty sure Vader knows that as well as we do."

"Granted." I-Five punched the hyperdrive controls. Space blurred, the stars becoming streamers of varicolored light. "And I suppose you could be right about

Vader—perhaps he *is* toying with Jax. Or perhaps he's simply wary of him. In either case, it begs a most interesting question."

"That being?"

"Why?"

Den was quiet for a moment. "I don't like that question."

"Maybe you'll like this one better, because it arises simultaneously: how well does Darth Vader know himself?"

Den was quiet for a longer time. At last he said, "It's a good thing you opted for indispensable metal sidekick."

"Yes? Why?"

"Because you *suck* at comedy relief."

In his cabin, Jax walked back through their brief stay on Coruscant—realizing how close he'd come to giving up the whole mission by affording Vader a chance to recognize him. More than ever, he longed for his Master's guiding hand, for Yimmon's quiet strength, for Laranth's cool, clean pragmatism. But as much as he hungered for their presence, he felt haunted by them.

He sat down before the miisai tree to steady himself, to work out their next steps, but his attempts to empty his mind of ghosts met with only limited success. He focused his awareness on the miisai tree—a fractal structure of pulsing light, shedding pale ribbons of Force energy into his small cabin. He reached out with his own awareness, touching the field generated by the tree, moving beyond it toward its Source.

He was forced to banish Laranth from his thoughts repeatedly, but finally succeeded in emptying himself into the Force, stretching his awareness out to sense, to listen, to feel. He let his consciousness float in the Force eddies—an island, both disconnected and connected.

In this state, he fixed his mind on Thi Xon Yimmon. If he reached out to the Cerean's powerful intellect, he might be able to sense him—the epicenter of tiny ripples in the fabric of the Force. But it made more sense—dangerous as it might be—to seek Vader. As a powerful Force-user, Darth Vader inhabited the Force in a way that Jax could detect quickly and easily; a much more noticeable presence than Yimmon, like a planet-sized dent in the space–time continuum as opposed to a small asteroid.

Anger—hot, swift, and unreasoning—swelled momentarily in his breast. *Why?* Why was Vader what he was? How had Anakin become the enemy?

If you touch him with that much rage in your heart, he'll know, the voice within him, thin and small and low-key, reminded him. *Or with fear consuming you. He'll know you're alive. He'll know how much he's hurt you. And he'll know he can reel you in.*

It was true. The clarity of the knowledge, the *certainty* of it, all but stopped Jax's breath in his throat. He was trapped by the rawness of his own emotions, for he could not go anywhere near Vader with either fear or anger dominating him. Somehow, between now and the time they reached Mandalore, he had to armor himself. He had to be able to sense Darth Vader without Vader sensing him—until it was too late.

He needed time. And he needed help. Whiplash was out, and he'd already jeopardized the resistance fighters on Toprawa more than he ought to have—never mind that there was a chance betrayal had come from that quarter. Something bothered him about that idea, but he couldn't quite put his finger on what it was.

Jax shook off the vague unease and tried to think ahead to Mandalore. Even with his Force sensitivity in play, their chances of being able to scare up any real intelligence with a haphazard approach could prove to be a time-consuming exercise in futility.

Where could they get such help? They were cut off. Cut off from the resistance and from Whiplash.

He felt a sudden kinship with Tuden Sal. The Sakiyan must have felt something like this when he was first expelled from his entrepreneurial support network. When he'd lost his family, his business holdings, his contacts—

Jax felt as if the universe had paused in its ceaseless movement, waiting for him to catch up.

Sal's contacts.

Jax knew the Sakiyan hadn't lost touch with *all* of them. In fact, he occasionally used them to provide information, to distract attention, to misdirect blackmarket arms shipments.

Jax rose and went forward to the bridge. He found his companions right where he'd left them, though now Den was staring moodily out of the forward viewport.

"How soon can we drop out of hyperspace?" Jax asked I-Five.

"I'd planned on it in approximately fifteen minutes and . . . four seconds. That way we'll seem to be adhering to our flight plan—if anyone's watching. Why do you ask?"

"I need to talk to Sal. Let him know where we're going. What we're doing."

"Isn't that rather risky?"

"We can encrypt the message. We can even bounce the signal and make it seem to be coming from somewhere else. If we take those precautions, we should be all right. It won't be much—just a quick exchange of information."

"As you wish."

"Good." Jax reached out and touched the droid's helm briefly. Then he sat down in the jump seat behind the pilot's station and joined Den in staring out the viewport.

"You okay?" the Sullustan asked him. "You seem . . . edgy."

"I'm fine. Just . . . I know what I need to do."

"Oh. Okay then." Den smiled at him, relief all but oozing from his pores.

At I-Five's precise mark, they dropped out of hyperspace and adjusted their course to point them into Mandalorian space.

The droid looked over at Jax. "We're parked. You can talk to Sal anytime."

"Good." Jax slid out of the seat and headed aft. "I'll use the comm console in engineering."

He saw Den's head swivel toward him as he slipped from the bridge. He felt . . . strange. He was being secretive, and they all knew it. And he suspected that neither Den nor I-Five would approve of what he was about to do. He doubted Laranth would, either.

Well, he'd deal with all that later. Every action carried risk, but he had to act.

fourteen

Jax both encrypted the communication and bounced the signal from the *Laranth*'s main communications array off a satellite orbiting the farthest-flung planet in the nearby Champala system. Someone would have to be in the room with Tuden Sal to receive Jax's unencrypted side of the dialogue and would—if they were able to trace the transmission—assume that it originated several light-hours from where it actually did.

"Jax!"

Tuden Sal's holographic image appeared as if standing in the middle of the ship's small engineering bay. The Sakiyan took a step toward the holo-emitter and lowered his voice. "What—where are you?"

"Outbound from Coruscant. Listen, I need to talk to you about resources. I—"

"We can't afford you any resources right now, even if I could get them to you. They're engaged elsewhere."

Jax frowned and followed the digression. "In what?"

"In a plan that you would also be a part of if you weren't trying so hard to win the war all by yourself."

Jax ignored the personal analysis. "What plan?"

Sal shook his head, crossing his arms over his chest. "If you were here to participate in it, I'd tell you. But you seem about to fly blindly off into disaster. If you were to be captured . . ."

Jax nodded. "Yes, of course. I understand."

Sal unfolded his arms and moved forward another step. He made a beseeching gesture. "Please, Jax. I don't know how far out you are, but please reconsider. What can you and your team do on your own? Stay connected to Whiplash—to the resistance. Out there, you'll just be roguing it. Here, you'll be part of a larger effort. Here, you can hurt the Empire far more than if you're gallivanting across the starlanes on some wild bantha chase. And you won't be costing us any further resources."

Jax cringed. "It seems to me that Whiplash has disconnected from *me*. And from Yimmon. But that's not why I'm contacting you."

"Where are you heading, Jax? What are you planning? If you're after Vader—"

"I don't want revenge, Sal. I just want to free Yimmon. Then I want to work toward freeing the entire galaxy from the Empire's power. I want to see the Jedi Order rise again. I want to be part of the effort to rebuild."

"Which is all the more reason for you *not* to put yourself in harm's way again," Sal argued. "What if you *are* the last Jedi, Jax? Have you thought about that? What if you're the only one left to rebuild? You may be the only person alive who can transmit the knowledge of the Jedi to future Padawans." Sal scanned the Jedi's face. "You *have* considered that, haven't you?"

"Of course. That doesn't change what I have to do."

Sal continued to gaze at Jax for a long, silent moment. Then his shoulders slumped perceptibly. "I'm sorry you feel that way. So . . . then you're committed to this . . . crusade."

"I am. Everything in me tells me I have to do this."

"Obviously, nothing I say will convince you otherwise." Sal made a weary, dismissive gesture. "I wish I could help you, but . . ."

"Actually," Jax said, "I think you *can* help me. You have contacts in Black Sun."

Sal's surprise was obvious. "I *did* have contacts in Black Sun. Before they stood by and watched the Emperor ruin me. I haven't been in touch with them since."

"I know that's not strictly true. You have been in touch with *some* of them."

"One or two. And only briefly. Why?"

"Black Sun operates openly on parts of Mandalore and Concordia. I need to start my investigation there. Maybe your contacts could help me out."

Sal snorted. "You'd do better to go in and tell them you'd shot me and mounted my head on your cabin wall."

"If you think that would work," Jax said quietly.

Sal's expression showed naked fear for a split second before he recovered himself. Perhaps he had just remembered that he was talking to the man whose father he had unwittingly betrayed.

"I'll give you a name and contact information," he agreed. "You'll have to figure out what approach is best to take. As I said, I'm not sure claiming me as an ally would be helpful. Except in one case—an Arkanian system lieutenant named Tyno Fabris. He actually seemed to have a conscience about what happened to me. Not enough of one to explain to me why Black Sun was suddenly doing the Empire's bidding, but enough for him to keep finding ways to make it up to me. One thing, though. I've always communicated with Fabris through a location scrambler. He doesn't know I'm on Coruscant. In fact, with the hints I've dropped, he believes I'm on Klatooine. He also thinks I'm an arms dealer."

"All right."

Sal took one more step closer so that he was face-to-virtual-face with Jax. "Jax, he *can't* know I'm on Coruscant. None of them can."

Jax nodded. "I understand."

"I know you do. And I'm hoping—"

Jax knew what he was hoping. "I won't betray you, Sal."

The Sakiyan dropped his gaze and stepped back. "I'm . . . I'm sorry, Jax. You can't begin to imagine—" He cut off and turned his head sharply to the left. "Someone's here."

Jax ended the transmission. A tug of some chaotic emotion—almost a mental static—pulled his attention in the direction of the bridge. Den. Probably fretting over being a sitting duck.

Jax grimaced and pinged the bridge. "Let's get out of here," he told I-Five.

"Didn't I hear Jax's voice?" Pol Haus stepped into the Whiplash conference room and looked around, pointedly. Tuden Sal was alone in the room, but the prefect had heard enough to know whom he'd been talking to and what about.

"Jax is offworld."

"Offworld? Already? What happened?"

The Sakiyan Whiplash leader lowered himself into a chair at the conference table. "He didn't say. Wouldn't even tell me where he was . . . or where he was going. But I suspect he's gone after Vader."

Haus wanted to ask Sal why he was lying about Jax's plans but knew that would reveal how much of the conversation he'd overheard. Instead he asked, "So they're not coming back for a while, then?"

"No. And I have to say, that may be for the best. He hasn't been right since . . ." He made a gesture that indicated the galaxy outside the train car.

"The kid has been through a lot in the last two years."

The Sakiyan's face flushed a darker shade of bronze. "Yes. He has. Which is why it may be to the benefit of all concerned if he's not involved in Whiplash activities for a while."

"You mean this new plan of yours?"

"Jax might endanger the mission."

Haus nodded. "He might at that. Speaking of which, I have some interesting intel for you. Vader has sent all but a handful of Inquisitors offworld."

He had Sal's entire attention. "A handful? How big a handful?"

"All but four or five, by our best count. And Vader headed out soon after."

Sal rose from the chair, zeal brightening his eyes. "Then the Emperor . . ."

"Is missing most of his deadliest defenders."

"Where is he?"

Haus took a deep breath. He could see that Tuden Sal was practically trembling with anticipation. "I don't know. Ostensibly, he's at the Imperial Palace. But there are rumors he may actually be elsewhere."

"I want to hear those rumors, Pol. Every last one."

fifteen

Mandalore was a culture divided. The wartime activities of a consortium of criminal elements known as the Shadow Collective had proved too much for the New Mandalorians to handle. Satine's government had fallen and a violently dissenting group calling itself Death Watch had arisen to give the members of the Shadow Collective—largely Black Sun and Hutt organizations—a titanic headache. After the initial paroxysm of hostilities had passed, a puppet Prime Minister had been installed, and things had quieted down.

Still, the atmosphere on Mandalore was one of simmering uncertainty. It was peaceful enough on the surface—even with the strong Death Watch presence—but the dissolution of the Shadow Collective had left a power vacuum. Into this vacuum, Black Sun—personified by the Falleen Vigo, Prince Xizor—had oozed like malevolent slime.

Tuden Sal's contact, Tyno Fabris, was the new Vigo's lieutenant, living a discreet existence in the old Mandalorian capital of Keldabe. So that was where Jax set the ship down—at a small landing facility in the considerable shadow of the MandalMotors tower. She was still the *Corsair* but now carried a Tatooine registry.

The discretion of Tyno Fabris's existence was a bit unusual. Arkanians were not the most humble of beings; they tended to think of themselves as the apex of

evolution. To find an Arkanian in Black Sun was unusual enough, but to find one who kept a low profile
was even more surprising.

Once on the ground, Jax slipped into a disguise calculated to make him fit into Keldabe's hardscrabble, chaotic environment. He wore a blaster at his hip, covered
his back and chest with lightweight body armor, and
had bound his lengthening hair back in a metal clasp.
He'd even gone so far as to fit himself with a contact
lens that made his right eye look as if it had been replaced with a cybernetic implant. An artful scar ran
down his right cheek, bisecting the eyelid.

He looked hard, like a mercenary . . . and like he
could have been Sacha Swiftbird's male twin.

The disguise didn't end with his clothing. It was also
a persona that he slipped into. Corran Vigil was a dealer
in precious contraband, a man who lived on the fringes
in a completely different way than Jax Pavan had done.
He'd had I-Five give him a record as both a smuggler
and a ruthless procurer of hard-to-find items. The record of his disreputable existence was buried in obscure
places because those were what I-Five could access
without raising alarms, but if anyone looked for Corran
Vigil, they would assume his obscurity was due to attempts to hide.

Jax had not told either I-Five or Den whose counsel he
was going to seek, and so sent them off to glean information about a possible Imperial presence on Mandalore
or Concordia, and to further aid I-Five's rebuilding. He,
meanwhile, headed for the *Oyu'baat* tapcaf, arguably
the oldest cantina in continuous service in Keldabe. If
there were Black Sun operatives on Mandalore, that
was a likely place for them to do business.

The *Oyu'baat* was a large establishment that took up
several floors of a building that looked like a museum
piece. It was constructed entirely of wood and stone

with swaths of plaster from which chunks had fallen, leaving artful gaps that displayed the history of the building's various façades—brown, pale gray, even an amazing shade of orange that Jax was certain had never existed in nature on any world. The wooden ridgepole that anchored the tiled roof was as big around as three men and jutted from beneath the eaves like the prow of a sailing ship. It reminded Jax forcibly that Keldabe had originally been a fortress.

He entered beneath the shadow of the cantina's massive portico, eyeing patrons who passed him on their way out even as they gave him calculating once-overs. The main room of the tavern was a noisy, smoky cavern of dark wood and vivid tapestries depicting various legendary figures and events from Mandalorian history. Red was a dominant color. There was a lot of bloodshed in Mandalorian history.

At the top of the broad, shallow staircase that led down into the main room, Jax paused to look around. The center of the immense chamber was dominated by two curving bars. One apparently served food, the other beverages—including the spiced caf that the *Oyu'baat* was famous for. Both bars were lined with customers, jostling one another for service.

Around the raised perimeter of the room, tables were scattered at intervals while booths ringed the walls; each booth had a sliding wooden screen that could be slipped across the opening for privacy. Behind the bars, at the far end of the room, was a fireplace he could have parked a small shuttle in. It was from a period in which it—along with a scattering of braziers—had provided heat for the frontier gathering place. At least a dozen people could have sat in the alcove around the main fire pit. It was a chilly day—flames leapt in the huge grate, and a number of patrons gathered around it.

Jax had to admit its light and implied warmth beckoned, but he had business to transact and no time for creature comforts.

He looked up. Overhead—far overhead—sunlight filtered in through skylights in the sloped roof, falling in dusty splendor onto the age-rich wood of the bars. Broad galleries marked the third and second floors. Tyno Fabris was far more likely to be up there in one of the more private areas than down here in the noisy main room.

Jax settled on an approach and strode up to the beverage bar. "Spiced caf," he told the bartender when he'd finally gotten his attention. "Hot. A tankard."

"You're new here," said a female voice practically in his ear. It somehow managed to be sharp enough to cut through the ambient noise in the room and yet give the impression of velvet.

He turned. The source of the sultry voice was a Balosar woman who was nearly as tall as he was. That, in itself, was remarkable—natives of the planet Balosar were often small and frail. This woman was sapling-slender but hardly frail. Her long hair was artistically braided and fell in a twilight cascade over one pale shoulder. She wore a hair ornament that almost, but not quite, disguised her antenepalps—both of which were homed in on Jax.

A frisson of wariness tingled at the back of his neck. Those antenepalps, he knew, gave the Balosar a form of empathy that would make her a most observant spy for some corporate, underworld, or Imperial entity.

"New to Mandalore, no," he said. "To Keldabe, yes. I usually make planetfall on Concordia. But things are a bit . . . unsettled there of late."

She smiled. There was a gem embedded in one of her upper front teeth—a pale lavender crystal that echoed the color of her hair and eyes. "What brings you into the *Oyu*? Not that I'm complaining."

"Business."

"Of course. Look, why don't you go find yourself a seat and I'll bring you your caf."

"That's not necessary."

"That's my job." She picked up a tray from the bar. "The bar guys get snippy when patrons clog up the serving area."

Jax acquiesced with a curt nod and moved to a table from which he could see the entire room, except for a small section behind the food bar. He watched the female server collect his spiced caf, pop it onto a tray, and begin her walk toward his table. She was flirting with him during the entire passage, exaggerating the sway in her steps and clearly desiring his attention and admiration.

He wondered why she found him of particular interest. Though he suspected that she flirted with all her customers in the hope of a large gratuity, he sensed something beyond that in the way she looked at him. He muzzled his wariness, channeled it into impatience.

She set the tankard of caf down on the table and he snatched it up.

She tilted her head to one side, eyebrow raised, and rested the tray on the curve of one hip. "Can I get you anything else?" she asked. "Food . . . some other stimulant, perhaps?"

No subtext there. "I'm not hungry. And I don't care to be stimulated. I need to keep a clear head for business."

She made a face. "Business. Good-looking man like you is going to waste your time on business?"

"Better than wasting my time flirting with you. There's no profit in that."

Ignoring the spark of anger that leapt to her eye, Jax reached into an inner pocket and pulled out a couple of small cabochons of aurodium. He held them out on his palm where the ambient light caught them, sparking a rainbow shimmer of color.

"Unless you can *help* me do business."

She eyed the gleaming nuggets, then glanced back at the bar. "What do you need?"

"I'm looking for a man named Tyno Fabris. An Arkanian."

Her eyes narrowed. "You know him? Or you'd only *like* to know him?"

"I'd like to do business with him. I hear he's . . . a force in this sector."

She smiled wryly. "He is that. Why Tyno?"

"Why *not* Tyno?"

She regarded him a moment longer, her antenepalps at attention—assessing him. She frowned and shook her head. "No reason. In fact, I suspect maybe instead of warning you about him, I should warn him about you."

"Why don't you?" He set the aurodium on the table in front of her and met her gaze. "Tell him we have a mutual acquaintance who recommended him to me."

She nodded, scooped up the aurodium, and pocketed it before returning to the bar. When Jax looked up a moment later, she'd disappeared. He took a deep breath and a long sip of the hot spiced liquid.

Would she or wouldn't she? He leaned back in his chair to wait.

Den stared up at the address on the building—displayed in meter-tall numerals above the entrance—then glanced down at his datapad.

"I think this is the place."

I-Five made an impatient scraping sound. "A physical address—how quaint. I often forget exactly how backward these Outer Rim worlds can be. I suppose I should despair of finding any parts worth purchasing."

"The advertisement said they had a plethora of parts to meet special needs."

"Hm. Probably special if one is planning an act of piracy."

Den pocketed the datapad. "Isn't that what we're planning, more or less?"

I-Five's head swiveled on its gimbal. "You have a point."

Den looked back at the droid uneasily, wondering if he should divulge what had been burning a hole in his head since before they'd landed. He wanted to give Jax time to make it right, though, he told himself. Wanted to be disabused of the idea that their Jedi friend was keeping secrets from his two closest companions.

He opened his mouth to say something, but words wouldn't come. If he told I-Five what he'd overheard of Jax's conversation with Sal, he knew what that would mean. It would mean he didn't believe Jax would come clean. That he didn't trust him.

He'd wait, he decided. Tonight when they rendezvoused aboard the ship, Jax would tell them he'd asked Tuden Sal for his Black Sun contacts. He'd tell them he hadn't found any. Or that he had, but that he couldn't work with them.

I'll give it today, Den told himself. *Just today.*

He and Five had little to report with regard to recent Imperial activity on Mandalore. If anything, Den's journalistic credentials had caused people to be less forthcoming than ever. He hoped they'd have better luck filling their parts manifest than they had squeezing intel out of the closemouthed citizens of Keldabe.

They entered the building and found themselves in a sparsely furnished lobby. A protocol droid of many recognizable parts—none of them from the same type—sat behind a counter next to the door. It looked up and regarded them with optics that glowed a rather sinister red-orange.

"You need?" it asked curtly.

"Parts," said Den, "for an I-5YQ protocol droid if you've got 'em. Though we are interested in other . . . uh . . . peripherals."

"We?" repeated the droid with a look at the DUM unit.

"I . . . mean me and my captain. I'm mech-tech aboard the freighter *Corsair*."

"Your captain being?"

"Corran Vigil."

"I am unfamiliar with your captain. Which means nothing. What sort of peripherals were you seeking?"

"Armaments," Den said. "Shielding. That sort of thing."

The droid seemed to blink—its optics going dark for a split second. "You wish to arm an I-5YQ protocol unit? That is unusual."

Den saw an opportunity to bolster Jax's reputation as a menacing individual. "My captain's idea of protocol is sometimes . . . dangerous."

There was a soft hiss as an old-fashioned hydraulic blast door opened at the rear of the lobby and a tall, dark-skinned human woman, dressed from head to toe in black synthskin, stepped into the room.

"Then I'd say you've come to the right place," she said. "We can weaponize just about anything here. Even *that*." She gestured at I-Five with her head. A lock of shockingly red hair fell over one eye.

The droid responded by turning his head toward her and uttering a shrill chirrup that could have taken the paint off the walls. Den cringed and the woman covered her ears with both hands.

"I already *have* weaponized him," Den said. His voice

sounded muffled and wobbly even from inside. "Down, boy," he told I-Five.

The droid made a muted rattling sound, causing the proprietress to eye him warily.

"I'm actually hoping to build the protocol droid from hell," Den told her. "Something that seems benign and inoffensive . . . but isn't."

The woman rubbed at her ears. "I'd say your little buddy there is plenty offensive. Come on through. I'll show you what we've got."

What they had was a warehouse full of machine parts that were nowhere near as well organized as Geri's store of droid mechanisms back at Mountain Home. The inside of the building had been all but gutted, and bits and pieces of robotic gear hung from racks and netting or sat on shelves that went up several floors. A quartet of powered staircases—one for each wall—gave access to the collection.

The woman waved toward a rear corner of the warehouse. "Protocol droids," she announced. "Or what's left of 'em. The ones on the lowest levels are the closest to complete. Some of them actually still work . . . after a fashion. Armaments and other specialized enhancements are on the eastern wall." She gestured in that direction. "And in a private area through the door to your left. That area has rather a heightened security presence, as you might imagine. I'm sure we have what you want."

"I dunno," Den said, frowning. "Looks like a lot of junk from where I'm standing. You actually sell much of this?"

If she was offended, she didn't show it. "We have the biggest collection of droid parts between here and the desert rim. In fact, I just sold a bunch of this *junk* to the Empire."

Score. "The Empire. Really. What the heck would they want with this stuff?"

"I don't know, exactly. Stormtroopers aren't known for being chatty."

"But they found what they needed *here*?" Den gestured at the room.

She shifted. Glanced away at the walls with their clutter of metallic debris. "Sure. Why not? I mean, most of it . . . Some of it. But, I mean, who stocks blast cages, really?" She frowned at her collection of droid bits, then turned to glare at Den. "You don't need a blast cage, do you? 'Cause I don't have 'em."

"We don't need a blast cage. I would be interested in knowing what the Imperials bought, though. Captain Vigil likes to keep the ship up to standard." He gave the proprietress a meaningful look.

"Yeah? He willing to pay to know what the standard is?"

"He'll pay. Especially if we find what we need."

The woman smiled. Her teeth, Den realized, had been filed to points.

Charming.

He smiled back and followed I-Five to the wall of droids.

sixteen

Jax was at the point of going in search of Tyno Fabris himself when the Balosar woman reappeared. She didn't say a word to him; she only caught his eye and beckoned. He picked up his half-finished tankard of caf and followed her between the two service bars toward the back of the room. He was surprised when she went right past the staircase that led to the second-floor gallery.

She caught him peering up the steep flight of steps. "Looking for somebody?"

"Just noticing that I don't see much of an Imperial presence here. That's a bit odd. You can't go anywhere these days without tripping over stormtroopers."

"They leave us alone, pretty much."

"When's the last time you saw any of them?"

She gave him a look over her shoulder. "A while."

"A while. Days? Weeks? Months?"

"Months. Years. Decades."

"Don't anger me, Balosar," he said softly.

That earned him a smile. "Tlinetha. My name is Tlinetha. And I like your anger. It has a pleasant heat."

He pulled the Force more tightly around his thoughts. "So you're saying there haven't been Imperials in Keldabe for a very long time."

"That's what I'm saying."

She was lying. Why was she lying? If Vader's troops

had come to Mandalore, they would almost certainly have come to Keldabe. This was where business began, where intel flowed like wine.

They were making their way toward the giant fireplace now. Jax saw, to his surprise, that the clutter of patrons who had been there earlier were gone. In their place was a quartet of people who were obviously security goons of some sort. They didn't dress like security goons, but they felt like them.

There were three men—two humans and a Devaronian—and a female Zabrak. The Zabrak and one of the human men lounged in a seating group before the massive hearth, trying to look romantic; the Devaronian and second human were at separate tables. The four of them offered more than enough protection for the individual who sat in the hearth alcove, sipping caf.

He had pale, almost translucent skin, high cheekbones, and white hair that flowed like silk over his shoulders. Most Arkanians had pure white eyes; Tyno Fabris had either had his altered or wore lenses—his eyes were black.

"This is the man," Tlinetha told Fabris. "The one who was looking for you—to do business, he says."

"Corellian," the Arkanian said without preamble. "Am I right?"

Jax nodded curtly.

"Business. What sort of business?"

"Mutually beneficial business . . ." Jax glanced around at the bodyguards, his gaze lingering pointedly on the Balosar server. ". . . which I'd rather discuss in private."

"This is as private as you get for a first meeting," said Fabris. "A man in my position can't be too careful. Tlinetha says we have a mutual acquaintance. Who?"

"Tuden Sal."

Jax caught the other's surprise. And hesitation. Both were good.

Fabris nodded and flicked a glance at the Zabrak woman. She rose and moved to face Jax.

"Your weapons." She held out her hands.

Jax hesitated, then gave them over to her. The hesitation was for show alone. There wasn't a weapon the Jedi wore on his person that could equal the weapon he was.

She took his blaster and vibroblade, held up one hand. A small, round device nestled in her palm—a weapons sensor of some sort. She waved it up and down the length of his body, even passing it over his head.

"Can't be too careful," she told him, then glanced at her boss. "He's clean."

Fabris responded with the lifting of one pale brow, then indicated the seat across from him in the alcove.

Jax slid onto the padded stone bench, his gaze following the other man's hand. Interesting. Four digits—an indication of ancient Arkanian stock—but something about the shape of the hand told Jax it had been surgically altered. The pinkie had been removed and the hand reshaped. There was a tiny amount of residual scarring. Tyno Fabris was a genetically modified Arkanian then, but clearly a man who took enough pride in his heritage that he wanted to minimize the appearance of that modification.

Looking up across the leaping flames, Jax noticed that Fabris wore his hair pushed back from his ears, which were elegantly curved and pointed, seemingly without artifice. The dark eyes, then, must be lenses, Jax suspected: filters against the harsh brilliance of sun and ambient light. The Arkanian homeworld was a dismal snowball, and its inhabitants' eyes were calibrated to see infrared. In short—Tyno Fabris protected himself, but showed his ears to make clear there would be no doubt that he was Arkanian to the soul.

Interesting the subtle ways in which people revealed character.

"You've seen Tuden Sal, have you?" Fabris asked.

"I spoke to him only days ago."

"On Klatooine?"

Jax smiled tightly. "Where I spoke to him is irrelevant."

"And what is Sal doing these days?"

"Recovering from his reverses. And doing a decent job of it, too, to all appearances."

"Really? In what pursuit?" Fabris knew, of course. He'd supplied arms to Whiplash—possibly without knowing or caring about that.

"He's in . . . transportation, you might say. He tells me you've helped him . . . move things from time to time."

Fabris turned to Tlinetha. "You can go."

She nodded in a way that suggested her obedience was a form of mockery, and returned to the bar. The bodyguards had gone back to their watchful pretense that they were not watching at all.

"What do you seek?" asked the Arkanian.

"Information, perhaps more. It depends."

"And on what does it depend?"

"On whether you can account for your serving woman's lies."

One snowy eyebrow rose over its pool of darkness. "Lies? About what?"

"About the presence of Imperials on Mandalore recently. I'm curious about what they did here and where they went after the fact."

Fabris leaned back against the stone wall of the alcove. "Curious? Why would you be curious about that?"

"I was recently on Coruscant and heard that Darth

Vader was enlisting mercs for a 'special project.' I heard he was also looking for—but failed to find—a very special substance intended to aid in the interrogation of particularly resistant minds."

After a beat or two of silence, Fabris asked, "And?"

"And I just happen to know of such a substance. I'm certain Vader would make it worth my while if I were to get it for him. Problem is, he left Coruscant before I could make certain of my intel and I don't know where he's gone."

The Arkanian nodded thoughtfully. "Worth your while. And, naturally, if I could get you this information about Vader, you'd make it worth *my* while."

"Naturally."

Fabris nodded again, then pecked at a bit of fluff on one sleeve with a four-fingered hand. "I see. And what makes you think Imperials came through here recently?"

"I intercepted a distress call from a resistance ship that Vader was after. It was apparently transporting some high-level resistance operative. From what I could strain out of the garbled messages, Vader captured the operative, destroyed his vessel and all aboard, and sent him in a convoy to Mandalore. But I also know they didn't stay here long."

Fabris considered that for a moment, then said, "No. They didn't."

Jax didn't react to the admission.

"They were here briefly. I suggested Concordia might better meet their . . . needs."

"Which were?"

The Arkanian shrugged. "As you said: Mercs. Weapons. They had special needs, they said."

"Which were?" Jax repeated.

A slow smile spread across Tyno Fabris's face. "Now, I suspect that information might be worth something to me, Captain Vigil."

Jax returned the smile. "It might be. Can you help me out?"

"Possibly. I'll need to . . . check your story insofar as I can. This substance you mention. What is it, exactly?"

"I couldn't say. That's above my pay grade. But the full information on it is contained on a holocron I happen to have in my possession."

Jax could feel the other man's heightened interest as a vague fizz of static. Saw it as threads of energy that strained toward him.

Fabris leaned forward, his obsidian-lensed eyes reflecting the light of the flames. "A holocron? A *Jedi* holocron?"

"A Sith holocron, actually."

"And you've seen this data?"

"The previous owner showed it to me."

"The previous owner . . . ," Fabris murmured.

"You wouldn't know him. And his name's not important to our business. *If* we're going to do business, that is. Do you know where Vader's people went after they left Concordia . . . *if* they left Concordia?"

"I'm sure I can find out."

"Then we can do business?"

"I'll consider it. I'll *strongly* consider it."

Jax made an impatient sound and moved to leave. "If you're not sure—"

The Arkanian raised a pale hand. "Please. I'm a very careful man. In my line of work, I have to be careful. Otherwise, I might end up like our mutual friend. Homeless. Without people or identity . . . transporting things. I'll let you know tomorrow. Will that be soon enough?"

No, Jax thought, *not nearly soon enough.* But he smiled and inclined his head.

"That will be fine."

Fabris made a subtle gesture and Jax found the

Zabrak woman standing at his left shoulder, holding out his blaster and vibroblade. His cue to leave. He slid out of the hearth alcove and claimed his weapons.

From the corner of his eye he caught Fabris's movement as he pocketed the hold-out blaster he'd had aimed at Jax throughout their conversation. It had been hidden from sight by the leap of flames—but not from the Force.

He sketched a salute at the four bodyguards and returned to the main room of the cantina.

Tyno Fabris leaned back against the stone of the hearth, considering this development. Interesting. Garan had pronounced the newcomer clean of weapons, and yet . . .

He looked up as Tlinetha rejoined him, an inscrutable expression on her face. He waved her to a seat across from him in the hearth.

"You seem . . . puzzled," he told her. "Are you uncertain of our new Corellian friend?"

She nodded slowly. "I can't quite put a sensor on it, but there's something . . . different about him. The air around him . . . shivers. It's as if it's . . . charged in some way."

"A personal force shield perhaps?" That might account for what he, himself, had sensed—or seen, really.

"No. Artificial fields resonate differently than natural ones. This was a natural one—for want of a better word. I've only felt it twice before in my entire life."

That piqued Tyno's interest even more. "When?"

"The last time—when Vader's men were here. They had that . . . thing with them." Tlinetha's antenepalps lay down almost flat to her head.

Amusing. "You mean the Inquisitor?"

She nodded.

"Clearly he's not an Inquisitor. You said you'd felt it twice before. What caused it the first time?"

"A Jedi."

Now, that *was* interesting. Virtually impossible, but interesting. But it still didn't explain what his infrared-sensitive eyes had picked up from Captain Vigil—that he carried on his person a very concentrated source of energy. Not a weapon—Garan's sensor sweep would have detected that—but something.

All in all, Corran Vigil was a most interesting person. At least Tyno found him so, and he'd be willing to bet his Vigo would find him so, as well.

Den and I-Five had turned the smaller of the *Laranth*'s two cargo holds into a machine shop, which was where they were when Jax returned to the ship. Den was so buried in his brown study of an I-5YQ torso they'd procured that he was unaware of the Jedi's return. In fact, he barely registered I-Five stopping his own work on an I-5YQ head and slipping out of the hold.

There had not been a single, complete I-5YQ in the vendor's stock. They'd had to content themselves with pieces from several droids that were, according to the proprietress, the victims of a particularly bad day in the court of the Desilijic clan on Nal Hutta. As a result, they still didn't have enough for one entire I-5YQ.

Oddly, Den's mechanical friend didn't seem to mind too much. He was rather taken with the portability the resistance mech-tech, Geri, had given his neural processor, and seemed to be contemplating a future in which he wore droid bodies the way people wore clothing. He had, in fact, found in the highly guarded regions of the armory they'd visited, some parts—specifically the repulsor generators and laser array—from a Trang Robotics N-101 Nemesis droid. I-Five's original chassis had had a single laser incorporated into each index finger; the other fingers had been revised more recently to include other defensive mechanisms, as well. But the forearms he had just acquired had an actual laser cannon and a repulsor ray generator that mounted on the basic unit. What they lacked in stealth, he told Jax, they more than made up for in raw power.

I-Five admired the Nemesis design, as well. Like his own current chassis, the Nemesis could collapse itself into a small unit, barely a meter in length. But the Trang droid's elongated and jointed helm was fitted with the acme of ablative shielding. When the unit dropped into its protective/stealth posture, it looked like nothing so much as a Neimoidian harvester beetle—in camouflage. It was ostensibly the camouflage part that gave Nemesis droids their high success rate as assassins. They were outfitted with state-of-the-art confounder units calculated to muddle the senses of targets, guards, and surveillance equipment alike.

Den looked up as Jax and I-Five entered the cargo hold. His first look at Jax left the Sullustan feeling disoriented and chilled. He'd forgotten that the Jedi had gone off in disguise, and for a moment—a mere breath, a heartbeat—he had thought the man who stepped into the hold at I-Five's back was a stranger.

"I-Five says you had a productive day," said Jax.

Den shook himself. "Yeah. For one thing, our helpful proprietor verified the Imperial presence on Mandalore in the recent past . . . and could you please take that kriffing lens out of your eye? It gives me the creeps."

Jax ignored the plea. "What did the arms dealer say?"

"She said the Imperials came to her shop looking for some special items—sonic traps, sensor webbing, something called a photonic bender . . . and a blast cage. She didn't have the blast cage, though. Sent them to Concordia for that." He hesitated before asking, "We're not going to have to go to Concordia, are we?"

"We might, but I'm not sure yet. It depends."

"On what?" I-Five asked. "What did you find out today?"

Jax blinked, and his prosthetic iris rotated around his pupil. It was like watching a blast door close. In that moment of hesitation, Den felt the planet tilt.

"Pretty much the same thing you did. The Imperials were here. They were looking for mercenaries and 'special' items of some sort. They were sent to Concordia."

"Logically, then," said the droid, "we should go to Concordia, too."

Jax shook his head. "I'm waiting on some information. I have a contact who may be able to tell us more."

"For example?" prompted I-Five. "We know what they purchased here and what they were looking for on Concordia. Unless my logic is faulty—which it's not— that tells us the sort of situation we're going to find Yimmon in . . . unless the blast cage and other items have nothing to do with his abduction."

"I suspect they have everything to do with his abduction. And you're right—that does tell us the sort of situation we'll be walking into. But right now, we're missing the most critical piece of information—*where* we'll be walking into it. And how we can do it without being killed."

"Wait," said Den. "Am *I* missing something? What does their shopping list tell us, exactly?"

"Do you want to tell him, or shall I?" I-Five asked.

Jax gestured at the droid.

"The 'shopping list'—as you call it—tells us that we'd be walking into a trap."

"What?"

"Sonic traps are a type of aural confounder," explained I-Five. "Photonic benders do the same thing for sight. And the blast cage is a container intended to defeat sensors. One can assume that the blast cage would be used to contain the hidden item and the other devices arrayed around it to keep people from finding said item either through the normal senses or through sensor sweeps."

Den looked from I-Five to Jax, relief spreading through him in a warm, cozy tide. "But . . . that sort of trap won't defeat a Jedi."

"No. I rather suspect that's what the Inquisitors are for."

"The Inquisitors are for the interrogation," Jax said quietly. He had moved to I-Five's workbench and was looking down with an impenetrable expression at the head the droid had been working on.

"I imagine they'd make good Jedi traps nonetheless," said I-Five. "If Vader expects you to come . . ."

"Vader thinks I'm dead." Jax brushed his fingers over the dull metal of the I-Five unit's face.

"Can you be sure of that?"

"He has no reason to think I'm alive. And I'm trying very hard to not give him one."

Den bit back a crack about Jax's foray into ISB headquarters and instead asked the question that was giving him indigestion. "So, who do you know that can answer that 'where' question, Jax? Who's got this information we need?"

"A man I met today at the *Oyu'baat* tapcaf. Local information merchant."

"A local information merchant," Den repeated, meeting Jax's gaze. "And where does he get his information?"

"I didn't ask." Jax turned abruptly from the workbench and headed out into the corridor. "I need to get this lens out of my eye."

Den watched him go in utter disbelief. "Son of a . . . fripping . . . This isn't right."

I-Five's head tilted sidewise, and his oculus rotated to pull the Sullustan into focus. "What isn't right?"

Den told him.

seventeen

Jax hated waiting. He wanted to act, to move, to *do* something. Not dangle upon Tyno Fabris's whim. What if the Arkanian decided not to sell him the information he wanted? What then? What did he have that might tip the balance?

He'd already mentioned the holocron, but there was no way he could actually let that fall into someone else's hands—least of all someone like Tyno Fabris.

He got up from his mat and moved to the tree, opening the small compartment in its vessel and removing the Sith artifact. It tingled against his palm, glowing faintly the red of oxidized iron. To someone not endowed with a sense of the Force, it would look like a pretty little puzzle box—a geometrical container with sleek, rounded vertices and elaborately incised faces. Something one might keep jewelry in.

Few knew what it really contained.

Jax stared at the object vibrating in his hand and wondered—not for the first time—if it might hold information he could use in his present situation. It contained—ostensibly hidden in layers of memory below the more recent additions pertaining to Imperial strategic moves—the writings and lab notes of the Sith savant Darth Ramage. Some of the information was irrelevant now—the information on using pyronium to increase the yield of a dose of bota, for example—but Jax had heard rumors of the sort of experiments Darth Ramage had done, and some of them held terrifying implications.

Ramage was alleged to have done experiments in the manipulation of time.

Jax ran a finger down one beveled, etched face. Impossible. Cephalons could see through time, into it, past it, around it. Everyone else was destined to live in its stream and, eventually, to drown there. No one could swim against it, or strike out across it to stand with the Cephalons—and the few other species who shared their abilities—on the far shore.

Jax had asked Aoloiloa once what his perception of the Force was. He had gotten an answer that was typically metaphorical and vague: "Force is sea. Force is drop. Force is all. Force is not all."

If time was a stream, then it flowed into that sea—drop by drop. Laranth's drop. His drop. Perhaps what he should have asked the Cephalon was *Could I swim to shore and, having reached the shore, walk upstream?*

It wasn't possible, of course, but if it were, would he want to take that walk? Who hadn't thought, *If I only had this to do over. If only I could turn back time, I'd do this right next time.*

If he could manipulate time, could he rewrite his past?

Even that was not the real question. The question that haunted Jax Pavan was: was there something he *could* have done—*should* have done—to save Laranth?

He thrust all the questions aside. It was human nature to want to rewrite past mistakes, but that fantasy did not alter the fact that Darth Ramage's holocron was rumored to contain some information that could be of great use to a Jedi. He just had to figure out how to open it.

Jax held the holocron up before his eyes, feeling the warmth and weight of it; feeling the power that shivered in it. Every holocron was different. A simple data holocron could be opened verbally or manually or electronically by anyone with the proper password, combination, or key. A Jedi or Sith holocron was a different sort of puzzle altogether, and the "key" could take any number of forms. Some required both a Force key and a physical one—often a crystal. The Force key opened the box; the crystal allowed the possessor to access its contents.

Jax had no idea how Darth Ramage had secured his holocron, but he suspected one would almost have to be a Sith to figure it out—or at least have some knowledge of the dark side of the Force.

Yet the artifact spoke to him, quivered in his hand, sent frissons of power through his bones. Maybe . . .

Holding the holocron flat on his palm, he closed his eyes and focused his attention on the heat and pulse of it. His hand throbbed with the energies in it as his Force strands reached out to wrap themselves around it.

A stab of alarm rippled through him. *What are you doing? You don't know what you're doing. This isn't right. Stop now.*

Thoughts disrupted, he opened his eyes and was startled to see the red glow of the holocron enveloping his hand, creeping up his wrist. The heat of it went to the marrow of his bones. He swallowed, closed his eyes again.

Stop. Stop!

The hatch panel pinged, jarring Jax's concentration. He tried to ignore it, but it pinged again. Frustrated, he swept his free hand at the hatch.

"Come!"

I-Five stood in the open hatchway, with Den beside him, the two so close in height and posture that it was almost comical. The warring urges to laugh and rage collided.

"What?" Jax asked, the word half growl, half chuckle.

I-Five didn't beat around the bush. "This contact you've made here on Mandalore—who is he?"

"I told you. He's a businessman. An information broker."

"His name? His affiliation?"

"Why is this important?"

Den stepped into the little cabin. "Tyno Fabris. That's his name."

Jax stared at the Sullustan. "How do you know that?"

"I overheard it. In a conversation you were having with Tuden Sal." He shook his head. "Why, Jax? Why didn't you tell us you've been in contact with Black Sun?"

"More to the point," said I-Five, "why do we need to be in contact with Black Sun in the first place?"

Now Jax almost did laugh. "Why not? What's my alternative? Reach out with the Force and poke around until I poke Vader? Do I need to remind you that if I do that, he may find *us*?"

Den muttered, "You'd get his attention, that's for sure."

"I don't want to get his attention. I want to catch him looking the other way."

"If you believe that can still happen, you're in denial. You thought he sensed you at the bureau."

"He sensed the Force, yes. But he saw an Inquisitor. He didn't strike at me or pursue me. He didn't even attempt to touch me. He thought I was one of his. If he hadn't, I'd have had to fight him then and there." That was what he'd told himself, over and over again in the days since his ill-advised infiltration of the ISB. Vader would have come after him with tooth and claw if he'd recognized Jax.

"I'm going to catch him by surprise. I just have to figure out how."

"And for that you need Black Sun?" I-Five asked wryly.

"I need—*we* need—whatever resources will help us find Yimmon."

"Yimmon? Or Vader?"

Jax shook his head. What was the droid talking about? "Where we find one, we'll find the other."

"And if not?"

"What do you mean?"

"If Vader and Yimmon have separated?"

Jax looked at the droid with honest perplexity. "I doubt that will have happened. He's sent his special legion through here to wherever he's holding Yimmon. He's sent his Inquisitors there. He's going there, himself. That's the only thing that makes sense. We just need to find out where 'there' is."

The droid was relentless. "What if Vader has left Yimmon somewhere and gone back to his other business? Which path will you pursue?"

Jax felt a niggle of irritation. He breathed it in and let it flow out again. "I'll go after Yimmon. And I'll find him. Whatever it takes. Even brushing shoulders with Black Sun. Why are you grilling me like this?"

"Forgive me," said I-Five. "I merely want to be certain that we're in agreement on the goal."

"The goal is to get Thi Xon Yimmon out alive and intact."

In the back of Jax's mind was the havoc Vader had wrought with his erstwhile Padawan, Kajin Savaros— what the Dark Lord had been able to do to the boy's mind. But Yimmon, he told himself, was not an unschooled child. He was a Cerean and unusually disciplined even for one of his species. He had displayed an almost Jedi-like ability to think above the physical dimensions and to shepherd his thoughts. Jax prayed that ability would help him withstand Darth Vader's formidable array of tools.

"We don't have to do this alone," I-Five said, "or with Black Sun. We could return to Toprawa and enlist the aid of the Rangers. We can trust them."

"We don't know that. Not for sure. One of them may have betrayed us to Vader in the first place."

"But you trust Black Sun?" Den asked incredulously.

"Not at all. Not one bit. But I *know* I can't trust them. And I won't. But with the Rangers . . . I can't trust them all and I can't treat them all as if I *don't* trust them. Paradox. And by trying to tread a middle ground, I'll put the traitor in a position of power and the loyal in harm's way."

"We can't talk you out of this?" asked Den.

Jax sighed. "Look, I'm supposed to see Fabris tomorrow to find out if he's even willing to sell us the information we need. He may still shut that door in our faces."

"And if he doesn't?"

"Then we'll see what the deal is. Frankly, I don't have that much to bargain with. I told a pretty glib fib to get my foot in the door."

"Great," Den muttered. "We're dealing with a demon and we've got no leverage."

Jax smiled wryly. "I didn't say we don't have leverage. I'll create leverage out of thin air and spit if I have to."

I-Five tilted his head, obviously focusing his optics on the holocron in Jax's hand. "Using that?"

"Using whatever it takes."

Pol Haus carefully read the report that had just dropped into his datapad. The ISB had been moving resources about in a most intriguing way, and now the Emperor was on the move, as well. In a matter of days he'd be going to a villa on the shores of the Western Sea.

Several members of the Imperial Senate were also planning trips to the seashore. Pol didn't believe for a moment that this was coincidental.

The Emperor's villa was small—at least compared with the Imperial Palace—and part of it sat out over the water. This last bit of information would likely be of interest to Tuden Sal. Pol could see that it might be possible to approach the villa by water with the right personnel and resources.

He returned the datapad to the pocket of his coat and looked up as the Whiplash Express—as he'd come to think of it—glided into the run-down transit station in a whisper of air.

Tuden Sal would view this windfall as a sign that it was time to put his plan into action . . . which was precisely why he should not know of it.

eighteen

Tuden Sal looked up from his drink as Acer Ash slid into the booth across from him and set his own beverage down, sliding it to the center of the tabletop. A data wafer was concealed behind the cup. The human pushed it over behind Sal's glass with one finger.

"Were you able to get everything?" Sal asked, palming the wafer.

Acer smiled. "Not everything, but most of it. *And—*" he added, before Sal could respond, "the rest of it is coming."

"The rest of it? How much of it?"

"The cloaking system you wanted has components that are illegal for public consumption. It will be a few days before I can get those. But I *will* get them, thanks to a little windfall."

Sal smiled, lifting his cup. "Good news. Here's to your windfall."

Acer touched the rim of his cup to Sal's. "To my windfall."

"What was it—your little stroke of luck?"

"Some Imperial security forces are going to be moving in a day or two, and that will leave certain facilities and routes less well patrolled than usual. Something is going on, looks like. Not sure what. There's some more intel about that on the wafer." He tipped his cup toward Sal's hand.

"Something? Any idea what?"

"Not a clue. All I know is it frees me up to make some propitious moves."

Sal raised an eyebrow. "Propitious? Isn't that a bit of a stretch for your vocabulary, Acer?"

The smuggler grinned. His canines—capped with aurodium—gleamed with rainbow hues. "It is. I'm trying to improve myself. It means—"

"I know what it means. I'm just surprised *you* do. But congratulations. What's the word for next week?"

"Haven't chosen one yet," Acer told him. "Got any suggestions?"

"Just my word of the week: insurrection."

Acer looked disappointed. "Oh. I already know what *that* means."

This time they met in Fabris's office, which was reached via a secret panel beneath a staircase in the cantina. Den and I-Five had wanted to come along, but Jax saw no reason to announce to all and sundry that they were a team.

"It raises our profile," he told them. "Which is the last thing I want to do. Better if you two work independently."

He could tell by the look on Den's face that the Sullustan was suspicious of his dealings with the Black Sun lieutenant, but he couldn't help that. He wasn't responsible to Den Dhur for his actions. The truth was, *he* needed to be independent to do whatever was best for the mission. Hence, he was alone when Tlinetha escorted him to meet "the Boss."

The office suite was a study in anachronism. The furniture was wooden—some of it hand-carved. The corners of the room were illuminated, not by ambient walls but by myriad small lanterns that dotted the room with pools of light. In the largest such pool, the Arkanian sat behind a huge desk in solitary splendor, watching Jax react to the opulent space. The colors were as vibrant as its occupant was pale—they assaulted the eyes. Vivid carpets in green and deep plum covered flamewood floors that glowed in the hues of a desert sunset.

Overhead, in the center of the vaulted ceiling, hung an antique chandelier of epic proportions and ornateness. It was strung with thousands of small crystals that caught light and sprayed it about the room in millions of tiny, colorful points. Its light was generated by real candles—hundreds of them. Above the chandelier, the ceiling seemed to pulse and crawl with living light and shadow.

A rainbow of tapestries from a dozen worlds decorated the walls. Jax guessed that several of them concealed doors: his Force sense told him that a handful of sentients occupied a space behind the tapestry nearest to Fabris's desk. This was no surprise—Tyno Fabris was, by his own admission, a careful man. Jax didn't react to their presence, but merely surveyed his surroundings with a cool gaze.

Too cool for Tyno Fabris, apparently. The man rose and made a sweeping gesture. "Well? What do you think? Most people at least comment on the colors . . . but perhaps with your prosthesis, you don't see color the way most people do."

Jax swung his gaze to the Arkanian. "Have you considered my offer?"

The pale eyebrows ascended. "All right, I guess we'll skip the pleasantries. Yes. I find your offer most interesting. Have you been able to open the holocron?"

"Tampering with such things naïvely can be dangerous. I had thought I might let Lord Vader open it."

Fabris shook his head. "That would be just as dangerous. If the information you promise him is not in it . . ."

"That's for me to worry about, isn't it?"

"Not if I'm to receive a portion of your 'reward,' Captain Vigil. If your reward is—oh, say—death and dismemberment, then I'll pass. I think it best if you open the holocron and make certain of the information before selling the device to Darth Vader. He does not react well to disappointment. And I will not be the one to disappoint him."

Jax hadn't counted on Fabris demanding that he open the holocron. Though he'd come near trying it the night before, he now found himself strangely reluctant. "I don't possess the . . . ability to open the holocron."

Again the raised eyebrow. "You don't?"

Jax's skin prickled with wariness. "No."

"Then how do you know—"

"It was taken from a Jedi who knew its contents."

"A Jedi. Does he have a name?"

"*Had* a name. He's dead now. His name was Jax Pavan." He didn't even blink at the mention of his own demise.

"Ah. And you removed the holocron from his dead body, I suppose."

"Something like that."

"May I ask how you—"

"Does it matter?"

Fabris shrugged and strolled about his office, seemingly admiring its décor, touching this or that object lovingly . . . or perhaps significantly. Jax tensed, assuming the people in the next room were monitoring all this.

"You're asking me to take a huge risk, Captain Vigil. You tell me a tale of a murdered Jedi, a stolen holocron, and an alleged substance that Darth Vader would be willing to pay for . . ." He glanced fleetingly at Jax.

"I didn't say the Jedi was murdered. Or that the holocron was stolen. And Vader need never know you were the source of my intelligence about his location."

"It is the nature of Lord Vader to know what he wishes to know. If your purpose is other than what you've said, or you fail to give him something he wants, he will discover who connected you to him. If I'm in your . . . revenue stream, he'll follow that stream right back to me." Again, the glance.

"If you're not willing to deal—"

"Didn't say that. Didn't mean it. I'd just like to structure the deal differently." The huge, dark eyes fixed on Jax's face. "I want payment up front."

"What sort of payment?"

"First, answer a question for me."

Jax tensed anew. He'd been aware of the Arkanian's intense curiosity; now he feared it might be more than that. "If I can."

"You've been cleared of weapons, and yet I detect a white-hot source of energy on your person. What is it?"

The pyronium. Well, that gave Jax some idea of the sort of genetic modifications Tyno Fabris had been given. He reached beneath the flexible body armor into the sash of his tunic and withdrew the gleaming, opalescent object, holding it out on the flat of his hand.

The light of a dozen lamps and a hundred candles shivered on the curving surface of the gem, and it absorbed even that meager energy, cycling through rainbow hues that rivaled those in Tyno Fabris's office. The Arkanian's eyes were so alight with it that Jax expected him to lick his lips.

"What is that?"

"Pyronium."

Fabris paused in the act of touching the nugget and looked up into Jax's face. Jax felt his sudden excitement like static in the air between them.

"Pyronium? I've heard rumors of it. Legends. It's said to be constantly absorbing electromagnetic energy in whatever environment it's placed. Storing it in virtually unlimited amounts in some sort of hyperspatial lattice."

"Those are its properties." Jax didn't mention that the trick was getting the rare metal to *release* the energy. The information on how to do that was also in the Sith holocron concealed behind the miisai tree—or at least that was the rumor that had come with the device.

Fabris's eyes were on the gem. "It's also said to be quite rare—vanishingly so, in fact. This is really pyronium?"

"Yes."

"Where did you get it?"

Jax's mouth twisted wryly. "Another Jedi who no longer exists. Are you interested in it?"

Fabris withdrew his hand. "I might be . . . Yes. Yes, I'm interested."

"Then we have an agreement? Darth Vader's whereabouts for the pyronium."

Fabris nodded, his eyes never leaving the jewel. "Where are you staying in Keldabe? I'll contact you as soon as I have something for you."

Jax folded the pyronium in his hand and tucked it away again. "I'm staying aboard my ship, the *Corsair*."

"*Corsair*," Fabris repeated, his gaze following the pyronium to its hiding place. "You're at the local port, I assume."

"You assume correctly. Until you have news, then."

The Arkanian favored him with a businesslike smile. "I don't expect it to take too long. Until then, enjoy your stay. I have it on good authority that Tlinetha is quite taken with you. She always did have a soft spot for pirates."

Jax laughed at that characterization of his alter ego and let himself out of the room. He contemplated exploring Tyno Fabris's domain a bit further, but sensed he was being watched carefully. He returned to the cantina the way he had come. Tlinetha met him beneath the staircase, her eyes confirming her boss's sense of her fondness for "pirates."

Tyno Fabris did not need to feel the flutter of the tapestry or hear the opening of the door behind it to know that someone else had entered the room. That one, he thought wryly, announced his presence only too effectively. He shifted in mild discomfort.

"Is that him?" the Arkanian asked, not bothering to turn around.

"Yes." The voice sounded faintly amused. "It would seem the rumors of Jax Pavan's demise are somewhat exaggerated."

"And?" Fabris turned.

Prince Xizor gave an eloquent shrug, his skin flushing green. "And . . . you should abide by your agreement. By all means, let's get him what he wants."

nineteen

Everything was going well. Better than expected, under the circumstances. The arms and equipment would be moved within the week, Darth Vader was off-world, and Jax had followed him. This last item was not what Tuden Sal would have called *good* news under normal circumstances, but since Thi Xon Yimmon's abduction, circumstances were not normal and probably never would be again.

Now, Sal was convinced, it was better that Jax be away, as well. That was a trifecta of goodness—things were aligning, and he needed but one more piece to fall into place.

Standing in the shadows of the old transit hub, he heard the maglev coming before it pulled into the station. He waited impatiently for it to glide to a stop before hurrying aboard. He went directly to his private quarters and popped Acer Ash's data wafer into his reader.

The contents accelerated his pulse—lists of much-needed equipment and the schedule by which they would be moved into "safe" areas scrolled down the display. This was followed by an aerial map of the routing information for the assorted shipments—information that would allow Sal to select where to have the items delivered or intercepted. He saw immediately that Ash was right—there were subtle and not-so-subtle changes in the corridors the traffickers were using to bring the contraband from the various spaceports.

Disbelief crept into the Sakiyan's excitement as he began to understand the nature of those changes. The smugglers were using corridors that ran very near the Imperial Palace and the Senate complex.

How was that possible? It spoke of a radical redeployment of Imperial military and police forces. Not to mention Inquisitors. And if they weren't guarding the thoroughfares around the Imperial power complexes, then what were they guarding?

He expanded the map view, looking for anomalies. He found them along the shore of the Western Sea. The trafficking corridors there that smugglers had used regularly had gone dark, marked as "avoid until further notice."

There was only one possible reason that Sal could see: What they were guarding had moved. His pulse accelerated further as comprehension struck. The Emperor had relocated to his villa at the Western Sea.

He was reachable.

Sal turned to his communications console, intending to call the Whiplash Council together, but stopped with his hand over the controls, stunned by a sudden realization. This information that Ash had given him was gleaned from local and regional security nets. Which meant that Pol Haus should have already had it . . . and relayed it to him.

Why hadn't he?

Tuden Sal activated his comlink and sent a scrambled signal to the district police headquarters.

In the engineering bay of the *Laranth/Corsair,* Den felt as if he had been consigned to some sort of machine shop limbo. He'd surely been sitting at this workbench fusing aural and visual synapses for days. It was mind-

less work, but in some ways he treasured the mindless-
ness. It kept him from thinking about Jax.

He found himself staring into the metal cranium he
was holding, laser tool on standby, looking for something to solder.

"I believe," said I-Five, "that you have completed the
connections."

Den put the laser solderer down. "I guess." He picked
up the topless I-5YQ head, then hesitated, uncertain
what to do next.

Five took the thing out of his hands and settled it atop
the neck and shoulders of the I-5YQ torso that sat on a
stool at the end of the bench. With several deft moves,
the little droid fastened it in place and stood back to
survey the work. "I also believe it is ready for a brief
trial."

"Trial?"

Den stared at the thing. It was pathetic. The head was
missing its crown and rear plate, and while the body
was intact, it had only one complete leg and the upper
half of one arm. The lower left arm was from the Nemesis assembly. The right one was a crazy quilt of parts
from a number of different droids. The left leg was, from
the knee down, just a thick durasteel rod with a roller
ball set into the bottom of it. If Five was seriously suggesting he take it for a test drive, he wouldn't be able to
walk so much as scooter along.

"You're joking, right?"

The pit droid's oculus swiveled toward him. "Joking.
Me."

"Okay. I take it back. What do we do next?"

"We take me out of here—" I-Five tapped his current
braincase. "—and install me in there."

"Right." Den slid off his chair at the workbench.
I-Five folded up into his compact form and tilted his
head forward. "I'm thinking we should install a second-

ary cortex in each of my chassis that will allow me to transfer myself as needed."

"Oh, I see. Thereby making me redundant and dispensable."

"Only you would choose to see it that way. I was thinking of your welfare. I thought it might be best if you didn't need to play mechanic every time a change was required. There might also be emergency situations in which you might not be available."

Den took a deep breath. "Emergency situations, yeah. I can see that."

I-Five tripped the catch on his helm and popped it open, allowing Den access to his cortex.

Den wiped his hands on his pants. "I don't mind telling you that this makes me very nervous."

"You've done it before."

"Yeah, but the R2 unit didn't have a fripping blaster built into its manipulators."

"I promise I will not shoot you. Please proceed."

Den carefully lifted I-Five's brain out of the DUM head casing and installed it in the hybrid droid. Its optics lit up so swiftly he was startled. He jumped, took a step back, and landed on his butt on the deck.

"Ah," I-Five said from the new unit. "Ah-*ah*. Calibrating. Hm. Optics are not optimal. We'll have to make some adjustments—in fact, I've been contemplating some upgrades."

"You sound . . . more like you," Den observed.

"My resonating cavity is larger and deeper," the droid responded. He turned his head. Shifted his shoulders. Flexed his elbows. Den flinched. The cobbled-together droid—Den was still having a hard time thinking of it as I-Five—curled his lethal fingers. Rotated his lone ankle.

Then he stood.

"Move aside and let me see if the legs work."

Den scrambled to obey, his eyes on the Nemesis blaster arm. "What about the draft?"

"The draft?"

Den pointed to the crown of his own head. "We're missing a piece of your skull, in case you'd forgotten. I'd hate for you to have an unfortunate accident and undo all of Geri's careful work. Not to mention losing your mind. Ha."

I-Five ignored the weak joke. "You can use the magnetic clips to attach the Nemesis carapace."

Den looked at the insectile shell doubtfully. "Seriously?"

"It may not be the ideal arrangement, but it will do for a test."

Den lifted the Nemesis helm, activated the magnetic latches, and placed it atop the I-Five head. It looked . . . ridiculous. It looked like the droid equivalent of a long wig.

Den was unable to stifle the laughter that bubbled up out of his throat. He laughed until his nose started to run and his eyes watered.

"I'm pleased," I-Five said when Den finally ran out of breath and mirth, "to be the cause of levity. You've been positively gloomy lately."

"Yeah? Can you blame me?"

"All things considered, no."

I-Five adjusted his carapace and experimented with motion. With one unarticulated leg and a roller, he could only scoot—which was just as funny as Den had imagined.

He felt another fit of laughter coming on, but his gut hurt. He shook his head as he watched I-Five testing his joints—picking things up and putting them down again . . . except for the ones he dropped. The Nemesis hand had a few bugs, Den noted.

He was suddenly struck by the sheer hopelessness of their situation.

"Why?" he asked.

The droid stopped scootering across the deck and turned. "Why what?"

"Why are you doing this? Why are *we* doing this?"

"Could you be more specific?"

Den made a frustrated gesture. "Why are we here sitting on Mandalore, turning you into a juggernaut, while Jax is playing games with Black Sun?"

"We may need me to be a juggernaut, and is that really what you think Jax is doing—playing games? I rather think his dealings with Black Sun are deadly serious."

"Yeah," said Den laughing nervously. "I guess that's what I was afraid to say. Why is he doing this? Why is he dealing with them?"

"He said it: He'll do whatever it takes to find Yimmon. Deal with whomever he has to deal with."

"And you approve?"

"Do you think I do?"

Den sighed and sat back down at his workbench. "No. But, blast it all, it feels *wrong*. Why doesn't it feel wrong to Jax?"

"Jax is a man driven by grief, outrage, and purpose."

"Jax is a Jedi!" Den objected.

"Yes, but he is still a man." I-Five glided back to the workbench again. "Here, put me back in my other chassis. We need to work on my optics."

"Yeah, and find you a real leg, or I'll have to start calling you I-Gimpy."

"You're not funny when you're depressed—you do realize that."

"Sit down and shut up."

For the second day in a row, Jax walked for kilometers around Keldabe, poking his nose into public houses and businesses that catered to spacers, asking questions and soaking up answers and the energies that went with them. He felt no real need of the answers at this point—he was marking time, waiting for Fabris to get back to him about Vader's possible whereabouts.

He hated it. Told himself he didn't; that he could be patient, watchful, calm. But inside, he was *buzzing*. His chest felt as if it harbored an expanding ball of static electricity that would—if left long enough—explode and short-circuit his entire system.

Nonetheless, some of the answers were interesting—stormtroopers had been here, seeking mercenaries with a particular skill set that included an extreme lack of sensitivity to the Force. That made sense; if Vader was planning on subjecting Yimmon to interrogation or guarding by sentients he'd hardly want them to be susceptible to the sort of psychic ricochets that could occur when powerful minds collided.

Yimmon, being a Cerean, was an unknown commodity in some ways. Jax had always suspected that the dual brains the species possessed allowed them to handle even small amounts of Force energy differently and perhaps more effectively than sentients with only one central processor.

Yimmon had been tortured once in his youth. Jax had asked him how he had dealt with it. He said something cryptic: "I hid."

"I don't understand," Jax had admitted.

"I hid," the Cerean had replied, tapping his skull.

Jax *did* understand the concept. Jedi were taught to absent the mind when exposed to extreme stimuli. Jax had even been able to practice it . . . once.

At the end of a long day, he returned to the ship, entering to the murmur of voices drifting up from engineering. He headed in that direction, intending to report what little he'd learned. The sound of Den's laughter brought him up short. Something had set the Sullustan off. His laughter came in gales.

Jax's reaction was disturbing even to himself. He felt a flash of deep, painful anger, as if there was something *wrong* in the laughter—something disrespectful. Beneath that was an equally intense longing—a sort of mindless envy—to experience something that could make him laugh.

He stopped just beyond the engineering hatchway and listened.

"It feels *wrong*," Den was saying. "Why doesn't it feel wrong to Jax?"

Jax didn't stay to hear the answer. He felt like an interloper, an outsider. Right now, perhaps he was.

He moved swiftly to his cabin, slipped inside, and locked the hatch. A soft, insistent chime started up in one corner of the small chamber. Puzzled, he looked around. The light on the miisai tree's container was flashing yellow.

He stared at it, stunned to the roots of his soul. How had he forgotten? He hurried to find organics to feed the converter. Here he'd been angry at Den for laughing in the shadow of Laranth's death, while *he'd* neglected the one tiny bit of her that he still had.

His hands trembled as he crumbled a protein bar into the container's food receptacle and closed the door of the converter. The chime went silent; the light returned to a calming shade of green.

Jax took a deep breath, wiped sweating palms on his tunic, and stepped back to the center of the cabin just as the cabin's comlink pinged.

He found Den at his cabin door. "There's a woman at the air lock asking for you. A Balosar."

Tlinetha. "Did she say what she wanted?"

Den's thick lips twitched. "You."

"I meant—"

"Yeah. I know what you meant. She won't say what she wants."

Jax nodded. "Bring her aboard."

"You sure?"

"She works for Tyno Fabris."

The big dark eyes were suddenly wary. "Oh. I see." Den glanced back down the corridor. "It's okay, Five. You can let her come aboard."

She appeared before the Sullustan could quite remove himself from sight. He ducked down the aft passage.

"Who was that?" she asked, nodding toward Den's shadow as he disappeared into his own quarters.

"Crew. To what do I owe the honor?"

Tlinetha looked past Jax into his quarters. "Tyno sent me."

"And?"

She met his eyes for a moment. "He wants to see you."

"He has information for me?"

She chuckled softly and slipped past him into his cabin. "You think he'd tell me? He just said, 'Bring him.' "

"Then let's go."

She looked back over her shoulder at him, smiling. "What's your hurry?"

Before he could tell her what his hurry was, she had swung back around, taking in the small quarters at a glance. Her gaze fixed on the miisai tree.

"I need that information, Balosar."

"*I* think you need to relax." She moved to the tree and reached out to touch one of the gracefully turned boughs.

Jax had crossed the space between them and grasped her wrist in a punishing grip before her fingertips could brush the silvery green foliage.

She turned on him, her smile deepening. "That's more like it."

"It's fragile," he said, dropping her wrist. "Don't touch it."

"That go for you, too?"

He turned away from her, gesturing at the door. "Tyno's waiting."

She hesitated for a moment longer, then shrugged and ducked past him into the corridor.

She took him directly to Tyno Fabris's office in the cantina, where the Arkanian awaited him, sitting behind his fabulous desk, his feet resting on its polished surface. He looked relaxed, lazy even, but that was a lie. Underneath the relaxed exterior was a strange watchfulness that put Jax immediately on alert.

"You have something for me?"

Fabris nodded. "It wasn't easy to get, my friend, but let's see if it's worth the price. Vader's forces came through Mandalorian space in three waves. The first, as you know, was close to a month ago. They made landfall on Mandalore and on Concordia. The second wave—three ships, so not much a wave as a ripple—came through roughly two weeks ago. They didn't stop—just dropped out of hyperspace on the fringes of the system, adjusted course, and took off again. The third wave was composed of only two ships. Also in a hurry. One of these ships sent two coded messages—one to Imperial Center, the other to a destination in Bothan space. I would assume that destination was where the ships were headed."

"Where?"

Fabris didn't answer, just continued his narrative. "The messages positively identified the ship of origin as a *Lambda*-class long-range shuttle—the *Questor*. I have it on good authority that Darth Vader himself was aboard."

"Where did he send the second message?"

Fabris sat up straight, feet on the floor, and spread his

hands in a gesture of bemusement. "Aren't you the least bit interested in what the messages said?"

"You were able to intercept and decode them?" Somehow Jax hadn't thought Fabris's resources ran to that sort of technology.

"No, but I know someone who did. I figured you might want to meet him. So I invited him to our little meeting."

A frisson of wariness scurried down Jax's spine. Who would have the resources to do that without Vader knowing it?

One of the hidden doors slid open and the tapestry covering it was swept aside by the brawny arm of a Mandalorian mercenary in full armor.

Jax took in his escape options in one swift glance—he was midway between the chamber's exit and a barred window fashioned of artisan glass in a rainbow of colors. Either would serve.

Jax knew whom he would see before Xizor entered the room: the heady wash of pheromones preceded him.

The Falleen was engaged, excited, but not, surprisingly, hostile. He held up both hands in a reassuring gesture. "Please, Jax. I'm here to deal, not fight."

"Deal? I seem to recall that the last time we met you tried very hard to kill me . . . with my own lightsaber."

"That was then. This is now. And even then, I didn't start out to kill you. You were worth far more to me alive, but you were unwilling to be captured and . . ." He shrugged eloquently. "Well, my life was in jeopardy. It was me or you. Nothing personal, believe me. It was just business. Then as now."

"And the deal?"

Again the shrug. "You want to know where Vader has gone to ground. I want . . ." Xizor advanced farther into the room, coming around to lean on the corner of

Fabris's desk, making the smaller man have to peer past him to see Jax. "Well, I'm not sure what I want yet."

"I offered Fabris, here, a pyronium gem in exchange for information."

Xizor glanced over his shoulder at the Arkanian. "Tyno has a puny imagination. He believes in *things*. I believe in people. You, for instance."

"Me."

"You're a Jedi. Possibly the last of a dead breed. Rare. Unusual. Powerful. I like rare, unusual, powerful things."

Jax's jaw tightened painfully. Where was this going? "What do you want?"

"I want to be able to name my price later. I want a . . . voucher. A promissory note."

"In other words, you want to own me."

Xizor laughed, but his flesh flushed an exultant violet. "Nothing so melodramatic as that. I just want to be able to call on you at some point to give me something or some service that I will—at that point in time—need more than I need a chunk of strange, glowing metal . . . or even a strange, glowing data device. Yes, Tyno told me about the holocron. And I suppose I could have you open it up for me—as I have every faith you can—and give me all that knowledge. Who knows—that might actually be what I ultimately want. But not today, I think. Today, I want to have a Jedi Knight indebted to me."

Everything in Jax rejected the idea—rejected it to the center of his soul.

"No," he said, turned, and walked out of the room.

He had no clear thoughts until he had regained the relative safety of his ship. Then, as the hatch slid shut behind him, his mind exploded with questions:

Was Xizor his only resource? Certainly he'd get no more out of Fabris without the Falleen Vigo's approval.

Was that avenue cut off?

Was there enough information in what the Arkanian had already told him to go on?

No, not nearly. Bothan space spanned more territory than he could possibly cover, even given a Jedi's trained Force sense. Might he learn more on Concordia? The first wave of Imperial forces had gone there for their needs—someone might have figured out where they were headed.

Not likely. Stormtroopers wouldn't give up that sort of intel.

What did that leave him? Not much.

He turned on his heel, punching the hatch open again.

"Jax?" Den stood just outside of the engineering bay, a frown furrowing his broad brow. "What's up?"

"I have to go out again. Keep the ship ready to lift, okay?"

Den took a step toward him. "What? Where are you going? Not back to that Black Sun lowlife."

"No. He's no longer of any importance."

Den let out a gust of breath. "Well, that's a relief. Who, then?"

Jax smiled—an expression that made the Sullustan's eyes grow rounder. "Don't worry about it. Like the man said: it's just business."

Den watched Jax stride out down the landing ramp, looking every inch the Corellian pirate he was supposed to be.

Scary.

He heard a telltale rattle behind him and turned to find I-Five—in his new half-finished chassis—standing in the access to their makeshift workshop.

Also scary. The Nemesis helm and forearm looked strikingly out of place with the protocol droid's dull silver torso. Den noticed absently that I-Five had replaced one of the standard optics with one of the odd optical units they'd purchased in Keldabe. The reflector was a bit larger, and the charged unit glowed a fiery amber.

Den had started to think of the new persona as I-Nemesis, but he'd yet to mention that to his mechanical friend. He'd almost begun to wish they'd opted for that LeisureMech Bobbie-Bot that Five had been so interested in.

"If I read the expression on your face correctly—and I do—you're worried," the droid observed.

"Aren't you? He says Tyno Fabris is out of the picture, but he's still got something going with Black Sun—I can feel it."

"Did he say that he was going to meet with someone from Black Sun?"

"You were eavesdropping on the conversation—you know what he said. He was . . . careful. When Jax is careful with his words, I think I have every right to worry." Den shook himself. "What do you think we should do?"

"I think we should be ready to move. Why don't you run the pre-launch sequence." The droid turned and scooted back into the workshop area.

Den wasn't even tempted to laugh. "What are you going to do?"

"I'm going to slip into disguise and do a little recon."

twenty

Sal put the train in motion the moment Pol Haus came aboard. A precaution, merely. There was no way of knowing what the police prefect might do if he thought he had been compromised. For all Tuden Sal knew, Haus was taking orders directly from ISB.

He gritted his teeth as Haus came through into the council car. Schooled his face to expressionless calm as the other man's gaze swept the empty chamber, at last returning to rest on the Sakiyan sitting at the head of the long table.

"Am I the first one aboard?"

"You're the only one aboard. Have a seat." Sal gestured at a chair along one side of the table.

Haus slid into a chair three seats down from Sal. "No one else could come?"

"No one else was invited."

Haus shook his shaggy head. "I thought we agreed there weren't going to be any closed meetings. That sort of thing leads to factions, internal division—"

"And what does disinformation lead to, Pol?"

The prefect raised an eyebrow. "I beg your pardon? I didn't quite catch that."

"The Emperor's forces have been redeployed. They've shifted their attention from the Imperial Palace to a villa on the Western Sea. You knew this."

To his credit, Haus didn't bat an eyelash. Sal had to admire his poise—albeit grudgingly.

"Yes. I did."

"And you—what? Thought it wouldn't interest me?"

The Zabrak chuckled; the sound grated on Sal's ears. "Oh, I knew it would interest you."

Sal sat in the silence that followed, resisting the desire to throw himself across the table and wipe that lopsided smile from the prefect's face. Sal was a Sakiyan: the veneer of civilization was painted very thinly on him. Beneath it, he could feel his pulse at his temples, fast and frantic. His *yithræl*—his clan-pride—was stirring angrily.

"Why? *Why* didn't you tell me, then? You knew I was waiting for an opportunity like this—an opportunity to get close to the Emperor."

Maddeningly, Haus nodded. "Yeah. I knew that, too."

"And didn't tell me. You withheld important information from me, Pol. What else haven't you told me?"

"That's a silly question, isn't it?"

Sal stood, his fists planted firmly on the table. The gleaming surface felt solid, steady. He needed that steadiness. "You intentionally undermined Whiplash operations—"

"Actually, I intentionally tried to keep *you* from undermining Whiplash operations, Sal. I hope I haven't failed."

"What are you talking about?"

The Zabrak looked up at him with annoying aplomb, his amber eyes showing an intensity that belied his relaxed slouch. "Stay away from the Emperor, Sal. Stop plotting to take his life. Our cause won't be won that way."

"Oh really? And in what way do you imagine it will be won?"

"I don't know. But not that way. You put our resources into that and the consequences could be horrific."

A chill settled into the marrow of Sal's bones. "Is that a threat?"

"No. It's a fear." Haus rocked forward in his seat, put his elbows on the table, and gave Sal a look that was disconcertingly direct. "If you try to assassinate Palpatine and fail—even if you succeed—it could cost us the entire network. Right now Vader's got Thi Xon Yimmon. What do you think would happen if he got more of us?"

"Vader's offworld."

Haus nodded, slowly. "Yes. He is. Which means that the Emperor is more closely guarded than usual."

"By Inquisitors, you mean? There are only a handful left. Or so you said."

The prefect tilted his head to one side. "There are. I wouldn't underestimate them, though."

"Is he guarded by your men, Pol? By you, personally, perhaps?"

Now Haus laughed out loud. "I'm not the Emperor's man, Sal. If I were, I'd've ratted you out long since. Can you imagine the cachet that would go with bringing down Whiplash and putting Jax Pavan—alive and well—into Vader's hands?"

Fear and rage warred in Tuden Sal's head. "Have *you* imagined it? Is that what this is about?"

"I repeat: I am *not* the Emperor's man."

"No, you've always been your own man, haven't you? Working your own agenda."

Sal stood back from the table, then turned and tapped a control on the system panel that dominated the forward right corner of the car. He kept one eye on Haus throughout. It would be only too easy for the police prefect to pull a blaster on him and blow him away. He'd taken precautions against that, of course, and

Haus would realize that. That didn't mean he might not test the proposition.

Sal turned back to face the Zabrak even as the train began to slow. "It's over, Pol. We're done. You're no longer part of Whiplash."

Something sparked deep in the Zabrak's eyes, but he only rose from his seat and rearranged his disreputable coat. "What, you're not going to shoot me?"

"If I had proof that you were in league with the enemy, I would. In a heartbeat. But I'm not sure you haven't just been working for your own ends. Protecting your own interests. You're right, after all. If you *were* in league with the Empire, we all would have been dead long since."

"Are you going to go after Palpatine?"

"I'm not stupid, Pol. You've hamstrung me. I can't exactly go forward with any plans I might have had now. You know what I might do. You've known long enough that even if I *did* shoot you, that information probably exists somewhere outside this room just waiting to be found."

"Naturally."

"Naturally."

"So what then?"

"So, I let you off at an unscheduled stop and you never see this train again. I've rerouted it, and I'll let the other members of the council know where to meet it as needed." The maglev was slowing to a stop. "And now, it's time for us to part ways."

"I won't betray you, Sal," Haus said solemnly. "Friends don't betray each other. But I'd like you to reconsider. If you're going to do something stupid, you should at least have a full complement of naysayers to keep you in check. And the best intel you can get."

Sal shook his head, resenting that the Zabrak had felt it necessary to make a veiled reference to his betrayal of

Jax's father. "Whatever we do now, we'll just have to do it without your intelligence, *friend*. Besides, you've demonstrated that I can't trust you to give me the best intel if it suits you to withhold it."

"I withheld it to protect you. To protect Whiplash."

"It's a nice enough story. I simply don't believe it."

The train had come to a full stop. The magnetic field that had cradled it was dissipated, and it dropped gently into the curved durasteel channel in which it ran.

Sal gestured at the forward doorway. "Good-bye, Pol. I sincerely hope I never see you again."

The Zabrak pulled himself to his full height. "If you *need* to see me again, Sal, don't hesitate to call."

Pol Haus went out through the forward door, there to be deposited on a deep service platform from which it would be difficult to extract himself quickly. If he had associates tracking him, the Whiplash Express would be long gone before they reached him.

Sal sat down at the table again, vaguely aware that the hovertrain had started moving. The rear door of the compartment hissed open and Dyat Agni came into the car. The Devaronian singer studied him for a moment, then asked, "Are you sure that he won't betray us?"

"I'm sure he *can't* betray us without betraying himself. He's worked too actively to protect Jax Pavan. Even if he turned coat now, the Emperor would never trust him. There would be too many unanswerable questions about why he waited until now to reveal what he knew. And people the Emperor doesn't trust—" He made a flinging gesture with one hand.

"Die," Dyat said simply. "So we stand down, then."

Tuden Sal smiled. "I think not."

The Devaronian's tilted red eyes widened. "But you said—"

The smile deepened. "I lied. Merely returning the favor."

Pol Haus stood in the dark on the abandoned service platform for long moments, considering his predicament. He had expected that Tuden Sal might eventually discover what Haus had tried to conceal. He hadn't thought it would happen quite so soon.

He could at least console himself that he'd cut Sal off from any attempt on the Emperor . . . maybe. He shifted the energy absorptive shielding he wore beneath his long, tatty coat and scratched at the spot where it met his collarbone. It was a good thing to know about Tuden Sal: that he would not kill a comrade he thought might have betrayed him, even if it meant giving up—or at least revising—a plan he had long hungered to put into motion. He could only suppose the Sakiyan felt his own betrayal of Lorn Pavan and I-Five acutely enough that it still affected his judgment and his behavior.

Well, it was a wrinkle, not a tear—a bump, not a breach. Tuden Sal was not to be rid of him that easily. Hopefully it would be some time before the Sakiyan realized that.

Haus smiled grimly. Sal really should have shot him down where he stood.

twenty-one

Jax felt as if he were being herded by Circumstance. Experience had taught him that Circumstance was a tool of the Force; now, that experience failed to translate into confidence. Whereas before he might have met the situation with his eyes open for opportunity, now he caught himself thinking reactively and defensively.

At the *Oyu'baat* tapcaf, he found Tlinetha at the beverage bar in the main room and had to work at ignoring her smug assertion that she'd known he would come back. She ushered him up to Tyno Fabris's offices, where Prince Xizor was waiting for him. The Falleen Vigo was alone in the room, sitting in Fabris's favorite chair, his booted feet on the desk, his eyes exploring the flame and sparkle of the chandelier overhead.

Despite Tlinetha's smugness, Xizor seemed surprised to see him.

"I was led to believe you've been expecting me," Jax said drily.

"Actually, no. I had rather imagined that when you said no, you meant it. What changed your mind?"

"I can't walk away from this, and I'm out of time to cultivate other avenues of approach. I'll grant you your promissory note, with one condition."

A blush of vermilion rippled across the Vigo's high cheekbones, sending a wash of warm static down Jax's spine.

"And what might that be?" the Falleen asked.

"That whatever you ask of me doesn't require me to harm the resistance or help the Empire."

Xizor shrugged. "I have no particular love or loathing for either party, certainly. Consider your condition met. But I have a condition, too."

"Which is?"

Xizor met Jax's eyes. "The truth. Obviously, the story you told Tyno was intended as subterfuge. You're a Jedi, not a pirate, and you clearly don't want to give Vader something he needs or wants. What's your real agenda, Jax Pavan? Why are you really pursuing Lord Vader?"

The urge to leave again was strong, but not strong enough to overwhelm his sense of duty.

"He has something I want."

"Some*one,* you mean. Remember, I was eavesdropping on your conversation with Tyno."

"Which, as you said, was subterfuge."

Xizor raised one graceful digit. "Ah, no. I said it was *intended* as subterfuge. But there was truth in it. Here's what I think happened. You didn't intercept a distress call from a resistance ship. You were *piloting* the ship. A ship that was, as you said, transporting a high-level resistance operative. Vader captured the operative, destroyed or damaged your vessel, and brought this person to Mandalore en route to parts unknown. How am I doing so far?"

"Pretty well." The admission was like ashes on Jax's tongue. He felt exposed, vulnerable. And despite what his life had been like since Flame Night, he had felt this way precious few times.

"I surmise you want this person back. Or at least that you want to keep Vader from extracting critical intelligence from him or her."

"Him. Thi Xon Yimmon. Head of—"

Xizor's eyes had widened. "Head of the resistance on

Coruscant. Yes, I know who he is. I try to stay informed. So, it seems you only overstated the damage to your ship."

"Not by much," Jax said. "I lost . . . the ship."

The Falleen's eyes narrowed, as if he were trying to read what hid behind the bland words and the slight hesitation. "So, you want to retrieve your associate. I'd suggest to you that getting in and killing him would be simpler, easier, and more likely to succeed, but I suspect your Jedi sensibilities rule that out."

Jax inclined his head.

Xizor laughed. "Be careful, Jedi. In dealing with me you may have just stepped onto the slippery slope to . . . well, the Force only knows, eh?"

Jax ignored the warning. "So, will you give me the intel I need?"

"Are you certain you don't want more than mere intel? From what I hear, you've got one small ship, one Sullustan crewman, and one pathetic little droid."

"I have sufficient resources, thanks."

A shrug. "If you say so. Here's what I know: The message Vader sent ahead was directed at the Bothan system, but neither Vader nor his forces have made landfall on any planet in the system. There has, however, been some extraordinary activity around Kantaros Station."

Jax frowned. "That's an old military outpost, isn't it?"

"Ex-Republic depot and medical facility. It still has a civilian population, but it's currently in use by the Empire as, apparently, a dumping ground for high-level prisoners of war."

Jax laughed humorlessly. "Except that we're supposedly not at war. The Empire is one big, happy family."

"Hm. And the family heir apparent seems to be in residence." Xizor pushed a data wafer across the top of the desk toward Jax. "Full intel—including complement, armaments, and station schematics. Are you sure you don't require additional assistance: ships, weapons?"

"All for a favor from a Jedi?"

"I'll be sure to make it a very big favor."

There was a sudden disturbance in the hall outside the office. A moment later someone rapped on the door.

"Come," said Xizor.

Jax turned to see Garan, Tyno Fabris's Devaronian bodyguard, shove an R2 unit through the doorway. The droid uttered a shrill protest, but didn't try to escape.

"What is it?" Xizor asked.

"I just caught this thing out in the hallway, snooping around the door."

Xizor turned an amused gaze on Jax. "Does it belong to you?"

"Yes. My crew probably sent it to find me." Jax turned to the droid. "Do you have a message?"

The droid uttered a series of trills that Jax interpreted as, *Take care.*

"I'm always careful, Five." He turned back to Xizor, feeling strangely more at ease with the droid at his back. "As you said, Xizor, Lord Vader is in residence at Kantaros Station. I need a way to draw him off. Keep him from going farther with Yimmon. I won't accept your offer of material aid, but if you could create a diversion—"

Xizor considered this. "A diversion that would draw Vader back to Coruscant? I think I can pull that off."

"How quickly?"

"Within hours."

"What—" Jax started to ask, but the Vigo shook his head.

"Better if you don't know."

Jax grimaced. Those were practically the same words Tuden Sal had said to him not that long ago. "Right. I'll be going then."

"And I'll be thinking of a really big favor for you to do me."

The Port o' Call Café Theater was tucked beneath the overhang of a relatively new tower near the Westport. At least the top of the tower was new. The theater sat just below the more recent construction on a seam between the old and the not-so-old, its façade an explosion of graffiti. The proprietors had taken advantage of the collection of spontaneous art to introduce intentional elements that glowed with the names of performers and their scheduled appearances.

The Togruta poetess Sheel Mafeen was on the program tonight; her name and an exaggerated likeness of her floated next to the door. The flicker of light from a variety of sources made the static image seem to move, while its eyes followed everyone who passed through the door.

Pol Haus paused to read over the night's entertainment, then nodded and entered. If anyone besides the effigy of Sheel watched him, let them think he'd just stopped by on a lark because he saw someone he liked on the billing. The café was a sea of darkness punctuated with flickering, holographic flames that seemed to float above each table. It was just over half full of patrons and cluttered with the sound of their conversations. The air stank of death sticks and other inhalants, most of them hallucinatory; he felt the slight beginnings of a buzz as he found himself a seat to the far right of the stage and ordered a hot, flavored caf.

The performances started within ten minutes of his arrival; he sat through a stream-of-thought singer, a parodist, and a human storyteller, before Sheel Mafeen took the stage. She performed three poems—two brief and one fairly long—while the prefect tried very hard not to yawn. He didn't really understand poetry. He understood songs.

She'd seen him halfway through her set and, though she was pro enough to be low-key about it, he saw her eyes light up. Once she'd finished her recital, she'd hopped off the stage and headed straight for him.

"It's good to see you, Pol!" she exclaimed, wrapping her hands around his. She slid into the chair next to him and leaned her head so close that it all but rested on his shoulder. "What happened?" she murmured, and smiled as if she'd just said something intimate or flirtatious.

Haus felt a tickle of attraction to the Togruta. It surprised him. And it was distracting. He stifled it.

"Our Sakiyan friend is a bit put out with me. Seems he was expecting a gift and I neglected to give it to him."

Her eyes fixed on his face. "A gift?"

"The gift of knowledge."

She considered that for a moment, then nodded. "What did he do?"

"About what I expected. He threw me out on my posterior. I'm no longer welcome in his elite club."

Her eyes grew round with worry. "What can I do? Try to patch things up between you?"

He shook his head. "That's not likely to happen, and you'd only make him mad at you if you tried. But I'd like to know what he's thinking. He got what he needed from a different source. I'm a little concerned about what he might do with it."

"I'm sure he'll be careful. You're sweet to worry about him, though." She leaned in and brushed his cheek with her lips, whispering, "He's called a meeting tonight. Late. On L-two-six-nine."

Haus nodded. So Sal had moved the maglev's stops to a different level of the city.

Sheel straightened. "Stick around for the next reading?"

He shook his head. "Gotta run, sorry. Duty calls."

She made a rueful face. "Doesn't it always? Later then?"

"Later," he agreed. "Uh, where? Where will you be later?"

"The Ellipse," she said, but her hand made a subtle gesture that told Pol Haus she would catch the train two levels below that establishment.

"I may join you . . . after."

"I'd like that. Give me a ping. If I'm free . . ." She let the sentence hang, rose, kissed his other cheek, and said, "You need a haircut, Pol. What sort of prefect looks like a street vendor?"

"One other street vendors are willing to share confidences with."

She laughed softly and disappeared behind the low stage.

Haus finished his lukewarm caf and left, wondering if all that subtext had been strictly necessary. Or perhaps wishing that it hadn't been. Tuden Sal knew that both Haus and Sheel were wary of his obsession with assassinating Palpatine, and though neither had expressed strong dissent, they had both cautioned him against haste. With Jax Pavan and Pol Haus both out of the picture, the Sakiyan might very well throw caution to the wind. Or he might bury his plans under layers of subterfuge. Or both.

If that happened, he might well take it into his head to exclude anyone he had the least doubts about from his most intimate counsel. Haus could only hope he had no doubts about Sheel Mafeen. If he did, it was going to be hard to guess his moves.

Tuden Sal watched his fellow Whiplash Council members take their places around the table. Only four now—Acer Ash, Dyat Agni, Fars Sil-at, and Sheel Mafeen. Fars and Dyat were already engaged in an argument about future plans. Dyat was advocating a bolder, more proactive approach through a series of lightning-fast hits on Imperial facilities all over Coruscant. Fars argued that given their recent loss, they ought to lie low, regroup, and retrench—possibly even consider moving their base of operations offworld.

The discussion grew spirited. Acer watched the by-play with obvious amusement, Sheel with inscrutable silence.

"You're both right," Sal said after letting the debate roll for a time.

Everyone turned to look at him.

"How's that work?" Acer asked. "Just curious."

"We *appear* to be lying low. Perhaps even to be defunct. But we use the quiet to strike at a target that is believed to be impervious. A target on the shore of the Western Sea."

"What?" Fars asked. "Why? What's on the shore of the Western Sea?"

Acer Ash's thin lips curved in a slow smile. "I know. It's the Emperor, isn't it? He's gone down to his villa by the sea."

Dyat's eyes lit up, and her face flushed a deep shade of rose gold. "You intend to strike the Emperor, after all?" She slapped the table with the flat of her hand. "Yes! *This* is the way we should operate. All our caution has bought us thus far is heartbreak and death. If the Emperor expects us to be cowed, let us surprise him and be bold! Let us surprise him to *death*." Having flung her challenge down before any who were inclined to timidity, the Devaronian turned burning eyes to Sal. "You have a plan?"

He nodded slowly. "The beginnings of one. For which we'll need explosives—" He flicked a glance at Acer

Ash, who grinned. "—and a couple of cars from this train."

Sheel Mafeen leaned toward him, her hands folded on the table before her, her expression rendered unreadable by her facial patterning. "You intend to blow the villa up? Surely anyplace the Emperor would live would be proofed to such an attack. How do you intend to get at him?"

"The specifics will be worked out with . . . special operatives. But before I go into great detail, I need to know that you're all behind this endeavor. Some of you have expressed . . . reservations about this sort of operation. I won't lie to you—this will be perhaps the most dangerous thing Whiplash has ever attempted. But if we succeed—even if we lose people—we will have cut the head from the Empire."

"What about the Dark Lord?" asked Fars Sil-at. "I'd say the Empire has two heads."

Sal curled his lip. "Vader is the Emperor's lapdog. Without his master, he will be without direction or purpose."

"He seems to be driven by his hatred of the Jedi," Fars observed. "If you'll recall, there is a Jedi associated with Whiplash. If we kill the Emperor, what makes you think Vader won't be even more driven to wipe out Jax Pavan and anyone connected to him?"

"In case you hadn't noticed, Jax Pavan is absent from our number."

"Yes," Fars said. "And so is Pol Haus. Where is he? What does he think of your plan?"

Sal looked down at his hands. "Pol Haus has parted company with us."

A ripple of disbelief washed through the group.

"What?" Dyat Agni exclaimed. "Why?"

"Yes, why?" echoed Sheel Mafeen. "Can you enlighten us?"

How much to tell them? Tuden Sal was stricken with uncertainty. Did he lie to soften the blow of the police prefect's betrayal, or did he impress them with his decisiveness?

He opted for the truth as he saw it. "Pol Haus willfully withheld critical information."

"Why would he do that?" Fars Sil-at demanded.

"I don't know. He couldn't explain himself."

"Which is why you changed the train route," Acer said, nodding. "That was wise of you. Do you think he's gone over to the enemy?"

"No. I think he's simply looking out for his own interests. The mission we're about to embark on is a dangerous one. Pol opted not to be part of it. He also believes his withholding of intel has derailed my plan. Which is good. If he should fall under suspicion in the eyes of the ISB, he will be able to tell them nothing."

He looked around again at the people seated at the table. "So, my friends, here we are. If, like Pol Haus, you don't want to be involved in this, now is the time to leave—before you know any more. Dyat has already given her support. Acer?"

"I'm in."

"Sheel?"

"Yes."

"Fars?"

There was a long moment of silence before the Amani wrinkled his broad nose, blinked several times, then let out a huge sigh. "Yes. Yes, I'm in. What else can we do?"

Sal held Fars's gaze for a long moment. "Good," he said. "Now, let me sketch out what I've been thinking."

Jax walked for several blocks in silence—I-Five rolling along beside him—before he spoke. What he said finally was, "Spying on me?"

"Providing backup," I-Five said quietly—R2 units were not supposed to have verbal mimicry vocalizers. "I thought you might need it."

"What would make you think that?"

"I reasoned that if Tyno Fabris was out of the picture, someone else must be in it. Someone with an even longer reach than Fabris. I didn't like the implications of that. So I followed you. If you recall, the last time you were in the same room with Xizor, he did his best to kill you."

Jax smiled. "Oh, he assured me that was nothing personal. Just business."

"Is this just business, too, Jax? Your involvement with Xizor?"

Jax wondered how much of their conversation the droid had overheard. Then he wondered why he cared. "I'm hoping that my 'involvement' with Xizor is at an end. He gave me the information I needed. Now we can act on it." He glanced over at the droid. "You heard him offer more, I'm sure."

"I did."

"Then you heard me turn him down. We're leaving Mandalore, Five. Immediately. We're going to Kantaros Station."

The droid rolled along silently until they reached the entrance to the spaceport's northern landing platform, then asked, "And when we get to the station? What then? I expect that its defender will be watching."

"Of course he will. But I'm counting on him not watching for Jedi simply because he believes all the Jedi are dead."

"And what if he's right, Jax?" I-Five asked. "What if you *are* the last Jedi? Putting your life in jeopardy—"

Jax stopped and wheeled on the little droid. "What other options do I have?"

"You could get help from the Rangers—"

"We've been over this. There are inherent dangers in that."

"You could stay here on Mandalore and let Den and me go to Kantaros Station."

"Unacceptable." Jax turned and started walking again, swiftly enough that the R2 had to scurry to catch up. He had crossed the platform and was halfway up the *Laranth*'s boarding ramp when I-Five stopped him.

"Jax."

He turned to look down at the battered droid.

"Do you *want* to die?"

Whatever question Jax had expected his mechanical friend to ask, it wasn't that one. "What?"

"It's not rich with subtext. Do you want to die?"

"What kind of question is that?"

"One you didn't answer."

"Of course I don't want to die."

"Really? Because you're acting like someone with a death wish. Going into ISB headquarters, putting yourself into close contact with Inquisitors—and with Vader. Coming here and courting Black Sun contacts. Throwing yourself in with Prince Xizor—who, for all you knew, might just as soon have shot you as talk to you. And now sailing off into a completely unknown situation after the most dangerous man in the galaxy . . ."

That jarred a laugh out of Jax. "Right now, Five, *I'm* the most dangerous man in the galaxy—because I have nothing to lose."

The droid rolled up the ramp toward him. "You're wrong. There is much still to be lost, Jax. The problem is, it's not yours to lose."

That stung. Mostly because he knew it was true and that what he had just mouthed were empty words. In a moment of epiphany, Jax realized that I-Five himself was one of those things that might be lost. If they threw everything they had at Vader in one go and failed . . .

"You and Den can stay behind in Keldabe. You'll be safe enough here."

"What—and cut your chances of staying alive even more? I think not."

"Fine. Then let's get this bird off the ground." He turned on his heel and continued up the ramp.

twenty-two

He had the dream in hyperspace en route to the Bothan system. It was different from previous dreams in that it did not begin in the chaos of *Far Ranger*'s ruined corridors. It began at the Jedi Temple on Coruscant, in the broad gallery that led to the great library. He was walking toward the huge, heavily carved doors, a wash of sunlight from the skylights laying a glowing, translucent carpet for his feet to tread.

He was aware that someone walked beside him, but when he turned to look, the figure—another senior Jedi Padawan in temple robes—was so bathed in sunlight that he couldn't make out who it was. He wanted to speak, to prompt the other Jedi to speak so he would recognize him or her, but though he opened his mouth, no sound came out.

He kept walking, the other beside him, stride for stride. When they reached the library, he would be able to see the other's face.

But they never reached the library. Behind them the broad corridor was shattered by a tremendous blast and filled with smoke and cries of alarm.

Jax was confused. Order 66 had been carried out at night, as had the operation that had resulted in Flame Night. What was this? *When* was this?

It didn't matter. Time didn't matter. He had to fight.

He drew his lightsaber and turned toward the chaos,

but a strong hand on his arm stopped him. He looked over at the robed figure beside him.

Green eyes met his.

"No," Laranth said. "We keep going." She strode toward the library.

Torn, he vacillated. What could be so important in the library that it should keep him from defending the Temple? They knew how this would end. They *knew*. The younglings and junior Padawans would all be killed. Anakin would murder them with his own hand.

"Jax," Laranth said, "it isn't time."

He felt the heat of flames on his face, watched the corridor melt, heard the screams of the younglings.

"When, then?" he demanded. "When?"

"Time is a spiral," Laranth said, and layered behind her voice was another voice, saying, *Time is/was/will be a spiral.*

The lightsaber was heavy and solid in his hand as he glanced, again, down the hall. Flames ran up the walls and dripped from the ceiling. The skylights were dark.

"Choice is loss—" the twinned voices said, and Jax screamed with frustration.

"Yes! Yes! I *know*! And indecision is all loss. I know that, too!"

"We have to go," Laranth said.

"Go where? You weren't there," he realized. That seemed important suddenly. "You weren't at the Temple when Order 66 was executed. You weren't *there*!"

"*You* were there. Now I was, too."

"I don't understand."

"Time," she said, and he didn't know whether she was telling him it was time to go, or that time had something to do with her witnessing the gutting of the Jedi Order. "Time," she repeated, and turned from him again.

He glanced once more at the deteriorating hallway, then turned to follow Laranth.

She was gone.

Heart hammering, limbs chilled, Jax sprang after her. The grand library doors were falling shut. In a moment it would be too late. He threw himself on the doors, forcing them open again and sliding through.

The library was gone, and Jax stood in the longitudinal corridor of his dying ship. Now the nightmare was familiar. He knew where Laranth was. She was dying in the dorsal weapons battery.

Wake up, he told himself, but he kept walking toward the heart of the ship. A billow of smoke obscured his view.

Again, a hand grasped his arm, halting him.

"I'm not there," Laranth said, but as before there was another voice only partly hidden behind the Gray Paladin's. A darker voice.

"I'm not there," the dark voice said, and now Jax recognized it and knew it came from the chaos of fire and destruction behind him. It was the voice of murder and rage. The voice of death.

The voice of Darth Vader.

He felt the impulse to turn, but that would mean putting Laranth behind him.

Choice.

"I'm not *there*," Laranth said emphatically from nowhere.

Jax woke to the realization that they'd dropped out of hyperspace.

"Jax," Den's voice said over the ship's comm, "we're in Bothan space."

He opened his eyes to his cabin, and for a moment he was disoriented. Tendrils of Force energy that were not his own enwrapped him. They were translucent yet vividly colored; in the same moment he saw them, they were gone, seeming to withdraw into the miisai tree.

He stared at the tree in confusion for a moment, then responded to Den's repeated message. "I'm on my way."

He wasn't, though. Not right away. He took several moments to connect consciously with the Force, to calm his pounding heart and center his thoughts.

Before he left the cabin, he glanced at the tree again. It did nothing extraordinary, but merely glowed faintly with the energy that only he could see—energy that fed into it continually from the Force.

Somehow Den had expected Kantaros Station to be like other Imperial depots he'd seen: low orbital platforms that floated in the clouds of otherwise inhospitable planets, or dirtside complexes that rambled over the landscape, burrowed under it, or rose out of it. Kantaros was none of those things. It wasn't tethered to a planet. It wasn't orbiting a planet. Nor was it floating in free space. According to Prince Xizor's last bit of intel, it was somewhere in the Fervse'dra asteroid belt that orbited Both system where the star's original third planet had been. Now it formed a formidable barrier between the sere, barren world of Taboth and the population center, Bothawui.

All this meant precisely one thing to Den Dhur—the station was going to be kriffing hard to find, dangerous to approach, and almost impossible to escape from with any speed.

They came at the asteroid field from the outskirts of the system, hiding in the gravity shadows of the outer worlds, then falling in among the commercial traffic as they came out from behind the purple gas giant, Golm.

What the Vigo had been unable to give them was the station's transponder frequency. He hadn't had it— something Den was sure wrinkled his universe. Black Sun runners supplied the station with some hard-to-get items, but they were guided to it on an as-needed basis,

entering the system with their own signal beacons pinging and waiting for Kantaros to contact them and pull
them in on autopilot. The Black Sun vessel *Corsair* was
on her own.

To approach the field from either above or below the
solar plane was just as suspicious. One of the ways
smugglers implicitly signaled their "honorable" inten-
tions was to relinquish control of their ships to the station. Every eye on Kantaros would have been upon
them from the moment they transmitted their call sign.

They made planetfall on Bothawui, took on fuel, and
turned I-Five loose in the Bothan Space Authority's
data banks. He could find no transponder code for
Kantaros Station; nor could he find any indication of
where it might be in the Fervse'dra field.

"Clever of Vader," Den said as they moved away from
Bothawui toward the ring of asteroids, "hiding his
depot in a bunch of tumbling rocks. How are we going
to find it?"

"It will still have an energy signature," I-Five said.
"We'll be able to pick that up on the ship's sensors."

"Oh, sure," said Den. "Once we're close enough to
register the energy output. Do you have any idea how
big this asteroid belt is?"

I-Five's R2 turret swiveled toward him. "It is three-
hundred-point-oh-six-million kilometers across at its
widest point and has a diameter of—"

"It was a rhetorical question."

Jax, seated at the helm, let out an audible breath.
"Den's right, though. It would take forever to scan this
whole structure, even if we took the inside orbit."

"It will take approximately five days, twenty-seven
hours, and—"

"That was also rhetorical. Add to that the fact that if
we don't give them remote pilot control, we might as

well come in with blasters blazing." Then Jax added, "That wasn't rhetorical."

"I wasn't keeping score," the R2 unit replied.

Den smiled, enjoying the fact that Jax had said something humorous. "So what do we do, then?" he asked. "Is there any way to extend our scanner's range?"

"This vessel already has one of the most advanced scanning systems I've encountered," I-Five said. "But even with that, we stand only a fifty–fifty chance of locating the station because of the width and depth of the asteroid belt. Which is," he added, "something of a misnomer—its range is almost sufficient to qualify it as a sphere, rather than a—"

Den was shaking his head. "I never should have installed that vocalizer."

Jax closed his eyes, looking suddenly exhausted. "So, up to four days *if* we scan from the interior of the field, and if we don't manage to locate the station . . ."

"Then we'll have to repeat the process on the outer perimeter, which will take roughly twice as long."

"Time," Jax murmured. "It's always a matter of time. Time we don't have." He opened his eyes and, after a moment's hesitation, switched to autopilot. "Den, you have the helm. I-Five, if you think it will do any good, you can target the asteroid field with the scanners and see if we get lucky."

"And what are you going to do?" I-Five asked as Jax slid out of the pilot's seat.

"I'm going to find the station . . . one way or another."

Den felt as if someone had poured an icy beverage over his head. "You mean you're going shopping for Force signatures. You're going to poke around for Vader. Do I need to remind you how dangerous that is?"

"Apparently," the droid muttered.

"You do not. But I may not have to poke around for

Vader. If the intel is correct, he's loaded up his little dungeon with Inquisitors. That's a lot of Force energy in one place. And one of those Inquisitors is Probus Tesla. Trust me—I will never forget that signature."

"There is every possibility," I-Five said, "that Tesla remembers your signature as vividly as you remember his. If he knows you're still alive, then Vader will also know it."

Jax paused by the cockpit hatch, his gaze on the transparisteel viewport over the control console. Den held his breath, hoping the Jedi would change his mind. But he didn't. He shook his head, his mouth a tight, grim line.

"That's a chance I'll have to take," he said, and disappeared.

Once in his cabin, Jax sat cross-legged on his meditation mat and contemplated the situation. What I-Five had suggested was a distinct possibility. Through a series of confrontations, Jax had become only too familiar with Probus Tesla's Force signature. It was an alien thing to him. He experienced the Force as threads, ribbons, tendrils of energy that twisted and wove themselves into a fabric of power and meaning. Tesla's energy did not weave; it boiled, surged, undulated. It had made him wonder if the other adept's experience of it was, as Kajin Savaros's had been, liquid in nature.

He had once heard it said that to understand another's sense of the Force was to understand how he or she could be defeated. He didn't need to defeat Tesla, only to pass by him unnoticed . . . or perhaps disguised.

He had closed his eyes and now opened them to gaze at Laranth's tree. The tree had its own Force signature—a singularly strong signature for a plant. Could he possibly use that to cover or obscure his own telltale energy the way the Inquisitors used the scales of the taozin to muddy theirs?

There was only one way to find out.

He rose and lifted the tree's pot out of the feeding container.

twenty-three

Probus Tesla breathed deeply and let his body follow the path of memory through the moves of the Soresu combat form. He wore a belted, sleeveless gray tunic and a fine sheen of sweat. He wielded a lightfoil, good for little beyond ritual combat and the practice of forms. He schooled himself, cooled his temper against the anger that seemed on the verge of swamping his self-control, and moved through the steps of the form and the lines of the Sith mantra.

Step.

Peace is a lie; there is only passion.

Cross-step.

Through passion, I gain strength.

Turn.

Through strength, I gain power.

Step.

Through power, I gain victory.

A sweep of the foil.

Through victory, my chains are broken.

Step—turn—twist.

The Force shall free me.

"Your movements are tentative, Tesla. I fear you are distracted."

Tesla did not open his eyes. He knew what he would see—his Elomin apprentice, Renefra Ren, standing in the doorway of the meditation chamber, no doubt wearing a bland expression that would somehow still manage to suggest both smugness and subservience. In Tesla's opinion, his apprentice was an obsequious snake.

But Ren was not the target of the anger he was struggling to master. It was the Dark Lord, himself, who had spurred his Inquisitor to a passion that was threatening to slip its leash.

"If I am distracted," Tesla said, still not opening his eyes, "it is because of my awareness of *you*. Why have you come?" He continued executing the movements of the form. Perversely, Ren's interruption was helping his focus; he executed a series of thrusts that were both powerful and smooth.

"To tell you that Lord Vader has returned to the station from his rendezvous on Bothawui."

Tesla's concentration splintered. He stopped in the midst of a sweep and turned to look into his apprentice's glittering black eyes. "I knew that, of course," he said, but he hadn't—his own inner turmoil had blocked him.

Renefra Ren's browridges arched, and his smile became even more smug. "Then I am surprised you didn't seek him out. I know you like to be . . . attentive to him."

"I was meditating," said Tesla. "And unlike some among our number, I do not feel the need to ingratiate myself with Lord Vader at every opportunity. I have served him long enough—and well enough—to know when he is open to approach. If he needs me, he will no doubt summon me directly."

The Elomin was silent for a moment, his black eyes unreadable, but his smile was gone. "No doubt; but he seemed . . . disturbed by something. There was a different scent about him, and I detected an undercurrent of fury in his voice as he spoke to his adjutant. I thought perhaps you also sensed this."

Again, Tesla was caught off guard. Had he been so intent on his meditations that he had mistaken his Master's agitation for his own? He reached out now with a trickle of Force sense and felt for Vader's aura. Yes, there was something there—something like dark static.

"Whether I did or not should be irrelevant to you, Renefra," Tesla said, using the Elomin's personal name to remind him of his station. "Again, if the Dark Lord wishes me to attend him, he will summon . . ."

The words deserted him as Vader's summons came—a strong, almost painful tug at his Force sense. He straightened, deactivated the lightfoil and put it back in the equipment rack, then fetched his deep red robe from a hook by the door of the chamber.

Ren's eyes widened. "He calls?"

So much hunger in those two simple words. Tesla smiled. "As I expected he would." He belted his robe, hooked his lightsaber to the belt, and swept from the room, leaving Ren behind to wallow in his longing.

The corridors of Kantaros Station were sterile durasteel that gleamed a ghostly, muted greenish white. Tesla found the color soothing. It reminded him of moonlight on the fields of grain near his boyhood home in Corellia's Denendre Valley. But the air in his valley had never had this scrubbed quality. The air on Kantaros Station was antiseptic and metallic, though Renefra Ren bragged he could smell the dust from the asteroid in which the station was embedded.

The heart of the station was the detention center where Tesla's Master kept persons and items of interest. The quarters Vader kept were very near this dark heart. And while the quarters, cells, common areas, and storage units were patrolled by both Imperial troops and Inquisitors, the Dark Lord's private rooms were guarded only by his own immense abilities.

Tesla chose to avoid the cells today, skirting them on

the broad inner hallway that described a circle around the center of the complex. Thinking about what Vader kept there—or rather, who—only served to remind the Inquisitor of the anger he had been trying to quell. Not only was Darth Vader the most powerful Force-user Tesla had ever known, he had always thought of him as a towering genius. But events over the last months had sown seeds of doubt. He had seen Vader inexplicably allow the Jedi Jax Pavan to provoke him to irrational acts. In fact, it had seemed to the Inquisitor as if Pavan's destruction was more important to the Dark Lord than the wishes of Emperor Palpatine or the putting down of the nascent rebellion. He had sometimes thought that given a choice between extinguishing the resistance on every world or wounding Pavan, Lord Vader would choose the latter.

When the Jedi had at last been destroyed, Tesla had expected his Master to be triumphant—to bend himself to eradicating the entire network of interfering "freedom fighters." Instead, Vader had taken Thi Xon Yimmon alive and insisted on handling his interrogation completely on his own, relegating his team of Inquisitors to surveillance and guard duty. There had been no sign of triumph; it was as if the destruction of the Jedi had not been a major accomplishment.

This was the source of Tesla's ill humor. He longed to interrogate the Whiplash leader himself, to show his Master the extent of his powers and his loyalty. But not only had Vader denied Tesla a chance to prove himself, he'd made no progress with the Cerean himself. Or at least he had reported none to the Inquisitorius. The one time Tesla had asked if he might assist, Lord Vader had made it very clear that he, alone, was privileged to work with such prizes as Thi Xon Yimmon. No one else was to be allowed near him.

His Master's rejection was hard for Tesla to take in

any event, but with the added presumption that he was not capable of breaking a non-adept, it was galling.

How capable were you with your last assignment? he asked himself. *How successful were you with Jax Pavan's Padawan, Kajin Savaros? How successful were you in protecting your Master's interests then?*

Not very. He supposed he should be grateful that Lord Vader hadn't dismissed him outright or left him on Coruscant with the least experienced Inquisitors and apprentices.

Tesla's ruminations ended at the outer hatch to his Master's quarters. He paused there and announced himself as a ripple on the surface of the Force. The outer hatch slid into the wall, and he entered the Dark Lord's rooms.

Vader faced him, standing just outside his private meditation chamber. The segmented entrance was even now closing. Tesla tried to catch a glimpse inside without appearing to do so. No one, to his knowledge, had ever seen the interior of Lord Vader's private sanctum. It was rumored that only within that specialized structure was the Dark Lord able to exist outside of his enviro-suit.

This close to his Master, Tesla was even more aware of the dark static that hummed just beneath the gleaming exterior of the suit's carapace.

"What is it, my Lord?" he asked, and felt as if he had been doused with hot and cold water almost simultaneously. He took a step back. He had never before felt anything like that from his Master. It confused him.

Vader turned and swept across the room to stand at a viewscreen that looked out onto an intimidating panorama of floating, rolling rocks, starkly lit by the system star.

"I must leave the station again," Vader said.

"But you've only just returned—"

"Things are transpiring on Imperial Center that I must attend to."

"Shall I go with you?"

"I think not. You will stay behind here and maintain close watch over our important guest. In fact, Tesla, I want you to attend him daily."

Tesla only barely kept himself from smiling. How long had he waited to hear those words? He wanted to throw himself at Vader's feet and thank him, but knew that the Dark Lord despised subservience in his followers. To cringe or quiver when Darth Vader appeared or spoke was to invite his contempt. Those who assumed he demanded complete servility in his underlings made a mistake that Tesla had seen end careers . . . and lives.

"Attend him, Lord? Then you wish me to interrogate him?"

"No. Nor are you to use your Force abilities on him except to read his moods and his passions. I want you merely to observe him."

The Inquisitor knew his facial expression had lost its equanimity. "Observe him? Observe him doing what?"

"Being. He is a man alone with his own thoughts and feelings. Learn them."

"Is this . . . Is this what you have been doing, Lord Vader?"

"After a fashion."

Tesla nodded. "I see."

"Do you?"

Tesla heard the dangerous note in his Master's voice, experienced it as an icy spray in his back brain. He stifled the fear it induced and squared his shoulders. "You wish to lull him into a false sense of security. To defeat his expectations of you. To . . . cause his own straying thoughts to betray him."

"You have learned something after all."

Tesla's relief was profound. So profound that he felt,

again, that warm tide flowing around him. He read it as his Master's approval, but it was supplanted almost as soon as he'd felt it by the cold static he'd felt from Vader earlier. Puzzling. The two sensations were so at odds, and yet seemed to overlap.

"As I said," Vader continued, "you shall attend and observe. Do not prepare questions, only ask such questions as you feel moved to ask. Do nothing beyond that. *Nothing.* Then you shall report to me what you observe and any impressions you take away from the session."

Tesla gave no outward sign that he was at a loss to understand the instructions. What sort of interrogation was this? "Of course, Lord. But if I might ask—what takes you back to Imperial Center? Is something wrong there?"

Dark amusement lapped at Tesla's consciousness.

"Something is always wrong on Imperial Center," Vader said. "What is wrong now is that someone appears to be plotting against the life of Emperor Palpatine."

Tesla left off musing about the nature of the observations his Master desired of him. "I am gratified that our spy network is so effective."

Vader uttered a sound that might have been a grunt or a laugh. "Our spy network? It is often next to useless, motivated by fear and ideology. This came from Black Sun, which is motivated by simple greed and opportunism. I trust their network—and their motives—far more than I do our own."

Tesla went away from the interview foundering in a mixture of pride and perplexity. He had been assigned the duty he had coveted, but with such narrow constraints! There was only one way to widen his influence with Darth Vader, and that was to be able to present him with some intelligence about Thi Xon Yimmon that the Dark Lord had not already gleaned himself.

Attend and observe. Probus Tesla had every intention of discovering a way to do more than that without it being apparent.

Jax sat back against the wall of his cabin, sorting through the impressions he had gleaned in his brief contact with the Inquisitor. Trepidation. Relief. Even a spark of exultation—all this had flowed through the momentary connections. But while the emotions of the Inquisitor were chaotic and confusing, his location was clear. As was his identity. Jax had a history with Probus Tesla that neither man was likely to forget.

Jax rolled to his feet, returned the miisai tree to its container, and made his way up to the bridge.

twenty-four

The core of Kantaros Station was buried in an asteroid. The asteroid itself was a halfhearted, lumpy attempt at a sphere that had failed due to lack of gravity.
The station was visible as a chaotic jumble of structures
that poked or peeked out of the native rock. Studying it,
Den saw what he took to be a control bridge, docking
rings above, at, and below the asteroid's natural equator, and some docking tethers and space bridges that
were used to debark and unload vessels too large to fit
into the docking bays but not large enough to make a
close approach suicidal.

Traffic around the station seemed strangely light. The
only ship nearby was an Imperial frigate that floated
serenely in the flow of stone, dwarfed by the ponderous
asteroids. There were no surveillance buoys or small patrol craft.

"How are they doing that?" he asked, peering at the
frigate. "You'd think they'd be crushed."

I-Five answered him. "Passive repulsor fields, most
likely, or possibly a tractor/pressor web. Either would
provide an energy cushion around the vessel that would
keep the asteroids from colliding with it and would keep
it moving along with them. I'd bet on a web, though.
More energy—greater stability."

Den grimaced. He'd bet on a web, too.

I-Five swiveled his domed turret toward Jax. "The

question is, is Vader there? I don't see his shuttle. Of course, the landing bays could be internal."

"He's there. When I . . . brushed Tesla, he was with Vader."

Den blinked his huge eyes, startled. "You don't think Vader . . . you know . . . recognized your, um . . ."

Jax shook his head. "I was camouflaged—in a manner of speaking. Tesla didn't seem to notice that I'd touched him. He was focused on something else."

"Why isn't there more of an Imperial presence?" Den asked. "Where are the perimeter patrols, and the surveillance outposts? Are they hidden in the other asteroids?" He squinted at a large specimen that tumbled past the smaller body they were using for cover.

I-Five uttered a series of rapid clicks as he read data from the sensors. "Not as far as our sensors can determine. Odd. So little protection."

"Not so odd, considering whose lair this is," Jax said. "The physical protection is all around us. Without the transponder codes, a non-Force-sensitive wouldn't be able to find this place except by trial and error."

That was a chilling thought. "Which sort of makes this place an ideal Jedi trap, don't you think?" Den asked.

"There are no more Jedi," Jax murmured.

Den bit back an angry retort, recognizing—in the instant it began to claw its way up from his gut—that it rested on a solid foundation of icy fear. "Then we'd better take good care of the one we've got," he said.

"How do you propose we proceed?" I-Five had swiveled back to the view of the station.

Jax studied the heads-up display. "That asteroid, there—the one closest to the station—would get us within several hundred kilometers of it."

"And then what?" Den asked. "We jump across like green fleas? It's not as if you can land on that thing undetected. I mean, if you had a shielded ship and a big distraction, then maybe . . ."

"We have a shielded ship. If we could slide past the dark side of the asteroid . . ."

"The frigate is on the dark side of the asteroid," I-Five noted. "Jax, I don't think we can do this unaided. I think we should return to Toprawa and enlist the help of the Rangers."

"There is another possibility," Jax said thoughtfully. "The station crew is composed of Imperial regulars, mercenaries, and some civilians. According to Xizor's intel, the civilian crew and the mercenaries get . . . extra supplies through the black market."

"You mean through Black Sun," Den said, not at all liking where this was going.

"Yes, and these black-market runners are allowed access to parts of the station."

"Not the parts we need," Den objected.

"Once we're aboard, I'll have to work that out. The real trick is getting aboard in the first place. We're flying a ship with Mandalorian ident codes. We might be able to pass ourselves off as Black Sun."

"Yes, we might. But we'd need to have a legitimate cargo . . . or rather an illicit one," Den observed. "Which we don't."

"Not now, but we could pick one up on Concordia."

I-Five emitted a high trill and rotated his turret back toward the sensor panel.

"What is it?" Jax asked.

"Activity in the Kantaros docking bays."

Den drew in a sharp breath. "Maybe they've spotted us."

"Unlikely," said I-Five. "We're shielded and our comm is silent."

Jax's hand hovered over the controls of the tractor beam that tethered the *Laranth/Corsair* to her hiding place. He watched as a portal opened in the lower hemisphere of Kantaros Station and a number of small, long-range fighters emerged, swarming around the station like gnats. They seemed to be in a holding pattern, awaiting command or perhaps a vessel they were intended to escort.

"Jax . . ." Den breathed the name out on a rising tide of unease.

Jax didn't wait to find out what their agenda was. He deactivated the tractor beam, fired the ion engines, and flipped the little freighter end over end, then fled toward the inner orbit, weaving among the floating obstacles with a speed that pushed Den's heart even farther into his throat.

As he sat in the cockpit of the *Laranth/Corsair,* watching the streaks of light beyond the transparisteel cowling, Jax did some hasty calculations. None of them was pleasant. Xizor had known when he'd handed Jax that data wafer and the Mandalorian ident codes that the chances of him being able to infiltrate Kantaros Station without assistance from Black Sun were nil. Coming here had been a waste of time and effort.

And yet, unavoidable. Jax had to own that if Xizor had told him this was what they would find, he'd never have believed him.

There were clearly only two ways to penetrate the station's defenses: a direct assault with significant firepower; or infiltration, which would require further assistance from Black Sun. The more he thought about it, the more he realized that with Probus Tesla on the station, his chances of blending in without a significant number of others to conceal himself would be suicidal. The Inquisitor knew him too well and had more legitimate reasons to hate him than his dark Master did.

Jax exhaled in frustration. Every answer he needed

seemed just out of reach. He was a Jedi, yes, but a Jedi whose education had been cut short by the Empire's persecution and destruction of his Order. There were things his Master had not lived long enough to teach him, things he'd had to learn imperfectly on his own . . . many of them from Laranth.

He had discovered on his own the ability to wrap his Force signature in the energies and colors of disguise. Now he wished he understood how to take that principle further. Was it a form of psychometry, perhaps?

When he had touched the Inquisitor, Tesla, he had first imagined himself passing through the miisai tree, wrapping ribbons of its life force around him, clothing himself in them—or perhaps mimicking them. He honestly wasn't sure which—if either—was the reality. He knew only that he had projected something "other" into the station—something that was not entirely Jax Pavan.

Now he had to wonder: Had his activity been sensed by either Vader or his apprentice? Is that what the sudden activity had been about?

It would be several hours before they'd emerge into normal space near Mandalore, where they were ostensibly going to reprovision and refuel before stopping off on Concordia in search of an illicit cargo.

Den and I-Five wouldn't know until it was too late to talk him out of it that he had no intention of going to Concordia at all.

twenty-five

Tuden Sal sat in a faux-wood chair in one of four themed cafés attached to the Hotel Sunspire. The name was not inaccurate—every suite and condo in the huge, glittering tower had a sunny view of the Western Sea. If you had the credits, you could bide there awhile. If you didn't, but dressed as if you did, you could pretend.

Sal was doing that now—pretending to be just another wealthy visitor to the seashore, sipping hot caf and reading the latest news from a datapad. What he was doing, in fact, was taking readings of direction and distance between the various points his people had identified as necessary connections in their plan.

And he was awaiting a signal.

Down along the docks of the rich, the famous, and the politically astute, there was constant need for upkeep. Machines scrubbed the docks, the boats, the water, and the shoreline, but someone had to mind those machines. And sometimes, when a machine broke down in the water—as happened now and again—someone, usually of an aquatic species, had to go repair it.

There was a maintenance crew in the water at the moment, in fact, engaged in the process of repairing a skimmer bot the sole purpose of which was to keep the surface of the water free of unsightly or potentially dangerous debris.

The crew was made up of a Nautolan and a Mon Calamari. The Nautolan was in the water with the broken bot, while the Mon Cal monitored the repair from the docks. As Sal watched, the Nautolan completed his repairs, sent the water skimmer on its way, swam back to shore in a series of effortless strokes, and pulled himself out of the water, the tips of two of his dorsal head tresses lifting to perform a serpentine dance.

Tuden Sal smiled. If all the control overrides and charges were planted that easily, bringing Palpatine's palatial seaside home down on his head was going to be simpler than he'd thought. When this was over, he decided, the Nautolans who had come up with the idea would deserve a Hutt's reward—the entire resistance movement would owe them that.

In the next several days, fifty of the little cleaning bots would come up for routine maintenance. Their team of Whiplash associates—all carefully inserted into the maintenance crew in ways both mundane and ingenious—could service roughly two-thirds of them. Others would seemingly "forget" their programming and run amok, necessitating emergency measures to set them right again.

In the end, Whiplash would have roughly seventy obedient, highly charged assassins on its hands. They would assuredly bring down a large portion of the Emperor's seaside palace and his landing pad. In the event that this failed to kill him, there was a contingency plan: If the Emperor attempted to flee by water, he would be the victim of a second wave of killer maintenance bots and Nautolan assassins. And if he tried to leave by surface streets, other Whiplash operatives in the area would surely be able to penetrate his weakened defensive forces and destroy him.

Emperor Palpatine's senses were clouded by arrogance. He thought far too highly of his own powers and those of his lieutenant, Darth Vader. He was about to find out how limited they were against a sly and unpredictable enemy.

Sal finished off his caf and pushed his datapad into his pocket. He felt good about his plan, despite what naysayers like Jax Pavan and traitors like Pol Haus might think. This was the right course of action. The *only* course of action that made any sense.

Yimmon and his executive council had been too timid—his being abducted while fleeing Coruscant was proof of that . . . and also, perhaps, a fitting reward for such timidity. It fell to stronger leadership to see what had to be done and simply do it.

Probus Tesla did not wait long to "attend" Thi Xon Yimmon in his cell at the core of Kantaros Station. He had been curious about the accommodations the Whiplash leader had been accorded, had imagined all manner of ways in which Darth Vader might seek to undermine the Cerean's rocklike calm once he'd emerged from his self-induced catatonia. This Yimmon had done, but apparently what Lord Vader had encountered in the other man's mind was not at all what he had expected.

Tesla knew nothing of either his Master's expectations or his findings. What he did know was that Vader had acquired a large blast cage intended to defeat electronic surveillance, kinetic energy, and psychic signals. He was surprised to find that the Whiplash leader was being held, not in that shielded environment, but in a cavernous room whose upper dimensions were cloaked so completely in shadow that, from Yimmon's perspective, the place must seem as endless and dark as space itself. But though the outer regions of the place were in utter blackness, the spot where Yimmon sat cross-legged on the floor—he had been given no furniture of any kind—was lit harshly from a single overhead source that beat down like a merciless sun.

This was puzzling. Tesla knew that sleep deprivation was a cardinal factor in a successful interrogation, but all Yimmon needed to do to find blessed darkness was walk away from the light. That may have had symbolic or spiritual significance to a religious zealot like Yimmon, but that certainly wouldn't have kept him from sleeping away his days and hours here.

Only when he had watched the prisoner for several minutes from his hidden gallery high along one wall did Tesla realize the ingenuity of his Master's devices: when Thi Xon Yimmon moved, the light moved with him, bathing him continually in harsh, white brilliance while leaving all beyond the cloak of radiance in utter darkness. In addition, he discovered that the blast cage had been incorporated into the watcher's gallery, thus minimizing the likelihood that the psychically sensitive individual in the room below would know he was being observed.

In the dim confines of Tesla's aerie, a soft tone sounded and a computer voice said, "Subject's heart rate has reached resting levels."

The room beyond was suddenly barraged with a chaos dance of light, movement, and sound. Tiny glittering lights spun and wove through the darkness, and a cacophonous blend of arrhythmic and atonal sounds swirled around the Cerean prisoner.

Yimmon rose from the floor and moved slowly to the outer perimeter of the room, finding the wall beneath Tesla's observation chamber and moving along it, trailing his fingertips over the surface. He never once opened his eyes.

Tesla was astounded. A frisson of some unnamable emotion scurried between his shoulder blades. Surely it was only coincidence that the spot Yimmon had navigated to lay directly below where his watcher was concealed.

The Inquisitor watched through the filtered and enhanced transparisteel of the observation chamber's wall
as the prisoner made his way steadily, even briskly,
around the outer perimeter of his huge prison cell. He
turned at the last corner and made his way up the wall
toward where he had begun, seemingly oblivious of the
spinning lights and the blare of sound.

Yimmon stopped walking in exactly the place he had
begun his sojourn. He stretched, rolled his large head on
his shoulders, then made a second circuit of the room,
again stopping in the exact spot he had previously.

Well, of course, he was simply counting footsteps. He
must have made that same circuit repeatedly in the time
he'd been there. There was nothing particularly note-
worthy about that, though the eerie serenity of the man
was disconcerting. Tesla wondered if the Dark Lord
found it so.

The Watcher turned from his window. Now was as
good a time as any to begin "attending" the prisoner.

twenty-six

"You gonna come with us to the little mercenary's store?" Den asked Jax as the Jedi put final touches on what Den thought of as his "pirate costume."

Jax inserted his faux-cyber lens and turned to look at him. "I've got another errand I need to take care of at the tapcaf."

Den shivered at the strangeness of the seemingly mechanical eye. "Yeah? And what might that be?"

"I need to talk to Tyno Fabris about something."

"Tyno Fabris?" I-Five asked as he entered the tiny crew's commons, wearing his pit droid persona. "Or Prince Xizor?"

"Does it matter?"

"Not really. Black Sun is Black Sun. One member is just as slimy and dangerous as the next."

Jax tied the closes of his jacket with extraordinary care. "Five . . ."

"What can you possibly have to say to him? You refused his additional help the last time you met, if you'll recall," the droid said. "I thought it was one of the smartest decisions you've made of late."

"Meaning?"

"Meaning I think it would be a bad idea to go back and deal with Xizor further. He can't be trusted."

"Except not to be trustworthy," Den muttered.

"Who said I trusted him? I don't. But I do need his resources. He can get us onto Kantaros Station with some of his smugglers. And he may be able to provide cover or camouflage for us if we should happen to need it."

"For which he will demand what, Jax?" I-Five asked. "Something you can't afford to give?"

"We've had this discussion before—"

"We apparently need to have it again."

Den looked back and forth between the Jedi and the droid. Under other circumstances he would have found the picture hilarious—a piratical human facing off against a meter-tall pit droid. Ludicrous. He could feel the tension between the two crawling on his skin; Jax was the definition of *grim,* and I-5YQ bristled with righteous indignation. It was almost like a standoff between a father and son.

Den swallowed an inappropriate chuckle when Jax observed, "This must be what it's like to have a father."

"Sometimes you seem to need one," the droid responded.

"What I need," Jax ground out, "is a Jedi Master, but I don't have that. What I *need* is Laranth, but I don't have her, either. What I *need* is not to have put Yimmon in harm's way, but I did. What I *need* is the training and the experience to go head-to-head with Vader—but I lack that, as well. The last time I faced him I had help—a lot of it. And even with all that help, it took Vader overreaching and Rhinann throwing his life away to even get us out of there alive. Right now, I've got Xizor and his resources and I'm willing to use them."

"This is a mistake, Jax," I-Five told him. "For a Jedi Knight to be in the service of a Black Sun Vigo . . ."

"I don't like it, either. But it's what we've got."

Den realized he'd been shaking his head for the last minute or so. "Jax, Jax, we *can't.*"

Jax fixed him with a cold gaze. "Maybe *you* can't, but *I* have to. If you don't want to be part of this, then don't be. I'm sure I can catch a ride on one of Xizor's ships."

"Then perhaps you should," said I-Five.

Jax slipped his lightsaber under the folds of his jacket and left the ship, leaving Den to stare after him.

"Come on, Den," I-Five said. "We, too, have errands to take care of. I think it behooves us to get my retrofit completed as soon as possible."

"Do you really mean to bail on Jax? Can't we . . ."

"Can't we what? Stick with him to the bitter end? Watch him sell his soul to Black Sun—to Prince Xizor? If he's determined to go after Yimmon using Black Sun resources, what can we do?"

"Sit here in Keldabe and hold our breath?"

"I don't breathe."

Was that a joke? "I'm not kidding, Five. I'm . . . I'm scared. Something's happening to Jax and I feel powerless to help."

"I don't think we *can* help. Not without getting help ourselves."

"What did you have in mind?"

"If he's intent on going to Kantaros Station, perhaps we should go back to Toprawa and gather some forces there. We might be able to mount an attack on the station that would give Jax some much-needed cover and provide a distraction for the Imperials while he extracts Yimmon."

"That sounds . . . insane."

"It probably is."

"Okay, let me put that another way: do you think we'd stand the slightest chance of success?"

"I don't know."

Those, Den thought, were the three bleakest words he had ever heard.

*   *   *

Jax arrived at the *Oyu'baat* tapcaf to find Tyno Fabris once more ensconced in his garish office. Tlinetha did her best to keep Jax from going up, but he sensed that had more to do with her own agenda than her boss's. At last she escorted him to the upstairs suite, dropping unsubtle hints about how exciting life on a smuggler's ship must be.

"Exciting?" Jax repeated. "Hardly. Cramped, boring, and dangerous."

"There are ways to alleviate boredom," she said, smiling.

He turned at Fabris's office door to give her a quelling look. "The last woman who shipped with me is dead," he said tonelessly. "What else would you like to know?"

He'd shocked her. Frightened her just a little—her energies curled away from him. Still, to her credit, she recovered quickly enough to ask, "Do you care that she's dead?"

The question, unexpected as it was, almost gutted him. Though he kept his face shuttered, he knew that the Balosar, with her sensitivity to shifts in emotion, was not fooled.

He shook himself. *Focus.*

"Let Fabris know I'm here," he said.

"Already have," she told him. "Go on in. He's waiting for you." She swung away and went back down the flight of rough-hewn wooden stairs, her long, pale hair flying behind her like a cloak.

Fabris's door opened at a touch. Entering, Jax scanned the room, but his eyes only confirmed what his Jedi senses had already told him: the Arkanian was alone.

"Where's Xizor?" he asked.

"Why would you expect to find him here? Yours is a done deal. You got what you wanted, and I had the distinct impression that you wanted nothing more to do with us. So did he."

"I *don't* want to have anything more to do with you. Unfortunately, I need to."

The Arkanian flicked a glance toward the tapestry to the right of his desk. "That's too bad, because I don't know if he'll see you. Prince Xizor is a busy man."

Jax took two long strides to the desk and slammed both hands down in the center of its broad, vivid surface, scattering flimsies, tablets, and writing utensils along with some of the knickknacks that littered the top. A statuette of a Dathomir warrior toppled and rolled off the desk and onto the floor, hitting the carpet with a solid *thunk!*

"I don't have time for games. Xizor will see me because I am potentially useful to him. Do you want to be responsible for depriving the prince of something he considers useful?"

Fabris's smile disappeared as if it had been vacuumed from his face. He chewed the inside of his lip for a moment, struggling with his temper. Clearly, he wanted to send the Jedi packing, but business came before pride.

Jax raised one hand and held it up before the other man's face. He summoned the fallen statuette to it, the sharp impact against his palm no less satisfying than Fabris's reaction to it—the Arkanian jumped as if he'd been shocked. Fear, sudden and raw, flooded his eyes.

"I'll let him know you've returned," Fabris murmured, his lips barely moving.

"I'd lay odds he knows already," Jax said. "In fact, I'll bet he was expecting me . . . this time."

He felt the tingle of pheromones before he heard the sound of applause from a single pair of hands. He turned as Prince Xizor entered the room through the hidden door, his Mandalorian bodyguard holding back the tapestry that had concealed it.

"Very subtle display of force, Jedi," Xizor said. "You continue to surprise me. You're wrong, you know—I wasn't sure I'd see you again. Did you go to Kantaros Station?"

"I did."

"Really? And lived to tell about it. I congratulate you. In fact, I congratulate you on even *finding* it. How did you accomplish that miracle?"

"How do you think I accomplished it?"

Xizor's smile was slow and altogether vile. "That is a marvelous talent you have, Jedi—to be able to sense the presence of other powerful adepts at such distances. Marvelous . . . and extremely valuable."

Jax quelled the rebellion of conscience the Falleen's words evoked. He needed Xizor—*needed* him—if he was going to infiltrate the station.

"Yes, it is."

"What do you want for it?"

"I want to get onto Kantaros Station. That should be easy to achieve, given that your ships go there on occasion. Beyond that, I'll need to get to Yimmon and get him into a disguise or some sort of container that we can then get back aboard the ship."

"How do you propose to even get to him? There are Inquisitors on that station."

"I'll take care of that. I've dealt with Inquisitors before."

Something kindled deep in Xizor's violet eyes, and his skin flushed toward copper. "Ah, another valuable talent."

"It's been that. Now, about when we go—"

"Now. The time is now—and for a very good reason. My distraction worked quite well. Darth Vader has left Kantaros Station to return to Imperial Center."

Probus Tesla stood just inside the great, barren chamber that was Yimmon's cell and regarded his prisoner with interest. The Cerean was sitting, as usual, in a

meditative posture, seemingly quite unfazed by the chaotic blare of sounds bombarding him. Something to do
with that dual cortex, Tesla suspected.

He'd mention it when his Master returned. Now he
raised a hand, causing the barrage of sound to cease.

Yimmon didn't move, though Tesla sensed a change
in the level of the other man's awareness of the outer
world. Tesla approached slowly, moving to stand before
the Whiplash leader where he sat under his cone of brilliant light. The Inquisitor stayed just at the edge of the
veil of shadows, knowing that he looked sinister and
imposing in his cowled robe. He regarded the Cerean
silently for some minutes and was bemused at his complete lack of response.

Curious, he reached out with a rivulet of the Force
and touched the other's consciousness. He met a serene
pool of calm with barely a ripple to mar its surface.
Mesmerized, he dared to explore the pool. It was so
calm and clear, he imagined he could see to its depths.
It was only when he had swum to the center of that pool
that he became aware of what he *couldn't* see. Aware,
in fact, that he floated above a fathomless unknown.

Tesla dragged himself forcibly back to the shore of his
own consciousness with the stunned impression that the
unseen depths of Thi Xon Yimmon's mind hid something unsettlingly alien. He'd felt . . . He shook himself.
He'd felt as if he, the Watcher, was himself being watched.

Perhaps this was why his Master had ordered him
only to "attend." Vader must have known what touching this alien consciousness would lead him to imagine.

And perhaps your Master underestimates you.

That was his pride talking, of course—pride that had
taken somewhat of a beating in his prior encounters with
Whiplash operatives, most especially with Jax Pavan. But
that did not cause him to dismiss the idea out of hand.
One thing he knew: he had been given the authority for

Kantaros Station in Lord Vader's absence. He would not let the opportunity to show his worth slip by.

He squatted half in the shadows, put back his hood, and gazed into Thi Xon Yimmon's face.

"I will know you, Cerean," he told him. "By the time Lord Vader returns, I will know you."

The amber eyes snapped open, boring into Tesla's. It was all he could do not to flinch.

"Do you know yourself?" Yimmon asked, his voice husky with disuse.

He closed his eyes again—and his mind.

Tesla waited a moment, but the prisoner said no more. He rose, then, replacing his cowl. He wanted to let the Cerean know he recognized his pathetic attempt at manipulation, but he realized before the words left his lips that even that much acknowledgment gave ground.

"Better than you can imagine," he told the prisoner, and withdrew from the room.

He pondered Thi Xon Yimmon as if the Cerean were a mathematical equation or a logical conundrum. He trusted his instincts, and his instincts told him that the secret to compromising the Whiplash leader lay in neutralizing his dual cortex. The strategy: divide and conquer.

He wondered if Vader had considered seeking some way to separate the Cerean's cortices. In pursuit of that information, he went over the record of Yimmon's interrogations and treatment. Though there was repeated mention of the power of his intelligence, there was no reference to its peculiar nature.

An oversight . . . or a test?

If it was the former, Probus Tesla would exploit it; if it was the latter, he would rise to it.

twenty-seven

"That is a most interesting . . . necklace."

Pol Haus looked up at the sound of Sheel Mafeen's mellifluous voice and smiled inwardly, knowing it was not the necklace she found interesting, but the Togruta skinsuit he wore that transformed him into a handsome male of her own species. She had recognized him, he knew, only by the fact that he was wearing a rancor tooth pendant, which—according to their prearranged agreement—he would be toying with.

"Thanks. You have the speaking voice of an angel." He reached over to pull a chair out from the small table from which he'd watched her performance. "May I offer you a drink?"

"I'd love one, thanks." She sat down opposite him, smiling. "You're new here."

"I saw your picture out front. Thought I'd see if you sounded as good as you looked."

"And?"

"Like I said, you have a beautiful speaking voice. And your selection of poetry is stellar."

They ordered drinks, talked flirtatiously, and left for Sheel's conapt. It was a nice place. But then, Sheel Mafeen was a well-known and much-admired performer in the sector. Haus reckoned she must do pretty well for herself to be able to afford a suite of rooms so high up in her resiblock.

A gleaming, carpeted hallway led to her door, which opened into a main room that was decorated in rich shades of green and furnished with pieces that looked as if they were fashioned of real wood.

She noticed him studying the furniture.

"Yes, it's real," she said. "I had it imported from my homeworld. The forest valleys of Shili are very dear to me."

"Very nice." He caught her expression and laughed. "No, I mean it. It's beautiful." He didn't mention that the greens clashed a bit with her rosy complexion.

She smiled, showing sharp canines. "Make yourself at home. I'll get us some caf." As she spoke, she removed her shoulder bag and withdrew from it what looked like a makeup case.

It wasn't, he knew. It was a portable sensor array—or SAP, as the military liked to call them, short for "sensor array, portable." As she crossed the cozy living area and went into the kitchen, he got out his datapad and activated its sensors. In less than a minute, he had ascertained that the living room was free of surveillance devices.

Haus relaxed, sat down on a forest-green divan, and scanned the room visually. It took him several moments to realize that the view outside of the large living room window was *real*. Those were the *real* spires of the Imperial Palace, not holographic images of them.

"Whoa." He was drawn to the window as if by a magnet, mesmerized by the play of light and shadow among the cloudcutters and skygrazers.

"Whoa, indeed. I bet you don't often get to see that view in your line of work."

Sheel Mafeen had reentered the room. Haus was surprised to see that she was carrying a tray with steaming mugs of caf and a dish of some sort of candied fruit.

"No. Not often. I've visited the Security Bureau a

number of times, but even then, I've never seen the Palace from this angle."

"The kitchen's clean," she said as he returned to the divan.

"Have you ever found surveillance bugs in here?"

"Only when I first moved in. I'd just made a splash in the local performance and art world and I think the Imperials wanted to vet me. I left the bugs there for a while to establish that I was a good, upstanding citizen, then 'accidentally' destroyed them when I had the place redecorated. Since then, nothing." She handed him a mug. "Did I mention that you make a handsome Togruta?"

He chuckled. "As opposed to a homely Zabrak?"

"I didn't say that—or mean it. You're a handsome Zabrak, too. Just a bit . . . scruffy."

She wrinkled her nose when she said it, and for a moment, he considered that perhaps he didn't need to always look like a demented street rat. Then again, it was such a useful thing—it nearly always caused people to underestimate him.

He took a sip of the caf. "What's the situation?"

Sheel's smile drained away. "Sal is going through with it—with the . . ." She shook her head, unable to frame the words. "Here's what really worries me: he's doing all this with minimal input from the full Whiplash Council."

"I'm starting to think that's the way Tuden Sal works," Haus agreed. "Divide and control."

Sheel nodded. "He's not only divided the authority among Whiplash leaders, but he's pieced out different parts of this . . . plan, as well; I think he's the only one who has the whole picture. Not even Acer and Dyat are in on everything, though I think he trusts them the most. He talked about ambushing the Emperor in the streets around the shore, but that doesn't tally with what I've seen. He's got field operatives in the shore and floor maintenance crews near the Emperor's villa. And Acer let it slip that he's been in receipt of large amounts of explosives—explosives powerful enough to bring down entire buildings."

Haus nodded. It didn't surprise him that the Sakiyan had effectively made himself the head of Whiplash, all the while giving lip service to support for a nonhierarchical authority. It was—according to his dossier, which the prefect had combed through thoroughly—the way he had run his corporate organization, as well. He was in the pilot's seat, while his underlings took care of discrete parts of the business with authority that only extended to their own small domain. No one except Sal himself had an overview of the entire operation.

In an organization like Black Sun, this kind of arrangement was offset by natural ambition; any and all subordinates were looking for ways to rise above their positions, pull off a coup, or work out their own competing plans. In an organization like Whiplash, however, in which the council members took the egalitarian nature of their cause at face value, Tuden Sal could make his own plans with confidence that no one else among the shared leadership would formulate competing schemes or imagine that he was withholding information. Haus remembered that the Coruscant resistance had chosen the name *Whiplash* out of a sense of irony—a constant reminder of the Imperial yoke they attempted to overthrow.

"I suppose it's possible he's just being careful," Sheel said, her hands wrapped around her mug as if her fingers were cold. "If I were him, I'd be afraid that maybe someone would slip up and reveal too much to the wrong person."

Reminded of his own unwelcome suspicions, Haus set his caf down on the carved wooden table more heavily than he'd intended.

"What is it, Pol?"

"What you were saying about slippage—it may have already happened. I can't be sure."

Maybe it was his imagination, but the Togruta's face seemed to go a shade or two lighter. "What do you mean?"

"One of my speeder patrols checked in early this morning with the observation that for the past two nights, they've seen Imperial security forces moving into the Golden Crescent area near the Emperor's villa."

"Well, of course, the Emperor is in residence—"

He shook his head. "He's been in residence for over a week. Why would they be moving now—and under cover of darkness? I also got a report from an operative who delivers supplies to the administrative offices of the Inquisitorius. She says the few Inquisitors that were left behind when Vader went offworld are no longer 'drifting around the place,' as she put it."

Now Sheel's pallor was definitely not imaginary. "You think they've gone to guard the Emperor?"

"Entirely possible. It's also entirely possible that, high-level Senate committee meeting or not, the Emperor himself may have been moved." He shrugged. "Or, knowing how arrogant he is, he may be lying in wait like a spider at the middle of a web."

"What do we do? Don't we have to warn Sal?"

"How? Do you think he'd trust anything I had to say? And if you go to him with this intel, he'll want to know how you got it. Worse—he may decide he can't trust you, either."

"What then?"

Haus stood. "I'll try to reach him. At least that will keep you out of it. I'll try to make him believe the warning is real and not my attempt to run interference. Chances are he'll laugh in my face, but I can't just let him run head-on into a rancor nest. I suppose I could arrest him on trumped-up charges or make up some reason to bring him in for questioning."

"Would you do that? *Could* you do it?"

"If I have to. But I'm not sure that would stop whatever it is he's set in motion."

Haus started for the front door, then paused and turned back. "Sheel, maybe you shouldn't attend any more Whiplash Council meetings."

She blinked. "He's called a meeting tomorrow morning. If I don't go . . ."

Forgetting that he was in disguise, Haus reached up to scratch his shock of badly trimmed hair. His fingers met a fake Togruta montral. "You're right. Stick with it, but keep your comlink handy."

She nodded, her lips drawn into a grim, ashen line.

At the soft chime of the HoloNet terminal in his personal quarters aboard the Whiplash hovertrain, Tuden Sal looked up to see who would be calling him at this time of night. He was honestly surprised to see Pol Haus's ident icon floating above the console.

He was even more surprised at himself: he actually answered the summons.

"To what do I owe the dubious pleasure, Prefect Haus?" he asked the holographic image of Pol Haus's head and shoulders that appeared once he had answered the call.

"To a report I got early this morning from a couple of my speeder patrols. Specifically, the ones routed around the eastern shore of the Western Sea in the Golden Crescent area."

"Oh, wait. Let me guess: they saw Darth Vader out walking his pet rancor beast. Or perhaps he was trolling the waters for Jedi."

Haus sighed audibly. "Will you shut up for a minute and hear me out?"

"Why? Nothing you have to say is of interest to me."

"If you've still got designs on Palpatine, it should be. There are Imperial security forces and possibly Inquisitors in and around the seashore near the Emperor's villa."

Sal was immediately wary. "Why should I care what happens near the Emperor's villa?"

"Don't play games, Sal. There isn't time. I know you're going after Palpatine, and chances are good that someone else suspects you are, as well."

Sal's pulse jacked up several notches. "How do you know? Who told you?"

"I have people all over the sector. They see things. They hear things. And what they see and hear they report to me—or to another prefect who then files his own activity report. The difference between those prefects and me is that I know who the Whiplash operatives are. And I know you. I didn't buy for a moment that you weren't going to act on that intel. Striking Palpatine while he's in residence at the villa is the best chance you're going to get."

Haus was right. His logic was impeccable. Sal sometimes forgot that Pol Haus wasn't the dense, lazy career detective he pretended to be.

"So you've called to warn me off. What are you thinking, Haus? That I'm an idiot?"

"I think you're a zealot, Sal. I think you're so focused on taking out Palpatine—so focused on revenge—that you're not thinking straight."

Anger, swift and hot, flared in Tuden Sal's breast. He knotted his hands against it, striving to keep a smile on his face and his tone level.

"Revenge? Is that what you think this is about? My own personal agenda? Palpatine didn't just ruin *me*, Pol. He ruined a *lot* of people. And murdered more. He's directly responsible for us losing Yimmon and Laranth and indirectly responsible for us losing Jax, I-Five, and Den. This is the man, Prefect, who took down the entire Jedi Order, leaving the way open for his unchecked, ironfisted control of all our lives. This isn't just my battle. It's *everyone's* battle."

"Yes. It is. Which is why you need to listen to me. If the Emperor's been tipped off to your plans, *everyone* suffers."

"You know what your problem is, Pol? You can't commit to anything. You glide around in the background, slither through the dark, pretending to be something you're not. Playing the foolish, clumsy police detective so that your enemies will fail to recognize you as a threat. I'm sure you think you do it to be clever and because it allows you to know things you wouldn't otherwise know. But that's not it, is it? You don't do it for any of those reasons. You do it because it keeps you safe. Other people die. You're already a ghost. The man no one sees. Fine, then. Be a ghost—be a coward. But don't expect the rest of us to run scared, too. The Emperor is going to die."

Haus was shaking his head. "Sal, listen to me. I want to be free of Palpatine as much as the next man—"

"Do you really?" An ugly suspicion struck Sal. "Or are you on his payroll?"

"If I was, would I warn you?"

Of course. That impeccable logic again. "No. You're right. You're no traitor. Just a coward."

"If you think you can get under my skin by calling me names—"

"I don't care about your skin. Frag your skin. I care about this mission."

"You don't know what you're doing, Sal—"

"*Wrong.* I know *exactly* what I'm doing. How about you? Are you planning on getting in my way?"

The Zabrak ran long fingers through his frowzy

mane, and for once, Tuden Sal read resignation in his sharp features.

"No," he said. "No. I won't get in your way. Good luck with this. I mean it. I hope you succeed. I'm just afraid you won't."

Sal cut him off.

In a spacer tavern near the Westport, Acer Ash shook wrists with Captain Donari Caron and felt a pleasurable flush of attraction as he touched the Zeltron's ruby skin. He held her wrist a moment longer than formality required, basking in her glow, while her large dark eyes glinted in acknowledgment of his silent admiration.

He was hopeful that their business might also involve a significant amount of pleasure; he was also on his guard. A Zeltron smuggler had a tactical advantage—she could pheromonically manipulate the emotions of her contacts, thus negotiating better conditions than someone without that capacity might arrange.

Ash determined he would not fall prey to that sort of emotional byplay. He knew Zeltrons craved physical affection as much as he craved profits. That was a bit of leverage he could and would use. He gestured the captain to a private cubicle in the dimly lit back room of the tavern that, owing to a deal with the tavern owner— a Whiplash informant—amounted to a private office. Meanwhile, in the large main room, a live band thumped out loud music to the cheers and jeers of their audience. The white noise generated by the audio confounders in the back room melted neatly into the chaotic drift from the tavern.

Their negotiations were cordial, notwithstanding the Zeltron tried several times to employ her pheromones to sway him toward purchasing or bartering for items he did not, in fact, want. He caught her at it, called her on it, and the two of them had a good laugh.

He made good deals all in all, for the mundane imports, but there were a few items for which Captain Caron had rather specific demands—such as several extraordinary pieces of art ripped from archaeological sites on other worlds and for which Acer Ash had eager buyers. What he did not have in abundance were the cutting-edge tech gadgets that Captain Caron's Black Sun contacts wanted for the artworks.

"How many units can you get me?" she asked, referring to an experimental palm-sized energy shield with a range of two meters that not only deflected energy weapons and projectiles, but turned them back on the attackers.

Ash returned the sample device to its little packing case. "I've got five of them, but I need to keep two back for another buyer."

The other buyer was Tuden Sal. He had requisitioned two of the devices for field operatives involved in the Mission. Profits were profits, but Whiplash came first even for someone of Acer Ash's mercenary bent.

"Only three?" She shook her head, sending a cascade of rippling saffron-colored hair over one shoulder. "My clients need them in the hundreds."

He shrugged, fighting his hormonal responses to her, and leaned away from her against the back of his chair, pulling his hands back to his side of the table. "They can disassemble the prototypes. See what makes 'em work. Make their own."

Donari Caron rolled her lustrous eyes; sweat broke out on Ash's upper lip. She was certainly an exemplary example of her species; a regular pheromone factory. He desperately wanted to lean into her—to draw closer—but he kept his relaxed pose, slouched in his chair, one hand toying with his half-empty glass of cinnamon liqueur.

"Without the specs? Please, Acer, my clients have

high expectations of me. I'd need twenty or thirty of the things at least if they're going to have to reverse-engineer them. Or all five of the ones you've got *and* the specifications. I'm sure you understand the imperative."

She put her hand over his on the table.

He withdrew his hand. "You're kidding, right? I can't get the specs. They're a closely guarded secret."

Her frustration was palpable. "What *can* you get? Can you at least get me ten of the devices?"

Ash laughed. "You seem to be under the impression that I *could* get you more of the bloody things if you offer the right incentives, but that I'm just trying to drive a hard bargain. I swear that's not the case. I can get them, but not quickly and not in great numbers. What with Palpatine, Darth Vader, the inquisitive Inquisitors, and the fraggin' Security Bureau, my supply lines are—shall we say—squeezed."

Her eyes lost their gleam and she sat back, withdrawing herself—and her considerable hormonal presence—completely. "That's bad news. I guess I oversold your ability to get things done. My clients will be disappointed . . . to say the least."

He shifted toward her, hungry for the warm flush he'd felt moments before, then realized she was using his own tactics against him. The knowledge didn't help much, though he was able to regain a bit of his poise.

"Donari, I can get things done, trust me. It's just that things are a little tight on Coruscant right now, security-wise. But that's going to change real soon."

"Really? And why is that?"

"Let's just say that Palpatine isn't going to be a factor for much longer, and once he's out of the picture, Vader and his spooks and his little black-shirted goon squad will be running around trying to figure out what happened. And while they're busy doing that, I'll take the opportunity to get all sorts of stuff out under their noses."

She blinked at him, then gave him a cockeyed smile that lit him up like a homing beacon. "You seem awfully sure of your intel. What do you know?" She leaned toward him again, elbows on the table, her eyes bright and speculative.

Ash shook his head, chuckling. "Sorry, Captain, but I can't tell you a thing about a thing. It's just a feeling I got. You know how it is with . . . feelings."

Her smile deepened. "I do, indeed. Now, what kind of deal can you give me for my temple art?"

They ended up striking a deal for three of the personal shields he had against one of the temple paintings she had with a promissory handshake for another set of ten shields. If he could produce the specs or another set of ten personal shields, a second artifact would be his.

They sealed their deal in the captain's quarters aboard her ship, the *Touch of Gold*.

Three days.

In three days, the last of the selected Senators would collect at Emperor Palpatine's villa on the shore of the Western Sea and enter into secret meetings. That was the day they would strike. To most men planning an operation of this type, the heightened security required for such a meeting might have argued against carrying out an assassination attempt. But Tuden Sal had observed many times over that the chaos caused by such events could afford the perfect cover for such a mission.

He was counting on it being so this time, as well.

There were multiple security organizations involved—Imperial forces, the Senators' personal bodyguards and security detachments, their administrative personnel—all of which created overlap and gaps, and distracted rote-trained forces from their daily routines and habits.

In such times as these, competing security protocols and agendas often came into conflict, and when they did it forced those involved to focus much more tightly on one another than on what was going on outside and beyond them.

It also put a whole group of operatives into play who were unfamiliar with what was "normal" in this neighborhood or in the waters that lapped at the Emperor's private jetty and swirled beneath his private dock.

Tuden Sal had taken seriously Pol Haus's claim that additional Imperial forces had moved into the area under cover of darkness, but none of his operatives in the coastal neighborhoods had reported any such activity, which led to the obvious conclusion that Haus was lying.

The Emperor probably suspected people were plotting to assassinate him all the time. He was right; very likely they were. But Palpatine was an arrogant man, so sure of his own powers and those of his dark-hearted protégé, Darth Vader, that he would never hide, even if he knew the hour and day of his planned demise. But he didn't know. Hence, Vader was offworld and the Emperor was having a private conclave with his favorite sycophants.

Thi Xon Yimmon, Sal thought, would have balked at killing the Emperor at the risk of so much collateral damage—the explosives Acer Ash had brought in would reduce the villa and its nearest neighbors to rubble—but Sal had no such qualms. The Emperor deserved the death he was going to get, and so did the Senators who willingly supported him.

So, the explosives were in place on their cleaning droids; the "cleanup" team of Nautolans and Mon Calamari had infiltrated the maintenance crews of the seaside resorts and had every reason to be in or near the water; the aerial assault teams were ready to pick off anyone who escaped the conflagration; the ground forces were armed and ready to take down anyone who might get out of the villa's grounds into the streets. Nor would there be any escape by water; the operatives who had planted the charges and reprogrammed the droids would be there to "help" any would-be escapees to a far quieter place.

Tuden Sal reached a hand out to the illuminated 3-D image of the Emperor's villa. Soon all those years of loss would be over. He would reunite with his family. He would have a life again. His fingertip passed through the holographic image, erasing it in a split second.

Three days.

twenty-eight

Tyno Fabris was smiling.

Prince Xizor recognized the smile the moment he entered his lieutenant's tasteful, if somewhat cluttered, office suite. The smile was of the *I know something you don't* variety, and the newly minted Vigo found it annoying. That annoyance made his skin prickle, though he managed to control his flushing reflex.

"You seem pleased with yourself," he commented.

"Well, not with myself, but with my intelligence network. Yes, I'm quite . . ." Xizor's attempt to control his reflexes was not entirely successful; the Arkanian's smile faltered as the shift in his boss's pheromone levels struck him ". . . pleased," he ended lamely.

"Do tell," Xizor said, and meant it as a command.

To his credit, Fabris took it as one. "Things are happening on Imperial Center, Vigo. Interesting things. Our rumor mill has not only drawn Darth Vader away from Kantaros Station, but has caused Imperial forces to be moved to the affected area."

Xizor shrugged. "That's to be expected."

"Ah, but that's not all—at least according to one Captain Donari Caron. When asked why she was able to produce only three of the prototype P-shields she was asked to procure, she reported that her contact told her that security on Imperial Center was tight at the moment, but that the situation would soon change when Palpatine was—how did she put it—out of the picture."

Xizor was momentarily speechless. Once he'd processed the information, he said, "What you're implying is that someone actually *is* plotting to kill Palpatine."

The Arkanian's smile was back, no less annoying. "It certainly looks that way."

On the bridge of the Black Sun vessel *Raptor,* everything was going according to plan. Jax watched from a jump seat at the rear of the bridge as the small crew went through their pre-launch protocols. The *Raptor* was one of three Black Sun vessels—well-armed black-market runners all. In under an hour, they would lift from Mandalore and make way to Kantaros Station.

He raised his eyes to the viewport, which gave a view of the other nearby vessels. Past the two Black Sun ships, he could see the *Laranth* sitting, her engines powered down and cold.

He was not unhappy that Den and I-Five would not be with him, he told himself. It was better that they stay behind, for a growing list of reasons. One was their own safety. What Jax was proposing to do was risky to anyone involved—including Xizor's operatives. A related imperative was that the resistance not lose more good people. If he went in alone and failed, Den and I-Five would be left to carry on. If they were with him and he failed . . .

No. It didn't bear thinking about.

There was a third reason for his decision to part from his closest friends—their distrust. It was palpable and it distracted him. Both distraction and distrust could foster indecision and, as he already knew, indecision resulted in loss . . . in death.

There is no death . . .

Jax shook himself, shoving doubt aside. Perhaps there was no death from the point of view of the dead. Perhaps death only existed in the minds of the living—the ones left behind.

Jax felt the thrum of the *Raptor*'s ion engines as they ramped up. He frowned and checked his chrono. Where was Xizor? The thrill-seeking Vigo had made his own presence on the mission a part of the deal, but he had yet to come aboard, though their departure was only minutes away.

There was a sudden shift in the atmosphere of the bridge. All of Jax's senses focused on the source of that change—the captain, a human named Breck, had straightened and raised a hand to the earpiece of his comlink, then tilted his head, sat back in his seat, and glanced back over his shoulder at Jax.

The hair rose up on the back of Jax's neck. Something was wrong.

The captain faced front again, uttered a word or two, then turned to his navigator. "Secure the ship. We're standing down."

Jax was stunned. He stood. "What do you mean 'standing down'?" But he knew what was meant before Captain Breck answered.

"That was the boss," the man told him. "He's pulled the plug on the operation. We're not going to Kantaros."

"Did he say why?"

The captain shook his head. "No. And I didn't ask."

"Then I will."

Jax strode from the bridge and off the ship.

"What's happening?"

Den Dhur peered through the *Laranth*'s transparent viewport at the activity on the tarmac—or rather, the lack of activity. The three Black Sun smugglers, which had been powering up, were suddenly ramping back down again. After a momentary stillness, the loading ramp of the largest ship lowered and Jax came down it. He crossed the tarmac in long, ground-eating strides. The expression on his face was terrifying, and would have been even without the fake cybernetic eye.

Den was terrified by it, at any rate. He pulled back from the viewport. "Something's wrong, Five."

"You've only just noticed?"

"I'm serious, frag it! Something's gone wrong. *Badly* wrong."

"Apparently."

Den turned to look at the droid, who was "dressed" in his new, not-so-shiny I-Five persona. "How can you be so sanguine about . . . whatever this is?"

"I'm not sanguine. In fact, I feel rather powerless to do anything. But consider what it might mean that Jax—apparently in a towering rage—has left the ship that was supposed to take him to Kantaros Station."

Den considered what it meant and was about to say he didn't follow, when he realized that he did. "Xizor's broken the deal."

"That would be my surmise."

"What do we do? Should we follow him?"

"In his present state of mind, I doubt Jax would take that gesture in the spirit it was intended. I think we should just sit tight."

Den clenched his fists atop the control console. "He could be in trouble, Five. He may be headed into a face-off with a Black Sun Vigo—one who almost killed him."

"Jax wasn't the same man then that he is now, and Xizor would be a fool to think that he is."

The tapcaf was closed at this hour of the day. Only a few people were in the street when Jax arrived at the front of the building. The locked door was no obstacle.

It opened at a gesture, letting him into the darkened ground floor. As he strode across the room to the staircase beyond the bar, a pair of startled employees—surprised in the act of polishing tabletops—glanced up but offered no objection.

He took the stairs two at a time and met his first resistance at the top in the form of a pair of Fabris's goons—the Devaronian and the Zabrak. They came toward him, hands already on their weapons.

"Stop!" the Zabrak ordered.

Her partner drew his weapon. Jax made a swiping gesture, and the blaster spun away over the banister into the room below. The Zabrak woman went for her weapon next—Jax's clenching fist caused the Force to twist it into an unrecognizable lump.

She flung the useless thing aside and lunged at him. He answered with a Force thrust powerful enough to toss her four meters down the corridor. Her Devaronian cohort, wisely, chose to run, scooping the Zabrak up and dragging her away.

Jax came down the hallway after them, doors flying open at his passing. When he reached the door to Fabris's office, there were no guards there to challenge him, though he sensed quite a few in the depths of the building.

He thrust one hand, stiff-armed, at the door. It ripped from its hinges, blowing inward in a rain of wood dust and plaster.

Fabris was not behind his desk. Not surprising.

Jax closed his eyes, scanning. There, behind that tapestry, behind a door and the wall, were life forces. Four of them.

Jax crossed the room in three strides. One gesture tore the tapestry from the wall and flung it into a corner; another shoved the inner door aside, making its machinery scream. He drew his lightsaber and stepped into the doorway, expecting to have to parry blaster bolts, but no one fired.

Prince Xizor stood in the center of the room, his hands held out from his body—whether to show he was unarmed or to dissuade his two bodyguards from doing anything rash, Jax wasn't sure. The Falleen was a stew of emotions, making his flesh shift colors rapidly. Tyno Fabris sat between the two guards, striving unsuccessfully to look composed. Sweat stood out on his brow, and his gaze was locked on Jax's lightsaber.

Jax shifted his stance, swinging his glowing blade in a slow figure-eight that made it hum menacingly.

"What game are you playing, Xizor?" he asked the Vigo. "Why have you scrubbed the mission?"

"Mission? My, my, how religious that sounds. There's no mission, Jedi. This is business, not a spiritual quest."

"Then let me put it in terms you'll understand. Why have you broken our contract?"

Xizor spread his hands in a gesture that said he had no choice. "The situation has changed radically. It no longer makes sense for me to involve myself in this . . . endeavor."

Jax stepped fully into the room and moved slowly to his right, forcing Xizor to turn to face him. The last time the two men had confronted each other, Jax's Force connection had been sputtering and inconsistent. Xizor had had the advantage. This time Xizor was pinned and he knew it.

"I'm going to let you explain yourself," he told the Vigo, "but first I want to warn you about what will happen if the bodyguards that are massing in the outer corridor try to enter Fabris's office. That big chandelier on the ceiling is going to come crashing down on their heads. Then I'm going to embed you in that wall behind you."

Smiling, Xizor locked eyes with him, reading him.

Apparently, the Falleen didn't like what he saw. His eyes flickered, trying to dodge. His smile faltered, became wooden. His lips drew back in a snarl. "Let me send one of my men out to hold them back."

Jax considered the idea, then nodded.

Xizor turned to the men flanking Tyno Fabris. "Brank, go out and forestall any attack."

"Tell them to withdraw to the lower level," Jax ordered.

"Fine. Tell them that."

Brank, a tall, broad-shouldered Mandalorian of indeterminate species, nodded curtly, growled, and lumbered out of the room.

"You were expecting me, Xizor," Jax observed. "Otherwise I doubt there would be quite so many guards lurking in the upstairs corridors."

"You've got me there. I figured my news would make you less than happy, but what can I do? I can't get you to Kantaros Station, Jax. Sorry. I mean that. I was looking forward to having a Jedi at my beck and call. I'd be the only Vigo in the history of Black Sun to be so endowed. So, you see, this hurts me as much as it does you."

"I doubt it. You said something changed. What changed?" Jax struggled not to connect with the roil of fury in his breast. If he could stay above it . . .

"Well, you see, a funny thing happened. As you requested, I employed my network of associates to draw Darth Vader back to Imperial Center. My people effected this by spreading seemingly credible rumors that someone was plotting to assassinate the Emperor."

Jax felt a clammy chill invade his gut. "And this changes things, how?"

"I'm a bit embarrassed about this, but it appears that someone actually *is* plotting such an attack. One of our captains was engaged in a business negotiation with a black-market supplier—a fellow named Ash, I think she said—and this supplier made a strange reference to Palpatine being removed from the picture."

Acer Ash—a member of Whiplash. Tuden Sal was going ahead with his insane plan, and there wasn't a thing Jax could do about it.

"The bottom line is that the rumors I had planted happened to be true. Now, let's imagine for a moment that this assassination attempt is linked with an arguably insane attempt to free Whiplash's captured leader. The fact that Yimmon's liberator arrived on a Black Sun vessel would not be lost on the Emperor."

"You could say that I stowed away."

The Falleen was slowly shaking his head. "A handful of valuable members within my organization know about this plan. If Vader were to question them, it would become immediately apparent that I was involved. I simply can't take that chance."

"Did you know? Did you even stop to think that rumors of that nature could impact the resistance?" Jax's voice was hard, cold, and quiet.

"It didn't occur to me, nor would I have cared if it had, to be perfectly honest with you. I simply reasoned that a credible threat to the Emperor would draw Vader away. It worked." Xizor spread his hands again. "Sorry, Pavan. Nothing personal, it's just business."

Just business. How many people had died—how many *would* die—because Black Sun was just doing *business*?

Jax was struck with a full appreciation of Den and I-Five's objections to his dealing with Xizor. To them it must seem as if he were neck-deep in his own version of "just business" as he pursued his goals.

Deep down inside him, something gave.

Xizor sensed it, for he took a step back and said loudly, "Brank! To me!"

Jax felt the sudden rise of adrenaline among the sentients in the tapcaf below. Of course, Xizor had kept a comlink open. He would have been stupid not to.

Jax turned and bolted for the outer room, reaching it as the first of the guards came pounding up the staircase. He knew others were coming along other routes, intending, no doubt, to cut off all egress. But they were dealing with a Jedi. Albeit a Jedi whom they had never seen show any sign of real violence.

Wielding his lightsaber, Jax sundered the rest of Fabris's tapestries, effectively blocking the remaining hidden doors with yards of heavy material. Then he whipped around, free hand extended, generating a Force thrust that swept every surface in the room, creating a storm of flying objects. The hail of glass, metal, and wood pelted the bodyguards who were even now rushing in through the unblocked office door.

Jax leapt away from the center of the room, reaching up toward the ceiling with his free hand. Overhead, the gaudy, oversized chandelier quivered and chattered. The candles flickered in their sconces.

"*No!*" Tyno Fabris wailed from the doorway of his hidden room. "Not that!"

"Stand down, Pavan," Xizor warned. "You're trapped. You've nowhere to go."

Jax met the Falleen's smile with one of his own—one he guessed was no more pleasant. "I guess you're right. There's no way out."

He deactivated his lightsaber and returned it to his belt, slanting a look at the heavily fortified stained-glass window behind him. He saw the bodyguards relax back, heard Fabris sigh in relief, felt Xizor warm toward gloating.

He glanced back at the Vigo. "But I can fix that."

Jax spun, thrusting with both hands. The barred window exploded outward over the street below, taking a big chunk of the wall with it. Colored glass sparkled in the morning sun like bright rain.

In the stunned moment of silence after, Jax glanced back at Xizor and his lieutenant. "Nothing personal, of course. Just business."

A last sweep of his hands wrenched Tyno Fabris's fantastic chandelier from its mounts and brought it down in a shower of crystal and flame. Then Jax stepped out of the empty window and let himself down into the street in the arms of the Force.

He knew a moment of regret when he saw the devastation his blast of energy had caused—blocks of masonry and shards of wood and glass lay scattered across the walkway and into the street; the few people out this early were either scrambling for cover or staring in utter disbelief. He felt no injured here, and hoped there were no dead as he broke into a run.

Less than half an hour after he'd left the spaceport, Jax reappeared at a dead run, looking no less fearsome than he had earlier. He came straight to the *Laranth,* boarded through the hastily lowered loading ramp, and made his way to the bridge.

Den looked up into that stony face, uncertain what to expect.

"Prepare the ship for departure," Jax said. "We're going to Toprawa." Then he turned and went aft.

Den stared after him, a strange, wild elation blossoming in his chest. Jax was back—again. They would soon be among friends. He sagged in the copilot's seat and looked over at I-Five, who was going into the pre-liftoff protocols with mechanical precision—using the one "normal" hand on his mongrel I-5YQ chassis.

"Is it too early to celebrate?"

"Far too early," I-Five said, nodding his still-misshapen head toward the commercial quarter Jax had just come from. "From appearances, I'd say Jax left some destruction in his wake."

Den peered out the viewport, his eyes immediately finding what the droid was talking about: a telltale plume of smoke curling up from the direction of the *Oyu'baat* tapcaf.

"I suggest we hurry," said I-Five, and activated the ion engines.

He had never felt like this—not after his Master's death, not after Flame Night, not after Kajin Savaros's near destruction, not even in the aftermath of losing Laranth and Yimmon. He was filled with a horrible, dark, quivering *desire*—but for what, he could not put into words. His whole life had been about self-knowledge, self-control, self-discipline. Now he knew nothing about himself except that he had none of those things.

In the moment the door of his quarters hissed shut behind him, the ravenous need swarmed him, swamped him, roared to be free. He let it, giving vent to a wild scream of alien passion. The room around him exploded in a cyclonic whorl of motion, sound, and violence. Whatever was not fixed to the decking or walls came loose, blown to the upper bulkhead. Whatever was fixed followed mere seconds later.

As swiftly as it had come, the tidal wave of emotion surged out again, leaving Jax empty in the center of his ruined cabin. He trembled as his eyes took in the devastation . . . and stopped dead at the sight of Laranth's tree lying on the deck, its roots naked and half crushed by the broken remnants of its container.

The Sith lightsaber he had concealed in the device lay gleaming on the deck plating, taunting him.

He fell to his knees on the padded flooring, pulling away the debris and lifting the tiny miisai into a cupped palm. He reassembled the feeding container as best he could, collected the soil, and set the tree back into it, watering it and feeding it energy from his own life force. Then he sat and stared at it, numbly aware of the ship's trembling as she lifted into the morning sky.

‑[PART THREE]‑

JOURNEY'S END

twenty-nine

The timetable was set. Sheel Mafeen had recited it to Haus just as Tuden Sal had revealed it to the Whiplash Council. She'd backed it up with a set of plans sliced neatly from the holo-terminal in the council chamber aboard the Whiplash Express.

Haus was in the process of setting up his own plans for derailing the plot when he got an unsettling piece of intel from a contact inside the ISB: Darth Vader had returned to Imperial Center without warning or fanfare.

In response, Prefect Haus pushed his own timetable up by two days. He assembled a special ops force of crack combat-trained officers and informed them that a dangerous cadre of criminals had set up operations along an abandoned maglev route. In the late afternoon—1500 on the chrono—they would follow an informant to a prearranged meeting place, intercept the criminals, and arrest them.

Simple.

Except that when said informant—Sheel Mafeen—entered the abandoned tube station at which the train was supposed to stop at 1515, it wasn't there. She waited; Haus and his men waited within sight of her. She tried to contact Sal; she got no answer.

She contacted Haus surreptitiously, fear clogging her voice. "This is all wrong, Pol. This is where the train was supposed to be at this time today. We were supposed to go over the plan one more time."

Haus blew out a long gust of air and squinted at the abandoned freight terminal where the meet-up was to have taken place. A suspicion was slowly dawning that Tuden Sal's paranoia had caused him to plant decoy plans in the event that his intent was discovered.

Comlink open, Haus said, "All right. All right. I'm gonna call it."

The words prompted a cloaked Sheel Mafeen to leave the terminal; it prompted Haus's people to prick up their ears.

"Sir?" asked his Bothan lieutenant, Kalibar Droosh.

"Send the crew in. Look for any signs of recent visits."

They found more than that. After taking a group of officers down the right-hand tunnel, Lieutenant Droosh appeared mere moments later, alone. Standing in the mouth of the tunnel, he waved to Haus.

"Sir? We've found something! There's an abandoned train car just out of sight in the tube here."

An abandoned . . . The hair rose up on the back of the prefect's neck, making him rub at it. "Just one?"

"Yes, sir. Just the one. Should I have the men board, sir?"

"No! Don't let them go near it! Get them out of there, Lieutenant! Get them out now!"

The lieutenant's long nose scrunched into an exclamation point of Bothan puzzlement. He shrugged, turned, and shouted, "Sergeant Amry! Come on back! Prefect wants you guys out of there."

A second later, the lieutenant was blown off his feet by a blast from inside the tunnel—a blast violent enough to bowl over Haus and several other officers engaged in searching the terminal area. In the chaos that followed, Haus picked himself up, already shouting orders to his uninjured men.

What had started out as a sting ended up as a rescue mission.

As soon as the emergency crews arrived and the situation was under control, Pol Haus put a slightly-the-worse-for-wear Lieutenant Droosh in charge, got into his aircar, and called Sheel Mafeen. He explained what had happened in clipped syllables, then expressed his worst fears.

"Sal set that ambush for me, Sheel, because he expected me or someone else to betray him. The fact that you weren't in on his plan makes it pretty clear he didn't feel he could trust you completely."

"He never . . . I mean, of all of us, he seemed the least trusting of Fars. Fars didn't want to do this. I wonder if Dyat and Acer knew—"

"It doesn't matter, Sheel. He's burned his bridges. Abandoned the maglev line. To me that suggests that he's set things in motion already."

Sheel gasped. "Oh, spirits of fire and air! What do we do?"

"You go home and wait for me to contact you. I'm going try to salvage this—if I can."

He took to the upper levels of traffic then, running with his avoidance system and chase lights on and making for the Western Sea. In the gray of twilight, he emerged from between the two last skyscraping resiblocks and saw the shoreline neighborhoods laid out before him. Here, only the most elite of the elite owned businesses or homes, and the buildings were strictly limited in height. So he knew even as he left the shadow of the towering resiblocks that something dire was unfolding along the shore in the Golden Crescent.

Fire reflected in the waters of the sea, scattering rubies and topazes across its choppy surface. Smoke billowed above the jetty of the Emperor's villa, but the villa itself seemed intact. There were ground troops in black uniforms and white-sheathed stormtroopers everywhere. The air was alive with military craft, while out on the water, Imperial launches and patrol vessels formed a barrier against the escape of a group of struggling figures they had trapped against the burning jetty.

He drew closer, falling in with a line of other constabulary vehicles that seemed, like his, to be arriving late to the party. One after another, they were stopped by ISB aircars and turned away. When it was his turn to be checked, he showed his ident to the security officer.

"Prefect Haus? You're from a neighboring prefecture, aren't you?"

Haus nodded. "I was pursuing a lead on a smuggling ring that caters to the rich and famous. Looks like you've got your hands full here. More than smuggling by the look of it."

"Rebels, sir. A plot against the Emperor, himself, I've heard. Not that I hear much. I'm just directing traffic." The young officer looked apologetic. "I'll have to ask you to move along now, Prefect."

"Sure . . . sure." Haus gave the security officer an amicable nod and took his aircar up and about, circling just low enough to be able to see the plaza in front of the Emperor's villa. Stormtroopers patrolled there, standing guard over a group of bodies laid out on the stones before an elaborate fountain. The vidcam could capture what the naked eye could not; Haus made a slow turn, his vidcam trained first on the bodies, then on the jetty.

He knew, even as he flew away, that one of the bodies in the courtyard was a Sakiyan. And he had recognized several others who'd thrown their lives into Tuden Sal's plan. In his blind quest for revenge, Sal had wiped out the remainder of Whiplash's guiding council and a number of its technically adept operatives. The fortunes of the resistance on Coruscant were fading with the smoke from the Emperor's jetty.

There was a sudden flurry of activity in the courtyard that Haus was now watching through his rear vidcam. A figure had stepped out into the walled enclosure to which every other person alive paid instant obeisance.

Darth Vader—as ever, at the center of it all.

thirty

The *Laranth/Corsair* made Toprawa three days after leaving Mandalore. In the dark of the local night, she disappeared into the back door of Mountain Home, her crew met on the landing platform by a welcoming committee that included Degan Cor, Sacha Swiftbird, and the little Rodian mech-tech, Geri.

Jax held his thoughts and emotions close and schooled his face to reveal nothing of the turmoil going on within. Regardless, Degan Cor took one look at him and apparently knew something was wrong.

"I take it things didn't go very smoothly on Mandalore," the resistance leader said as Jax stepped off the loading ramp.

"No. Not at all smoothly. We know where Yimmon is, but as far as how we get to him . . . we're back to square one."

"Back?" Sacha Swiftbird glanced from Jax to Den, who had come down the ramp behind him. "Then you tried to get to him?"

"We . . . I was poised to do that. Thought I had found a way of doing that. But the plans . . . went up in smoke."

Den uttered a short bark of laughter, then coughed apologetically. "Sorry. That was inappropriate."

I-Five reached the bottom of the ramp at that moment, still in his patchwork I-5YQ/Nemesis persona. Standing on mismatched legs—his single I-5YQ limb

paired with a unit cobbled from a 3PO-series droid that
had seen better days, he had his pit droid chassis tucked
under one arm. Geri let out a squawk and squeezed
through between the two human Rangers.

"Wow, Five! You look . . . really awful."

"Thank you. Perhaps instead of criticizing, you might
suggest further modifications?"

"Oh, uh, sure." He glanced up at Degan Cor. "After
you guys—y'know—have your war council, why don't
you come on up to the shop?"

"Perhaps we could go now. I would rather not carry
this—" I-Five hefted the pit droid. "—around indefi-
nitely."

Geri nodded. "Sure. C'mon up."

Den and I-Five both moved to follow the Rodian into
the core of Mountain Home. Jax was glad to see them
go. It took too much effort to be with them right now.
His head was full of dark, woolly thoughts trying to
claw their way toward some glint of light; he had neither the words to describe them nor the desire to explore them.

He moved automatically into step with the two resistance operatives, aware of their intense regard. Degan
hurried to the communications center to summon Aren
Folee, who was currently away in Big Woolly. That left
Sacha to guide Jax to the council chambers.

"You look pretty rough," the engineer commented as
they moved through the corridors beneath the mountain. When he didn't reply, she went on, "Look, just
knowing where they're holding Yimmon is a big deal.
It's a victory and you know it. We'll put a team together.
We'll go back and we'll get Yimmon out."

Jax almost smiled. Here he was—a Jedi Knight—and
a washed-up Podracer was trying to cheer him on. "It's
not quite that simple," he said. "You'll understand when
we go over the data. Kantaros is . . . a closed system."

"Yeah. But it's a *system*. Any system can be cracked, sliced, and screwed up royally."

He turned to look at her. She was in deadly earnest.

"Could you do it without anyone being the wiser?"

"For a while." She shook back her hair, revealing the silvery scar that bisected her left eyelid.

Jax looked away.

"Want some caf or *shig*?" she asked as they entered the informal council chamber. "You look like you could use something bracing."

"Thank you. *Shig*, please."

Jax sat down in one of the formchairs, tilted his head back, and considered what Sacha had said.

Any system can be cracked.

That was true enough, and his flirtation with Black Sun hadn't been entirely a loss. He now knew that Black Sun had regular dealings with the crew at Kantaros and that Xizor's ships docked there without issue. That gave them an "in." With I-Five's talents and the selection of ships available here in Mountain Home, they might credibly pass as a Black Sun runner.

Jax smiled wryly at the thought that Xizor might end up being connected to Yimmon's rescue whether he liked it or not.

"Here."

He opened his eyes to find Sacha holding out a cup of steaming liquid to him. He took it, thanked her, then said, "Let's assume we can arrange to dock at Kantaros Station and I can pinpoint where Yimmon is in the complex. It's a big complex—built into a good-sized asteroid. If we get in the way I'm thinking, we'd be restricted to the docking bays pretty much—maybe allowed onto the crew's levels. How would you propose we go places we're not supposed to without drawing attention?"

She sat down next to him, a cup of *shig* in her hands. "Misdirection and selective slicing. You don't defeat systems you don't need to defeat. Take surveillance cams—you can cause those to develop hiccups with the right energy pulses. If you only mess with one or two cams at a time, it's hard to pick up." She shrugged. "Of course, you could also make the cam think it's seeing something it's not."

"An empty corridor."

"Yeah. Or a corridor with someone in it who's actually supposed to be there." She paused to sip her drink. "You could tell it that it saw intruders—but not where the intruders actually were. Of course, you'd need to plan something like that carefully. Takes time."

"Which we don't have a lot of."

"Yeah. Your droid could probably pull off a simple looping effect . . . or I could."

Jax ignored the woman's obvious bid to be included, then looked up as the door of the chamber slid back to admit I-Five and Den. Degan Cor arrived practically on their heels with a look on his face that brought Jax to his feet.

"What?" Sacha asked. "Deg, what is it?"

He shook his head, made a gesture that was eloquent of impotence and frustration. "While I was in the communications bay, we got an urgent message from Coruscant. Whiplash . . . Whiplash has been shattered. There was a botched attempt on the Emperor's life. Apparently, the Imperials were ready for it. They wiped out . . . dozens. Dozens of operatives and most of the leading council."

Jax felt as if someone had set off a stun grenade in the room. His lips tried to form words, but failed.

I-Five had no such problem. "Who sent the message?"

"Guy who called himself 'the Constable.' He said he didn't know how many dead there were, and that, as far as he knew, he and someone he called 'the Poet' were the only members of the Whiplash Council left alive. He said . . . Vader was there."

Den Dhur sat down on the floor—hard.

"Pol Haus," murmured Jax. "And Sheel Mafeen."

Whiplash was effectively gone. Dead.

Why?

And who had started this chain of events? Who had tipped Darth Vader off to Yimmon's move in the first place? Had it been Pol Haus?

"Lord Vader will turn his attention to other resistance hubs now that he's crushed Whiplash," said I-Five. "He'll try even harder to squeeze intel out of Yimmon."

"Yimmon knows about the cell here on Toprawa," Jax said. "And the one on Dantooine. We *have* to get him off that station."

Degan nodded. "I'll have the communications crew try to get us more information about the situation on Coruscant. We need to know what Vader is doing, where he's going . . ."

"I need sleep," Jax said.

That drew silence. Then Degan Cor nodded. "Yeah. You're probably right. Trying to plan something in the middle of the night is not a great idea. Let's grab a couple of hours of rest and come at this fresh in the morning."

They withdrew, then, to their quarters, but Jax had no intention of sleeping. He waited until the others had been bedded down for close to an hour before he retraced his steps to the great cavern and went aboard the *Laranth* long enough to pick up his kit and consign Kantaros Station's last position to a data crystal. Then he found his way to the Jedi starfighter. It had been completely stripped of paint since he'd seen it last and was now a uniformly satiny silver, though he could still see the telltale signs of its last firefight on the port bow.

A nudge with the Force caused the ship to drop its landing ramp and turn on its interior lights.

Jax stepped up onto the ramp, then took a look back at the cavern. A pair of night-duty mech-techs watched him with uncertainty rippling between them. He waved at them, smiled, and went aboard the sleek, bladelike ship. He had no idea what they did once he'd fired up the engines and lifted away from the landing pad. His mind had already leapt ahead to where he would go once he had escaped Toprawa's atmosphere.

thirty-one

Pol Haus watched the forensics team work their way over the blast area, picking up and bagging bits of debris, sweeping the twisted wreckage of the train car with sensitive scanners. Certain that the team was focused on the task at hand, Haus turned and walked down the tunnel, firing up a small, wide-area hand lamp as soon as he got out of sight.

Ostensibly, he was heading to see if any debris had been flung farther from the bomb blast. His real intent was to discover where Tuden Sal had hidden the rest of the Whiplash hovertrain. It was probably a vain hope that he had secreted it anywhere near the site of his parting shot of sabotage, but then Sal had a perverse way of doing the unexpected.

The durasteel surface of the old subway was still relatively smooth, though it was dull in places from the lack of maintenance. As he went, Haus tried to walk through Sal's thought process on where to hide the train. He might have chosen to put it within walking distance of any of the abandoned terminals they used, or even hide it close to the old freighter landing pad that was part of the larger Whiplash Underground Maglev escape system they used to get people offworld.

He might have done that, but it made more sense to the prefect—in a twisted sort of way—for the Sakiyan to have hidden the cars where most authorities would be least likely to look for them. And that might just be near the scene of a police investigation.

He had walked for perhaps two hundred meters and was considering turning around and going back when he noticed that the beam of his lamp was reflecting strangely off the curving wall of the tube—there was a definite, if diffuse, bright spot just where the right-hand wall curved out of sight, as if the light were reflecting off a surface other than the left-hand wall.

Haus took a deep breath and moved forward again. For a moment, he thought he heard another set of footsteps behind him in the tunnel. He halted to listen.

Nothing. The tube breathed, the chill air moving listlessly. That was normal. Beyond that, all Haus could hear was the faint, intermittent hum of the forensics team's voices far behind him.

He shook off the tingle of paranoia and moved forward again, clamping down on his imagination. Who'd follow him down here without calling for him? Refocusing on the tunnel ahead, he rounded the curve.

Powered down, the hovertrain lay cradled in the floor of the tube; no light peeped from the horizontal slits that served as windows on the outside world. Haus approached it carefully nonetheless, drawing his blaster. Theoretically, any Whiplash members who might be hiding here were his allies. But he knew how often theories failed.

He rounded the premier car, raising a hand to its sleek surface. There was no hint of vibration—the train's power was off.

At the door, he hesitated. Was this yet another booby trap? He returned his blaster to its holster and pulled out a scanner. If the train was generating even the tiniest amount of electric or electromagnetic signal, the scanner would detect it . . . theoretically.

It detected nothing.

With a wry grin, Pol Haus moved to the forward portal, pocketed the scanner, and got out a device that was—to the police and emergency services personnel among whom it was a closely guarded secret—a literal lifesaver. Casually known as "the hostage's best friend," the electromagnetic manipulator and phantom power unit allowed defunct mechanisms—such as dead doors— to be operated even if their power supply was completely drained or had been destroyed. It virtually eliminated the need to blow doors in with firepower, or force them open manually.

Naturally, the units were greatly in demand on the black market by people who made their living at the dubious art of breaking and entering.

Haus pressed the palm-sized device to the side of the train car just to the left of the irising portal, activated its sensors, and moved it slowly around the perimeter. It vibrated gently when it found the locking mechanism. He activated the magnetic clamp, pressed the activation button to start the power flow, and turned the device clockwise. Then he leapt aside, hunkering down low on the train's curving flank.

The door's lock vibrated in response, and the iris opened.

No big bang.

"So far, so good," Haus muttered, and swept his lamp's golden beam into the darkness of the car.

Nothing twitched. He swapped the EM unit for his blaster and stepped up into the train. He scanned the interior for life-forms and found none. He swept it visually, as well—one could only trust machines so far.

Assured that no one was hiding in the first car, he made his way to the car in which the Whiplash leadership had held council. It was spooky and more than a little sad.

Haus shook his head. He had only just been accepted

into the group, and it was now effectively dead. Sure, there were still cells of resistance—still souls dedicated to helping asylum-seekers offworld. But there was no one directing traffic. No one to keep the avenues of escape open.

Directing traffic. He smiled grimly. Sounded like a good detail for a police prefect.

He found himself standing at the communications console and wondered what it would take to power it up. There would be a redundant power supply, of course; it was just a question of activating it. And if he did—what then?

The big boom?

No. This was Sal's backup plan. His bolt-hole. He'd expected to return to it. But wouldn't he have left someone on the train, just in case?

A stealthy sound from the next car made Haus's hair stand on end. That was *not* his imagination.

Shielding his lamp in the pocket of his coat, he glided to the intersecting door between the two cars. The doorway was open into darkness. He paused in the short transitional corridor to listen again. From there he could see that the door to Tuden Sal's quarters was also open.

He moved with all the stealth he could muster, cursing—not for the first time—the long-coat that swirled around his legs. He really ought to consider giving up that affectation. One of these days it was going to get him killed.

He made the entrance to Sal's quarters and paused to listen again.

Complete silence.

No . . . not complete. He could hear someone breathing, and he was convinced whoever it was knew he was there. A frisson of unease hit him as he detected a new sound—a stealthy sound—from the conference room in the car he'd just left. He turned, pressing his back against the bulkhead, and palmed his lamp. He focused all his senses on the cabin and thrust the lamp into the empty doorway so that it illuminated the room beyond.

"Out where I can see you!" he commanded.

"Well, well. The traitor returns to the scene of his treachery." Tuden Sal's voice came from a corner of the room to Haus's left.

The prefect could only vaguely make out a form that might have been the Sakiyan. "I'm no traitor, Sal. I don't know who was, only that it wasn't me."

"Of course you'd say that. You want me to come out where you can shoot me."

Haus lowered his blaster. "I'm not going to shoot you, Sal."

"I don't suppose it matters, really, does it? I should have died with the others."

"I thought you had."

The Sakiyan uttered a dry laugh. "No, no. A general doesn't go into battle with the troops. I sent them on a suicide mission and watched from a safe distance. Watched it all go wrong. Watched them die."

"I tried to warn you, Sal."

A beat. "You did, didn't you?"

Tuden Sal came out of hiding then. He was armed—a small hold-out blaster that was barely visible in his hand. He made no move to use it.

Haus kept his own weapon lowered.

"I should have listened," Sal told him. "If I had, none of this would have happened."

"Why didn't you?"

"I told the others it was because you might be a traitor to the cause or that you were a coward." He shook his head. "It was because I knew you'd do whatever you could to stop me. The Empire took my life away from me, Pol. My business. My family. I only saw one way to get it back: kill Palpatine."

"So in the end, you used Whiplash for your personal vendetta."

"I did." Sal's face worked, and for a moment, Haus thought the Sakiyan might weep. Instead he simply said, "I did worse than that."

"What do you mean?" Haus asked, then stiffened at a minute sound from the corridor behind him.

He turned. His Bothan lieutenant, Kalibar Droosh, was framed in the doorway, his blaster leveled at his prefect's midsection.

"A very revealing conversation, sir," the lieutenant said in his hissing, oddly accented Basic. "One I'm sure the Imperial Security Bureau would be most interested in hearing."

"And you're going to relay it to them?" Haus asked.

"Of course. I'm sure there will be great rewards for the man who captures . . . or kills . . . the remaining members of Whiplash."

"He's not a member of Whiplash," Tuden Sal said acidly. "He was merely a hanger-on."

The lieutenant shrugged. "Close enough. And there was that woman, too, the so-called informant you brought here before. I assume you've got some way to contact her, sir?"

Haus felt bile rising in his throat. Sheel. This sorry specimen would go after her next.

"Why do you want to do this, Lieutenant? What love do you have for the Empire?"

"They pay me. Good credits for faithful service. More, if I can give them items of interest. I've been watching you for a while, Prefect Haus. Since I transferred into your prefecture. I was taken with how unusual your friends are. I expect you'll generate quite a bit of interest among my superiors. Maybe enough to get me assigned permanently to the ISB."

Haus sighed and started to turn his blaster butt-first so he could hand it to Droosh.

"Oh, no, sir. You keep that. It's important for this to look—"

There was a ragged scream from Tuden Sal as he flung himself out from behind Haus, firing as he moved.

Haus extinguished the hand lamp and dived to his left. Two more blaster bolts ripped through the darkness in swift succession—one from the doorway and one from the center of the cabin.

Eyes dazzled, Haus lay still and listened, his own blaster up and leveled at the door. He heard the hiss of tortured breathing to his right. Nothing from the outer corridor. The hot stench of burnt flesh, hair, and fabric hinted at what he'd see when he turned on his lamp and blinked his eyes.

Through the slashes of afterimage, Haus saw Tuden Sal lying against the rear wall of the cabin. He wasn't dead, but he wasn't likely to live long, either. Droosh's blaster had caught him in the ribs, leaving a charred hole.

Of Droosh, he could see only the man's boots. He got carefully to his feet, light and blaster aimed at the fallen officer. From the center of the cabin it was clear Droosh was never going to get up again. Sal's shot had caught him right between the eyes.

Haus knelt next to Sal. "You didn't have to do that," he said.

"Oh, *you* would have?" Sal grunted. "You'd've let him shoot you. This called for another suicide mission. Mine . . . payback."

"Sal . . ."

The Sakiyan raised a trembling hand to Haus's sleeve. "Hide . . . the train. The data . . ."

"I'll take care of it. Sheel and I will take care of it."

Sal drew a shuddering breath, his eyes losing their focus. "Stupid . . . so many mistakes."

He was gone before Haus could ask him what mistakes he was referring to, and if they might impact his own continued existence.

Haus sat in the darkness for a long moment, trying to herd his thoughts into some semblance of order. When the chaos had settled and logic reasserted itself, he stood and considered the grim task ahead of him—disposing of the bodies.

After that . . . well, how hard could it be to hide a train?

thirty-two

The Delta-7 *Aethersprite* dropped out of hyperspace just within the orbit of the Fervse'dra asteroid field and moved into synchronous flow with the nearest body. Jax had considered his approach to Kantaros Station all during the four-day journey to the Both system. With Darth Vader on Coruscant, he had a window of opportunity, but possibly only a very narrow window.

The first order of business was to find the station. He had returned to where the station had been; it was not there now. He input the telemetry of the station's last position, which he'd gotten from the *Laranth*'s navcom, into the starfighter's system and had it extrapolate its current location.

He found it more or less where the navcom said it would be, and parked his ship on a slowly tumbling asteroid roughly one hundred klicks behind it in the flow of stone. He wedged the *Aethersprite* in between two projections of icy rock. That should be enough to preserve him from accidental detection, but if there were patrols that came this far out, or an approaching vessel overflew his position, his energy shielding would be useless. He set the ship's sensors to their widest possible spectrum and brought their perimeters in to the point that gave him just enough time to scurry out of sight if anyone entered the area. This gave him decreased range, but increased sensitivity. A lone speeder, life pod, or drone would vibrate his sensor web.

Then, hands on the controls of the ship—ready to lift off at a moment's notice—he settled into a meditative state, preparing to reach for Thi Xon Yimmon's consciousness.

For a fraction of a second, his mind swerved to the idea Xizor had raised—that it would be easier to destroy Yimmon than to save him. Everything in Jax rebelled against the thought. Rebelled so emphatically that, for a moment, he was physically ill. He righted himself with a will, closed his eyes, and sank, once more, into meditation. He missed the miisai tree and found himself calling its shape to his mind's eye.

Jax couldn't afford detection, so he reached out delicately, carefully. He missed the tree at this point, too, because he had used it before to cloak his own Force signature. All he had now was the memory of the miisai, his native talents, and the skills he'd developed in training them.

And he had the Sith holocron.

In the stillness that came with the thought, Jax fetched the thing out of the inner pocket of his surcoat. As if his regard had touched off a response in the artifact, it warmed in his hand. When he closed his eyes, he could still see it as a locus of diffuse light and heat . . . a Force signature.

Balancing the holocron on his palm, he stretched out his energies with more confidence—long, trailing ribbons of the Force wove through the ambience generated by Ramage's device and sought their goal.

He found Yimmon, at length, ironically, by using Vader's seemingly random array of deflection fields to triangulate. He found it interesting that Vader didn't realize that randomness was a chimera. Patterns were so woven into the fabric of the universe that they emerged despite the most rigorous attempts to avoid them.

Jax was amazed at the Cerean's mental state. He was calm. Almost too calm, considering the circumstances. Had they drugged him?

No . . . there was no sense of confusion or sluggishness, just serenity. And watchfulness. He frowned, trying to shake the feeling that he was being observed in some way. It was not unnerving, merely unexpected. As if . . .

With a suddenness that stole his breath, Jax sensed another presence—no, more than one: a strong Force signature, unrecognizable, pushed aside the recognizable consciousness of the Whiplash leader. Then, before he could half grasp that—

—*Listen. Indecision is all loss. Yimmon's separation destroys us all.*

The voice that was not a voice was clear, strong, and insistent. And undeniably alien. Cephalon, in fact.

Aoloiloa? How could that be? How could a Cephalon stationed on Coruscant reach out to him here in this Mid Rim asteroid field?

He felt of the Cephalon's communication. It was equal parts familiar and unfamiliar. Aoloiloa, but *not* Aoloiloa. It was, Jax realized, with a jolt of adrenaline, not just one Cephalon, but a living network of them, linked together to send him this message.

But you've already told me this, he thought. *What more can I do with it? Why do you keep repeating it?*

—*Separation destroys us all.*

Separation destroys . . . what did that mean?

"I have to get him back," Jax murmured aloud. Which meant he had no more time to delay. He must move *now.*

—*Separation destroys us.*

But wait. The message had changed subtly with every

repetition. Jax swallowed a groan of pure frustration. Why, in the name of the Force, could the Cephalons not just say things clearly?

—*Separation destroys,* insisted Aoloiloa and his networked kin.

I shouldn't do this alone? Is that what you mean? Is it my *separation that destroys?*

Jax put the question to the Force, to the living universe. The answer came in the form of a sense—so strong he almost cried aloud—that he was not alone in the confines of the *Aethersprite's* cockpit.

—*Seek,* said the Cephalons, *communion. Seek sisters.*

Communion? Sisters?

For one dreadful moment Jax was certain he was losing his mind. In one sense Laranth was a sister—a fellow Force-user. But Laranth was dead, returning to him only in dreams and memories. Still, he was frozen in his seat, afraid that if he opened his eyes, Laranth would be sitting beside him in the jump seat.

And equally afraid that she wouldn't be.

He unfroze when the ship's perimeter alarms went off. There was a small vessel entering the system. Only a slow-moving freighter, but it had an escort of Imperial TIE fighters and it would soon overfly his position.

Without pausing to think, Jax released the soft docking clamps and gave the ship just enough of a push from its ion drives to turn it away from the oncoming convoy. Then he dived in the opposite direction, out of the plane of the ecliptic, and wove his way through the asteroids. He engaged his hyperdrive once free of the field, only half noting what course he'd set.

He'd used the Force to make that last course setting and hoped he was right and that, on some level, he'd understood what the Cephalons had been trying to say.

What did that mean: *Seek sisters?*

Whose sisters? The Cephalons'? The only known species that could be considered "sisters" of the Cephalons were the Celegians. They were a rather isolated species and there were few among them who had engaged in training their Force abilities, notwithstanding their natural use of telepathy and telekinesis. They seemed, though not genetically related, at least endophenotypically connected.

Sisters in the resistance? Aren Folee or Sacha Swiftbird fit the bill, as did Sheel Mafeen. That made logical sense. It made so much sense, he leaned forward to check the coordinates he'd set, expecting the navigational array would tell him he'd be on a heading back to Toprawa.

His hand was hovering over the nav panel when a third possibility occurred to him: that by "sisters" was meant other Force-users. He could think of only one such group that could be considered "sisters" of the Jedi and the Gray Paladins: the Witches of Dathomir.

He shook himself. That was a ridiculous thought. Dathomir was not a safe place for Jedi. Especially male Jedi. Though there were exceptions, most of the Dathomiri clans were extremely matrilineal and matriarchal. In many, if not most, men had been reduced to virtual slavery. And though the Witches were strong in the Force, they were understandably hostile to outsiders.

Still, they were allied with the light side of the Force, and their mantra—handed down from their alleged ancestress, the banished Jedi Knight Allya—was "Never concede to evil."

Jax's sense of irony was still operant enough to permit a wry shake of his head at a species that didn't include the concept of slavery in its definition of evil.

There had been two unabashedly evil orders among them, though. These were the Nightsisters and Nightbrothers— many of them human–Zabrak hybrids, and all outcasts from existing tribes. In the years leading up to the Clone Wars, they had allied themselves with the Sith, but not before they had used the serendipitous discovery of the interstellar portal called the Infinity Gate in an effort to destroy Coruscant, which was then the seat of the Republic.

The Jedi had brought them down and destroyed the Star Temple that contained the Gate on Dathomir. Since that time—thirteen years earlier—Dathomir had been all but quarantined. Not fair to the majority of clans, but they were hardly friendly to begin with, and they had neither strategic position nor natural resources that the Empire might envy, nor technology that it might fear.

Jax closed his fingers. The Witches were strong in the Force; that they chanted spells to employ it hardly mattered. They were Force-users—but Force-users who lived and worked beyond the more regimented existence of the Jedi Order, even as Laranth and the Gray Paladins had.

Sisters, indeed. What knowledge might they possess that another fringe dweller might find of use?

Jax made the decision emotionally before his reason capitulated. He dropped out of hyperspace at the edge of Bothan space and put his hands to the navigational controls again, this time to set a course for Dathomir. He was both exhilarated and chilled when he realized that was the course he had already laid in.

thirty-three

Probus Tesla orbited his Cerean captive as a planet orbited its star. He had begun his pacing around the Whiplash leader in a moment of frustration with the other's impassivity. But when he sensed that the constant movement was actually having an impact on Yimmon, he kept it up.

He had lost track of how many times he'd circled the still figure—probing with tiny trickles of Force sense—when he decided to make a more assertive move. The trickle became a stream and he pressed, seeking a chink in Yimmon's psychic wall. To his surprise, the Cerean flinched away mentally, withdrawing from his approach.

Tesla curbed his excitement and increased the pressure.

"What's wrong?" he asked aloud. "Why are you suddenly shy? Is it something I've said? Something I've done?"

He was tempted to tell Yimmon what he'd learned from his last communication with his Master—that Whiplash was dead, broken. He stopped himself. Hadn't his Master told him to do no more than watch?

He flooded the connection between himself and the Cerean, seeking an inlet. But the other was barricaded behind a seawall of calm.

Tesla's lip curled. Yimmon wasn't a Force adept, and his pitiful mental defenses were lumpish, inert, rocklike. Water eroded rock, Tesla mused; entered its chinks, built up pressure, and blew it apart. The Inquisitor called such images to mind and brought the Force to bear. His physical and mental eddying must have somehow disconcerted the stolid rebel. Perhaps he had only to keep up his assault.

Yimmon's defensive barrier seemed to yield and contract . . . and then it held.

Tesla sought a way to breach it. He settled on a means that was not quite in violation of his Master's instructions.

"What if I were to tell you that there has been a coup on Coruscant?" He let the question hang and was rewarded with a sudden spark of interest from Yimmon, as if he had poked his head above his barricade.

"What if I were to tell you that there had been an attempt on the life of the Emperor. Perhaps you already knew this?"

No response, but the other's pulse quickened; his breathing shallowed.

"And what if I were to tell you that the perpetrators of this attempt were crushed utterly and their entire organization shattered?"

Ah, yes. Now, *that* was a reaction. He could sense how much Yimmon wanted to open his eyes, to see Tesla's face, though he would be unable to read anything in it.

"Has such a thing happened, you're wondering? Let's assume that it has. And that resistance operations on other worlds are next. And that they will fall, one after the other. Would you warn them if you could? Ah, but of course you can't. You have no way to reach them."

Having put that suggestion in place—having invited Thi Xon Yimmon to think about his resistance colleagues on their various worlds—Tesla monitored the comparatively nervous activity behind the Cerean's calm façade for a moment more, then pressed ever so gently at it. Then he withdrew . . . apparently. At least it should feel to Yimmon as if he had withdrawn.

Suiting physical action to mental suggestion, he turned as if to leave the room—and was flayed by a flash flood of Force energy. It pattered against him like static rain. Electrifying. Shocking.

As swiftly as it had come, it was gone, leaving Tesla feeling winded and chilled. He hesitated, and felt an instantaneous tickle of interest from the man seated cross-legged on the floor behind him. He forced himself to keep walking, his feverish thoughts held tightly to him. Was it possible that this Cerean was a secret adept? He thought again of the course of action he meant to put to Darth Vader on his return to Kantaros Station—the physical separation of Yimmon's dual cortices. If Yimmon was a Force-sensitive, what effect might that have?

Tesla hurried out of Yimmon's cell, curiosity curling deliciously. He was eager for his Master's return so that, together, they might dissect Thi Xon Yimmon's psyche and expose its secrets.

thirty-four

In low orbit above Dathomir, Jax carefully considered where to land. The planet was still largely uninhabited, and the existing populations were confined to the broad coastal region of one of three continents. There were a number of clans of so-called Witches tucked into the landscape. New ones formed occasionally, too, peopled by outcasts, ex-slaves, or renegades.

The Nightsisters had been such a renegade group, and there were at least two clans rumored to be made up of men and women who had rejected the matriarchal hierarchy of the female-dominated clans and who aimed to create a more egalitarian society. They might be more kindly disposed to a visit from an outsider than their more isolationist kindred, but he doubted either of these clans could provide him with what he wanted—access to the ruins of the Star Temple.

No, he would have to brave arousing the ire of the Singing Mountain Clan—the tribal group that claimed the territory above the devastated high plain where the temple had once sat.

Any doubts he might have had about his choice of destination were dispelled as he flew over the vast ruin that dominated the Infinity Plain. Tucked into a deep pocket in the skirt of his surcoat, the Sith holocron resonated with the decaying energies of the place. It wasn't much, but it was enough to alert Jax to the fact that the crumbling field of slag and rocky debris still held residual power.

The Singing Mountain Clan capital lay in the lap of a major peak in the range that gave the clan its name. The walled township's avenues wandered the lower slopes of the mountain, hemmed in by a sparse forest.

That the clan would be at full alert by the time he landed, Jax had no doubt. He brought the Delta-7 down on a flat table of rock that lay just beyond the township gates and stepped from the cockpit into the chill mountain air . . . and into the full sight of half a dozen warriors—all female and all, no doubt, deadly.

He didn't hesitate, but simply strode to the bottom of the narrow landing ramp, his hands in plain sight, palms out. He moved to within conversational distance of the women and surveyed them carefully.

Two were armed with static lances, each tipped with an energy bolt. Two carried cortosis staffs. The pair at the center of the group were unarmed . . . unless you counted the Force as a weapon. One was decidedly human; the other was a Dathomiri Zabrak and wore the facial tattoos that declared her adulthood. They ringed her eyes and the bases of her horns and connected the bridge of her nose, upper lip, and chin.

Though neither woman was dressed for battle, Jax had no doubt they were as well-trained in the art of defense as they were in the arcane nuances of Force manipulation.

Sending out gentle ribbons of sense, Jax learned only that these two women saw themselves as co-equal and in the service of another.

"Please," he said, quietly, "I seek an audience with your clan leader."

The women exchanged glances. The Zabrak tilted her tattooed chin toward the *Aethersprite*.

"You fly a Jedi craft. Yet you cannot be Jedi."

"I am."

A pause, then: "We have heard rumors of the destruction of the Jedi Order by the Empire."

"The rumors are exaggerated. I *am* a Jedi."

"We felt their dying echoes in the Force."

Jax ignored the twisting in his guts. "As did I."

He felt the touch of the others' Force sense as questing hands that brushed his temples, then swept across his forebrain. He shielded himself against the intrusion.

"You are a Force adept, at least," the human observed. "Only an adept could block so effectively. Show me your weapon."

He knew she wasn't asking to see the blaster he wore in plain sight on his belt. He held his right hand out and called his lightsaber to his open palm. It flew from beneath the thigh-length panels of his coat and landed solidly in his hand.

"Activate it," the Zabrak commanded.

He did. The blade surged into existence with a hum of raw power—bright, gleaming, and the color of sea foam under a full moon. All but the Zabrak took a step in retreat.

She nodded and exchanged a glance with her human counterpart.

"A Jedi weapon."

Jax breathed a sigh of relief and sent a silent message of gratitude to the Force that he and Laranth had had time to construct a new lightsaber for him before they'd left Coruscant. Otherwise, he'd have been facing these bitter enemies of the Emperor with a Sith blade in his hand. He doubted he'd have been able to talk himself out of that one. Fortunately, he'd left the Sith blade aboard the *Laranth*.

The Sith holocron he'd concealed aboard the starfighter might also pose a threat to his credibility, but he'd meet that challenge when he got to it.

"His weapon may signify nothing," the human Witch said. "He might have stolen both the ship and the weapon from a dead Jedi." She turned her gaze to Jax. "You will enter the citadel and allow yourself to be scanned . . . or you will leave."

Jax deactivated the lightsaber and inclined his head in acquiescence. "Whatever it takes."

She held her hand out for his weapon. "This is what it takes. Give me your lightsaber."

He handed it over to her without hesitation. It would return to him at will, so he had no concern on that count . . . unless she locked it away somewhere.

She took a step back and gestured for him to pass through their group. He bowed deferentially and moved toward the now-opening gates.

"What's your name, Jedi?" the Zabrak asked.

It would be futile to lie. "Jax Pavan."

"Why have you come?"

Why had he come? What did he hope to find? "That's what I need to discuss with your leader."

They escorted him into the citadel and swung the massive gates closed behind without the intervention of either being or machine. In the broad plaza just inside the enclosure, Jax felt the pinprick regard of many eyes. The buildings were no taller than three stories, but people—mostly women and girls—watched from every window and doorway. The streets, too, were filled with onlookers.

His guards took him straight across the plaza to a roundhouse that seemed to be an official greeting center. Its conical, two-story roof was supported by huge columns carved from native tree trunks and capped with metal-clad ornamentation. Each column was adorned with a medallion of worked metal that bore the sigil particular to a neighboring tribal or clan group.

Jax supposed it was auspicious that he hadn't been

immediately marched into a stockade from which he would then be forced to escape. He had no doubt that escape from here would not be easy.

He moved to the center of the roundhouse floor and turned to look back at his hosts. The two women who'd spoken—somehow the term *lieutenants* seemed to fit them—moved to stand one on each side, facing him. The other four took up positions around the circle.

The two closest to him raised their arms in a parody of an embrace, then the Zabrak uttered a series of tonal words he didn't understand. He was immediately assailed with the sense that someone had poured a bucket of warm water over his head so that it flowed down into his brain, trickled down his spine, and pooled in his gut. It was at once a soothing and nerve-racking sensation, and when it left him, he felt winded and invaded.

He had closed his eyes. Now he opened them to find both women regarding him with increased wariness.

"You say you are Jedi," the human said, "but there is darkness in you—a confusion of shadow and light."

Jax took a deep breath and spoke words he had not intended to say. "I lost a companion. My . . . my mate. A Force adept of great talent. Her death has disturbed the balance of the Force in me. I also lost the leader of my . . . clan, but not to death—to the Dark Lord. These are losses that must be . . ."

"Avenged?"

The voice floated down to him from the second-floor gallery that ran the entire circumference of the roundhouse.

He looked up, seeking the source. His eyes found a woman of perhaps fifty-five or sixty standard years watching from above. She was tall, regal, with hair the color of moonlight held back from her handsome face with a circlet of aurodium.

He turned to face her and bowed. "Not avenged, but redeemed."

She shook her head. "Redemption, Jedi, is a difficult thing to bring about."

"As you, yourself, know," he guessed. "You are Augwynne Djo, are you not?"

Her smile was a reflection of the deep sorrow that covered her sere, serene inner landscape like a thin coat of snow. Jax felt an immediate sense of concord with the woman; he sensed that she, too, had been a victim of betrayal and loss. The two Force-users stood, measuring each other, for a long moment—long enough to make the Zabrak warrior move restlessly. The movement drew her mistress's gaze.

"Bring him up to me," said Djo. She turned from the gallery rail and disappeared into the shadows.

Her two acolytes immediately flanked Jax and led him to a flight of stairs that connected the ground floor of the roundhouse with the gallery. At the top of the stairs, two hallways ran away at a forty-five-degree angle to each other. The roundhouse, Jax realized, was connected to the building or buildings behind it. His guards took the hallway to the right and they passed along it briskly, following the flickering shadow of their clan matriarch.

Their destination was a large chamber with walls of reddish stone and a central hearth whose fire burned bright and warm but consumed no fuel. Augwynne Djo was already seated on a wide, padded chair hewn from the same native stone as the slab and bricks that made up the walls and floor.

Jax's guardians ushered him into the room and placed him before her.

"Thank you, Magash, Duala." The clan matriarch nodded at each woman in turn. "You may leave us now."

The Zabrak, Magash, started. "But, Mother, he is a stranger. And a *man*."

Jax couldn't tell which bothered her more.

"He is a Jedi," said Augwynne Djo, as if that was all that need be said. She held out her hand to Magash. "His weapon, please."

With a glance at her companion, the Zabrak came to her mistress and handed over Jax's lightsaber. Then the two young women bowed and took themselves out of the room.

"Sit, Jedi," said the Witch, gesturing with one graceful, long-fingered hand, "and tell me why you have come to us."

Duala Aidu had returned immediately to the roundhouse to dismiss the guardian warriors there. In her colleague's absence, Magash Drashi found herself pacing the corridor outside the Clan Mother's rooms in deep distress. She had never known Mother Augwynne to be so receptive to visitors.

Yes, perhaps this visitor really *was* a Jedi, and yes, the Jedi were—at least in theory—aligned with the Dathomir Witches against the Sith and the darkness they brought. But he was . . . well, a *man*.

She would have to be Force-blind not to have felt the strange sense of familiarity that flashed between her matriarch and this outsider. It had something, she was sure, to do with his revelation about his lost mate.

Her native curiosity kicked in hard, then. What sort of partnership could exist between female and male Force-users? In her culture, men were subservient and inferior to women. They were gatherers of food, workers, breeding stock. Why, they could no more channel the Force than a rancor could study philosophy! But apparently males of other worlds *could* channel the Force. Jedi, Magash knew, were subservient to no one. Jedi males were apparently as free as their female counterparts to train in the Force, or even to teach its use.

She found herself wanting very much to be in close company with the Jedi Knight, to watch him, see him use the Force without casting spells—something she could hardly imagine—hear his thoughts on his place in the universe and his connection to the Force. She'd felt the Force in him, had seen him summon his Jedi weapon and activate it.

Could he do more? She hungered to know.

A part of her scoffed at her own naïve interest in an outsider. What sort of thoughts could a man have about anything, after all? They thought about eating, sleeping, breeding, working, and spending their few leisure hours playing games with abstruse rules that resulted in the winners mocking the losers. This was her first exposure to a male from another world—another culture. Could they really be that alien?

Well, replied an argumentative voice, *doesn't this Jedi's behavior demonstrate how different he is from any Dathomiri clansman? The very fact that he flies such a complex spacecraft—*

Her thoughts were arrested by the thought of the Jedi starfighter sitting on the apron of rock beyond the gates. With a swift glance at the doors of Augwynne Djo's chambers, Magash Drashi hurried away to get a closer look at the stranger's vessel.

thirty-five

Den Dhur stared at the patchwork droid as if he'd begun speaking Huttese. "What did you say?"

"I said, Jax is gone. Which somehow doesn't surprise me as much as it should."

Den glanced from I-Five to Sacha Swiftbird, who stood behind the droid in the doorway of Geri's workshop. "What does he mean—Jax is gone?"

The woman grimaced and crossed her arms over her chest. "He fired up the *Aethersprite* and took off in the middle of the night. A couple of night-duty mech-techs saw him, but—" She shook her head.

The cold flush of dread that coursed through Den's body sat him down hard on his stool. "And no one thought to stop him?"

Swiftbird shrugged. "He's Jax Pavan. That makes him a bit of a hero around here. You don't stop a hero who's off to do heroic things."

"I thought no one was supposed to know who he was—outside of the leadership here."

She rolled her eyes. "Oh, come on. In a tight-knit community like this? Give us a break. Secret intel is the daily bread around here. I'd reckon that within a day of your first landing, everyone knew there was a Jedi among us. They just didn't talk about it."

Den shook his head, looking to I-Five for something

to stop his world from wobbling. "So he grabbed the starfighter and took off—to where?"

"I've no idea," said the droid. "He didn't bother to file an itinerary with Mountain Home flight control. Remiss of him."

"Don't be flip," Den retorted. "You always get flip when you're angry."

"I'm a droid. Droids don't get angry."

"Oh, don't fall back on that stupid dodge, Tinhead. You're mad and you karking well know it."

I-Five's optics flashed brighter and he uttered a disgruntled noise, preparatory to issuing a further comment, but Sacha cut him off.

"You two are like an old married couple. This is a waste of time, aye? Pavan has gone missing and we're down a fighting vessel. Thi Xon Yimmon's situation hasn't changed, guys. He's still at the mercy of the Dark Lord and his slimy little toadies. We need to regroup and figure out what can be done to salvage the situation. Any *constructive* ideas?"

Both Sullustan and droid turned startled gazes on the ex-Podracer.

A stifled grunt of laughter reminded Den that he hadn't been alone in the workshop when I-Five and Sacha had burst in. He and Geri had both brought their breakfasts down here to eat and had been noodling with ideas to customize I-5YQ's Nemesis parts. Now the little mech-tech was watching their byplay with undisguised mirth.

"Sorry," he said, looking as contrite as his Rodian features would allow. "It was just . . . y'know . . . funny."

"Hence the laughter," said I-Five. "But Sacha is correct. We have no idea what Jax is doing, or where he's bound. We can only try to deal with the situation as best we can."

"How?" Den demanded on a rising tide of frustration. "As you said, we have no idea where Jax is going."

I-Five came fully into the chamber. "Either Jax has returned to Kantaros Station or he has not. If he has, he'll need our assistance. If he has not, then Yimmon still needs to be rescued."

Sacha Swiftbird sauntered into the room on the droid's heels and slid onto the stool next to Geri to pick at the leftovers of his breakfast. The Rodian youth offered no protest.

"Great," she said. "So, it sounds as if you're thinking we should go back to Kantaros Station and rescue Yimmon ourselves."

"We?" I-Five asked.

"You need a pilot, right? I'm a pilot. One of the best, as it happens. I'm also a fantastic engineer."

"Oh, but you'll need a mech-tech, too, won't you?" Geri asked. "I mean, you can't engineer while you're piloting, right?"

"No," the others said in perfect unison.

"Sorry, kiddo," Sacha said. "This is a dangerous mission."

"C'mon, Sacha!"

"Aren and Degan would never give you permission. You thinking of disobeying your superiors, cadet?"

Geri screwed up his face. "I guess not."

Sacha turned back to Den and I-Five. "But Degan's already offered me to you once. You need redundancy in engineering and at the helm. Which means I'm going with you. Like it or not."

"Who said we didn't like it?" Den asked. "Did we say that?"

"Great," Swiftbird said, polishing off the last of Geri's breakfast. "So what's the plan?" She gave I-Five her entire attention.

"I'm surprised you don't have that covered already."

"Curmudgeon," she called the droid. "I figure we're going back to Kantaros Station. And since we know that Black Sun ships are welcome there, we'll go in as a Black Sun ship. How'm I doing?"

"Quite well," I-Five admitted. "Now that we're clear on the mission, I suggest we depart as soon as possible. As much as I'd like to hang around here and continue my refit, we can't afford the time. Can you clear a departure with your leadership?"

"I can do better than that. I can get us an escort and backup."

"They'll only be able to escort us so far. Trust me, the area around the station is well patrolled."

"They'll be like shadows. Vader's forces will never know they're there—unless we want them to."

Den felt as if he'd been left completely in the dust. "Back up! What do you mean we're clear on the mission? I'm not clear on anything. What exactly is it we're proposing to do?"

If I-Five had had an eyebrow to raise, he'd have raised it, Den was certain. "Exactly what Sacha suggested. We're going to pose as a Black Sun freighter and dock at the station just as if we had every right to be there."

Den shook his head. "And what's going to convince them they shouldn't just blow us out of the sky? Any incoming Black Sun ships have to send ident codes to the station in order to gain admittance. We don't have Black Sun ident codes."

"Actually, we do," the droid said, sounding about as smug as it was possible for a droid to sound. "While we were sitting on the landing pad in Keldabe with Prince Xizor's little fleet, I took the liberty of slicing a few ident codes. As far as the Kantaros command and control is concerned, we'll be the *Raptor* out of Mandalore."

Den nodded, grateful, at last, for an explanation that made sense. "I see. That way, once we invade the station and rescue Yimmon, we can get away before they—" He blinked his owlish eyes. "Wait—*what*?"

thirty-six

The Jedi starfighter was beautiful, Magash admitted. Even her faded and scored finish did not detract from the sleek lines and arrowlike profile.

The Zabrak Witch was not the only member of her community who found the vessel intriguing; there were several sisters—even a handful of children—observing the Jedi vessel from a safe distance.

Magash felt a niggle of irritation. By the Mountain, they were *afraid* of it! Well, she would not be. She marched up to the ship and stood in the shadow of one backswept wing, wishing that the visitor had left his landing ramp down. She would not have hesitated for a moment, she told herself, to walk up it and peer into the cowled cockpit.

She considered a Force jump up onto the foredeck but backed away from such a bold move. Male he might be—stranger he might be—but he was a guest of the Matriarch. Such an act would be a breach of courtesy. So instead, she merely raised a hand and caressed the forward surface of the wing where it melted into the fuselage.

A tingle of something like dread coursed up her arm. She pulled her hand back with a sharp intake of breath.

What was that?

She glanced quickly over her shoulder at the timid ones who stood watching her. Had they felt her involuntary withdrawal? Did they read it as fear?

Clenching her teeth, Magash reached up and laid her fingertips against the shiny metal. The whisper of dark energy returned, making her suck in another breath. She murmured the words and melody of a calming spell—

"I call on thee, O Unformed.

"Let no harm befall me in times of trial.

"In moments of danger, guide my steps.

"Inspire me. Purpose me."

She kept her hand in contact with the ship's hull until she thought her every nerve would scream out with the urge to shut out that whisper of dark power. Then she withdrew it casually, as if her jaws did not hurt from the clenching of her teeth—as if she did not want to snarl with unnamable distress.

She stepped away from the ship, turned, and strode back into the citadel, taking care that no one could see her compulsively wiping her hand on the front of her tunic. She had gone past curiosity. Now she wanted desperately to know what haunted the Jedi's vessel.

Jax Pavan seated himself upon the divan Clan Mother Djo indicated and considered how to answer her question: why had he come to them?

I don't want to put a name to what brought me here, he thought, but that was not an answer she would accept . . . nor would he, ultimately, because he knew it was a dodge.

"I was led here, mistress. In part, by my mate, Laranth—a Gray Paladin."

Augwynne Djo's gaze was serene, but Jax felt a sudden sharpening of her focus on him. "You mentioned her before. Her death. Yet you say she led you?"

"I had a vision of her—no, less than a vision, an impression—while I was in contact with my Cephalon allies. Their message was: *Seek sisters.* Other than Laranth, herself, only the Witches of Dathomir might be called 'sisters' of the Jedi."

Djo's regard intensified. "You were in contact with Cephalons? We have heard of these beings. It is said they live outside of time."

"I don't know if they live *outside* it, but they certainly have a different perspective on it."

Jax leaned toward the Clan Mother, willing her to an openness he knew must be difficult for her, given her circumstances. The Witches of Dathomir were essentially a community in exile on their own world.

"Clan Mother Djo, while I was still immersed in this contact, I was forced to lay in a course rather hastily. I didn't think about what course to set, I simply did it. When I dropped out of hyperspace, I realized that I'd set a course for Dathomir."

Djo's eyebrows rose toward her coronet. "*Seek sisters*," she quoted softly. "Yes, I see. But what do you expect to find here?"

"I'm not sure. I only know what I need."

"And that is?"

"A tool. A weapon. A strategy to use against the Dark Lord. I also mentioned that I lost my own leader to him. I can't bring Laranth Tarak back from the dead, but I *must* free Thi Xon Yimmon."

Augwynne Djo nodded. "And you believe you will find that . . . weapon . . . here?"

"Yes. And I think it may have something to do with the ruins out on the plain."

The Clan Mother stood and paced away from him, but he had seen the fleeting distress in her expression, and he felt it as ripples in the fabric of the Force that stretched tightly between them.

"The ruins of the Star Temple? We avoid them. Assiduously. You believe what you would find is there?"

"There's some residual energy, possibly from the Infinity Gate. Some . . . eddies in the Force . . . possibly in time, itself. I . . . I feel the need to understand them." He didn't mention the Sith holocron or its reaction to the ruins of the Gate.

"Then you intend to go there—to visit the ruins?"

"If you will permit it, Clan Mother."

She turned back to look at him, a tiny spark of humor in her pale eyes. "And if I were to say no? If I were to deny you access to the ruins?"

He stood. "Then I'll go away. I'll find another way to . . . to discover whatever it is I need to discover."

"No other clan can grant you access to that place. We are its guardians."

"I know."

She considered the proposition silently, never taking her gaze from his face, never breaking the Force connection she had established with him since he had been ushered into the roundhouse.

"You may visit the ruin, Jax Pavan, but you must have one of the Sisterhood with you."

He inclined his head. "Thank you, Clan Mother."

Augwynne Djo turned toward the doors of her chamber. Jax saw the filaments of Force fly from her—bright fibers of energy, issuing a summons. Then she returned to her seat. She'd no more than resettled herself when her chamber door opened to admit her human lieutenant— the one she had called Duala.

"You summoned me, Mother?" the woman asked.

"I have granted our guest permission to visit the ruins." She tilted her snowy head toward the plain that lay beyond the city walls to the northwest.

The younger Witch threw Jax a startled glance, but all she said was, "Yes, Mother Augwynne."

"I wish him to have a companion from among the Sisterhood. The ruins are . . . a dangerous place."

"It will be difficult," Duala said, "to find someone willing to go with him."

"I will go."

Jax, Augwynne, and Duala all turned at the sound of the voice. Djo's Zabrak lieutenant stood in the doorway, her gaze on Jax. The intensity of that gaze caused the Jedi to raise a cautious shield.

"Are you certain, Magash?" asked her mistress.

"I am curious about the ways of the Jedi," the Zabrak said. "I would like to understand them better, that perhaps I might learn something of value to the clan."

"A noble sentiment," Djo said approvingly, then addressed Jax. "It is past midday. When the sun sets, the temperature will fall and the ruins will become more dangerous, even to those immersed in the Force. Will you go there now, or wait until morning?"

"Time, Clan Mother, is not something I have to waste," he said. "I would go now, if that is acceptable."

Augwynne Djo nodded her permission. Then she held out her hand, Jax's lightsaber balanced across it.

He raised his own hand and called the weapon to him. It settled against his palm with a comforting weight. He secured it to his belt.

"I'm sure I don't have to tell you to be careful," said Djo.

Jax smiled. "No, Clan Mother. You don't." He bowed to her and started for the door and his unsmiling guardian.

"Jax Pavan."

He turned back at the sound of the Matriarch's voice.

"If you should find something in that ruin that might be of benefit to us . . ."

"Rest assured, Mother Djo, that I will share anything I learn that can serve the Sisterhood."

Jax went first back to the starfighter to retrieve the holocron. He had no idea how he would explain it to Magash and her sisters, and wondered if he might somehow conceal its presence.

The *Aethersprite* extended her ramp to him at a

thought and he went up into the cockpit. He secreted the Sith holocron in the deep pocket of his surcoat, calling on his memory of the miisai tree to help him create a Force veil to dampen the artifact's signature. Then he rejoined Magash Drashi on the rocky plateau.

She gave him a strange look as he reached the bottom of the landing ramp and triggered its retraction. He was mystified when she stepped briskly forward and touched her fingertips to the vessel's wing.

She pulled her hand back and turned on him. "It's gone. What have you done with it?"

"What's gone?"

"The Dread Thing," she said, and he felt a prickling sense of what she meant.

He bit the inside of his lip. The Witch was incredibly sensitive to the texture of Force energy.

"I'm not sure what you mean—the Dread Thing?"

She made an impatient gesture. "It was aboard your vessel—or it was part of your vessel. A dark flutter, like the tread of a predator you cannot see. It was there. Now it's not."

Jax glanced about. They were the focus of attention from a number of women who had come out to watch them.

"Not here," he told his guardian. "I'll explain later. Now, what's the best way to get down to the ruins? Do we have to walk?"

"Yes. That is, unless you wish to try riding a rancor beast. They suffer the sisters to ride them. To my knowledge no *man* has ever tried . . . successfully." She smiled, showing sharp, white teeth.

Jax's answering smile was wry. "We'll walk. Which way?"

thirty-seven

"You don't mind using Jax's quarters?" Den stood uneasily in the hatchway of the Jedi's cabin, watching Sacha Swiftbird examine it.

"I don't if he doesn't. And he's not here to ask—so, no. I don't mind."

She moved to the miisai tree and brushed her fingertips over the delicate branches. "This was his?"

"Yeah. Uh. She gave it to him . . . Laranth did. He used it—uses it—to meditate."

"Looks like it's had a rough time." She fingered a broken branch, then patted some loose moss into place around the base of the little trunk.

"Yeah, it . . . met with an accident."

Den was going to ask if he should take it off her hands when she reached into the front flap of her pack, pulled out a packet of energy nuggets, and proceeded to crumble one into the planter's feeding receptacle. Okay, so she was the nurturing type.

"Well, I'll leave you to it," Den said. "Come up to the bridge when you're settled in."

"Sure thing."

Settling in took Sacha longer than Den expected, and I-Five was inexplicably absent, as well. Sitting alone on the bridge, Den had begun to wonder if he was the only one who felt any sort of time pressure when he heard the landing ramp retract.

Well, finally.

A minute or two later, I-Five slipped onto the bridge in his pit droid persona.

"Where the heck have you been, Ducky?" Den asked. "I thought we were in a hurry."

"We are, but I had to consult Geri about some . . . further modifications."

"Modifications to you, you mean?"

"Yes. Are we ready for liftoff?"

"As soon as our new engineer shows up."

As if on cue, Sacha appeared in the hatchway. "Sorry," she murmured. "Just settling in."

"Ah," said I-Five. "There you are. Would you like to put the *Laranth* through her paces?"

"Love to."

Den vacated the copilot's station and watched her slide in behind the control panel. She seemed . . . troubled. Or at least introspective.

"I think the wisest course of action is to put in at Keldabe to pick up some actual cargo and to establish our point of origin as Mandalore," the droid continued as the Ranger checked over the controls. "That way, if the folks at Kantaros Station check our back trail . . ."

Sacha was nodding. ". . . it reinforces our disguise as a Black Sun carrier," she finished for him. She took the yoke and checked their heading. "We should be at a good jump point one-point-two-five hours out."

"That's what I make it, too," I-Five said.

Den, sitting behind Sacha and to her left, found himself watching her. She seemed edgy . . . or ill at ease. Her hands were working the steering yoke—fingers flexing, tapping, rubbing. Her jaw seemed tight.

Den had opened his mouth to ask if anything was wrong when she said, "Um. I . . . ah . . . I found something kind of . . . unusual . . . in Jax's cabin. Not quite sure what to make of it."

"Unusual?" I-Five repeated.

"What?" Den asked, his mouth suddenly dry. The last thing he wanted was to have their new colleague tell him something scary about Jax to add to all the other scary things about Jax he'd come to know.

"There's a hidden drawer in the casing of the planter that little tree is in—which I found while I was making sure the water-to-food ratio was set right," she added when Five swiveled his head to look at her. "Anyway, there's a lightsaber in it." She hesitated. "A Sith lightsaber."

There was a profound silence while she waited for their reaction. Den broke it by bursting into laughter.

Sacha gave him a strange look. "That's funny?"

"No. Not funny." Den swallowed the inappropriate mirth. "Just a relief."

"A relief that our Jedi friend has a Sith weapon hidden in his quarters."

"Listen, Sacha, with all that's been going on with Jax, I was afraid you were going to tell me—I don't know what—but something I couldn't cope with."

Her look became more perplexed. "Hello? Sith? Dark side? Not Our Friends? The Enemy, in fact."

Five interjected: "Jax received the lightsaber from an anonymous source prior to confronting the assassin Aurra Sing. You may have heard of her."

Swiftbird nodded. "Piece of radically deadly work. Yeah."

"Jax theorized that the blade might actually have belonged to Sing. When he faced her, *she* was carrying a Jedi weapon."

"You mean they . . . swapped somehow?"

"Jax's lightsaber had been destroyed. He used the Sith weapon until he and Laranth were able to build a new one."

"But he kept the Sith weapon, anyway?" The idea seemed to disturb her.

"The plan," Den said, "was to locate a new crystal for the hilt and remake the weapon for some future Padawan. It just never happened."

Sacha Swiftbird nodded slowly, processing the information. "Okay. Thanks for explaining that. I was a little leery of my new quarters. . . . I'm not likely to find any other surprises in there, am I?"

"Hopefully not," I-Five said.

"But you never know," Den murmured.

In some parts of Coruscant, night was brighter than day. With the artfully refracted and reflected sunlight gone, artifice took over completely and turned the streets to gold, to copper, to silver, to rubies and emeralds, to rainbows. False day reigned in all its varied splendor.

But here, in the abandoned recesses of the antique maglev system, night was night. Black on black.

Pol Haus knew that there were things surviving down here that never saw any sort of daylight—false or otherwise. Things that fled light and sound, scent and vibration . . . unless they were hungry.

It was just such a place he had chosen to hide the Whiplash train. He had let go all but the first three cars—sacrificing the tail to save the body and mind—and had brought those to the lowest level still accessible from the tube where Sal had originally left them. He chose a length of track that only seemed to be cut off from egress but actually had a well-hidden "back door." He had also rigged the computer core with a number of destructive software and hardware devices; if discovered, and cut off from that back door, he could irretrievably vaporize every jot and tittle of information in the system.

He hoped it wouldn't come to that, but he had no way

of knowing for certain if his Bothan lieutenant had been alone in his activities. Instinct said yes. Droosh's motivation had, ultimately, been greed. Greedy people tended not to want to share their potential sources of wealth and/or power with others.

But again, one never knew.

So, as he and Sheel Mafeen made their way into the bowels of the old maglev system, hundreds of feet below the original tunnels Whiplash had used, he rehearsed in his mind what an escape might look like if they had to flee before they'd extracted all the information from the system.

Haus pulled his two-person speeder into the lee of the rearmost car and got out, blaster in hand.

Sheel slid out behind him. That she was nervous was obvious in the way her voice trembled when she asked if the train seemed as he'd left it.

"Yes. And since I took the precaution of setting up a sensor perimeter, I can guarantee that no one has been here." He deactivated the sensors as he spoke and approached the hatch that gave onto the rearmost car—the one that held Tuden Sal's quarters.

They boarded, and he reset the external sensor field, which was implemented by a set of small discs magnetically clamped to the sides of the train cars. Cheap as dirt to acquire, easy to install, and quite effective.

Once inside, they each had a predefined task. Haus went to the main computer console to begin downloading data to several HoloNet nodes at various locations elsewhere in the city. Sheel, meanwhile, tackled the standalone unit in Sal's personal quarters. She had a handheld retrieval device for that; they'd theorized that Sal's personal data would be only a fraction of what was in the main node.

They'd been at their jobs for perhaps half an hour—

Haus was switching to his tertiary backup node—when Sheel uttered a cry of surprise or distress.

Haus was out of the main car and standing at the door to Sal's quarters before he'd half realized he'd moved. The room still smelled like death, or perhaps that was only his fertile imagination.

"Sheel, what is it?"

She turned to look up at him from Sal's private console with an expression of such anguish on her face that he felt a primal need to touch her, to reassure her. He reached her side in two strides and laid a hand on her shoulder.

"What's wrong?"

In answer, she held her retrieval unit out to him, tilting the screen so he could read it.

"I prioritized the download," she said, "and had it sequester anything that mentioned Jax, Laranth, Darth Vader, or the Emperor. This entry is from Sal's private correspondence."

Frowning, Haus took the handheld and peered at it. There was no holographic data—it was text only. The sent message read: *Urgent. Att'n Lord Vader. Some reason to suspect movement of Pavan and "persons of interest" through Myto's Arrow.* This was followed by a range of dates that included the time period Jax and his companions had been moving Thi Xon Yimmon . . .

"Through Myto's Arrow . . ." Haus murmured. He shook his head. "I don't get it. What . . ."

"He sent this," Sheel said urgently. Her eyes were sparkling with unshed tears. "*Sal* sent this. To the Imperial Security Bureau—to Lord Vader. It was encrypted. One of maybe a dozen encrypted messages, and the only one that mentioned both Jax and Vader—which was why I sampled it. Sal sold them out, Pol. He sold *us* out."

With a world-shuddering impact, the information hit home. "Why?"

"I don't know. I don't think it was for reward. He did this anonymously—encrypted the message, sent it via shadow link so it went through a host of nodes before getting to the target. It's text only—clearly he didn't want to be recognized . . . and he gives only minimal location and timing data, when he knew exactly what *Far Ranger*'s itinerary was."

Haus leaned heavily against the bulkhead and stared at her. "He could have sent the Imperials to Toprawa on the exact day of Yimmon's arrival there."

"But he didn't."

"Again, why?"

Sheel sat down on the edge of Sal's bunk, her feet inches from the stain left by the dying Sakiyan's blood. "Maybe he didn't intend them to be caught, but only . . . I don't know . . . scared off, perhaps?"

Haus nodded. "His plot against the Emperor. He knew Yimmon and Jax would never have allowed it to go forward. If they were running from Vader—hiding out away from any resistance cells—he could do whatever he wanted and they'd be none the wiser until it was too late." He tried, unsuccessfully, to loosen his jaw. "He could do exactly what he did do."

"Except that with Yimmon captured . . ."

Haus closed his eyes, understanding at last why Sal had been so committed to assassinating Palpatine. "He couldn't abort his plans, no matter what happened. The only way to keep Yimmon's capture from shattering the resistance would be to kill Palpatine and destabilize the Empire."

Sheel got to her feet. "We need to finish this up and get out of here, Pol. We need to go over all of this as carefully as we can. And we need to try to reconnect with our allies. We can't let this kill the resistance on Coruscant. Whiplash can't have died in vain."

He gazed at her, admiring her courage—her sheer stubbornness. He liked stubbornness.

"Died?" he repeated. "I'm not ready to hold the funeral just yet."

Probus Tesla had made an impression on his prisoner, that much was clear. The Cerean's thoughts, while hidden behind his still-impressive calm, were more emotional, more unsettled. Tesla sensed trepidation, sorrow, hope, regret.

Now, what to do about it?

Lord Vader had given explicit instructions to him not to interact too directly with the Whiplash leader, but only to observe. Tesla believed he could truthfully say that he had done just that—though perhaps he had given himself something to observe by making veiled suggestions to the rebel that his colleagues were in distress.

Which was only the truth.

It made sense for him to proceed, next, to offering simple reminders of what had already been lost. With that in mind, literally, Tesla visited the holding cell in which Yimmon was imprisoned, and at an unusual time—while the other man was eating his meager meal. Surprise, Tesla knew, was an effective tool in the interrogation process.

Even as he entered the room, Tesla felt the rewards of his effort. The Cerean was startled, momentarily off center. He had not expected this visit at a time he was usually left alone and so soon on the heels of their last encounter. He hastily raised a mental barrier, but Tesla had felt of his inner turmoil. He was thinking of his possibly dead allies back on Coruscant.

Perfect.

Tesla came and sat cross-legged before his prisoner, facing him.

"You have suffered much loss" was his opening gambit.

Yimmon glanced up at him only momentarily, then returned his attention to his meal. He ate slowly, in tiny, careful bites.

"You realize you will suffer more."

No response.

"Laranth Tarak, Den Dhur, Jax Pavan—all dead."

A brief flicker of the Cerean's eyes and emotions caught the Inquisitor's attention. Tesla pressed on: "You are utterly alone."

Thi Xon Yimmon raised his gaze to Tesla's face, his eyes sharp, clear, disconcerting. "Am I?"

Tesla was puzzled by the tickle of emotion he sensed from the Cerean. It was all wrong. Yes, there was sorrow, but not a bottomless pit of despair. Yimmon had . . . hope.

Hope of what? Hope from what source? Tesla almost asked the questions aloud.

The Cerean pulled his gaze away, and Tesla knew.

"You believe Jax Pavan is still alive? You think he's going to rescue you? I tell you, he's dead."

Yimmon shrugged. He actually *shrugged.* As if they were debating a meaningless difference of opinion.

"Why do you persist in this vain hope, Yimmon? You were there. You saw the condition the vessel was in. You saw the explosion when it was finally sucked into the nexus between the two stars. All life aboard that vessel was obliterated. Utterly destroyed."

Again, the artless shrug. "Believe what you will. I will believe what I will."

Tesla trickled more of his Force energies into the gaps in Yimmon's consciousness. He felt something far stronger than mere hope. Certitude. It was absurd. Infuriating. Mad . . . yet there it was.

Tesla sat back in sudden disappointment. Is that how

Yimmon proposed to escape Vader's efforts—by diving headfirst into insanity?

The Cerean met his eyes again, calm, serene, certain . . . implacable. His faith in the Jedi and in the Force was complete. Tesla perceived flashes of it from Yimmon's perspective: how the young Jedi Jax Pavan had outwitted the Inquisitorius and disrupted Darth Vader's plans repeatedly . . . how he had snatched Kajin Savaros from under Tesla's nose . . . how—at their last encounter—Tesla had been forced to flee.

The Inquisitor did not try to hide his disgust. He stood slowly, until he towered over the seated prisoner. Then he deliberately pulled back his cowl, revealing his expressionless face and shaved head.

Here is the face of your enemy, Cerean.

"How sad," he said aloud. "Lord Vader will be disappointed that you've crumbled so much mentally as to harbor these . . . vapid fantasies. But I suppose that will make it easier for him to prise the information he needs from your mind."

He felt Yimmon's barriers fly back into place, and smiled inwardly. Too late. Tesla not only knew Thi Xon Yimmon's emotional weakness, he also saw how it could be exploited.

He replaced his cowl and left the chamber, wondering if he should contact Lord Vader and announce his breakthrough. His dilemma was solved when he received a communication from his Master: having dealt the rebels on Imperial Center a mortal wound, the Dark Lord was returning to Kantaros Station.

Tesla decided he would wait to share his insights. For now, he had to calculate how best to use what he had discovered about the prisoner's mental condition.

Sequestered in his quarters, he sat in meditation on the subject of Jax Pavan. It was more difficult than he'd expected—every time he tried to ruminate on how he could use Yimmon's mad faith to advantage, he was forced to face his own deep hatred for the Jedi, forced to remember the stinging humiliation of their last encounter.

It was a shame Jax Pavan was already dead, because Tesla would have liked very much to be the one to kill him.

thirty-eight

"Your mate . . . she was a Jedi, too?"

Magash watched the Jedi out of the corner of her eye, catching the sudden, delicate tightening of the muscles in his face and the flutter of the Force energies around him.

"She was a Gray Paladin. A Force adept but, like you, not trained by the Jedi Order. She . . . lived by the same principles as Jedi, but the Paladins were less . . . rigid in their approach to certain things."

It did not escape Magash that the Jedi picked his way through those words as carefully as they now picked their way across the treacherous defile that led down to the Infinity Plain.

"What sort of things?" she asked.

"Oh . . . weaponry, for example. The Jedi have used lightsabers as their primary weapon for so long, it's become part of who we are. The weapon attuned to the warrior, I guess you could say. The Gray Paladins believe that a Force adept should be independent of any specific . . ." He paused, smiled wanly. ". . . prop," he finished, and gave her a sidewise glance. "The Gray Paladin might choose a primary weapon and attune her fighting philosophy to that."

Magash nodded. "The warrior attuned to the weapon."

"Yes, but for a Jedi, learning the forms of lightsaber

combat is considered key to harnessing and channeling the Force."

"It is part of your discipline, then. As incantations are part of ours."

The Jedi nodded.

"So, these Gray Paladins are undisciplined warriors? That seems unwise."

He shook his head. "No. I didn't mean to give that impression, Magash, believe me. Laranth . . ." He paused again, swallowed. "Laranth was very disciplined. In some ways, more disciplined than I am. She taught me a lot about what it means to be a Jedi."

Magash was pleased with this assessment. This Jedi, it seemed, was more open to different forms of Force channeling than she'd expected. "So," she asked, "what do you believe? Is the lightsaber the only proper weapon for a Jedi?"

He laughed. "A year or two ago, I'd probably have said that, of course it was. But since then I've used . . . ah . . . a variety of weapons. And I've used no weapons at all. What I believe . . ." He stopped walking and gazed out over the crazy quilt of slag, rock, and sand. "I believe that a Jedi doesn't *need* any weapon. I believe that a Jedi—or any Force-user—*is* the weapon. What he or she uses as a tool or a focus is secondary."

He started walking again, his eyes on the rocks beneath their feet. Magash kept pace.

"What do *you* believe?" he asked her.

"I?" The question startled her. Why would a Temple-trained Jedi care what a Dathomiri Witch believed?

"You have opinions on the subject, I'm sure." He was smiling at her, now, not at himself. Maybe he was even laughing at her.

She lifted her chin. "I do. I believe . . . very much what you've said. It is the purity of the channel that is important, not what tool she uses to facilitate her channeling."

She was surprised to hear herself say that, certain that what should have come from her mouth was an endorsement of channeling the Force through spells and incantations. Yet she knew—as surely as she knew the Force flowed through her—that spoken or sung incantations were only a device to focus the energies a Witch wielded.

"The most critical thing," she added, "is never to concede to evil."

She felt a shift of energies in the man beside her, as if something had caught within him.

"What?" she said. "Does that not match with your Jedi teachings?"

He nodded. "Yes. Yes, certainly the words do."

"But?"

He shook his head. "That's an opinion I shouldn't share."

She took two quick steps past him and turned, blocking his path. "I have asked you to share it. I *demand* that you share it." She wanted to understand the rift that lay between Jedi and Witch.

He met her gaze, letting her see a bit of the ambivalence behind his eyes. Then he said, "When you look at me, what do you see?"

"What do I *see*?"

"Yes. Am I a fellow Force adept or am I . . . an inferior being?"

"You—" She halted. "You are a Jedi."

"That's not an answer, Magash."

She reached into her own thoughts and tried again. "You are . . ." She stopped and looked at him—*really* looked at him. She saw a tall, slender, young human male with longish dark hair, eyes that were all colors at once, and a weariness and sadness in his face that usually came with great age or hardship.

He was attractive. She saw that, too, and realized that were he among the men of their village, she might consider him as a mate.

Behind that was the Force. It shone from him just as it shone from her sisters or Mother Augwynne. And that was who she had been conversing with these last several minutes, she realized. The Force adept.

"You are unique in my experience," she admitted. "It's true that when you first arrived, I took you as an inferior. But now, I see you as a rare companion in the Force. An adept."

"But that's just it, Magash. I'm *not* rare." He shook his head wryly. "Well, okay. Maybe I am now. But I *wasn't*. In the group of Padawans I grew up with and trained with, there were easily as many males as females. From dozens of worlds and hundreds of cultures. When I set foot on your world, I became, if only for a short while, an inferior being. If I were born here or exiled here, I'd be a slave, just like all the other men of your tribe. I'd have no freedom. I'd be permitted no thought of channeling the Force, no matter how accomplished I might become if trained. I would never, on this world, reach my potential as a Force adept . . . or as a sentient being. I would be poorer for it . . . and the clan would be poorer for it. If that's not evil, what is it?"

Her anger was swift and hot. She opened her mouth to retort, but she was struck silent by a vast, ageless sadness that seemed to open up in the Jedi's eyes—as if he held within him the mingled sorrows of all past Jedi.

She fell back on the lesson learned from birth. "Men of our clan can't channel the Force."

"Have you allowed any of them to try? In any event, is that reason enough to enslave them?"

"They are little better than beasts," she argued.

"Taught to use the Force, they would only use it against one another—against us."

"Have I used *my* ability against you?"

"You are not of this world. You've been trained in a spiritual discipline . . ."

"Fine. Then let them learn spiritual discipline and wisdom before you teach them how to wield the Force. Let them learn it from childhood. That's the way all Jedi are taught—*were* taught. The first thing I learned at the feet of my Master was what sort of person a Jedi must be to accomplish good in life and to avoid falling to the dark side. Channeling the Force came after. If the Jedi could teach that, why couldn't the Witches of Dathomir? What prevents it?"

He stepped around her and continued down the rocky slope.

She stood and looked after him, then past him at the demented wilderness beyond. Steam and smoke rose through deep vents opened up in the native rock by the cataclysm that had destroyed the Star Temple and the Infinity Gate. They trailed like wraiths over the scorched ground, and wound around the shards of stone and slag that were all that was left of the Nightsisters' horrific weapon.

Suddenly Magash was not so eager to venture out there with this young-old Jedi. She was not afraid of the ghosts of this place, she told herself, but only angered by this man's censure.

Coward, she called herself, and followed him onto the plain, glassy flakes of obsidian grinding to dust beneath her feet. She reached him just as he stepped out into the debris field, then jerked her head up at a familiar sound.

Rancor.

She could hear them now. One, maybe two. She swiveled her head—there, to the east, in the lee of the great mountain.

"Rancor?" the Jedi asked. He had stopped and turned back to look at her.

She nodded. "I'll go ward them away. I wouldn't want you to be eaten while in my care," she added, flashing a toothy grin.

Liar, she called herself as she picked her way across the slag toward the fringe of forest. Rancors never came up onto this devastated plain, but the Jedi was not to know that.

Jax directed his steps toward the center of the plateau. He reckoned it was about a dozen kilometers long from end to end, perhaps five across. To the west, the plateau seemed to drop off the edge of the world; to the east, it merged into a forest of smoke-colored trees.

That was where his escort had headed. He could see her leaping lightly over obstacles, once executing a stunning somersault before touching softly down atop a boulder the size of a rancor's head.

He wondered at her reason for parting from him. There were no signs of rancors out here—none. Indeed, there was no reason for a rancor—who was an intelligent beast, after all—to venture onto this blasted landscape. He knew he'd driven her away. Perhaps he'd done it instinctively, just as he'd set course for Dathomir.

He turned his gaze back to the center of the high plateau. Several shards of native rock and twisted metal— each as long as the *Aethersprite* and as big around as a Toprawan cedar—jutted out of the tortured ground, their crowns canted toward one another like saber points saluting a coming battle. Just beyond and to the east of that structure was a gash in the surface into which a ship twice the size of the Delta-7 could have disappeared without a trace. A cascade of black rock was frozen in its plunge over the edge like a waterfall made of glass.

Jax took a deep breath and struck out toward the two features, feeling the tug of energies of which he could only dimly discern the contours.

Yes, this area was the source of the displacement he'd sensed in the Force. But where should he start? Indeed, what should he do when he found where to start? The sky was darkening as the Dathomirian sun kissed the mountaintops. Clouds scudded overhead through the silver sky, and a ground mist was beginning to rise out of the shadowed vales. Darkness would come in two hours, maybe less.

Jax pulled the Sith holocron out of his pocket, hoping he might use it like a compass. But while it was clearly reacting to the energies eddying about this place, it offered no indication of which of the features of the destroyed temple he should explore.

He had just closed his eyes and sent out the first ribbons of Force sense when something tugged at him. He opened his eyes and turned them toward the rock spires to the west, many meters away. A graceful figure moved among the titanic saber points, halting when his gaze touched it.

How had she done that? How could Magash have possibly gotten from the last place he'd seen her—almost a klick away—to the broken temple? More to the point, *why* would she? Showing off her prowess for the inferior being, perhaps?

His heart beat faster. Maybe she'd found something. Maybe she knew more about this place than Mother Djo suspected. The Matriarch had said the sisters avoided the ruins, but Magash had been eager to accompany him, and watching her navigate the uneven ground, Jax could well believe this hadn't been her first trek out here.

All right. He'd follow her lead, then. He made for the spires, using the Force to avoid falling into the increasingly alarming rents in the surface of the plain.

He looked up at the formation as he drew nearer. The woman was waiting for him, all but obscured by the rising ground mist, seeming, at times, as if she were part of the vapor herself. He covered the last several meters in a series of Force-assisted bounds and reached the spot where she had been.

She was gone.

"Magash?" He paused to listen. A cold breeze wended its way among the glassy spires, crying disconsolately.

He hesitated. Had he angered the Witch so much that she might ambush him? She could pretend he'd fallen into a crevasse or been eaten by a rancor. He'd felt her anger, but nothing so lethal as hatred.

"Magash!" he called again.

When there was still no answer, he drew his lightsaber and stepped into the shadow of the spires. Almost immediately his senses were caught in a wash of warm static. He found himself panting, disoriented.

He spun at a touch on his shoulder, but there was no one there.

Yet . . . yet, in that split second before he'd reacted, he'd expected to see Laranth standing behind him. Standing *with* him. Now, not seeing or sensing her, he was bereft.

Jax groaned aloud. What *was* this place? What forces lingered here to tear at him in this way?

In his right hand, his lightsaber hummed, bathing the shadows in cool aquas. In his left, the Sith holocron spiked with sudden heat and cast the molten gleam of fire over the slick surfaces of the half-fallen stone spears that met above his head.

He turned slowly, watching the clashing wash of radiance slide over the glassy rock. He stopped, facing the largest of the massive shards, seeing himself in it. Seeing, fleetingly, the reflection of the woman standing behind him.

Not Zabrak. Twi'lek.

Not Magash. Laranth.

He spun.

The space behind him was empty. The closest thing to him a curl of ground mist.

He turned back to the twisted mirror—

—and stepped into the fore-and-aft passage of his dying ship. The lightsaber still hummed, shedding radiance into the semi-darkness; the orange light was not from the Sith holocron, but from the fires eating the *Far Ranger's* bone and blood. And there, before him in the flickering darkness, Laranth stood beneath the open weapons bay, with Den Dhur at her side, struggling with the ladder.

He took a step forward. Another. And another.

"Laranth! Den! Now! It's over! Let's go!"

They looked at him. Den said something to Laranth, then ran aft, toward Jax.

"Laranth! Now!" Jax put the full energy of the Force behind the words. "Yimmon needs us."

She glanced up into the weapons bay, looked at Jax . . . and came aft to safety.

The reflections wavered, eddied, re-sorted themselves. Laranth lay on the deck, dying, a shard of metal piercing her neck.

Jax uttered an inarticulate roar of anguish, emptying himself utterly, until he felt as if he'd been turned inside out. Before he could draw breath again, the images eddied once more, and Laranth was standing before him . . . and Laranth was lying dead at his feet.

He sucked in a cold breath. Two paths. Two pasts. The one he had created through indecision and choice; the one he might have created had he not hesitated. He wished with every last atom of his being that he could take one more step and make that choice anew.

For a fraction of a second it seemed to him that he could, and in that second, he stepped forward again, crying Laranth's name.

He stumbled in the rocky debris and went to his knees. His lightsaber deactivated, the holocron tumbled from his hand. He put out the hand to arrest his fall and hissed in pain as a shard of obsidian sliced through his palm.

He rocked back on his heels and looked up. He was fully among the ruin of the Star Temple. All remnants of the past were gone. Wind moaned through the spires, shadows lengthened.

Had it been real? Was he really standing in some sort of temporal nexus? Or was it something else? And if the nexus were real, could he somehow force it open again?

Focus. You came here for Yimmon.

Had he? Or had he come here for something else? *Someone* else? Hadn't he had, in the back of his mind, some idea that there must be some way to cheat Death? To cheat time?

There is no death; there is the Force.

He shoved the thought away, even as he recognized that it must be accepted. And he *had* accepted it . . . once. Or thought he had.

Now he wasn't sure.

He took a deep breath and tried to reorient himself. He looked about again, realizing that he was kneeling on some sort of artificial structure—a flat, reasonably level piece of bedrock that might have formed part of the floor of the temple, or an altar—or a control matrix.

He looked around near where he knelt and recognized the peculiar character of the stone shards lying about him. They seemed to have some sort of writing or drawing on them. He clipped his lightsaber to his belt and reached for one of the glistening chips of black rock—a piece the length of his hand. It *did* have some sort of symbols on it, and he realized, as he turned it in the amber light of the late-afternoon sun, that its contours were too regular for it to be natural.

His pulse accelerated. He suspected he'd been led to very near the heart of the Star Temple. Which meant . . . what? That energies were unstable here? Might time, itself, be unstable?

A flash of radiance in the corner of his eye caused him to turn toward the holocron, which lay roughly half a meter away. It was pulsing, its facets and engraved surfaces running with beads of light.

He reached over and picked it up, balancing it in the palm of his undamaged hand. Here, atop the slab of stone on which he knelt, the pulsation of the Sith artifact deepened, and now he could feel the reverberations in the Force. The Star Temple, too, teemed with energies— energies that had driven the Infinity Gate and that had been bent to the service of the dark side.

The holocron responded to them, but did that mean it was any closer to opening?

Jax concentrated his own energies on the holocron, letting his Force sense touch it, sample it, taste its texture. It was acid and oil. It was quicksilver and glass. It was fire and ice.

He closed his eyes, still seeing the artifact in his mind's gaze. With tendrils of the Force, he followed the facets, traced the intricate etched ideograms, pressed and pulled. Where his mind touched, the sigils leapt to brilliant life.

He was close. He could feel it.

He raised his left hand over the apex of the holocron, bracketing it, as he focused all his senses on it, wrapping it in a fabric of Force energy. And suddenly, suddenly and far too easily, a panel slid open and another folded back. A holoprojection filled the air before him, alphanumerics and complex formulas rising upward.

Jax remembered I-Five speaking of watching Yanth, the Hutt crime lord, skillfully manipulating the holocron's exterior plates, to reveal information in the electron lattices of the holocron's outer shells. But holocrons were composed of many layers—almost infinite, in fact—and the Sith had been devious beyond time and space. I-Five had posited that a catalyst of some sort might be necessary to expose the deeper layers.

A drop of blood fell from Jax's wounded palm, struck the crown of the artifact, and traced a zigzag down the incised face.

The Force within and around Jax shuddered, and the holocron beat with a single sanguine pulse. The bottom corner facing Jax turned on an unseen axis.

A catalyst.

Stunned, Jax dropped the holocron.

Magash never reached the forest. Her steps grew slower and slower still, until she was literally dragging her feet. She berated herself for being seven kinds of a coward. The Jedi had threatened her sense of identity, and she had abandoned him to the heath.

She stopped and stared at the smoke trees.

No. He hadn't threatened her identity—but only upheld his own. If that was enough to cause her to disobey her Clan Mother . . .

She turned back to the blasted plain. He had confused her, that was all.

No, she had *let* herself be confused.

But what, realistically, was the alternative? If she was not willing to sift through his ideas and confront the ones that merited confronting, what more could she do but ignore them? Was that the way of the Singing

Mountain Sisterhood—to shrink from unpleasant ideas in preference for unruffled ignorance?

The Jedi had asked what prevented the Dathomiri sisterhoods from doing what the Jedi Order had done—teaching adepts of all genders to channel the Force. Magash did not know the answer to that because she had never contemplated it.

What if what the Jedi proposed was true? What if there were, among the male denizens of Dathomir, potential Force-users who were withering because they were not allowed to develop? What if potential talent was being wasted . . . because of fear?

Wouldn't Mother Augwynne know this? Wouldn't she—and even Magash, herself—*know* if a male in her presence possessed latent Force abilities? Or did the expectation that there were no abilities to develop and the fear of dire consequences ensure that none were found?

Magash turned back toward the ruins. She could see the Jedi moving about the base of the fallen black spires. A shiver coursed down her spine.

You are *afraid!*

She freely admitted it, then. As often as she had stolen out here to sample the strange atmosphere, seeking any hint of the ancient knowledge that might remain in the Kwa temple the Nightsisters had plundered for their own ends, the place still unsettled her. So much so that she had allowed the Jedi to wander the ruins alone because he made her uncomfortable. What if he found what she had sought? Or what if he were injured or killed because she wasn't there to prevent it? In either case, how could she explain to Mother Augwynne why she had abandoned him?

With a snort of disgust at her own weakness, Magash Drashi headed back to the ruins. She had gone no more than two strides when the black pinnacles across the Infinity Plain were lit by warring bursts of aqua and crimson light. The whipcord response in the Force almost knocked her from her feet, and her soul was raked by a raw wave of anguish from the Jedi.

Cursing herself, Magash moved faster.

Blood.

Darth Ramage's holocron was sealed with blood.

Knees drawn up to his chest, retreating into himself, Jax stared at the holocron where it lay atop the black slab of rock in a pool of pulsing crimson light.

Anathema.

It shouldn't have surprised him as much as it did. Ramage had been a Sith, and a particularly ruthless Sith, at that. His science had centered on the destructive use of power and had been steeped in darkness.

How much blood does it require? Jax wondered. *And what kind?*

He glanced at his hastily bandaged hand. The holocron had responded to his blood, of course, but that trickle had caused only one corner closure to respond—and then only to open slightly. That hinted that a significant amount of blood was necessary. Clearly, if the adept opening the holocron was also the one whose blood facilitated its opening, the drain on his neurological processes would make it difficult, if not impossible, to wield the Force as needed to probe the artifact's arcane locks.

What then?

The implications were sickening.

Jax got to his feet. There was only one way to test the ideas that were making chaos of his thoughts.

He extended his Force sense, probing the nooks and crevices around the ruin. There was life, he found, even here. Some sort of large insect there, a reptile here, and *there* beneath that tumble of small rubble, a weak mammalian energy. He found himself moving toward it before he'd half thought through what he meant to do. He raised a hand over the rubble—small rocks lifted and sand shot away to reveal the nest of an endothermic rodentlike creature not much larger than the holocron itself.

The creature, suddenly dispossessed, tried to scurry away, but Jax caught it with the Force, lifting it into his hand. It peered at him out of huge glittering eyes, its nostrils wide in alarm, trying to understand what sort of monster had plucked it from the safety of its home.

Jax carried the little rodent over to the holocron and reached out with the Force, tracing the artifact's energy pathways, facets, and incisions as before. Then, jaw clamped so hard it hurt, he picked up one of the shards of slagged obsidian and quickly, deftly nicked the animal's tail. The creature struggled, and a large drop of blood welled and fell onto the holocron.

There was no reaction—none.

Jax sat down, hard, on the rocky altar. Almost reflexively, he sent the rodent a calming, healing—and apologetic—touch. Then he released it. It scurried away to disappear back into its slag heap.

Icy as was the wind that rose around the temple, chilled as he was, Jax was sweating. He wiped perspiration from his forehead with his bandaged hand.

Not just any blood then, apparently, would appease Darth Ramage's little crimson god. It wanted the blood of a sentient. Most likely the blood of a Force-user. But the amount of blood necessary would cripple the would-be knower of Ramage's secrets so much that he would lose the ability to draw them out; the key had to be the combined application of spirit and matter.

The intent was clear: Darth Ramage intended that the seeker of his dark knowledge commit a dark act—the sacrifice of another Force-user's blood. Possibly enough blood to kill. Perhaps his intention was to make sure that no one from the light side would ever make use of his research.

I should destroy the thing, Jax thought. *I should take it and throw it down a deep, dark hole.*

There was such a fissure only meters away.

But within the artifact was potentially the salvation of Thi Xon Yimmon and the resistance.

Jax pressed his forehead to his knees, wrapped his arms over his head. It was impossible. It couldn't be done.

Wrong, the still, small voice within him whispered. *It can be done, but* you *can't do it. You can't even* think *of doing it.*

"Jedi? What's wrong?"

Jax raised his head to see Magash Drashi standing at the edge of the altar, the Force strong and bright within her.

thirty-nine

The *Laranth/Corsair* had been at Keldabe for less than a day, but in that time they had refueled, arranged for the delivery of cargo, and picked up some small arms. Sacha Swiftbird looked with favor on the DH-17 blaster she'd purchased, but found, when she was in Jax's quarters, that her gaze went again and again to the weapon he'd left behind.

At first, she had returned the Sith lightsaber to its hiding place. That had lasted only hours, though, and she'd brought it out again, fascinated by it. She'd propped it up beside the miisai tree in the wall niche, where it would be invisible to anyone standing in the doorway. She picked it up at intervals, turning it in her hand. The hilt seemed to fit her hand well, which made her wonder if it might have been a woman's weapon.

In a rare moment in which she'd been alone on the vessel while Den and I-Five oversaw the loading of cargo, she'd timidly activated it . . . and turned it off seconds later. The power that flowed from the thing— that seemed to connect her hand, her arm, her entire body to it—had been overwhelming.

And unsettling.

And *exhilarating*.

The truly odd thing, in her mind, was that she'd felt no evil from it. Power, yes, but no evil. No darkness. Puzzling, that. She wondered if there was some deficit in her own mishmash of virtues that made her incapable of sensing evil.

No. She'd been in proximity to Inquisitors. She knew evil when she felt it.

Maybe, as Jax Pavan's ownership of the weapon indicated, the Force was agnostic about such things. The difference was in the person who wielded the weapon. She had heard Force-users argue endlessly on the subject: Was there indeed a dichotomy of intention? Or was the Force merely raw power, the distillation of the cosmic Will, and as such above sentient concepts of right and wrong? Or was it beneficent, requiring the venal desires of sentients to use it to dark purpose?

The next time Sacha activated the lightsaber, she held her ground, though her hands trembled and her bones vibrated and her brain itched. She held it, moved with it—albeit gingerly—and finally ventured out into the larger engineering bay to pretend at fighting with it. She loved the way it balanced in her hand. It felt more natural there than any blaster she'd ever owned.

So caught up was she in her dance that she barely registered the sound of the cargo ramp clamping shut. Only when she heard voices in the passageway beyond engineering did she hastily deactivate the lightsaber.

She tucked it into the front of her jacket just in time to hear I-Five say, "Peculiar."

Two seconds later he and Den appeared in the engineering hatchway.

"What's peculiar?" Den was asking.

"Yeah," Sacha echoed, leaning nonchalantly against a circuit panel. "What's peculiar?"

I-Five fixed her with his pit droid oculus. "I heard something from within this chamber just before we arrived. It sounded like a lightsaber."

Sacha laughed, knowing her face was flushed.

"What's so funny?" Den asked, blinking at her.

Sacha recovered her balance, gesturing at I-Five. "Him, talking to me. I can't get used to the idea of Ducky with a genius-class brain."

"Ducky doesn't have a genius-class brain," I-Five said. "The genius-class brain has Ducky."

"Yeah. Right." Sacha cleared her throat. "We ready to fly?"

"Ready as we'll ever be," Den said. He wiped his hands on his coverall. "Which is to say, *not*."

Sacha patted the Sullustan on the shoulder as she swung out of engineering to head for her cabin. "Ah, we'll be fine. When we step off this ship at Kantaros Station we'll look like we were born and raised in Black Sun. I'm gonna go make sure my cabin's buttoned down, then I'll join you on the bridge."

She went aft, whistling, feeling the pit droid's monocular gaze burning into her back until the turn in the corridor. Inside Jax's cabin, she quickly returned the lightsaber to its hiding place and stroked the miisai's boughs, cursing her carelessness.

"Swiftbird, don't do stupid stuff like that as a matter of habit. Deal?"

She sketched a salute at her reflection in the miisai's container, then hastened to the bridge.

She'd no more than dropped into the copilot's seat when the communications array pinged. "Incoming," she said, peering at the display. Then she gave Den a startled glance. "From Coruscant."

I-Five activated the unit. He was careful, Sacha noted, to establish one-way visual communication—they would see their "caller" if an image was sent, but would not be seen.

The holographic display showed a Zabrak man and a Togruta woman. Sacha recognized them, but their setting was obscured—probably with purpose, in case someone else was sampling the message. Not likely, but it could happen.

"Jax," the man said, "Jax, it's Pol Haus and Sheel Mafeen."

I-Five activated the visuals from their end, then nodded at Den, who swallowed and said, "Hi, Pol. Uh, Jax isn't with us at the moment. We . . . uh, how bad are things there? Is it . . . is it as bad as you thought?"

"Yes and no," the Zabrak said with a glance at his companion. "The Whiplash leadership is gone, except for us. Tuden Sal . . . died rather heroically, as it happens. But not, as I first supposed, during the assassination attempt on Palpatine. There are still lower-level operatives around, though. People who have supported the effort for years but who, thankfully, weren't inside Sal's plot. That's the good news—there's some remnant left of Whiplash, after all. Though not much. And we were able to retrieve all of the data from HQ and destroy the physical evidence."

"I take it that means there's more bad news—apart from Sal and the others being dead."

Haus nodded and Sheel Mafeen said, "Sal was the one who tipped Vader off that Yimmon was leaving Coruscant."

Sacha felt as if all the blood had drained out of her face. "I don't understand. He put Whiplash, the resistance, and the Ranger operation on Toprawa in danger . . . for what?"

"Revenge," the Togruta said, her voice unsteady. "He wanted the Emperor dead that badly."

Haus added: "To be fair to Sal, we don't think he meant for Yimmon to be captured or for anyone to be killed. We think he meant only to force Yimmon and Jax into deep hiding so they couldn't interfere with his assassination plot. So I tried to interfere with it. What I didn't realize was that when Yimmon was captured, Sal had no way out. He had to go through with it."

"That," said I-Five, "explains a lot."

Sacha found herself nodding. "Like why Vader's knowledge of *Far Ranger*'s route was only approximate."

"Exactly," the droid said. "If it had been a Toprawan operative, he would have known exactly where to intercept us, which he didn't—apparently until he sensed Jax and Laranth through the Force."

"We thought you should know," said Haus. "Tell Jax he can trust his allies on Toprawa."

"If we ever see him again," Den murmured.

forty

Jax sat cross-legged beneath the apex of the cairn, eyes open, hand and mind cradling the planes and vertices of the Sith holocron. He felt the Force rise up within him, quivering in the twilight that wrapped around him like a soft cloak. With questing tendrils of sense he prodded at the artifact's locks—following the sigils on the incised planes.

He trembled as the liquid warmth of blood ran from the holocron to pool in the palm of his hand before cascading to the rock on which he sat.

The holocron responded just as he had suspected it would—as he followed the tracery of arcane symbols with his senses, the caps on the vertices turned, one after the other, the one at the apex last of all.

The holocron opened like a blossom and revealed the data crystal within.

The soft, musical chanting that had filled the ruined chamber ceased. Jax lowered his left hand, looking up to meet the gazes of the three women who knelt with him, their hands joined above the holocron, their blood mingled with his on its etched surfaces.

They withdrew their hands and Duala made quick work of binding first Augwynne Djo's wounds, then Magash's. Magash returned the favor, wrapping her sister's hand before turning her attention to Jax.

Jax barely felt her ministrations. His entire focus was

on the open fountain of knowledge in his hand; he couldn't have looked away if he'd tried. The holocron had him, and was pouring its Force-sealed contents into his mind. A thousand lights pulsed; a thousand voices whispered, a thousand tendrils of the Force attached themselves to his spirit—to his mind.

He was drowning in the flood of knowledge, and he could not look away.

"Is it readable, Jedi?"

Duala Aidu's voice came to him as if from a great distance.

Readable? He almost laughed. The physical crystal, he had no doubt, could be inserted into a holoreader, granting the user access to some of the more mundane information it contained. But this river of knowledge was meant only for the Force-user who had opened it—a Force-user Darth Ramage would have assumed must be aligned with the dark side to even contemplate the act he believed necessary to open his cache.

Jax doubted Ramage could have imagined that a group of Force-users would freely cooperate and com-mingle their lifeblood to that end.

"He is reading it, child," Augwynne Djo murmured. She leaned toward him, staring intently into his face.

Jax saw her through a veil of amber light, her own Force energies seeming to form a bright halo around her. He wanted to thank her, but he could neither speak nor move. He concentrated on the flow of images, ideas, experiments. Surely there must be a way of choosing the sort of information that might be of benefit to him. Or at least of sorting through it to winnow it out.

Fear niggled at him. What if he couldn't understand what he was being fed? What if there was too much? What if there was, after all, nothing of use to him?

Pain shot through his head.

Breathe!

The command seemed to come from within and without simultaneously.

No fear. No ignorance. No chaos. Only the Force. Breathe.

He breathed, opening himself to the knowledge, letting it flow through him, over him, into him, without attempting to sort it or filter it or impede it. He was a bottomless pool being filled with water. He offered no resistance to the flood.

With the suddenness of a door slamming shut, the flow of information ceased. Jax knew a moment of silent, dark stillness before he lost consciousness.

forty-one

"This gonna work?" Den asked, his eyes on the wall of floating rock that dominated the vista from the ship's forward viewport.

They'd entered hyperspace near Mandalore and exited in the Bothan system, flying the ident codes of the *Raptor*. Now they skirted the Fervse'dra asteroid field, looking for the best point of entry.

"Do you want the odds?" I-Five asked. He was back in his augmented I-5YQ chassis, manually copiloting the ship and feeding navigational data directly to the navcom from his own matrix via his right index finger.

"No, thanks," Den said, "I'll pass. It'd probably just make me squirm."

"As you wish."

The droid's optics blinked and a holographic tactical display of the asteroid field appeared over the control console.

"According to my calculations, Kantaros Station will be there." A blossom of red bloomed amid the field of tumbling rock, which was called out in blue-gray on the display.

"And we are here," Sacha said from the pilot's seat. She nodded at the bright spot of amber on the outer rim of the field, matching speed with the asteroids.

"There are a number of ways to approach this," said I-Five. "Laterally, from the front, from the rear . . ."

"I say we skim underneath the field," Sacha said, "until we're in hailing distance of the station, then come up from below and behind. Less chance of getting creamed by a big one that way. If we're traveling with the flow of debris, it'll be easier to stay out of its way. Or . . ." She pointed at a third point of light that had just appeared on the screen. "We could follow *that* in."

That was a large Toydarian freighter scuttling along the top of the asteroid field like a fat beetle.

"I'd be willing to bet," she said, "that they've done this before. And if we follow in their wake, we'll have the benefit of their navigator's familiarity with the protocols."

"What if they *haven't* done this before?" Den asked.

She shrugged and threw him a gamine grin. "They'll clear the way for us either way. Ship that size has gotta have repulsor shields brawny enough to shove a few rocks out of its path."

"And if it doesn't?"

"Boy, you are quite the little pessimist, aren't you?"

Den glared at her in mock outrage. "Who're you calling *little*?"

She laughed. "If they don't have strong enough repulsors, they'll still clear the rocks out of our way. I'm not gonna get so close that we'll get skragged if they blow, okay?"

"Promise?"

"Promise. So what'll it be, boys?" she asked, putting both hands firmly on the steering yoke. "We going in after 'em?"

"Aye," said I-Five.

"Sure," Den said. "Why not?"

Sacha handled the ship like a pro. It moved gracefully and deftly under her hands. It was almost, Den thought, like having Jax at the helm. Who knew, maybe this particular Podracer had some Force sensitivity. That might account for her success in the sport.

Whatever the reason, at the helm of the *Laranth* she was nothing short of amazing, weaving balletically through the upper strata of asteroids to settle in behind the Toydarian, where she kept the perfect distance and aspect. There was no sense of tension, no uncertainty. It was as if she did this every day of her life.

"The Toydarian just started sending," I-Five said.

"Then so should we," Sacha told him.

"Aye, Captain." The droid began sending their own set of ident codes—or rather the ones he had lifted from the real *Raptor*.

In a matter of moments, they were hailed by the docking authority and their ident codes acknowledged. Their amber locator blip was joined by a bright green one buried in the depths of the asteroid field. It overlay I-Five's predicted location almost exactly.

Den practically held his breath as they followed the homing beacon to Kantaros Station. The very sight of the Imperial craft that were synced with the installation made his dewlaps sweat. But they glided serenely in abaft the larger freighter, their only communication with the station coming in the form of a docking bay assignment in the "southern hemisphere" of the station.

"Not bad," Sacha said, turning the helm over to the automated docking beacon. "Small size does have its advantages."

"As I've often said," murmured Den.

"Chiefly that we get to dock closer to the heart of the operation."

"Uh-huh—and then what?"

"Then," I-Five said, "we blend in, get the lay of the land, do some eavesdropping, and start snooping around."

"Blend in," Den repeated, eyeing the droid skeptically. "You expect to blend in—in that getup?"

To say I-Five looked peculiar—and menacing—would be to understate the case. He was a gleaming nightmare—one-third protocol droid, one-third Nemesis assassinator, and one-third who knew what. One arm seemed almost normal—it wasn't—and the other, in pristine white, looked like a rocket launcher, which was not too far from the truth. One leg was silver, one was gold; both were augmented with antigravity repulsors. The long, helmetlike cowling that formed the back of his head was encrusted with short, conical spikes—he could kill someone simply by falling over backward on them.

Diplomacy with an evil twist.

The droid had all sorts of surprises up his metal sleeves, Den was sure. During their recent stay on Toprawa, he'd acquired the ability to move from chassis to chassis on his own and, therefore, work on his "upgrades" by himself. Den had lost control—and even knowledge—of the modifications from that time on. I-Five might have battle droid parts installed beneath his metal skin for all the Sullustan knew.

"I think he'll be brilliant," Sacha said. "We'll all be brilliant. We'll look so Black Sunny that no one will have any reason to question us."

"Black Sunny?" Den repeated.

"You know—scruffy, but well-heeled; hard-boiled, but eccentric. Colorful."

Den peered at her. She was colorful, all right—from her formfitting black-and-red coverall to the artful streaks of silver she had introduced into her shoulder-length hair. She wore a blaster on each hip, carried a hold-out pistol in her right boot, and had a vibroblade hidden in her left. Only she knew what else she'd secreted in the inner pockets of her flight jacket.

Den was no less "eccentric" in dress—she'd made

sure of that. He was covered from neck to toes in black synthskin. He was also armed to the teeth—all Black Sun operatives were armed to the teeth.

They looked as much like pirates as Jax had.

Den experienced a sharp pang of loss, wondering where Jax was now, and what he was doing.

And if they'd ever see him again.

forty-two

The place Jax Pavan stood was dark. He had the impression of a vast space and reached out with the Force to augment his eyes. Gradually, the place came to light—literally—as soft areas of multihued ambience bloomed in the darkness. These vague lights fanned out away from him on both sides in orderly rows that rose to a great height. They were too regular to be stars.

He knew—and had loved—this place. It was the great library at the Jedi Temple on Coruscant. It no longer existed.

He swept his gaze over the darkened walls with their spectral lights—lights that were growing in brilliance with every passing moment. They were the "books" lining the library shelves—datacubes, memory chips, holocrons, light scrolls, even old books composed of bound flimsi and ancient scrolls of flowing text on plant fiber.

He had been standing in the broad doorway of the vast chamber; now he stepped forward toward the center. Among the ranks of lights, some grew brighter. Here, an amber halo surrounded a datacube; there, a datascroll gleamed like a tube of palest gold. He wondered at their contents . . . and found himself many meters in the stygian air, reaching for a datascroll, knowing it contained a treatise on Force projections.

Useful. He took it from the shelf, feeling its warmth—
and it dissolved into his hand.

Startled, he stared at his palm. It glowed with the residual aura—almost obscuring the already healing slash
that cut diagonally from the heel of his hand to the base
of his fingers.

The knowledge contained on the scroll emerged into
his semiconscious mind like an island rising from a retreating sea. Of course, it made sense. It would require
practice and discipline, but it was a similar discipline to
the Force cloaking he had already been using.

He returned his eyes to the shelves. They weren't
really shelves, of course; he realized that. He wasn't
really in the library. The library was gone—swept away
in an orgy of horrific and senseless violence. He was in
his own head, choosing the knowledge he would bring
to conscious light, having chosen the metaphor through
which he acquired it.

There, a bright white luminescence many tiers up. In
a heartbeat he was there, looking at a datasphere that
shone like a tiny moon. It was a record of Darth Ramage's
experiments with energy—with pyronium, specifically.

Jax snatched it up and assimilated it.

He chose several other points of enlightenment—
a treatise on healing, acquired from Jedi long dead, another on the sort of Force cloaking he'd stumbled upon
when meditating on the miisai tree, another by an ancient Jedi Master on the nature of the Force, another on
Force communications, yet another on something Darth
Ramage called "tunneling," which allowed the Force-
user to concentrate his focus so tightly that he touched
nothing but the target of the focus.

During this time, Jax was aware he was working his
way toward a great, red brilliance high up on the curving wall of his mind's library. It was a holocron—
a cube that pulsed with energies that told him this was

the soul of Darth Ramage's work . . . if the work of such a madman could be said to have a soul. He had been avoiding it, he knew, afraid of what it might tell him— what it might force him to know. Nonetheless, he found himself facing it, reaching for it, touching it. *Knowing* it.

It was a treatise on the manipulation of time.

His heart clenched. He wanted this as much as he feared wanting it. If Darth Ramage had been at all successful at manipulating time, what might Jax Pavan, Jedi, do with the knowledge?

Careful, Jax. Careful. Could this knowledge help Yimmon?

He drew his hand back, hesitated, then thrust it out again. There was no way to know if it might help Yimmon without knowing what it was.

He lifted the ruddy cube from the shelf, felt it submerge into his hand to emerge in his mind.

He saw time not as a stream, but as a vast ocean teeming with myriad currents. On its deceptively placid surface, islands bobbed. The first thing he understood about the islands was that they were not all alike. Some extended their roots to the floor of the sea; some floated freely. There were fixed points—nexuses—and floating points that drifted about them.

The second thing he understood about these "islands" was that they did not march in a straight line. Indeed, they were not all even held by the same currents. How, then, did one move them or move among them?

Islands move not, unless the currents move them.

The assertion—embedded in this new knowledge— brought Jax up short. It had the texture of one of Aoloiloa's mystical pronouncements.

The moment the thought flickered through his mind, Jax knew with horrible certainty that Darth Ramage's knowledge about time manipulation had come at the expense of Cephalon lives and minds. Hundreds, perhaps even thousands of them.

Separation destroys us.

He could feel the echoes of agony in the interstices between visualization and articulation. Darth Ramage had ripped this perception of time in its extended dimensions from the minds of Cephalon victims, but in so doing, he had cut them off from their network of joined consciousness, leaving the individuals horrifically alone, isolated in this vast temporal sea.

Aoloiloa must have known it. Had he foreseen that the knowledge would be useful to Jax? Or had he foreseen something else—*someone* else that such information might be useful to?

If Jax, in possession of this knowledge, fell into Darth Vader's hands—into the Emperor's hands—what then?

Jax pulled his consciousness away from the knowledge—but it was too late, of course. It was fixed in him like a hot, red star. He closed his eyes and the library vanished.

Magash paced the council hall below the Clan Mother's chambers, her mind roiling. She knew nothing of what the Jedi was experiencing in his catatonia, but she could feel the repercussions of it in the Force.

Why had he felt it necessary to pry into that holocron? He knew it vibrated with dark energies. What contents could possibly have been so important that he was willing to risk his life—and their lives? Knowledge that would save his friend, he'd said. Knowledge that would benefit anyone allied against the Empire; that could help to bring the Empire down.

As much as Magash wanted to see the Empire fall, she realized there was a part of her that didn't care what happened to the rest of the universe as long as her small part of it was spared. She was not naïve enough to believe in that possibility, though. The Nightsisters and

Nightbrothers had already brought Dathomir to the attention of the Sith. That could not be undone. And perhaps, just perhaps, when the Jedi woke—*if* the Jedi woke—he would have knowledge that would also benefit the Singing Mountain Clan.

She felt a frisson of awareness ripple up her spine and swung about to face the steps that led up to the second-floor gallery. Jax Pavan stood at the top of the stairs, regarding her solemnly.

She moved to look up at him, wary. What effects might the knowledge he'd assimilated have on him?

"I wanted to thank you, Magash, for going with me to the Infinity Plain. For being willing to help me pry knowledge out of the holocron. For standing by me and befriending me."

She blinked. "What have you learned?"

He smiled. "Mother Djo wants to see you."

The Clan Mother wanted to see her? Then why hadn't she simply summoned her through the Force?

Frowning, Magash, started up the stairs. The Jedi turned and moved up the broad hallway in front of her. At the door to Mother Augwynne's chambers, he turned . . . and disappeared.

Magash stopped dead in her tracks. Is *that* what the holocron had taught him to do? Teleport? Render himself invisible? Walk through walls?

The door of the chamber opened and the Jedi stood before her. He wasn't smiling now. He was studying her face. She knew what he must see there—stunned disquiet.

"What was that? What did you just do?"

He held the door open for her to enter, and now she did feel Mother Augwynne's summons.

She entered the chamber and turned to face the Jedi. "Was that teleportation?"

He shook his head. "No. Projection. That was one of

the things Darth Ramage was experimenting with—
using a personal Force projection to make it seem that
he was somewhere he was not. Which, I suppose, opens
up all sorts of possibilities about the stories of his demise."

"So you were in here, projecting the version of you that
came out to speak to me. But you didn't seem to hear
what I said to you. You didn't answer my question."

"I didn't hear your question, Magash, because I
wasn't in here projecting that at the same time you were
seeing it. I was speaking to Mother Djo."

Magash felt as if there were wool in her head. "I don't
understand."

"It was an autonomous projection. I programmed it,
I guess you could say, to do just what it did. And only
what it did. Beyond that . . ." He shook his head—
wearily, Magash thought.

"But still, wouldn't it have required you to be projecting
it while I was seeing it?"

"No, because of something else Ramage was experimenting with: manipulating time."

Even as he said the words, Magash could feel the unease that quivered in the Jedi's aura. She looked at him
sharply, wanting to pierce the shell of control he wore.

"This knowledge . . . unsettles you. It disturbs you.
Why?"

"I couldn't even begin to explain." He glanced aside
at the Matriarch, who was watching from her chair
near the hearth. "Suffice it to say, it's potentially devastating knowledge . . . in the wrong hands."

Magash found herself filled with warring emotions—
dread, excitement, curiosity. She took a step toward the
Jedi.

"You can travel in time? You can change things that
have been or will be?"

"Travel, no. Influence, maybe. I have to be honest

with you." He included the Clan Mother in his glance. "I don't know, right now, what I might be able to do with this knowledge. But I know what Darth Vader might do with it. So, I wish to beg a further favor from the Singing Mountain Clan."

"And what is that?" Augwynne Djo asked.

"First of all, I wish to leave the Sith holocron with you. I know that you will neither attempt to use it for ill nor allow it to fall to the forces of the dark side." He locked each woman's gaze with his own—first Mother Augwynne's, then Magash's.

"That is acceptable to me," said the Clan Mother. "What else do you wish?"

"If I survive my . . . attempt to rescue my friend, I wish to return here and have you purge this knowledge from my mind. Utterly purge it, so that it will never be misused, either by Vader or by me."

The words chilled Magash's soul and she became aware, again, of the shadows that clung to this man.

"As you wish," Mother Augwynne said.

The Jedi bowed to her in a gesture of deference. "Then, with your permission, I would like a place I might meditate before I leave Dathomir."

The Clan Mother returned the Jedi's bow.

Magash bowed to them both.

"Do you really fear that you would misuse the knowledge you have gleaned?" Magash asked as she escorted Jax to the meditation chamber he had been accorded.

"I fear I would be tempted."

"To undo your mate's death?"

Perceptive of her, but not unexpected. Magash Darshi, Jax thought, would make an outstanding Padawan.

Catching his nod, she protested, "But what would be wrong with that? If I understand your situation clearly, if you were to undo what was done at that time, there would be no need to mourn your mate, rescue your friend, or even fear acquiring such dangerous knowledge, because in that time line, you would never have had the need—"

She broke off and met Jax's eyes. He could see she had stumbled upon the paradox. "You would never have needed to acquire it . . . But you would still have had this holocron, yes? So you *could* acquire it."

"For what reason? And once having used it—even assuming I *could* use it in that way—how easy would it be to use it again . . . and again? How many wrongs could I right? How many *would* I right? How many would I *have* to right simply because I could not foresee all the consequences of the time lines I'd already touched?"

Magash led him into a small balcony room high up on the flank of the main tower. As luck—or Augwynne Djo's sensibilities—would have it, it overlooked the Infinity Plain.

She turned to look at him. "You don't know how the time manipulation works, then?"

"Not yet. I may never fully understand it, which might be a great mercy." *Or a great tragedy.* "Right now, Magash, I have a storm of knowledge in my head. Flotsam and jetsam. Disjointed pieces, flying every which way. I need to try to get the pieces to fit together somehow."

She nodded. "I will leave you then. I wish you success, Jedi, in your endeavor."

He chuckled at the continued formality in her tone. "Jax, Magash. My name is Jax."

"Jax," she repeated, and bowed to him before leaving the room, as if he were her equal.

In his meditation, Jax saw himself as sitting at the hub of a great wheel. The bodies of knowledge sat at the ends of spokes, separate. He must somehow connect them.

The connection between the Force projections and

time was simple enough to see, but the nature of the time manipulation suggested by Darth Ramage's research was, at first, impenetrable.

Jax found himself looking down on his "islands" in the ocean of time, contemplating how one could move the floating points. He let his mind dive into that ocean, imagining the pull of tides and currents, seeing them fall into almost artistic fractal patterns.

Then, with a suddenness that stole his breath, the patterns fell together with a soul-deep thrill of comprehension: in order to move an island in time, you had to change the currents that affected it, and in order to change even one current, you had to make minute changes in the ones around it—especially the ones that preceded it and from which it was born.

There were "mother" currents, Jax realized. Currents in time that spun off child currents—and local currents as plentiful as moments. With that epiphany came another, less welcome one: *You can't alter one current without altering every downstream current—and island—to which it is connected.*

It wasn't a trickle-down effect, or a domino effect. It was a cascade effect. And as quickly as he realized that, he understood what Darth Ramage must have also understood: that such complex manipulation—or even comprehension of time—could be achieved only by a network of powerful minds that were, themselves, not entirely in the time stream.

Minds like the Cephalons'.

Ramage's reasoning was clear, too, then. The Cephalons formed such a network—that was what gave them their perception of time. Their sub-brains were each linked to various aspects, patterns, waves—each word was equally applicable—of the time sea.

Jax shuddered with the awareness of the experiments in which Darth Ramage had psychically cut individual

Cephalons off from their fellows, to prove that the network existed. Ramage had concluded that if the Cephalons' network gave them the ability to *see* currents in time and find the islands, a similar perception might give equally powerful minds—minds of dark side Force-users, say—the ability to *alter* those currents.

Jax was surprised by his own bitter laughter at the irony of the situation. The tool Darth Ramage would have needed to run such an experiment didn't exist in Sith experience. Even perceiving time as the Cephalons did required the deeply cooperative efforts of a host of powerful minds. Such a collective would be impossible to achieve for a group of dark side Force-users, in which fear, distrust, and ambition made up the air they breathed.

Impossible now for the Jedi, too, Jax thought. He was growing ever more convinced that there were no Jedi left to cooperate with.

He thrust the thought aside and gazed down on his time islands. The island bearing the *Far Ranger* and her crew was out of reach to a single Jedi. But a closer island both in time and space—a small island in a local current . . .

He thought of the brute-force projection of himself that had fooled Magash briefly. He hadn't considered currents then; he had simply cut across them. That near to the present moment, they were barely eddies. But what if he looked closely at those eddies? Could he affect them significantly without sufficient power? The Cephalons' power to see time as they did arose out of their network, and he had none. That suggested what he needed was more raw power.

Of course. The pyronium.

He turned what he now knew about pyronium's interaction with bota over in his mind. There was no bota. Not anymore. The bota plants that now existed had

mutated so that they no longer had the capacity to enhance a Force-user's abilities.

But the bota was irrelevant. What was relevant was
what it *did*: it enhanced Force connections. So the real
significance of pyronium was that it could somehow be
harnessed by or channeled through Force energies. It
was theoretically an unlimited source of raw physical
power—as the Force was theoretically an unlimited
source of psychic energy.

Darth Ramage's interest in the bota had been that it
presumably could heighten or deepen the Force energies
needed to condition that power and apply it.

Meaning what?

Jax took the pyronium out of his belt pouch and held
it out on the palm of his hand. It appeared to his eyes as
a milkily iridescent gem the size of a small egg—a flattened ovoid. The Force was not an engine you could
plug into. It was a field. An emanation.

A *source*.

Acting on an impulse, Jax extended Force tendrils to
the pyronium, then lowered his hand, leaving the pyronium nugget floating before him in midair. It began immediately cycling through the visible spectrum—yellow,
orange, red, violet, indigo, cyan, green, and back to yellow, after several beats in its opalescent form where, Jax
realized, it was likely making a few stops on a part of
the spectrum he couldn't see.

He fed more Force energy into the gem, and the colors
brightened and cycled more swiftly. Of course, it was absorbing the kinetic energy from the Force. But it was
doing more than that. It was cycling the energy out again,
thought-directed into an impulse that buoyed it up.

Jax sat back and withdrew his Force energies from
the jewel. Instead of tumbling to the floor of the little
room as he might have expected, it stayed aloft . . . be-

cause he'd touched it directly with the Force, surrounded it with the Force, and given it direction through the Force. It continued to follow that direction.

At the outer edges of the conceptual wheel in which Jax sat, a shimmering rim burst into being, connecting the spokes.

forty-three

Docking at Kantaros Station was simple and straight-forward. Doing business there was—if not as simple—at least a fairly straightforward matter of the appropriate level of bluster and bribery. Den Dhur was reasonably good at bluster—one had to be good at it to be a journalist, and he had been a journalist most of his life.

Sacha, it appeared, was also good at it. Looking diamond-hard and piratical, she strode into the station-master's office and offered up their wares, which—as they'd ascertained on Mandalore—were sought-after items on the station.

The stationmaster—a corporate functionary whose name, according to his badge, was Cleben—was human. This, Den decided, was a distinct advantage, since it meant the man had no trouble keeping his attention on "Captain" Swiftbird.

But, naturally, there had to be a wrinkle.

"You're a week early, *Raptor*," he said. "And what happened to Captain Vless?"

Without missing a beat, Sacha grimaced. "I guess you wouldn't have heard. Vless had quite the run of luck. Got promoted to a cushy position on Mandalore. Merchant commandant, if you please."

Cleben looked impressed. "So you inherited his ship?"

Den tried not to panic. A simple scan of the docking bay would show that the *Raptor* had more than a new captain; she had a whole new everything. He started to open his mouth to utter a glib lie.

"Nope," Sacha said smoothly. She shook her head, trailing dark, silver-streaked tresses over her shoulders. Cleben seemed fascinated. "He took his ship with him. All *I* inherited was his ship's ident codes. Seems he'd always fancied naming his bird the *Rancor's Heart*. A merchant commandant gets to pick things like that. Captains take whatever they can get."

"Really," said Cleben. "You can't even name your own ships? I thought the Black Sun was a little more flexible than that."

"Depends on what Vigo you fly under," Sacha said. "I pilot for Xizor. He likes to control pretty much everything."

Cleben nodded. "Yeah, I hear that about Xizor." He looked at Sacha speculatively. "Maybe you can confirm something else I've heard about the prince—that he's in deep with the Imperials."

Den threw Sacha a significant glance.

She didn't bat an eyelash. "Oh, now that's the sort of rumor I can neither confirm nor deny." She flashed a smile.

Cleben grinned back as if she'd just issued him an award. "Yeah, I get it. Look, I'll need to go over your manifest. Assess my . . . I mean, *our* needs. The Toydarian's first in line, but as soon as I've dealt with him. I'll gladly take a look at your . . . cargo. That okay?"

"That's fine," Sacha said, smile intact. She tossed the datachip of the manifest onto Cleben's console. "In the meantime, we'll go check out the facilities."

"This your first time here?"

She nodded.

"Eh, you might find it vaguely interesting. Since you're new here, I'll issue the standard warning. You're restricted to the civilian areas of the station. Stay away from the Red Zone. Imperials only."

Sacha made a pouty face. "Hey, even Imperials have itches to scratch. I've got some premium glitterstim—"

Den glanced at her sharply. Was that a lie, or had she really smuggled glitterstim onto the ship? He'd noticed a couple of crates of cargo that *he* hadn't loaded . . .

The stationmaster was shaking his head. "Uh-uh. Don't even think about it. They bring in their own forms of diversion. We supply them with the basics— food, beverages, medicinal supplies. Everything else, they take care of themselves. And they are dead down on glitterstim, especially when *he's* here."

"Darth Vader, you mean?" Den asked.

"Who else? And be careful down in the cargo bays. Every once in a while someone stumbles across the divide into their domain. That's never pretty."

"Killjoy," Sacha said playfully, smiling.

"Seriously," said Cleben. "These are not nice people. Any place their habitat touches ours is potentially dangerous. I wouldn't want to see you get fragged, sweetheart."

"I'll try not to, *honey*." Sacha returned the man's come-hither gaze with a sketchy salute and strode out of the office, trailing her crew of two.

They wandered into the commercial section of the station where the support staff lived and amused themselves when they weren't on duty. It was composed of a broad, curving arcade with various businesses along either side. There were inns for visiting crews, two cantinas, several eateries, a mercantile, a clothier, a repair shop for droids and mechanisms, and a gaming shop that featured amusements from a dozen worlds. Peripheral corridors radiated out from the main gallery at intervals, each color-coded and numbered.

At the very end of the commercial arcade was a wide,

sealed portal with a rather understated version of the Imperial sigil decorating the control panel to its left. Even as Den watched, the doors slid open and a pair of stormtroopers issued out. In fact, there were more stormtroopers and Imperial officers here than Den was strictly comfortable with, so clearly there was no rule against fraternizing with the civilian staff.

Sacha chose one of the eateries and led them in for a meal and a vantage point from which to watch the comings and goings of the patrons—paying special attention to the stormtroopers and Imperial officers. Her interest in the Red Zone portal made Den nervous, but it was I-Five who remarked on it.

"I hope," the droid said, fixing his monoculus on the Toprawan's face, "that you're not planning on sauntering down there and trying to get in."

"Heck no. Even I'm not *that* much of a risk-o-phile. I'm thinking the cargo area might afford better access."

"So, what's our next move?" Den asked.

"Lay of the land. There's got to be some way to come by the construction plans for this place. Those schematics Jax got from Xizor are a bit hazy on the Imperial side of the station."

"Indeed," said I-Five. "I hope it will merely be a matter of me having a brief discussion with the maintenance AI."

Jax did not so much meditate on his way to the Bothan system as he ruminated, working at further assimilating the knowledge that the Sith holocron had poured into his head. His agenda was fairly simple: determine where Yimmon was, then send a projection in to make the Inquisitors and their non-adept fellows look in the wrong place, while he headed for Yimmon from the opposite side of the facility.

Simple in theory. In practice . . . who knew?

He was more than aware of all the traps Vader had set around his prisoner. That probably meant that there was only one real access to wherever they were holding him and that the traps made any other avenues impassable— or at least they were meant to do that.

The blast cage was of no particular concern. It might muddy the Cerean's biological signature, but it couldn't touch what Jax felt through the Force. If Yimmon were to be placed in the blast cage, it would make Jax's job a bit more difficult, but not impossible. Of even less concern were the sonic devices intended to confuse and distort scanners. In fact, given what he now knew about Force projection, they might be more a help to an invading Jedi than a hindrance.

Much hinged on Vader's certainty of Jax Pavan's demise. Presumably, the inclusion of Inquisitors in the Dark Lord's party was his nod to the possibility that Jedi yet lived who might challenge him, but what if there were more? What if Vader were prepared to turn back a Jedi invader?

Jax bit down on that grim thought. Well, so what if the Dark Lord were prepared for a Jedi? He couldn't possibly be prepared for a Jedi who had opened Darth Ramage's holocron and absorbed its contents.

It was Sacha Swiftbird's personal opinion that the *Raptor,* late of Keldabe, Mandalore, could not have drawn a better assignment in Kantaros Station's cargo bays than the one she'd gotten.

The freighter bays were arrayed in long arcs, two levels deep, that began beneath the manufactured part of the station and ended in a series of caverns that burrowed into the flank of the asteroid. The bay in which the faux-*Raptor* sat was within the asteroid itself, below the equator. Between her and the so-called Red Zone, there was but one ship—a fat, insectile ore carrier out of the Mimban system.

The ore ship had settled into the hangar bay stern-first, so that her swollen backside hung over the broad interior walkway, putting the smaller *Raptor* in her shadow and effectively shielding her almost entirely from the view of the Red Zone portal on this level. The portal was broad enough to take three antigrav pallets at once, and twice the height of the two stormtroopers guarding it.

On the other side of that barrier, Sacha knew, were Imperial ships . . . and the entire Imperial complex.

The exact shape of that complex was hidden, even from the Kantaros maintenance AI. The maintenance system and its automated minions had only sufficient intel on the layout of the Imperial facility that they could perform the most basic of upkeep functions. The various corridors and chambers were viewable only as part of a tactical display; there were no live images or even area designations available. The Red Zone's internal systems were segregated from those of the main station and operated and maintained from within the zone itself. That meant they had to trust the schematics Jax had gotten from Prince Xizor.

Not a happy thought.

Now, standing at the bottom of the cargo ramp waiting for Stationmaster Cleben and his droids to take possession of the cargo he'd purchased, Sacha kept one eye on the portal and one on Cleben.

He liked to talk. When he talked, he liked to invade her space.

The third or fourth time he leaned into her and tried to put an arm around her waist, she pretended to see Den giving I-Five's Ducky persona a mistaken order and moved swiftly to intercept.

"Hey! Hey! That crate's mismarked! It's not Corellian spice wine, it's three-oh-seven ale. These guys can't handle that rotgut! Put it back!" She slipped between the droid and the Sullustan, squatting to inspect the crate and change the label with her inventory handheld.

"This guy takes the biscuit," she murmured so that only her companions could hear her. "Pushy sleaze. I wish I could get rid of him."

"You did flirt with him back in his office," Den observed unhelpfully. "I'm sure he's just following up on his promise to handle your, um, cargo."

Sacha glared at him. "I'd like him to keep his hands *off* my cargo, thanks. Any actual help would be appreciated."

Cleben had wandered over to them at this point and was standing right behind Sacha as she rose—close enough that she could feel his breath fan her hair. She grimaced. Unruly droids she could handle, unwholesome speeds she could handle, bar fights she could handle. In fact, if this guy were this annoying in a bar, she'd simply deck him. Alas, she was on his territory and he had the authority to toss them all off the station.

She turned on her heel and offered Cleben a smile.

"Leave the crate," he said, leaning in to put a hand on it. It bobbed gently in the grasp of its antigravity field. "I assure you, there isn't an ale made that the lads on this station can't handle . . . well, *my* lads anyway. Can't vouch for those Imperial types."

"Sure," Sacha said. "The crate's yours. Ducky, let him have the crate."

I-Five obeyed immediately, releasing the antigravity containment on the crate and allowing it to crash to the deck of the bay . . . and onto Stationmaster Cleben's left foot.

The result was spectacular and gratifying, in Sacha's opinion. Cleben shrieked and hit the deck, "Ducky" re-engaged the antigrav unit, and Den watched it all, wide-eyed, his mouth hanging open. Sacha took charge of the situation, cursing at the little droid and shouting for assistance.

In short order, a couple of Cleben's men had arrived to carry him off to the infirmary and the cargo was hauled away by a team of efficient droids. It was during their departure that a couple of R2-AG units wove their way past the departing crates and beetled in the direction of the Red Zone portal.

Sacha, her head bent over her inventory tablet, watched through a veil of hair as the two droids bustled through the portal without so much as a nod on the part of the stormtroopers guarding the checkpoint.

Beside her, I-Five made a peculiar noise that sounded suspiciously like a purr.

"You saw it, too, huh?" she asked as she turned back toward their ship and started up the cargo ramp.

"Saw what?" Den asked. "What did you see?"

I-Five swiveled his oculus to focus on the Sullustan. "How we're going to get inside the Red Zone. Or at least, how *I'm* going to do it."

Less than ten minutes later, his carapace polished to a gleaming finish, "R2-Five" rolled out of the shadow of the Mimban freighter. He approached the Red Zone portal without hesitation and zipped through just as the previous droids had, disappearing from view beyond the guards.

Seated in the *Laranth*'s engineering bay, Sacha made a rude noise. "They're probably fast asleep inside those little plastic shells." She leaned forward, her eyes on the flat-panel display set into the communications console. "Didn't so much as twitch."

Den mirrored the movement, his eyes following I-Five's progress into the Imperial docking bays. "Cams above the doors."

"I see 'em," Sacha murmured.

"I make five ships here," I-Five said—his voice generated internally so that it was heard only aboard the ship. "Several empty bays. As you can see, the largest is the one closest to the interior access."

They could see that. The empty bay, Den thought, was big enough for a *Lambda*-class long-range shuttle. Darth Vader's shuttle.

Beyond the empty bay along the arc of the huge chamber was a second checkpoint, this one unguarded, but with obvious sensor arrays and surveillance cams. As they watched I-Five's approach, the doors parted to expel an Inquisitor and an Imperial officer—a lieutenant. They were in conversation—something Den thought peculiar enough—then stopped and exchanged a few more words before the officer made his way to one of the docked shuttles and the Inquisitor turned and went back into the heart of the facility.

Neither of them noticed the little R2 unit going about its business, its turret swiveling this way and that. When the R2 stopped at a maintenance port to insert a connecting rod—presumably making a status check or receiving orders from the system—the Inquisitor continued on into the Imperial sector of the station. After a beat, the R2 unit followed at a respectful distance.

"Five, is that wise—following that Sith lackey?" Den asked, his stomach beginning to tie itself in knots.

"If I hope to find Thi Xon Yimmon, I believe so."

"There's no way to know if he's going anywhere near Yimmon," Den objected.

"There's no way to know anything more than what I gleaned from my momentary contact with the AI on this side of the checkpoint. I believe I know where the detention center is."

"That's where the dark side *peedunkey* is headed?" asked Sacha.

"The dark side *peedunkey*?" Den repeated.

"It's Huttese," Sacha said. "You don't want to know what it means."

"I don't know if that's where the Inquisitor is going," I-Five said. "But if he's not, I won't bother to follow him farther."

Seemingly endless corridors of mind-numbing sameness unfolded before I-Five's oculus. They were uniformly silvery gray in color, with textured floor coverings underfoot, and occasional portals—all open—that could be shut to seal off lengths of the corridor in case of emergency. Along these hallways were color-coded and labeled doors leading to other chambers, none of which seemed of interest to the mechanical spy. Some had surveillance cams mounted above them for extra security. I-Five continued to tail the Inquisitor, passing other droids, stormtroopers, and the occasional Imperial officer.

Just as Den was feeling as if his eyes would fall out from lack of blinking, the Inquisitor whom I-Five was following finally took a turn that the droid ignored. The Inquisitor stopped, turned, palmed a door control, and entered what I-Five's swift glance revealed were private quarters.

The R2 unit rolled on without pause, taking a cross-corridor to the left that would lead to the bowels of the station.

Den swallowed a sudden nervous lump in his throat. "Careful," he murmured.

"Not to worry."

In moments the corridor I-Five traversed took on a decidedly fortresslike aspect. The bulkheads were thicker and textured like honeycomb. Within some of the hexagonal cells, small blinking devices sat guard.

"Sonic distortion units," I-Five told them. "My sensors are useless here, unless—"

He didn't get to finish the thought. The corridor erupted with sudden activity—droids bustling this way and that, half a dozen stormtroopers and an Inquisitor hastening past him going the opposite direction. The sound of klaxons bleated through the connection between I-Five and his two companions aboard the *Laranth*.

The Inquisitor glanced down at the droid as he swept by, affording the watchers a glimpse of his face.

"Tesla!" Den sat up straight on a chill bolt of recognition.

Sacha ignored him. "What is it? What's happening, I-Five?"

The point of view swung to the retreating troops. "Do you want me to find out? Or find Yimmon?"

Den and Sacha exchanged glances. "Yimmon," they said in unison.

The view swung back to the corridor. The R2 unit rolled about five meters farther along, then stopped before a short, broad T-intersection and turned. At the end of the corridor was a portal warning in graphic characters that access was restricted to Imperial Security personnel by order of Darth Vader. There were security cams here, too. Anyone who entered the access corridor would be caught on them.

"That it?" Sacha asked. "Is that the detention area?"

"That would be my guess," I-Five said. "And it is at the dead center of the asteroid. Shielded very effectively, I should say, unless one happens to be a Jedi."

"Or a droid with more moxie than sense," Den murmured.

"I heard that." I-Five completed a visual sweep of the portal and its environs, then swung back around the way he'd come.

"Distance to the inner door?" Sacha asked.

"Four meters."

"Four meters—four seconds," Sacha murmured. "Standard lock interface?"

"Yes."

"Which you should be able to open."

"Probably not without alerting security. Do you have what you need, Sacha?"

"Yep. If you've located all the security sensors."

"If?"

She chuckled. "I've got what I need. Come on back before you get swept up in whatever's going on over there."

The droid obeyed immediately, trundling back through the Red Zone's hallways. He had made the turn at which he'd parted company with the Inquisitor he'd followed when the stormtroopers reappeared, marching in perfect unison toward him.

In their wake were the Inquisitor, Tesla, and Darth Vader.

Den got a way-too-close look at a reflection of R2-Five in Vader's black mask as he passed by and licked suddenly parched lips. "We just ran out of time."

forty-four

Tesla had served the Dark Lord long enough to know when the Sith was agitated. He felt his Master's present agitation as a chaotic, eddying current that seemed to have neither direction nor destination. He did not let on that he felt this, however. Nor did he ask what was disturbing his Lord. To hint that he thought Darth Vader was in any way shorn of his usual cold, imperturbable self-possession could prove disastrous.

And yet Probus Tesla knew better than most that his Lord was a being—somehow the word *man* seemed inadequate and inappropriate—of towering passion . . . but a passion that, like an incipient volcanic eruption, was shielded within the walls of an impenetrable furnace. It was what gave Darth Vader his aura of power, Tesla thought—that sense that there was a deep, hot molten core beneath the icy exterior.

Now, as they made their way toward Vader's private quarters, Tesla simply waited for his Lord to make his wishes known—which he did not do until he had dismissed the stormtroopers and given the Imperial officers orders to extend the station sensors farther into the asteroid field.

"You followed my orders regarding Thi Xon Yimmon?" Vader asked him when they were alone.

"Yes, my Lord. I observed him carefully and closely." True.

Tesla expected Vader to ask next what he had observed.

He didn't. Instead he asked, "Did you sense any . . . disturbances in the Force while I was absent?"

What *had* he sensed? That he was being observed, probed by rivulets of Force sense? "Not that I couldn't account for. Why do you ask? Has something happened, Lord Vader?"

The gleaming, black mask was opaque, but Tesla did not imagine the momentary stillness behind it, as if the Dark Lord were calculating how much to reveal. He felt a tickle of disappointment. Darth Vader didn't trust him, that was clear. He swallowed the disappointment; he would win that trust.

"A door opened," Vader said, "and out of it poured light and darkness . . . twilight. Like the moment before dawn. It was . . . unexpected."

"I don't understand," Tesla said stupidly.

Vader made an abrupt gesture. "You didn't feel it, then?"

"When would—"

"No matter. If you had felt it, you'd know. You wouldn't need me to put a time or date on it. You would *know.*"

Tesla bit his lip, using the pain to focus his emotions. Once again he had been found wanting, but he would not allow it to affect him. "You asked about Yimmon. If I had observed him."

Vader moved restlessly, then turned to face his Inquisitor. "And what did you observe?"

Tesla had thought much about this—about the peculiar feeling of being watched when he was in contact with Yimmon. But how to explain it to his Lord without revealing the depths of that contact?

He did not answer the question directly. "The dual cortex possessed by the Cereans is a significant adapta-

tion," he began. "It allows them, I think, to be . . . quite
above the sort of tactics we have used. I believe that
whether he is experiencing pain, sensory deprivation, or
anxiety, our 'guest' is able to literally detach himself
and rise above what he is feeling. It's as if he is able to
allow one part of his brain to feel the emotions connected to his suffering, then buttress it with the strength
of the other."

Vader's masked face was turned toward Tesla, but of
course he could read nothing in the opaque optical
shields. He cleared his throat and forged on.

"It has been theorized that a Cerean's lower faculties
reside in one cortex and his higher ones in the other."
He had researched that exhaustively and was pleased
with his findings.

Vader stirred, and Tesla had the absurd idea that his
mind had been elsewhere.

"That would be a remarkable adaptation," Vader said
now. "Let the primitive lower brain absorb the physical
and psychic shocks, then soothe it with the higher faculties."

"My thought, Lord Vader," Tesla said, taking a quick
step toward the Sith, "was that it is an adaptation that
could be used against him."

Vader was still watching him. "You found contact
with him . . . disturbing."

It wasn't really a question, and Tesla hesitated, knowing that he had allowed something to seep from beneath
the shield he'd erected around his own emotions. "Yes.
I did. Until I determined why he made me uncomfortable."

Vader's regard was swift and piercing. "A sensation of
being watched."

Tesla felt as if every bit of blood had drained out of
his head. Could Darth Vader penetrate him that easily?
"I . . . I find that an accurate description."

Vader turned away and moved to stare at the view-screen that showed the prisoner in his expansive cell, sitting, as ever, in meditation. "Could he be the source of . . ." He didn't finish the thought.

"The source of what, my Lord?"

"Of the strange . . . twilight effusion I felt in the Force."

Tesla shook his head. "I don't know, Lord."

"No. You don't." Vader swung about to face him. His gaze, as always, was inscrutable, expressionless—still, Tesla felt sweat break out beneath his heavy robes. "That is, Master, I have no reason to believe him a Force adept as such, though . . ."

"Yes?"

"When I was in the room with him, I did sense *something* beyond what I expected. I believe that to be the result of a combination of his extreme intelligence and his species' dual cortex. In fact, the answer to breaking Thi Xon Yimmon—to making him permeable—might lie in surgically disconnecting his cortices so that the one cannot defend or buttress the other."

Darth Vader was still for a long moment, so still for so long that Tesla felt a vague annoyance that he should have come to what he felt was a remarkable idea, only to have his Master focus less on what should have been of vital interest—crushing the resistance—and more on some freakish "twilight effusion" of the Force that Tesla had not even felt.

Vader abruptly turned back to the viewscreen in a swirl of black robes. "Arrange for our 'guest' to be taken to the infirmary. I will program the surgical droid myself."

Tesla fought to muzzle the burst of accomplishment—of pride. He had done it; he, Probus Tesla, though but an Inquisitor, had solved a conundrum that the Dark Lord himself had been unable to solve. "Yes, Lord

Vader. At once." He turned and strode toward the entrance to his Master's quarters.

Vader's next question was soft, almost purring; yet Tesla felt it as a bucket of ice water poured down his back. "Tell me, Tesla—how did you come to know what you have told me about Yimmon?"

The words arrested him just shy of the door. "I . . . I have done a great deal of research—"

"You sensed this. You *felt* the dual regard."

"I . . . Yes."

"Yet I did not," Vader said musingly. "Perhaps because I was working to contain him, while you *were* contained. You walked through the intersection of his dual consciousness."

"I—I realize that you told me to observe only, my Lord. Which I did, though I admit I got closer to him than I intended. For that I am truly—"

Vader seemed not to have heard him. "Interesting. That the experiences of even an inferior Force-user may prove instructive."

Inferior? Anger flared in Tesla's breast, then quickly guttered. Of course he was inferior. For one blinding second he'd forgotten to whom he was speaking. That was dangerous. *Extremely* dangerous.

Vader continued, "You walked through his mind. Did you leave your footprints there?"

In an obscure corner of Probus Tesla's consciousness, the part that was not quaking in scalded fury cowered in terror. "My Lord, I . . ."

"Tell me."

The compulsion was stronger than mere words, leaving Tesla with the impression that Vader held his will in one gloved hand.

"I—I merely suggested that Whiplash had fallen. That his network of friends and associates on Coruscant was gone. That it was only a matter of time before the entire resistance was as dead as Jax Pavan."

The release was sudden and violent. Tesla reeled back against the wall, gasping for breath.

Vader's voice was once more unnervingly calm. "Go. Prepare for the surgery."

Tesla went, wondering if it had been his disobedience that had caused that flare of rage in his Master . . . or the mention of a dead Jedi. He had a feeling it had been the latter.

forty-five

The mechanical part of the plan was the hardest in some ways. Having ascertained that an Imperial corvette was entering the Bothan system and making for Kantaros Station, Jax traced its path and placed his Force-cloaked vessel directly in it. It was possible that even this minimal use of the Force—the equivalent of waving a closed fist at someone behind their back—might alert Vader if he were near, but Jax couldn't let himself worry about the extent of the Dark Lord's abilities at this juncture.

When the ship overflew his position, Jax tried his hand at Force projection: a swiftly spinning chunk of ice and rock the size of a long-range shuttle seemed to ricochet out of the orbit of the larger asteroid field and tumble into the corvette's path, causing its helmsman to brake tens of kilometers early.

Pacing the corvette, Jax brought the *Aethersprite* into contact with the keel of the Imperial ship so gently that he doubted the contact had even registered on the ship's systems. A moment later the larger vessel raised its shields, enfolding Jax within them as it dived into the asteroid field.

Perfect. Now even the most sophisticated sensors would read the energy profile of his ship as part of the output of the corvette. The trick now was getting onto the station.

The corvette wouldn't enter the space docks—it was too large. It would use a refueling rig flown from the station to replenish its fuel. Any personnel and cargo that needed to be off-loaded would make use of shuttles to enter the docking bays.

That was where things got tricky. Entering one of the station's docking areas Force-cloaked was out of the question. Shuttles docked close enough to one another that one of them would be almost certain to collide with him if he seemed to be an empty space. The only possibility was another application of Force projection. A more prodigious one this time: the Delta-7 had to pretend to be a docking shuttle or courier vessel.

And so it did. When the Imperial corvette's shuttles left for the station, there was an additional courier in their number that was directed to a diplomatic bay in the northeastern hemisphere of the station's Imperial sector. It landed stem to stern with another courier, docking in the other vessel's shadow, just within the docking bay's perimeter force shield.

It was, as far as the Imperial operatives in the area were concerned, unremarkable in every way.

"Sacha, he's not coming back out." Den stood in the hatch of the ship's engineering bay, his stomach feeling as if he'd swallowed a nest of jellyworms.

She looked up from whatever she was working on and let out an expletive that made the Sullustan's dewlaps quiver and his ears flush. "Where the hell did Jax get that fragging crisper in the first place? He sure doesn't act like any droid I've ever known."

"Jax inherited I-Five from his father. Can you come talk to him? He seems to feel now that he's downloaded his data he should continue surveillance."

"Maybe he's right."

"Maybe he's right?" Den echoed in disbelief. "How're

we supposed to get into the facility if he's not with us? Someone's got to take out the stormtroopers while he messes with the cams at the checkpoint, right?"

She grinned at him. "Actually, I'm gonna mess with the cams." She snapped a cover onto the item she'd been working on and held it up for him to see. "My patented sensor recursor."

The "patented" recursor was a thin rectangular object about the length of Sacha's index finger. It had a touch pad on it and a tiny vid display.

"Your what?"

"Recursor. It'll basically cause whatever cam or sensor it's aimed at to loop until it's told to stop. One of the clever things you can do with ionite."

"So you're saying we don't need Five to come back."

She shook her head, pocketing the recursor and striding to the communications console. "Didn't say that. We absolutely need him to come back. But additional surveillance would be good, too."

Den grimaced. "Meaning we need two of him."

"At least." She opened a connection to I-Five. "Hey, Tinnie. Your sidekick here tells me—"

"They're moving Yimmon," I-Five announced.

Den imagined he could hear tension in the mechanically generated voice. Impossible, of course. But he could see by the sudden stiffening of Sacha's body that she'd had the same reaction.

Both of them glanced up at the viewscreen above the engineering console. The view I-Five had online showed a group of six stormtroopers and an Inquisitor leading a shambling Thi Xon Yimmon down a short corridor through a set of sliding doors that closed with a snap behind them.

"Where is that?" Den asked.

"Medbay. Two levels up from the high-security area and almost as well protected."

Even as he answered, I-Five rolled up to an AI port and inserted his data wand. He withdrew it mere moments later and began to move away down the hall.

"They've got an OR set up in there. All I could get out of the medbay AI is that they're planning on performing neurosurgery on him. The AI knows nothing about the nature of the procedure—access to that information was sealed by Darth Vader himself."

Den felt as if the worms in his stomach had turned to ice. He and Sacha exchanged glances.

"I'm returning to the outer docking portal," I-Five said, not waiting for them to respond. "There are two stormtroopers there and security apparatus. I need you to come in at the exact moment I'm going out."

"Yeah, yeah, so the portal will be open. I get it," said Sacha. "Then what?"

"There is a small life pod under repair just to your left as you enter the portal."

"Yeah. Saw it when you went in."

"We should be able to use it to cover our activities. If we can take out the troopers swiftly and quietly, we should be able to make use of one of the uniforms and gear to get you inside. Sacha, you spoke of creating a device that would confound the cams—"

"Done. If we time it right, the surveillance system will never know we're there." She quickly explained how the recursor worked, for which I-Five applauded her with a single word of praise.

"Elegant."

"Not really. But it was all I could do on such short notice."

Den's gaze was on the display above the console. It presently showed a set of turbolift doors that hissed open as he watched. The R2 was out like a shot, nearly colliding with a pair of technicians. He rounded them, and continued darting through the mazelike corridors at high speed.

"You might want to slow down a bit, Five," Den advised. "You don't want to draw too much attention to yourself."

"I'm behaving like all the other R2 units I've seen here. Bustling little tin cans. No one even notices them—" His voice simply stopped, though the scenery continued to fly by. After a pause, he said, "I'm approaching the inner docking bay doors. Time to scramble."

Sacha closed the connection to the console, picked up a comlink from the collection above it, and keyed it to I-Five's frequency. Den did the same. Then they headed for the portal that gave onto the Imperial docking bays.

They wandered up to the checkpoint, stopping just short of the area the cams covered. The stormtroopers turned their heads in unison to track Sacha, proving that there were actual men inside the white shells.

Sacha smiled. Waved. "Hi, boys. Tell me, do you ever get bored standing there like that?"

They ignored her.

Den's comlink pinged. "Now," he said.

Sacha targeted one surveillance cam, then the other, starting them on an endless loop that showed two bored guards standing there in their little plastic outfits.

"Hey!" said one of the guards. "What's that in your hand?" He raised his weapon.

The portal slid open and an R2 unit appeared. It stopped in the exact center of the doorway, effectively holding the doors open. It was enough to distract the guards: Den stunned the one to his right; Sacha took out the one to his left.

Checking to make sure the concourse behind I-Five was empty, Den and Sacha dragged the two unconscious stormtroopers back into the Imperial docking bay and into the lee of the life pod I-Five had identified as the best hiding place.

"I hope that worked," Den muttered, watching Sacha peel one of the stormtrooper's gear off.

"It worked," I-Five said, "because neither of these guards had a chance to call in an alarm. And even if someone should actually be monitoring the surveillance equipment at the various checkpoints, it would be unlikely they'd watch one post long enough to notice the repetitive nature of the guards' movements."

He swiveled his turret toward Sacha, who was mostly encased in the lightweight, sturdy plastoid of the stormtrooper's uniform. "Den is your prisoner," he told her. "I am your escort."

She nodded, put on the helmet, strapped on the Imperial weapon, and bundled the guard—clad only in his all-covering body glove—into the life pod with his partner. She gave each an infuser full of something she'd produced from a pocket in her own formfitting coverall.

"What is that?" Den asked.

"Something I picked up in the medbay."

"Do you—"

"Yes, I *do* know what it is, what it does, and how long it will take them to wake up and be able to move their joints and use their vocal cords."

She held up two Imperial comlinks. She opened one and removed its guts, stomping them to shards, then scooted them beneath the life pod's soft-docking skirt. Then she rose and crept to where she could see the full sweep of the concourse.

She knelt there for a moment or two, watching something going on down the way, then rose and beckoned to Den and I-Five. When they reached her, she drew her weapon, pointed it at Den, and nudged him along the causeway toward the inner portal. I-Five, in his astromech camouflage, scurried along at her side.

They were in the middle of the Imperial docking bay and had just come in sight of Vader's shuttle when I-Five spoke softly.

"He looked at me."

"Huh?" Den grunted.

Sacha said, "What? Who?"

"In the corridor earlier. When he was coming in from his shuttle. Vader looked at me as he passed by." He let a beat go by in which time Den's insides had once more gone squirmy, then added, "No one notices droids."

forty-six

Jax was wary of reaching out through the Force so close to Vader and his nest of Inquisitors, but he was hopeful that if he "tunneled," as Darth Ramage had called it—focused so tightly on a particular energy that he glided past all others—he might go undetected. The chief drawback of the discipline was that it kept the practitioner from being aware of any energies other than the one targeted. In seeking one Force-user, he might miss the presence of another.

For Jax, that was an acceptable risk. He knew there were Inquisitors on the station—suspected that Vader might even be here—though making absolutely sure would cause him to reveal himself.

What his tunneling told him as he sat in stillness aboard the starfighter-*cum*-courier was that Thi Xon Yimmon was no longer surrounded by sensor-confounding equipment. They had moved him. And, Jax realized as he felt the Cerean's patterns of consciousness alter inexplicably, they had drugged him.

Pursuant to what?

It didn't matter. Jax could wait no longer to move.

It would take many minutes to work his way to where Yimmon was being held. Ten. Perhaps fifteen. Perhaps longer if he met with unforeseen obstacles. There was no way to be sure when a decoy would be the most needful, so he would have to guess. He would also have to trust the station schematic he'd gotten from Xizor. The thought made him realize how dependent he'd gotten on I-5YQ for some things—I-Five would be able to check the schematic against the reality held in the Imperial AI, for example.

Jax would be less than honest if he didn't also acknowledge how much he missed the droid—and Den.

He stilled himself further, reaching for the knowledge he'd assimilated from the Sith holocron. It continued to appear in his mind's eye as a "library" containing a collection of books. Now he opened the Book of Time, plotted an angle of approach—the "southern hemisphere" that could be accessed from the commercial docks made the most sense—and felt of the local time currents.

Then, with the pyronium nugget suspended before him in a field of Force energy, he considered what a berserker Jedi might do to rescue a friend.

Tesla calmed himself with a will, imagining a cool stream of water pouring over his head. He was not nervous, merely excited. His Lord had requested that he oversee the prisoner's preparation for surgery while Vader, himself, conferred with the Emperor.

Tesla would be here at the Dark Lord's triumph; they would pry Thi Xon Yimmon's dual cortex open like a clamshell and extract pearls of information. They would have the resistance in the palm of their hands.

The Inquisitor checked the brain pattern readouts at the head of the table on which the prisoner lay.

Fascinating.

The twinned brains were even reacting to the anesthetic differently. One was in a soporific state; the other seemed much less affected. In fact, as Tesla watched, the more robust brain wave surged. At the same time, he felt a ripple in the Force, like a pebble dropped into a lazy pond.

Odd.

Which cortex was reacting, and what was it reacting to? Which brain handled the autonomic responses and which the higher reasoning faculties? He could make an educated guess, but there was no way to be certain.

Unless . . .

Tesla reached out a tentative rivulet of the Force to probe the Cerean's consciousness.

Up in the northern Imperial docking ring, in the bays reserved for small craft, a courier vessel opened her outer hatch and extended her landing ramp. An officer descended and made his way to the portal that led into the Imperial facility proper. He moved with a purposeful stride into the interior, passing other officers, a handful of technicians, a group of stormtroopers. Other than saluting superior officers, he interacted with no one.

In fact, Jax had no idea what he would do if someone decided to stop him. After setting up his decoy, he had used the pyronium to power the *Aethersprite*'s disguise. This meant the illusion was, to all intents and purposes, eternal, but it also meant that he didn't have the pyronium with him to extend his use of the Force. With it, perhaps he would be Darth Vader's equal; without it, he could only hope that something he had assimilated from the holocron would give him some small advantage, however fleeting.

He shook the dire thought away. He'd made the decision that keeping the Delta-7 cloaked was of paramount importance since it removed a potentially disastrous random variable—the sudden discovery of a Jedi vessel in an Imperial facility—and held open his only avenue of escape.

The projection of himself as an Imperial officer, while

effective, was difficult to maintain, given that he also had to tunnel to keep himself focused on Yimmon. He needed a different means of cloaking himself, one that would leave him free to employ the tools Darth Ramage's holocron had given him.

Letting go of Yimmon, he quickly scanned for an empty room, found one, and slipped into it. It was a small commons of some sort. No, rather, a meditation chamber—the lightfoils and other nuances confirmed this was where the Inquisitors practiced their various disciplines. It was empty just now, though Jax could sense the residual energies of its most recent and powerful occupants. Tesla had been here not that long before; the Jedi could feel the prickly texture of the Inquisitor's agitation.

He pushed the sensory fabric aside. An Inquisitor would be perfect for Jax's purposes—or rather, his outer garment would be.

He scanned again, seeking a Force signature nearby. He found one mere meters away.

Back out in the corridor, he located the doorway that hid the Inquisitor and signaled for admittance. After a moment of hesitation—during which he sensed an interruption of the other's meditative state, annoyance at having been interrupted, and hope that it would not be an interruption of long duration—the door slid aside to reveal a tall figure in the robes of an apprentice, still adjusting its cowl.

Surprise in his tone, the Inquisitor asked, "Yes, Major? What do you want?"

"A word with you," Jax said, and stepped through the door and around behind the Inquisitor—an Elomin. He raised a hand as the other man turned, touching his fingers to one bony temple.

Caught completely unawares by the psychic jolt, the Inquisitor folded up like an emptied sack and dropped to the floor. Jax considered taking the robe he wore, but changed his mind when he saw that others like it hung in a small closet next to the refresher unit. Better yet. That way, the Inquisitor would not be certain, on awakening, what had happened to him or why. If Jax was lucky, he wouldn't notice that one of his robes was missing.

He moved the unconscious Inquisitor to his bunk, then donned the borrowed robe swiftly, settling the hood over his head. As tall as he was, it was large on him and puddled a bit about his feet. Jax adjusted the folds of fabric to minimize that effect, then moved back out into the corridor. It was empty, so he took a moment to check his chrono; his decoy would activate in less than a minute.

Jax resumed his journey toward Yimmon, focusing completely on the Cerean's consciousness. What he found there surprised and perplexed him, for it was not Thi Xon Yimmon alone that he touched upon, but another consciousness, as well—subliminal, but clearly that of a Force-user.

In a chaos tumble of impressions and emotions, Jax understood three significant things: Yimmon was in a medical facility for some reason, he felt himself to be in immediate danger, and he was in mental contact with the Inquisitor Tesla.

Jax withdrew instantly. His feet continued to move forward, but his mind was roiling. If Tesla was probing Yimmon's drugged mind in some way, might he have sensed Jax's undisguised touch?

Jax reached out tentatively again, this time drawing on the residual personal energy of the robe's owner to muddle his own Force signature. No, Tesla's Force sense seemed focused elsewhere. Still, Jax felt a buzz of annoyance beneath the spiky texture of his curiosity about the nature of Yimmon's consciousness.

Duality. He was focused on its duality. On separating—

The intent of the Inquisitor's interest hit Jax like a bolt from a disruptor as he discovered yet another meaning of the Cephalon's riddle.

Yimmon's separation destroys us all.

He knew it as surely as if Tesla had spoken the words aloud into his ear. Darth Vader was going to surgically separate the two halves of Thi Xon Yimmon's brain.

Tesla kept his mind on the Cerean, his annoyance checked only by his sense of purpose. Trust Renefra Ren to try to snoop into Tesla's domain. He had felt the questing touch of the odious apprentice and had ignored it.

Vader would be here in mere minutes to oversee the clipping of Yimmon's neural pathways. If the operation was a success—if it yielded the information the Dark Lord needed and wanted to take down the resistance— Tesla could not help but be elevated in his Master's eyes. And when, at last, the Emperor died and Darth Vader moved to choose an apprentice—or if Vader were destroyed and the Emperor had to choose a new champion . . .

Tesla did not explore either avenue of thought. It was heady, and he was wary of falling into hubris. He was too smart—too cautious—to do that.

Some external stimulus vied for his attention. A noise he thought he recognized. It called him sharply, but he steeled himself against it. It was only Ren, most likely, trying to distract him from his responsibility to Lord Vader.

He would not let himself be distracted.

Sacha was sweating inside the stormtrooper's disguise. She was a tall woman, so it fit her reasonably well, but she felt restricted by it. She didn't know how to make use of the aural and visual enhancements built into the system, so the headgear only made navigation trickier.

"How far?" she asked I-Five.

"Four-hundred-eighty-two-point-oh-three meters," the droid responded.

"You can approximate."

"Why should I?"

"Quicker."

The R2 unit turned left. Two men in blue coveralls passed by, peering curiously at the Sullustan prisoner and his two guards. Neither spoke, though one did cast a glance at them over his shoulder.

Several meters along the new corridor, an Imperial officer—a commander, judging by his pips—passed by, then stopped.

"Who's this?" he asked Sacha, gesturing at Den.

She shot to attention, her mind fixing on one very important fact—she was female. Stormtroopers were all male. Her natural voice was a dusky contralto, but no matter how low she pitched it, it was still a woman's voice.

And yet she heard herself say in a clear baritone—without even moving her lips: "Sullustan spy. Tried to slip in through the portal in the commercial dock down on Level One. He was carrying an unknown device." Sacha had the presence of mind to raise the hand holding the recursor. "We suspect he may be a resistance operative."

The officer glanced at Den. "You aren't taking him to Lord Vader, are you?"

The last time Sacha had seen a look that cold, her Podracer had blown up within the next five minutes.

Again, the male voice issued—seemingly—from her lips. "No. I was told to take him to an Inquisitor named Tesla for questioning."

"Questioning. *Strip-mining* would be a more accurate term. And better than he deserves. Vermin. Carry on, then." He gestured down the corridor, turned on his heel, and paced away from them.

"Five?" Den asked softly as they resumed their walk. "Was that you?"

The droid responded in a series of beeps and whistles.

"Thanks," murmured Sacha. "I hadn't counted on being stopped—"

She drew up suddenly, hesitating. She couldn't have said why she was hesitating except that something had . . . *shifted* in the atmosphere of the station. It was like a sudden itch somewhere that she couldn't scratch. She shook herself mentally, squared her shoulders, and started to say something about being suggestible, but I-Five had stopped, too, and seemed to be staring at her.

"Oh, don't tell me you felt that, too," she murmured. "You couldn't have."

"Felt what?" Den asked, looking back and forth between the two of them.

I-Five set himself in motion again. Sacha followed suit, giving the Sullustan a gentle nudge toward their destination.

"Have you ever been tested for Force sensitivity?" the droid asked subliminally; she heard his voice over the stormtrooper uniform's audio receiver.

"When I joined the Rangers. It's . . . well, I'm no Jedi. But I get—you know—feelings. What about you?"

"Droids don't have the Force."

"Yeah? What *do* you have?"

"You know," Den said in a quietly aggrieved voice, "this is like listening to one half of a comlink conversation. What are you two talking about?"

Sacha turned the corner into a cross-corridor and halted yet again. What stopped her this time was a swiftly moving figure that shot into an intersection some ten meters distant, hesitated, then glanced in their direction.

Den let out a yelp of surprise. "Jax!"

If the Jedi saw them, he gave no sign of it. His gaze swept the corridor in which they stood, then he bolted out of sight.

"That was Jax!" Den cried. "Blast it, that was Jax!"

"Yeah, but where's he going?" murmured Sacha.

A handful of seconds later, alarms began to sound, and security lights raced along the floor and ceiling. I-Five took off toward the intersection with surprising speed. Sacha shouldered her blaster rifle and followed the droid, leaving Den to keep up as best he could.

"If that's Jax," the Sullustan said from behind her, "what the hell is he doing?"

She didn't answer, but broke into a run, arriving at the intersection at the same time I-Five did. She turned and looked down the corridor. Jax was nowhere in sight. The only turn he could have taken that would have "disappeared" him that swiftly would have been into one of two turbolifts between here and the next intersection—the wrong direction if he intended to get to Yimmon. Yimmon was on *this* level.

Was it possible he didn't know about the move? That seemed unlikely.

Was he running interference for them so they could get to Yimmon? That, too, seemed unlikely.

The thunder of boots against metal hauled Sacha's attention back to the present. She turned and dragged Den in front of her, clamping an ungentle hand on his shoulder and jamming the muzzle of the blaster into his back.

A moment later half a dozen stormtroopers raced by, ignoring them completely. The Imperials hesitated at the lift to eye the control panel, then dashed into the one across from it.

Sacha breathed out a long sigh of relief, then hurried her own team down the corridor toward the next junction, feeling that nasty itch between her shoulder blades again. She paused to give the lift panel a glance. It had, indeed, stopped two levels up.

What would happen, she wondered, if Jax realized his mistake, reversed course, and led the stormtroopers—and their boss—back this way?

"We're going to take the lift," she told Den.

"But we're already on—"

"I know, but if Jax realizes he's off course and heads back this way, we'll be overrun. We'll go down, get to a closer lift hub, and then go back up."

She activated the left-hand lift, then herded everyone into it, praying—perversely—that Jax *didn't* come back this way.

forty-seven

Jax stopped at the sound of the klaxon's wail. He wondered if there were some protocol that Inquisitors were supposed to follow under such circumstances—battle stations to go to, that sort of thing. It hardly mattered. He knew where he was going.

He was peripherally aware of the response to his decoy, felt the shift of attention to the part of the station where he had set his illusory doppelgänger to show itself—fleetingly—to surveillance equipment, before fading to nothing. While his "ghost" would seem to be coming up from the freight bays adjacent to the commercial sector toward the detention area, meanwhile the real Jax would arrive from the small-craft bays higher up on the northern hemisphere—almost the opposite direction. And he was targeting the medbay two levels below the lockup.

Now that he knew where he was headed, he took a moment to make a general sweep of the area for Force-users. He could do so nervelessly; it would be perfectly reasonable for an Inquisitor to check for the location of his compatriots in such a circumstance.

He opened himself to receiving the energies and was almost knocked from his feet by their violence. It was like being flayed by icy, malevolent whips of pure darkness. The regard of the Dark Lord was like a thick, viscous cable of frigid malice directed toward the Force projection. Around it, in spiraling tendrils of hostility, the energies of the Inquisitors whipped in the same direction. The attention of the stormtroopers and Imperial officers came in unfocused bursts like brittle slugfire.

Jax smiled grimly. So far so good.

To Probus Tesla, the Cerean's consciousness was a thing of wonder. With one cortex effectively dormant and the other in a dreaming state, the Inquisitor was able to get a real "look" into the rebel's mind. It was not the mind of a Force-user, certainly, but it was complex, with layers of ideation that overlapped like the currents of the deep.

Moving among the thought-eddies was like trying to glimpse the activity within a series of translucent bubbles that bobbed and moved with the current. The glimpses were tantalizing, and Tesla was certain that if he could but break one of the bubbles open and spill its contents—something he was sure the surgical procedure would facilitate—he would understand the workings of this exquisite mind.

Then, Lord Vader would realize Tesla's power and potential.

On the heels of this exhilarating thought came a chill stab of doubt: *What if the Dark Lord sees that power and potential as a threat to his own position? What then? Perhaps being clever around Darth Vader is not the best of strategies.*

Tesla felt Vader's summons even as he struggled with this dark epiphany. It was not the sort of summons he was used to. Instead of the usual steely command, what he received was a burst of intense *awareness*—a strange, dense admixture of disbelief, cold rage, excitement . . . and puzzlement. But all that was gone in an instant as if a door had slammed shut on the flow of sensation.

What was left was a visual image: Jax Pavan.

Tesla staggered mentally and physically, putting out a hand to steady himself on the side of Yimmon's bed.

No. It *couldn't* be. Pavan was dead. Tesla had seen the ship ripped apart by tidal forces. He had felt the sudden silence from the Jedi. The sudden stillness. He sensed nothing, now, that he recognized as a Jedi Force signature.

He wrenched his mind from its contact with Thi Xon Yimmon and stumbled to a comlink, suddenly aware of the bleating of the intruder alert. He shut down the alarm to the medbay and hailed the command center. "What's happened?"

"There's an intruder, Inquisitor," the officer of the watch said, telling him what he already knew.

"What intruder? How did he get in? Where's he heading?"

"I don't know how he got in, sir. He simply . . . appeared on our monitors. He seems to be heading for the detention block."

Tesla smiled. Yes, of course he was heading for the detention block. Because he thought that's where his colleague was. The Inquisitor shot a swift glance at the unconscious Cerean, shut down the comlink, and left the medbay, careful to lock it down at the exterior hatch.

He rounded the corner into the main corridor and found himself face-to-face with a tall apprentice Inquisitor. Renefra Ren, of course. Who else would be so arrogant as to forsake protocol to follow personal promptings?

"What are you doing here, Renefra?" Tesla snarled. "You're supposed to attend our Master under such circumstances, not follow me around. Come, the prisoner is secure and Lord Vader has summoned me."

He strode past his apprentice and moved down the hallway, realizing belatedly that the wretched creature hadn't moved. He swung back.

"Are you deaf? Or do you somehow think you can ingratiate yourself with our Master by hovering about his prisoner? Jax Pavan is on the station."

"Yes," said Renefra Ren in someone else's voice. "He is."

As Tesla registered the alienness of the voice, two things happened: Renefra Ren seemed to shimmer and shrink, and the turbolift to his right opened, revealing an armed stormtrooper, an R2 unit, and a Sullustan. The stormtrooper stepped out of the lift and took aim— pointing his blaster rifle right at Tesla's head.

"Back against the wall," the stormtrooper said in a female voice.

"Sacha, look out!" the Sullustan cried. "There're two of them!"

The white helm swiveled toward the unknown Inquisitor. Tesla acted reflexively, sweeping his left hand up and out. He Force-wrenched the rifle out of the fake trooper's hands, lifted her off her feet, and threw her against the wall of the lift.

"*No!*"

The roar of fear and rage hit Tesla's ears at the same time the emotions behind it struck his consciousness. An accompanying wave of Force power slammed into him and blew him heels-over-head down the corridor. As he surged to his feet, he heard the sizzle of a light-saber activating, saw the clear aqua beam of light, and knew that the approaching blur must be a Jedi—must be, in fact, Jax Pavan.

Tesla flung himself up and over the Jedi, careening along the ceiling before dropping back to his feet opposite the lift. A swift glance showed that the woman in the stormtrooper disguise was still out. The Sullustan was kneeling next to her.

The droid . . . where had the droid gone? If it was

really Imperial, it would be sending a call for assistance. If it was with these rebels . . .

Tesla drew his own weapon and turned to face his attacker. The indigo robes were gone now, and there was no question that it was Jax Pavan he faced.

"This is impossible," Tesla said. "You're . . . you can't be here. You're—"

"Dead?" the Jedi asked, then shook his head. "Sorry, no."

"You were up on the detention level."

"No." Pavan's face lit in a slow smile. "*He* was."

Tesla shifted his eyes momentarily to where the Jedi pointed. A second Jax Pavan—identical to the first—stood in the intersection of two corridors, lightsaber gleaming in his hand. The instant of distraction was enough; when Tesla turned back, the real Jedi was mere paces away, his lightsaber already in deadly motion.

Tesla had neither heard nor sensed the movement, and the realization both galled and chilled. He brought his Sith blade up to meet the Jedi weapon, barely in time. The two blades clashed in a shriek of energy.

"I don't have time for this, Tesla," Pavan growled. He glanced up over the Inquisitor's shoulder, that same taunting smile on his face, inviting his adversary to look.

Tesla refused the invitation. He didn't know how the Jedi had done this, but there could be only one Jedi and only one Jedi blade.

He smiled at Pavan. "Clever. But, of course, he can't be real. You're the last Jedi, and you have the last Jedi lightsaber."

He swung his blade down and around, whipping Pavan's weapon aside and shoving him backward. Pavan stumbled back a step. Tesla, grinning fiercely, continued his own blade's arc, sweeping it up and over, letting the Force augment the power of the downward stroke that would cleave Pavan in two . . .

Tesla's moment of triumph was interrupted by the sound of a second lightsaber, activating so close he could feel static crawling on his skin. He spun about . . . and was stunned to realize it was a red blade—a Sith blade—sweeping toward him.

His last fleeting emotion was puzzlement; his last fragment of thought was, *Impossible* . . .

forty-eight

Tesla was dead.

The agent of his demise stood over him with a Sith lightsaber in her hands, her dark, silver-streaked hair damp with sweat, her body still encased in a stormtrooper's armor.

Her pale gaze moved from the body to the blade. She deactivated it, bringing a strained silence to the corridor. Then she looked up at Jax. "*Wow,*" she said. "That was—effective."

Jax glanced down at the dead Inquisitor. The maroon cowling around his neck was a smoking ruin. "Help me get him out of sight."

"Here!" Den called from the medbay access corridor. He'd armed himself with the discarded blaster rifle. "Five's got the doors open."

Sacha and Jax dragged the corpse as far as the outer hatch of the access, but then Sacha stopped him from stepping into the short corridor and waved a handheld device at the cams over the doors.

"Just in case someone's watching," she said.

They entered the corridor, dragging Tesla's body between them. I-Five—in his R2 persona—had indeed opened the medbay doors, then disappeared. Jax and Sacha deposited their burden just within the medbay, but out of sight of the door.

"Den, lock the medbay doors and stand by," Jax said

tersely, then followed Sacha in search of the droid. They found him talking to the computer in control of Thi Xon Yimmon's autonomic processes.

Jax quashed a surge of emotion at the sight of the Whiplash leader—that this powerful intellect had been reduced to a sleeping hulk. He was struck anew by the horror of what Vader had meant to do.

"Can you wake him?" he asked I-Five.

"I've stopped the flow of anesthetic and programmed a mild stimulant. Beyond that—"

"Can we move him like this?" Sacha asked. "When Vader realizes he's chasing a phantom, this is the first place he'll go."

"He already knows," Jax said grimly. "Which means he's going to be casting around for me. I've managed to blur my Force signature, but it won't take him long to figure it out. He's too powerful. We need to get Yimmon out of here *now*."

"Jax . . ." The voice, a mere whisper, came from Thi Xon Yimmon's lips. "Spirit willing. Body . . ." He raised a shaking hand, focused his eyes on it, then let it drop.

"We have to move you now," Jax told the Cerean. "Can you stand?"

"He won't need to," I-Five said. He brought an antigrav medical gurney over to Yimmon's bedside. "Given the circumstances, what could be more natural than for the Inquisitor on duty to order the prisoner moved to safety?"

Thi Xon Yimmon was a big man. It took Jax, Sacha, and I-Five to heave him onto the gurney.

"What ship did you bring and where is it?" Jax asked Sacha.

"The *Laranth*—well, she's the *Raptor* now. Five stole their codes. She's in the commercial docking area one slip away from the external doors to this lovely place."

Jax groaned aloud. "That's where I started the decoy."

"Yeah, I know. We saw it."

Jax made a clutch decision. Reaching out with a dart of Force sense, he sought Darth Vader . . . and found him—on the same level and heading right for them. As soon as the connection was made, he knew he'd given up any hope of cover. Vader was alone—the stormtroopers and Inquisitors were sweeping up from the lower levels of the station, presumably driving any intruders in their path up into the northern hemisphere.

Had Vader not communicated the deception to them?

"Okay," Jax said. "We're going to have to take an alternative route out of here. Do you know where there are other exits into the main station?"

"Sure," said Sacha. "First thing we did when we got here—plot all the access points."

"If you go back the way you came, you're going to run into a horde of stormtroopers and Inquisitors."

She shrugged, rattling her body armor. "Fine. We'll keep to the upper levels."

"Good. Whatever I do, you need to get Yimmon to your ship and get him out of here. Understood?"

Sacha and Den both stared at him.

"You're not coming with us?" Den asked.

"I may not be able to. For one thing, I left the starfighter up in the shuttle bay. I'd really rather Vader not get his hands on it."

"And we'd really rather he not get his hands on *you*," said Den.

Jax closed his eyes. They had no idea. "I won't let him."

Moments later, an apprentice Inquisitor, a stormtrooper, and a droid exited the medbay with their two prisoners and got into the nearest turbolift. They headed up. Three levels later, they got off the lift and headed toward the commercial sector of the station. With the bulk of the Imperial forces concentrated below, there were few enemy soldiers on these levels and, though

they'd been alerted, they'd be looking for a Jedi interloper, not a security detachment encumbered with two
prisoners.

The Empire's penchant for paranoid secrecy was a
two-edged blade. No one they passed in the corridors
accorded them more than a glance.

Nor would Darth Vader, Jax thought . . . except that
there was a Jedi with them.

As they neared a junction approximately halfway to
the outer perimeter of the Imperial facility, Jax peeled
off the Inquisitor's robe and draped it over the gurney.

"Jax," Den asked, "what are you doing?"

Jax didn't answer. Instead he put a hand on I-Five's
turret. "Get them back to the ship, Five. Get them out
of here."

Then he sprinted away down the cross-corridor.

I-Five uttered a single, long note that sounded to Den
like a moan. The Sullustan shivered. He watched Jax
disappear down the corridor, feeling as if his personal
store of courage was disappearing right long with him.
He shook himself, kept his feet moving. He couldn't
think like that. They had a mission to carry out.

He glanced up over his shoulder at Sacha—for all the
good it did. Encased in her white plastoid armor, she was
all but invisible. But he knew she was thinking the same
thing: Keep moving. Keep to the plan . . . such as it was.
He had no idea what I-Five was thinking, but knew it
must be all the droid could do not to take off after Jax.
He didn't, though. He just kept moving along—steering
the gurney.

It struck Den as absurdly funny, at that moment, how
blithely they had waltzed in here expecting to break
Yimmon out. If Jax hadn't been there, *they* would have
come face-to-face with that Inquisitor. The surprise
would have been on *them*.

He started to laugh and found, once he'd got going, that he couldn't stop.

"What is it?" Sacha murmured and I-Five uttered a series of sharp tweets that Den was pretty sure meant "shut up."

He felt his hysteria subsiding. "I-I-I . . . What were we thinking? If it hadn't been for Jax—" He clamped his mouth shut as they passed a trio of Imperials moving briskly in the opposite direction.

"Huh," Sacha said softly when the corridor was empty again. "I see what you mean."

They went as far as they could on that level, then Sacha herded them all into a turbolift for the journey down toward the docking level.

"You don't intend to try to exit the way we came in?" I-Five asked her. "Chances are that empty checkpoint has been discovered."

"Yeah. I was thinking the same thing. Yimmon, how're you feeling right about now? Think you can stand?"

In answer, the Cerean sat up and swung his legs over the edge of the gurney. "I believe I can." He slid off the gurney, holding on to it for support.

Sacha stopped the lift one level above the docking bays but kept the doors closed.

Den looked up into Yimmon's face. His color wasn't good, and he was sweating. He moved so that the larger man could put a hand on his shoulder.

"What d'you think?" he asked. "Try a step?"

The Cerean tried two. Wobbly, but not dangerously so.

"Great." Sacha scooped up the Inquisitor's robe and handed it to him. "Try this on. Sorry we don't have one in your size."

Yimmon smiled and did as instructed. The robe was a bit tight through the shoulders, but it was long enough, and the draped cowl—tailored to afford room for an

Elomin's horns—covered his large cranium adequately, though it left his chin exposed.

Sacha pulled out the Sith lightsaber and put it into Yimmon's hands. "You'd scare me."

"I scare myself," Yimmon said gamely. He put a hand on Den's shoulder. The Sullustan grunted as the Cere-an's weight shifted.

"We ready?" Sacha asked.

Den nodded. "Let's go."

Sacha opened the doors and they moved out, heading for one of the exits that gave onto the civilian sector of the station. The gate guards gave them a once-over, seemed to find them of little interest.

Just as they crossed the threshold into the civilian side of the station, the stormtrooper on the right spoke to Sacha.

"Do you know if they caught the infiltrator?"

She turned and I-Five came to the rescue yet again, throwing his voice so that it seemed to be coming from inside the helmet. "Not yet. But it's only a matter of time."

"Heard a rumor it was a Jedi."

"A Jedi? The Jedi are all dead. Probably just one of those resistance crazies."

"Yeah. That makes more sense, I guess."

"Enough chatter," the tall Inquisitor said. "We have an appointment to keep." He gave Den a sharp shove that sent him stumbling into the civilian sector, then followed in a swish of indigo robes.

Sacha and I-Five moved crisply after him.

Den supposed he should relax once they'd moved out of sight of the checkpoint and into one of the commercial areas, but he didn't. His heart hammered in his chest, his mouth felt dry as a desert, and he was certain that any second an alarm would be raised. If the storm-troopers they'd anesthetized had been found and revived, they'd remember having seen a Sullustan at their checkpoint.

But no alarm went up on this side of the station, and they made their way back down to the cargo bays without mishap. Indeed, people seemed to keep scrupulously out of their way.

I-Five now shifted to be their advance guard—moving so swiftly that it was hard for Den, with his short legs, to keep up. He was panting by the time they got back to the ship and followed the little droid up the loading ramp.

Den finally relaxed when they were aboard and behind sealed doors—well, relatively relaxed. It wasn't as if sealed doors meant squat if Vader came for them, though Den suspected the Dark Lord was too focused on Jax to spare a thought for possible accomplices.

He felt a moment of absolutely hideous relief at the notion, and clamped down on it so hard his jaws spasmed.

Sacha peeled off her armor and headed for the bridge to prep for departure. After a brief argument about his physical condition—which Yimmon won, hands down—the Cerean followed her.

Den made his way back to engineering to make sure everything there was battened down. He was surprised to find the engineering bay empty. No I-Five. He checked the tiny crew commons, the cabins.

He stopped just short of opening up the hold to call the bridge. "Hey, Sacha, is I-Five up there with you?"

"Er . . . no. He's not in engineering?"

"No. Not a sign of him." Feeling the beginnings of worry, Den punched in the code to open the hold.

"Then where is he?" Sacha asked.

The hatch slid back on the nearly empty cargo bay and its mechanical occupants: a dormant pit droid, I-5YQ's souped-up I-Nemesis chassis, and an equally dark R2 unit.

It took Den a moment of silent gawping to realize that there was an open crate lying on the floor of the cargo bay—a crate roughly six feet long and about two feet deep. An empty crate. The words LEISUREMECH BB-4000 were printed on the side in Geri's careful block script.

Den's mind scrambled to make sense of what he was seeing. When could Five possibly have—

He remembered, then, how the droid had excused his belated return to the ship as they were preparing to leave Toprawa: "I had to consult Geri about some . . . further modifications."

"Further modifications, my dewlaps."

Den turned to head up to the bridge when he realized something else: the I-Nemesis was missing its arm-mounted blaster assembly.

forty-nine

Making his way back toward the medbay, Jax paused long enough to throw two more Force projections along his back trail to mislead the body of pursuers he could sense below and before him. Trying the same trick on Darth Vader would be fruitless—Vader had sensed him through the Force now, and there was nowhere to hide.

So he headed straight for the dark signature of energy he felt ahead of him, his mind tumbling through a series of absolutes: He must absolutely not allow Vader to retrieve Thi Xon Yimmon. He must absolutely not allow Vader to keep the Jedi starfighter.

He must absolutely not allow Vader to capture him.

If the knowledge in Yimmon's mind would wreak havoc on the resistance, the knowledge in Jax's would bring destruction of another order of magnitude. What it would mean to the Cephalon species alone was terrifying.

Coming to a branching of corridors, Jax hesitated. Go right and try to escape in the Delta-7? Or go left and face Darth Vader—and maybe, finally, end this.

The things he knew about time currents alone should give him an advantage over the Sith Lord. Vader could have no idea what Jax was capable of. The local time currents were manipulable. Maybe just manipulable enough to confuse his adversary.

Maybe.

For a moment, Jax stood on the edge of a precipice. If he could destroy Darth Vader—even if he sacrificed his own life in doing it—it would be worth it. Vader's death would serve to inspire more people to resist the Emperor's will. More important, it would deprive Palpatine of his greatest weapon . . . and it would avenge the destruction of the Jedi Order, the deaths of so many brilliant Force-users.

And Laranth.

I would be vengeance.

He looked to the left. Took a step that way.

Anger, hot and unexpected, scalded its way through him. He could not even begin to name its source.

Is that what it means to be a Jedi? Maybe the last Jedi? Is that what you want to die for, Pavan—revenge? Passion? Those emotions are from the dark side.

Gasping, Jax stumbled back against a bulkhead.

Then he took the right-hand turn and ran.

Jax's path through the corridors twisted and turned as he altered direction to avoid confrontation. His thoughts mirrored his flight. If he could reach the ship, he could blast his way out of here. If he couldn't do that . . .

He could feel Vader now—an ice-hot presence coming at him.

Ahead of him he suddenly sensed a quartet of sentients. They must have just stepped out of a lift. Two of them were Force-users—Inquisitors. He was surprised to realize he could feel the texture of their ability. One was soft, weak . . . new. An apprentice, maybe. The other was stronger. Not Tesla's equal, perhaps, but not inexperienced.

He could not avoid them without doubling back toward Vader, but if he engaged them . . .

No choice. He activated his lightsaber, stepped around a corner, and there they were: two stormtroopers and two Inquisitors. The troopers reacted to him swiftly, raising their blaster rifles and firing.

Jax easily deflected the blaster bolts while the Inquisitors drew their weapons. The smaller of the two wielded only a lightfoil, which marked him as an apprentice. Its tip quivered. Of course it did—the young adept was scared senseless. He had probably never seen a Jedi before, let alone faced one in combat.

That made him the obvious target.

Lightsaber spinning, Jax came right at the young Inquisitor, who reacted by dodging between the two stormtroopers, his cowl slipping to reveal a pale humanoid face with glittering, frightened eyes.

Jax darted after him, deflecting blaster bolts as he went.

The older Inquisitor did exactly what Jax expected him to do, as well—he slunk along the bulkhead, looking for an opportunity to get behind the Jedi. Jax ignored him for the time being, going directly at the stormtroopers and the terrified apprentice. He made a diagonal sweep with his lightsaber, slicing right through the blaster rifles and reducing their muzzles to molten nubs.

The Inquisitor behind him naturally chose that moment to attack Jax's seemingly unprotected back. Not content to merely rush the Jedi, he gathered the Force about him and leapt.

Jax dropped, rolled, and flicked out a whip of the Force to yank the apprentice forward several steps, right into the path of his superior's blade. The young adept bleated, blocking futilely with his lightfoil; the lesser weapon went spinning away to ricochet off the wall. The apprentice hit the floor.

The older Inquisitor executed his own twisting somersault and landed lightly on both feet, ready to come at Jax again.

One armed opponent. Better odds. No time.

Jax took a deep breath, steadied himself . . . then whipped around to face the turbolift. The doors slid open and Darth Vader stepped out into the corridor, turning his insectoid gaze on Jax.

The Inquisitor reacted by deactivating his blade, bowing his head, and backing hastily away.

That was all the time Jax needed. He gave the projection of Darth Vader a final surge of the Force, enough to hold it together a moment longer as he turned, vaulted over the stormtroopers, and raced away down the corridor.

His adversaries would wait for their Master to direct them, he knew. In the amount of time it would take them to realize the deception, he would be out of sight.

Two cross-corridors down, he stepped into a turbolift and took it up to the level of the shuttle bays. It was only when he'd had time to gather himself that he realized he could no longer sense Darth Vader's regard.

What did that mean? Had the Dark Lord turned his attention elsewhere? Had he realized that Yimmon was no longer with Jax and gone after the Cerean? Or had his recent unfamiliar use of the Force begun to deplete Jax's resources?

The turbolift doors swept open and Jax stepped out into the broad lift core that gave access to the short-range shuttle bays. He started forward—and was stopped dead in his tracks by a dark curl of intense curiosity . . . and an iron Force grip on his throat.

"Impressive." Darth Vader stepped out of an open lift to Jax's left. "Is this display of power the result of some knowledge you've sampled? From where, I wonder?"

Vader paced slowly toward him, his lightsaber held, deactivated, in one gloved fist. The lights of the lift core gleamed on his helm.

"This is dark knowledge you possess. I can feel it

on you—*in* you. Just as I felt it when you acquired it from . . ."

Lava-hot tendrils of the Force surrounded Jax, trying to pry into his mind. Recalling what he had felt from Tesla as the Inquisitor had attempted to invade Yimmon's consciousness, he rearranged the weave of his own thoughts and allowed Vader a glimpse behind the veil in his mind.

"Ah. A Sith holocron." Vader's honeyed tones seemed actually tinged with slight respect. "And not just any such repository, but one of Darth Ramage's works." Vader stood before Jax now, his cloak and biosuit seeming to draw the soft pearlescent light into him, soaking it up like a thirsty sponge.

"I'm surprised at you, Pavan. Surprised you'd sully yourself with such knowledge from the dark side. What could have driven you to that, I wonder? The death of your Paladin?"

Jax tried to keep from reacting to the taunt, but it was beyond him. Fine. Let Vader imagine he was a quivering wreck. Maybe he was exactly that.

And maybe not.

"You don't need to die, you know," said the dark, velvety voice.

Jax found his own voice. "No?"

"No. In fact, it would be . . . unfortunate . . . for you to die with all that knowledge in your mind."

"And you're going to offer me a deal, right . . . Anakin?"

The grip on Jax's throat tightened. The coldness of interstellar space invaded his core. If he could see Vader's face—Anakin's face—what would it reveal? Anger? Hurt? Torment?

"Anakin Skywalker is dead," Vader said. "Burned to a cinder and blown away by the winds of betrayal."

Jax dared to laugh. It sounded thin and wheezing. "Betrayed? You? No. *You* were the betrayer. You betrayed the Jedi Order. You betrayed us all. You betrayed *yourself*."

The grip tightened more now. Jax gasped, the bay area growing dark. Vader's tone remained amused, but with an edge to it. "Do you suppose your opinion of me matters?"

"Hardly."

The Dark Lord relaxed his hold a tiny bit and activated his lightsaber. The vivid red of the blade slashed across Jax's gaze. The Sith drew closer to his captive. Closer still, until Jax could see his own pale face as a warped reflection in the curved obsidian surface of Vader's mask.

"I sense that you already dance at the edges of the shadows, Pavan. Come into them fully, share this knowledge with me, and you can live. Your cause is lost in any case. You might as well salvage something."

"And Yimmon?"

"I have you, now. What do I need with him?"

"You won't torture him anymore? You won't kill him?"

"Is it so important to you at this moment?"

"If you want what's in my head, it will be important to you, too."

The Dark Lord hesitated. "Where is he?"

Jax flicked a glance at the lift doors to his extreme right. The doors parted, revealing Thi Xon Yimmon and Den Dhur. Yimmon leaned against the wall of the lift; Den, looking horror-struck, supported him.

The unexpected sight was enough to break Vader's concentration. The blast of Force energy that Jax then unleashed sent the Dark Lord staggering back, one, two, three steps.

Not much. But enough.

Jax dropped prone, his body hovering horizontally six centimeters above the floor. He coiled and hurled himself past Vader, accelerating through the open portal of the docking bay.

Vader recovered swiftly and strode through the doors, his robes billowing about him in an inky cloud.

"You've progressed, Pavan. I hadn't imagined you could wield such knowledge so well. It won't do you any good, of course. I can see through you. I always could see through you."

Jax came lightly to his feet and turned to face the Sith Lord. Lightsaber poised and activated, he continued to move backward deeper into the bay, keeping one eye out for Imperial troops. He saw none—only a handful of terrified crew huddled in a far corner.

"I'm that transparent, am I?" he asked Vader.

"Perhaps not, but your illusions are. You neglected to give them life signs." The Dark Lord swept a hand back at "Yimmon" and "Den"—still standing in the open turbolift—as if to dismiss Jax's careful mirage. They blurred about the edges, but did not evaporate. That Vader had expected them to do so was evident only in the slightest halting of his step, the sudden tilt of his helmeted head, the twitch of his gloved fingers.

Jax quashed the bubble of elation that bloomed in his heart at having thwarted the Dark Lord's expectations. He held the projections long enough to make the point that he could, then dropped them. The images of the Sullustan and the Cerean vanished like smoke.

"Proud of yourself?" Vader asked. "Perhaps you're entitled. You've exceeded my expectations, I'll allow. But . . . how interesting—the projections of your comrades are gone, yet I can still feel the texture of an illusion . . . somewhere . . ."

The helm tilted upward as if the Dark Lord was scenting the air, and Jax realized his mistake. Having touched and felt of Jax's projections, Vader could now recognize them. And there was a pyronium-powered projection buried in a far corner of this bay.

"What is it?" Vader asked Jax, moving slowly, inexorably closer. He was mere meters away. "What are you hiding, Jedi? What have you concealed in here? More to the point—*how* are you concealing it?"

Jax hesitated. He had hoped he could foil Darth Vader with a combination of thrust, parry, and projection, but that now seemed naïve. Now Vader stood a good chance of having not just the Jedi ship, but the pyronium, as well.

Ironic. Anakin Skywalker had been the one to give Jax the pyronium in the first place. For safekeeping, he'd said. That had been before—before he had become this towering pillar of darkness, this . . . *thing*. What might such a conscienceless creature do with that inexhaustible power source now?

The black helmet canted toward the corner of the bay where the Jedi starfighter sat, half concealed by the vessel that had entered the bay before it.

"Ah! The pyronium, of course. *That's* how you're doing it. That's how you're powering all your projections. Stupid of you, Pavan, to carry it with you."

"Oh, but I'm not."

Jax Force-grabbed the first thing he could find—a discarded length of shielding from a nearby shuttle under repair—and flung it at the Dark Lord. When Vader whirled out of its way, Jax followed it by wrenching the entire shuttle off its repair struts and tumbling it onto the Sith.

Without stopping to see the results of his efforts, Jax darted to his left, away from the telltale signature of the projection around the Delta-7. He was cut off from the lift core by his own hand, but he knew that there were, in every docking bay, hatches in the deck used to lower large pieces of machinery and cargo from one level to another. If he could just find one . . .

He heard the shriek of metal on metal behind him as Vader dealt with the shuttle. He spent no more of his precious Force sense on that, instead probing ahead as he ran.

There! There was a hatch, five meters ahead—but closed.

Not for long. Using the Force, Jax ripped the thick durasteel grating up and flung it back on its groaning hinges. Then he leapt, throwing himself into the open maw. He landed lightly, one level down, on the bow of a docked shuttle, then turned a quick somersault and vaulted to the deck.

What would Vader do?

If he believed the pyronium was in Jax's possession, he'd pursue Jax. Then the starfighter and the pyronium would be safe . . . for the time being. If he believed the pyronium must be aboard the vessel, if he failed to give chase, Jax could cause the nameless ship to self-destruct and maybe—a slim maybe—he could catch Vader in the blast.

Jax knew, now, what the endgame would have to be. He told himself he'd know when the moment arrived for him to give up fighting for his life.

The lower bay was laid out just like the one above it, with a portal that gave onto a lift core. Jax headed for that, chose a lift at random, and took it up two levels. He would head back toward the civilian sector of the station, hope that Den and Sacha had disobeyed after all, and waited for him.

As Den had waited, once before, in the corridor of the *Far Ranger* . . .

Off the lift, Jax headed to his left—west, in the geography of Kantaros Station. He'd have to work his way back down a number of levels once he'd gotten farther from Vader, but for now he just wanted distance.

He dashed past crewmates, stormtroopers, and officers, knowing they saw him as one of their own—an anonymous grease monkey hurrying about his assigned tasks. He hesitated when a trio of Inquisitors stepped out of a lift ahead, then dodged left and found himself in a galley.

It was a long, gleaming room, redolent with cooking smells and furnished with durasteel tables and equipment. The droids that staffed it were busily preparing meals for the crew. They paid him no heed.

He was halfway across the galley when the far door into the canteen swept back and Darth Vader appeared, his lightsaber vibrating the air around him. The droids ignored him, too.

"The problem with those projections, Pavan, is that I now know their scent. You left a trail a blind bantha could follow."

From the corner of his eye, Jax saw ranks of pots, pans, and metal utensils hanging above a center prep area. Beneath them were stacks of meal trays. Realizing the only escape was behind him, Jax coiled the Force in his hands and swept every pot, pan, utensil, and tray at Vader in a hail of metal.

Not done, Jax scooted back the way he'd come, using the Force to turn the droids in the galley to his own uses. He turned them on Darth Vader, with their knives and chopping blades, pestles and cook pots. There were a good half dozen of them, now intent on the Sith.

Jax had no doubt that the Dark Lord, with his mastery of the Force, could repel the attack, but it gave him time to flee. This time he didn't use a projection. And this time, he was spotted by the enemy. A handful of stormtroopers led by a corpulent lieutenant turned to give chase.

That decided his course of action. He headed back toward the docking bays, hoping Vader might believe he had gone the opposite way.

It was a forlorn hope. He heard the uproar as the Dark Lord entered the corridor outside the galley, felt the disturbance among the Imperials at the sight of him, heard his voice of command as he made it clear that this Jedi was his to dispose of.

"Leave him to me!"

Leave him to me.

Was it that inevitable?

Fine—endgame, then.

Lightsaber activated, Jax raced back to the docking bay in which the Delta-7 sat hidden. He entered the huge chamber and turned as Darth Vader came through the portal behind him.

"Your last chance, Pavan. Come willingly and live. Resist, and die. It makes no difference to me."

That was a lie and Jax knew it. It *did* make a difference to Darth Vader, because it made a difference to Anakin Skywalker. Jax understood, at last, that if he capitulated, he would vindicate Anakin in his fall to the dark side. If he resisted to the last and died, there could be no vindication. The Jedi Order—the thing that Vader lived to crush—would be gone, true enough. But Jax knew that merely killing it would not be enough for Darth Vader. No, the last Jedi had to do more than just die.

He had to be *broken*.

If not—if he made Vader end him—the Dark Lord's thirst for vengeance would remain unslaked, and there would be no one left for him to avenge himself upon. Even if there were other Jedi still alive—it was a big galaxy, after all—the man who had been Anakin Skywalker could search for a lifetime—a thousand lifetimes—and never find them.

He would be without purpose.

Like you were?

Something deep within Jax Pavan resonated with that. Didn't he also seek revenge for Laranth's death? Yes, of course—he'd come to rescue Yimmon, but hadn't he ultimately wanted *this*?

He met Vader's opaque gaze, stared into the gleaming black lenses. If he died, would that put an end to Vader's purpose? If Vader died, would that put an end to Jax's?

There was no time to answer the question. The Dark Lord was coming at him with long strides.

"Choose, Jedi!"

Jax chose. He flung himself at the Sith, lightsaber cutting the machine-scented air of the docking bay. Vader parried and the blades locked, slid apart, arced, and locked again. The air sizzled with their power.

Again, again. Thrust, parry, fade. Thrust, parry, fade.

Jax worked his way slowly, inexorably back toward the *Aethersprite*'s berth. He was careful not to seem as if he'd given up the fight. If Vader realized he was being lured, there was no telling how he'd react.

So Jax fought. Quite as if he expected to win.

He pelted his adversary with small objects—anything that wasn't bolted down, and a few things that were. Vader parried them with his lightsaber, slicing everything that came at him into shards of slag. He answered by treating Jax to the same rain of metal.

Crew scrambled to get out of the way; but, prisoners of curiosity, most of them continued to watch from the far sidelines.

And that gave Vader the advantage he sought.

With a flick of his free hand, the Dark Lord Force-lifted one of the deckhands off his feet and hurled him at Jax.

Jax froze for a split second, his weapon raised, then

twisted out of the way of the screaming crewman. Anakin knew him too well—knew what he would and would not do.

Maybe.

With a supreme effort of will, the Jedi felt the local time currents around him, stirred them to eddies, then dropped and rolled beneath the fuselage of a small shuttle that lay between him and the *Aethersprite*.

Vader's next barrage of ordnance was aimed at where Jax had been, not where he had gone.

Jax shot to his feet and pelted toward the Jedi starfighter where it lay tucked behind its Imperial look-alike. He was panting with the effort now, drained by the effort it took to harness so much energy.

The deafening groan of metal from behind him caused Jax to turn. The small vessel he'd just rolled beneath was ripped from her moorings and flung aside as if she were a bit of stray debris. Darth Vader came at him out of her wake, his Sith weapon shedding lurid light.

"You amaze me, Pavan. The things you have absorbed from that dark well of knowledge, the ease with which you use them. You are truly wasted on the light side. Your continued existence and what you have done to ensure it confirm this."

The observation cut deep, but Jax would not let Vader see him bleed. "What I've done, I did to free Yimmon. Having done that, I've served my purpose."

He was close enough to the Delta-7 now that he could feel the energies of the pyronium-fed projection as a humming tremor in the Force around him. He was certain Vader must feel it, too.

"Served your purpose?" the Sith echoed. He made an elegant gesture with gloved hands, the lightsaber describing a graceful arc in the air. "Then surrender."

"I'll die before I let you have what's in my head, Anakin."

Vader was completely still for a moment, then raised his lightsaber for an attack. "As you wish . . . Jax."

As Vader swept toward him, Jax reached back and felt of the connection between the pyronium and the ship. A simple command—a simple trigger—was all it would take to end this.

He was startled by the sudden flash of light that exploded along the hull of the starfighter's nearest neighbor. It was as if someone had opened a door between the two ships, letting sunlight pour through.

Vader stopped, his attention half on the newest intrusion. "Is this another of your projections? I won't be fooled by it . . ."

The dark voice trailed off as the Dark Lord must have sensed what Jax did: the new presence had a Force signature of its own—weak, but steady.

The glow intensified, and Jax could see a figure at its heart. A humanoid figure. Had Sacha—

"Run!"

It was a familiar voice, but he hesitated to obey. He knew what he had to do. He had to destroy the starfighter, himself, and Vader with him.

"*Run!*"

A volley of blasterfire streamed out of the radiance between the two ships, targeting Vader. The Dark Lord Force-leapt from the station deck in an arc that took him over Jax's head. He touched down in a swirl of black robes and rolled beneath the *Aethersprite*.

The rapid blasterfire followed him, sweeping the length of the vessel and melting its port landing struts. The Jedi ship sagged toward the deck, then dropped its bow with a metallic groan.

Jax ran.

He ran toward the light and found, at its center, not

Sacha but a stranger—a man. No, not a man, he realized as his eyes and Force sense took in the details of the face and body.

It was a droid—a human replicant droid. It could only be I-Five, his android arm encumbered with the Nemesis blaster rifle.

Jax stopped beside the droid.

"Keep moving," I-Five said, his humanoid face showing grim determination. "I am *not* losing you the way I lost your father."

Jax kept moving.

Behind him, the blasterfire intensified. He heard a roar of Force-backed rage, then felt the air quake as something exploded in his wake. The blast tumbled him off his feet. He pitched up against the landing strut of a small courier vessel.

Stunned, he tried to peer into the fiery aftermath of the explosion. There was no sign of Vader. And I-Five . . . he caught the shimmer of silvery metal as the lower half of the droid's leg—stripped of its synthflesh—toppled into hungry flames.

No. No, not that. Not Five.

Jax surged to his feet, started back toward the blast, and kicked something hard that lay on the deck. He looked down. I-Five's HRD head stared up at him from the decking. One ear had been blown away, but the durasteel skull was intact.

As Jax reached for the head, its eyes blinked and it gave a very human grimace.

"This," said the droid, his voice muffled and small, "is getting old."

Jax smothered his quaking elation and gathered the head up.

He became fully and suddenly aware of the chaos around him. The fire was spreading. Klaxons were going off, lights flashed, and over it all a voice repeated a dire warning: "Evacuate docking bay! Evacuate all personnel and vessels from the docking bay! Explosion imminent! Evacuate docking bay! Evacuate . . ."

Jax needed no further encouragement. With I-Five's head tucked under one arm, he hauled himself up into the courier—a tiny two-seater—and set I-Five's head on the second seat.

"The *Laranth*?" Jax asked, as he fired up the engines.

"On her way into the asteroid field . . . if they obeyed my last instruction set."

"Let's hope they did."

Jax navigated the little ship away from the burning wreckage and maneuvered easily among the shuttles fleeing the burning docking bay. As they zoomed clear of the station, he spared a backward thought to the crippled Jedi starfighter.

A moment later the docking bay was racked by a second explosion as the *Aethersprite* sacrificed itself. The ruined ship was shot out into the void of space by the blast, and vanished as if it had been sucked up by a vacuum. In a sense it had—the pyronium had devoured the energy of the blast and now was just one more tiny, glittering bit of flotsam jettisoned from the Imperial shuttle bays. A very powerful bit of flotsam.

Jax doubted even Darth Vader would be able to track it down . . . if he thought to look for it. Right now, the Dark Lord would have other things on his mind. And Jax knew without question that that mind had survived—he could feel the waves of cold rage even now.

Jax located the *Laranth* amid the flotilla of commercial vessels that had evacuated the station in the wake of the "accident" on the Imperial side. He made a soft dock with the little freighter and transferred aboard before setting the courier adrift in the lee of a slowly moving asteroid.

It felt strange to be back aboard the *Laranth*. He was

caught up in a daft combination of joy and trepidation. After all that had happened—after all he'd done—would the others be welcoming or wary?

He stepped through the hatch onto the cramped bridge, I-Five's head still cradled in his arms. Sacha, Den, and Yimmon all turned to look at him for a long, heavily silent moment.

"Oh, for pity's sake!" Den said, his gaze lighting on what Jax was carrying. "Are you planning to make a habit of this?"

The droid snorted through its slightly flattened nose. "I'm pleased to see you, too."

"Yeah, right." Den pulled himself out of the copilot's seat and came back to the hatch, holding his hands out. "Give him to me. I'll go put him in one of the, umm . . . other chassis."

Jax handed over the head.

Den slid past him, grumbling, then paused to look up into his face. "Welcome back, Jax. If you *are* back."

Jax nodded. "Yeah. I'm back. For good, this time." He turned to Sacha, who was still watching him warily from the helm. "Set a course for Dathomir. I've got an appointment to keep."

epilogue

The stop on Dathomir was relatively brief; just long enough for Augwynne Djo to keep her promise to relieve Jax of Darth Ramage's dark knowledge. It was risky, trusting a Dathomiri Witch to restore some balance to his mind, but that act of trust was, itself, a step back into the light.

Now back aboard the *Laranth*, prepping for liftoff, Jax probed his mind for memories of what he'd done on Kantaros Station. The events were there—clear and crystalline. How he had influenced them was a blank—a fuzzy hollow. He could no longer sense time currents, though the concept of their existence was still in his memory. The rest of Ramage's ideas were mere vapors—thin to transparency.

Beside him, in the copilot's seat, Sacha moved restlessly. "You . . . you all clear? Your head, I mean. You got all the . . . dark stuff out of it?"

"Well, at least the dark stuff Darth Ramage contributed."

"Where to now, Jax?" Den asked from the jump seat behind him.

"We'll take Yimmon back to Toprawa, get in touch with Pol Haus and Sheel Mafeen on Coruscant, do what needs doing."

He turned his gaze to Sacha Swiftbird. "You don't need me for liftoff, do you?" he asked.

"Not for liftoff, no." She shot him a cockeyed smile, the scar across her left eye wrinkling. "You got a hot date?"

"In a manner of speaking. I haven't meditated in a long time."

She nodded. "The tree's right where you left it. Five and I have been taking good care of it for you."

"Thanks." He returned her smile.

"Um," she said, oddly diffident, "about that red light-saber . . ."

"Why don't you keep it?"

Jax climbed out of the pilot's chair, brushed the top of I-Five's helm with his fingertips, laid a gentle hand on Den's shoulder, and went aft. He hadn't returned to his quarters since coming aboard. He'd let Sacha continue using them, and had bunked with Den and Yimmon.

The Whiplash leader had also been in need of the Da-thomiri Witches' ministrations, even once clear of the Imperials' drugs. When Jax asked how he had with-stood the Sith interrogations and seemingly lulled Tesla into a false sense of security, he smiled benignly and said, "I had an unfair advantage—two brains instead of one. And he wore his desires—and his fears—too close to the surface. It was easy enough to leave a trail where he would follow. But," he added, his expression sober, "Tesla had quite correctly suspected that separating my cortices would rob me of that advantage. Had he not invaded my mind one last time . . ."

Yimmon's recovery was aided by many hours spent in a meditative state. Jax, however, hadn't wanted to med-itate until the dark stain of Darth Ramage's knowledge was sponged from his mind. Now, finally, he was ready.

The tree *was* right where he'd left it, but it looked significantly healthier. Sacha's care was evident in the repaired feeding and watering device. She'd even re-turned the Sith lightsaber to its compartment.

Jax moved to the tree, put his face to its soft, silver-green foliage, and inhaled deeply of the piney scent. He took the tree, pot and all, out of the feeder and sat with it on the floor of the cabin, falling back into the arms of the Force.

It flowed like sap through this tree, he realized, roots to needle tips and out into the atmosphere; it permeated the planet beneath their landing struts, the space they would soon leap into . . . and him. It was the endless, changeless connective tissue of the universe, and it had connected him, and always would, to the Jedi who had gone before him . . . and the Jedi who would come after him.

It had connected him, and always would connect him, to Laranth.

He had not wanted to let go of her. Now he knew, with the strength of epiphany, that he had no need to hold on to what would always be there.

There is no death; there is the Force.

How often had he thought or spoken those words? Only now did he truly understand what they meant. They meant that there was no cause for grief, no need for revenge.

In his mind's eye, the tree's aura pulsed and he felt an infusion of warmth. For the first time in what seemed an eternity, he felt fully connected to the Force—rooted in it, just as Laranth's tree was. He'd cut himself off, he realized—uprooted his own "tree." He'd been exhausted after the battle with Darth Vader, but the Force was inexhaustible. He had forgotten that; had forgotten *himself.*

In the midst of his meditations, he sensed another presence in the room. He opened his eyes and saw a man, handsome if somewhat stern of countenance, dressed in a simple tunic and leggings. After a moment, Jax recognized him; not by his appearance, but by the unmistakable aura of the Force that he exuded. Jax stared at him, this droid who was his closest friend, who had kept the faith that he would return when nearly all others had given up.

"I'm sorry," Jax told him. "I know I . . . went off into the woods for a while. Like father, like son, I guess."

"No, fortunately. You had tools your father didn't."

"I had you."

The droid was silent for a moment, then said, "You had the Force. And the contents of that Sith holocron. And the ability to use them for good. That projection you used to distract Vader right at the end was very effective."

Jax stared at the droid. "What do you mean? What projection? The *Aethersprite*?"

"No. I meant the spectral image you used to cover my approach. That burst of light. Vader didn't see me until it was too late."

"I . . . I didn't do that," Jax said. "At least, not consciously. I thought that was you. I felt a Force signature behind it. So did Vader."

The droid shook his head. "It wasn't me."

"Then what—" Jax stopped, gazing down at the tree sitting before him on the deck. "There is no death; there is the Force," he murmured.

I-Five cocked his head; a quizzical gesture that was simultaneously eerily familiar and completely new. "Meaning?"

"Meaning, I guess, that we go on. In whatever form—" He paused to look at the humanoid droid. "—in whatever capacity. We work in whatever way we can. We never concede to evil. And we never surrender to the darkness."

As he said it, Jax could feel the truth of his statement. It was true that the old order of Jedi had been swept away, but that didn't mean it was gone forever. It just meant that a new Jedi Order would arise, sooner or later, from the ashes. Whether he would be around to help usher it in or not, only the Force knew.

He looked down at the miisai tree, then back at I-Five.

"What?" the droid asked.

"I remember," Jax said, "when I first sensed the Force from you. It was back in our old digs on Coruscant, when Tuden Sal had talked you into trying to assassinate Palpatine."

"Yes. Just before Vader blew me to smithereens for the first time."

"It's accepted dogma by everyone who knows about the Force," Jax said quietly, almost as if speaking to himself, "that the Force is manifested through living things by midi-chlorians. The higher the cell count of midi-chlorians, the stronger the connection to the Force."

"And yet . . . ," I-Five said.

"Right. Your neuroprocessor has no organic components—or at least it shouldn't have them. Neither did your original I-5YQ chassis or those interim bodies you used. This HRD body comes the closest, but it's still just synthflesh and nanomolecular electronics. You have no midi-chlorians, I-Five."

"This is true."

"But the Force lives within you. How do you account for this?"

"It would appear," said I-Five, "that the Force works in mysterious ways. Or at least that my neuroprocessor does."

They both sat quietly for a time. Then Jax picked up Laranth's tree and rose in one graceful movement. He put the tree back into its feeder and headed toward the hatch.

The droid turned to follow him. "Where are you going?"

"To send a message to someone in the Singing Mountain Clan. Someone with a lot of potential and an open mind. After all, someone's got to rebuild the Jedi Order. If I *am* the last Jedi, that responsibility falls to me."

I-Five chuckled. "It would seem that humans *are* teachable, after a fashion."

"What about you, Five? How does being human suit you?"

"It has its advantages," the droid admitted, following Jax. "I rather like being able to scowl menacingly."

Jax laughed . . . and wondered if he might be able to teach a droid the ways of the Force.

Read on for an excerpt from

STAR WARS:
Dawn of the Jedi: Into the Void

by Tim Lebbon

Published by Del Rey Books

At the heart of any poor soul not at one with the Force, there is only void.

    –Unknown Je'daii, 2,545 TYA (Tho Yor Arrival)

DARK MATTERS

Even at the beginning of our journey I feel like a rock in the river of the Force. Lanoree is a fish carried by that river, feeding from it, living within it and relying upon the waters for her well-being. But I am unmoving. An inconvenience to the water as long as I remain. And slowly, slowly, I am being eroded to nothing.
—DALIEN BROCK, diaries, 10,661 TYA

She is a little girl, the sky seems wide and endless, and Lanoree Brock breathes in the wonders of Tython as she runs to find her brother.

Dalien is down by the estuary again. He likes being alone, away from all the other children at Bodhi, the Je'daii Temple of the Arts. Lanoree's parents have sent her to find him, and though they still have some teaching to do that afternoon, they've promised that they will walk up to the boundary of the Edge Forest that evening. Lanoree loves it up there. And it scares her a little, as well. Close to the Temple, close to the sea, she can feel the Force ebbing and flowing through everything—the air she breathes, the sights she sees, and all that makes up the beautiful scenery. Up at the Edge Forest, there's a primal wildness to the Force that sets her blood pumping.

Her mother will smile and tell her that she will learn about it all, given time. Her father will look silently into the forest, as if he yearns to explore that way. And her little brother, only nine years old, will start to cry.

Always, at the Edge Forest, he cries.

"Dal!" She swishes through the long grasses close

to the riverbank, hands held out by her sides so that the grass caresses her palms. She won't tell him about the walk planned for that evening. If she does he'll get moody, and he might not agree to come home with her. He can be like that sometimes, and their father says it's the sign of someone finding his own way.

Dal doesn't seem to have heard her, and as she closes on him she slows from a run to a walk and thinks, *If that was me I'd have sensed me approaching ages ago.*

Dal's head remains dipped. The river flows by, fast and full from the recent rains. There's a power to it that is intimidating, and closing her eyes, Lanoree feels the Force and senses the myriad life-forms that call the river home. Some are as small as her finger, others that swim upriver from the ocean are almost half the size of a Cloud Chaser ship. She knows from her teachings that many of them have teeth.

Perhaps her brother is asleep. She bites her lip, hesitant. Then she probes out with her mind and—

"I told you to never do that to me!"

"Dal . . ."

He stands and turns around, and he looks furious. Just for a moment there's a fire in his eyes that she doesn't like. She has seen those flames before, and carries the knotted scar tissue in her lower lip to prove it. Then his anger slips and he smiles.

"Sorry. You startled me, that's all."

"You're drawing?" she asks.

Dal closes the art pad. "It's rubbish."

"I don't believe that," Lanoree said. "You're really good. Temple Master Fenn himself says so."

"Temple Master Fenn is a friend of father's."

Lanoree ignores the insinuation and walks closer to her brother. She can already see that he has chosen a fine place from which to draw the surroundings. The river curves here, and a smaller tributary joins from the hills of the Edge Forest, causing a confusion of currents. The undergrowth on the far bank is colorful and vibrant, and there's a huge old ak tree whose hollowed trunk is home to a flight of weavebirds. Their spun golden threads glisten in the afternoon sun. The birdsong compliments the river's roar.

"Let me see," Lanoree says.

Dal does not look at her, but he opens the pad.

"It's beautiful," she says. "The Force has guided your fingers, Dal." But she's not sure.

Dal picks a heavy pencil from his pocket and strikes five thick lines through his drawing, left to right, tearing the paper and ruining it forever. His expression does not change as he does so, and neither does his breathing. It's almost as if there is no anger at all.

"There," he says. "That's better."

For a moment the lines look like claw marks, and as Lanoree takes a breath and blinks—

A soft, insistent alarm pulled her up from sleep. Lanoree sighed and sat up, rubbing her eyes, massaging the dream away. Dear Dal. She dreamed of him often, but they were usually dreams of those later times when everything was turning bad. Not when they were still children for whom Tython was so full of potential.

Perhaps it was because she was on her way home.

She had not been back to Tython in more than four years. She was a Je'daii Ranger, and so ranging is what she did. Some Rangers found reasons to return to Tython regularly. Family connections, continuous training, face-to-face debriefs, it all amounted to the same thing— they hated being away from home. She also believed that there were those Je'daii who felt the need to immerse themselves in Tython's Force-rich surroundings from time to time, as if uncertain that their affinity with the Force was strong enough.

Lanoree had no such doubts. She was comfortable with her strength and balance in the Force. The short periods she had spent with others on retreats on Ashla and Bogan had made her even more confident in this.

She stood from her cot and stretched. She reached for the ceiling and grabbed the bars she'd welded there herself, pulling up, breathing softly, then lifting her legs and stretching them out until she was horizontal to the floor. Her muscles quivered, and she breathed deeply as she felt the Force flowing through her, a vibrant, living thing. Mental exercise and meditation was fine, but sometimes she took the greatest pleasure in exerting herself physically. She believed that to be strong with the Force, one had to be strong oneself.

The alarm was still ringing.

"I'm awake," she said, easing herself slowly back to the floor. "In case you hadn't noticed."

The alarm snapped off, and her Peacemaker's ship's grubby yellow maintenance droid ambled into the small living quarters on padded metal feet. It was one of many adaptations she'd made to the ship in her years out in the Tython system. Most Peacemakers carried a very simple droid, but she'd updated hers to a Holgorian IM-220, capable of limited communication with a human master and other duties not necessarily exclusive to ship maintenance. She'd further customized it with some heavy armor, doubling its weight but making it much more useful to her in risky scenarios. When she spoke to it, its replies were obtuse. She supposed it was the equivalent of trying to communicate with a grass kapir back home.

"Hey, Ironholgs. You better not have woken me early."

The droid beeped and scraped, and she wasn't sure whether it was getting cranky in its old age.

She looked around the small but comfortable living

quarters. She had chosen a Peacemaker over a Hunter because of its size; even before she flew her first mission as a Je'daii Ranger, she knew that she would be eager to spend much of her time in space. A Hunter was fast and agile, but too small to live in. The Peacemaker was a compromise on maneuverability, but she had spent long periods living alone on the ship. She liked it that way.

And like most Rangers, she had made many modifications and adaptations to her ship that stamped her own identity on it. She'd stripped out the pre-fitted table and chairs and replaced them with a weights and tensions rack for working out. Now she ate her food sitting on her narrow cot. She'd replaced the holo-scan entertainment system with an older flatscreen, which doubled as a communications center and reduced the ship's net weight. There had been a small room beside the extensive engine compartment that housed a second cot for guests or companions, but because she never hosted either, she removed it and filled the space left behind with extra laser blaster charge pods, a water recycling unit, and food stores. The ship's several cannons had also been upgraded. At the hands of the Cathar master armorer Gan Corla, the cannons now packed three times more punch and had more than twice the range of those standard to Peacemaker ships. She had also altered and adapted the function and positions of many controls, making it so that only she could fly the ship effectively. It was hers, and it was home.

"How long to Tython?" she asked.

The droid let out a series of whines and clicks.

"Right," Lanoree said. "Suppose I'd better freshen up." She brushed a touch pad and the darkened screens in the forward cockpit faded to clear, revealing the starspeckled view, which never failed to make her heart ache. There was something so profoundly moving about the distance and scale of what she saw out there, and

Tim Lebbon

the Force never let her forget that she was a part of something incomprehensibly large. She supposed it was as close as she ever came to a religious epiphany.

She touched the pad again and a red glow appeared surrounding a speck in the distance. Tython. Three hours and she'd be there.

The Je'daii Council ordering her back to Tython meant only one thing: They had a mission for her, and it was one that they needed to discuss face-to-face.

Washed, dressed, and fed, Lanoree sat in the ship's cockpit and watched Tython drawing closer. Her ship had communicated with sentry drones orbiting at two hundred thousand miles, and now the Peacemaker was performing a graceful parabola that would take it down into the atmosphere just above the equator.

She was nervous about visiting Tython again, but part of her was excited as well. It would be good to see her mother and father, however briefly. She contacted them far too infrequently.

With Dal dead, she was now their only child.

A soft chime announced an incoming transmission. She swiveled her seat and faced the flatscreen, just as it snowed into an image.

"Master Dam-Powl," Lanoree said, surprised. "An honor." And it was. She had expected the welcoming transmission to be from a Je'daii Ranger, or perhaps even a Journeyer she did not know. Not a Je'daii Master.

Dam-Powl bowed her head. "Ranger Lanoree, it's good to see you again. We've been eagerly awaiting your arrival. Pressing matters beg discussion. *Dark* matters."

"I assumed that was the case," Lanoree said. She shifted in her seat, unaccountably nervous.

"I sense your discomfort," Master Dam-Powl said.

"Forgive me. It's been some time since I spoke with a Je'daii Master."

"You feel unsettled even with me?" Dam-Powl asked, smiling. But the smile quickly slipped. "No matter. Prepare yourself, because today you speak with six Masters from the Council, including Temple Master Lha-Mi. I've sent your ship the landing coordinates for our meeting place twenty miles south of Akar Kesh. We'll expect you soon."

"Master, we're not meeting at a temple?"

But Dam-Powl had already broken the transmission, and Lanoree was left staring at a blank screen. She could see her image reflected there, and she quickly gathered herself, breathing away the shock. *Six Je'daii Masters? And Lha-Mi, as well?*

"Then it *is* something big."

She checked the transmitted coordinates and switched the flight computer to manual, eager to make the final approach herself. She had always loved flying and the untethered freedom it gave her. Almost like a free agent.

Lanoree closed her eyes briefly and breathed with the Force. It was strong this close to Tython, elemental, and it sparked her senses.

By the time the Peacemaker sliced into Tython's outer atmosphere, Lanoree's excitement was growing. The landing zone was nestled in a small valley with giant standing stones on the surrounding hills. She could see several other ships, including Hunters and another Peacemaker. It was a strange place for such a meeting, but the Je'daii Council would have their reasons. She guided her ship in an elegant arc and landed almost without a jolt.

"Solid ground," she whispered. It was her first time on Tython in four years. "Ironholgs, I don't know how long we'll be here, but take the opportunity to run a full systems check. Anything we need we can pick up from Akar Kesh before we leave."

The droid emitted a mechanical sigh.

Lanoree probed gently outward, and when she sensed that the air pressures inside and outside the ship had equaled she opened the lower hull hatch. The smells that flooded in—rash grass, running water, that curious charged smell that seemed to permeate the atmosphere around most Temples—brought a rush of nostalgia for the planet she had left behind. But there was no time for personal musings.

Three Journeyers were waiting for her, wide-eyed and excited.

"Welcome, Ranger Brock!" the tallest of the three said.

"I'm sure," she said. "Where are they waiting for me?"

"On Master Lha-Mi's Peacemaker," another Journeyer said. "We're here to escort you. Please, follow us."

They led the way, and Lanoree followed.

"Forgive us for not welcoming you back to Tython in more . . . salubrious surroundings," Temple Master Lha-Mi said. "But by necessity this meeting must be covert." His long white hair glowed in the room's artificial light. He was old and wise, and Lanoree was pleased to see him again.

"It's so nice to be back," Lanoree said. She bowed.

"Please, please." Lha-Mi pointed to a seat, and Lanoree sat facing him and the other five Je'daii Masters. This Peacemaker's living quarters had been pared down to provide a circular table with eight seats around it, and little more. She had already nodded a silent greeting to two of the Masters, but the other three she did not know. It seemed that things had moved swiftly while she had been away, especially when it came to promotions.

"Ranger Brock," Master Dam-Powl said, smiling. "It's wonderful to see you again, in the flesh." She was a Master at Anil Kesh, the Je'daii temple of science, and during Lanoree's training she and Dam-Powl had formed a close bond. It was she more than any other who had expressed the conviction that Lanoree would be a great Je'daii one day. It was also Dam-Powl who had revealed and encouraged the areas of Force use that Lanoree was most skilled at—metallurgy, elemental manipulation, alchemy.

"Likewise, Master Dam-Powl," Lanoree said.

"How are your studies?"

"Continuing," Lanoree said. She built a workspace in her Peacemaker ship, and sometimes she spent long, long hours there. Her skills still sometimes felt fledgling, but the sense of accomplishment and power she felt while using them were almost addictive.

"You're a talented Je'daii," Master Tem Madog said. "I can sense your experience and strength growing with the years." It was a sword forged by this master weapons-smith that hung by Lanoree's side. The blade had saved her life on many occasions, and on other occasions it had taken lives. It was her third arm. In the four years since leaving Tython she had never been more than an arm's reach from the weapon, and she felt it now, cool and solid, keen in the presence of its maker.

"I honor the Force as well as I can," Lanoree said. "I am the mystery of darkness, in balance with chaos and harmony." She smiled as she quoted from the Je'daii oath, and some of the Masters smiled back. Some of them. The three she did not know remained expressionless, and she probed gently, knowing that she risked punishment yet unable to break her old habit. She always liked knowing who she was talking to. And as they had not introduced themselves, she thought it only fair.

They closed themselves to her, and one, a Wookiee, growled deep in his throat.

"You have served the Je'daii and Tython well during

your years as Ranger," Lha-Mi said. "And sitting before us now, you must surely believe that we mean you no ill. I understand that this meeting might seem strange, and that being faced with us might seem . . . daunting. Intimidating, perhaps? But there is no need to invade another's privacy, Lanoree, especially a Master. No need at all."

"Apologies, Master Lha-Mi," Lanoree said, wincing inwardly. *You might have been out in the wilds,* she berated herself, *but be mindful of the Je'daii formality.*

The Wookiee laughed.

"I'm Master Xiang," one of the strangers said. "Your father taught me, and now I teach under him at Bodhi Temple. A wise man. And good at magic tricks."

For an instant Lanoree felt a flood of emotion that surprised her. She remembered her father's tricks from when she and Dal were children—how he would pull objects out of thin air, turn one thing into another. Back then she'd believed he was using mastery of the Force, but he had told her that there were some things not even the Force could do. *Tricks,* he'd said. *I'm merely fooling your senses, not touching them with my own.*

"And how is he?" Lanoree asked.

"He's fine. He and your mother send their best wishes. They'd hoped you could visit them, but given the circumstances, they understand why that would be difficult."

"Circumstances?"

Xiang glanced sidelong at Lha-Mi and then back at Lanoree. When she spoke again, it was not to answer her query. "We have a mission for you. It's . . . delicate. And extremely important."

Lanoree sensed a shift in the room's atmosphere. For a few moments they sat in almost complete silence— Temple Master Lha-Mi, five Je'daii Masters, and her. Air-conditioning hummed, and through the chair she could feel the deeper, more insistent vibration of the Peacemaker's power sources. Her own breath was loud. Her heart beat the moments by. The Force flowed through and around her, and she felt history pivoting on this moment—her own history and story, and that of the Je'daii civilization as well.

Something staggering was going to happen.

"Why do you choose me?" she asked softly. "There are many other Rangers, all across the system. Some much closer than me. It's taken me nineteen days to get here from Obri."

"Two reasons," Xiang said. "First, you're particularly suited to the investigations required. Your time on Kalimahr brokering the Hang Layden deal displayed your sensitivity in dealing with inhabitants on the settled worlds. The assassinations on Nox saved many lives and prevented many awkward questions for the Je'daii. And your defusing of the Wookiee land wars on Ska Gora probably prevented a civil war."

"It was hardly a defusing," Lanoree said.

"The deaths were unfortunate," Lha-Mi said. "But they prevented countless more."

Lanoree thought of the giant apex trees aflame, countless burning leaves drifting in the vicious winds that sometimes stirred the jungles there, the sound of millennia-old tree trunks splitting and rupturing in the intense firestorm, and the screams of dying Wookiees. And she thought of her finger on the trigger of her laser cannons, raised and yet more than ready to fire again. *It was me or them*, she thought whenever the dream haunted her, and she knew that to be true. She had tried everything else—*everything*—but in the end, diplomacy gave way to blood. Yet each time she dreamed, the Force was in turmoil within her, dark and light vying for supremacy. Light tortured her with those memories. Dark would let her settle easy.

"You saved tens of thousands," Xiang said. "Maybe more. The Wookiee warlord Gharcanna had to be stopped."

Lanoree glanced at the Wookiee Master and he nodded slowly, never taking his eyes from hers. He had great pride, and he carried his sadness well.

"You said two reasons," Lanoree said.

"Yes." Xiang seemed suddenly uncomfortable, shifting in his seat.

"Perhaps I should relay the rest of the information," Lha-Mi said. "The mission first. The threat that has risen against the Je'daii, and perhaps even Tython itself. And when you know that, you will understand why we have chosen you."

"Of course," Lanoree said. "I'm honored to be here, and eager to hear. Any threat against Tython is a threat against everything I love."

"Everything we all love," Lha-Mi said. "For ten thousand years we have studied the Force and developed our society around and within it. Wars and conflicts have come and gone. We strive to keep the dark and the light, Bogan and Ashla, forever in balance. But now . . . now there is something that threatens us all.

"One man. And his dreams. Dreams to leave the Tython system and travel out into the galaxy. Many people desire to do so, and it's something I understand. However settled we are in this system, any educated being knows that our history lies out there, beyond everything we now know and understand. But this man seeks another route."

"What other route?" Lanoree asked. Her skin prickled with fear.

"A hypergate," Lha-Mi said.

"But there is no hypergate on Tython," Lanoree said. "Only tales of one deep in the Old City, but they're just that. Tales."

"Tales," Lha-Mi said, his eyes heavy, beard drooping as he lowered his head. "But some people will chase a tale as far and hard as they can, and seek to make it real. We have intelligence that this man is doing such a thing. He believes that there is a hypergate deep beneath the ruins of the Old City. He seeks to activate it."

"How?" she asked.

"A device," Lha-Mi said. "We don't know its nature, nor its source. But it will be fueled by dark matter, harnessed through arcane means. Forbidden. Dreaded. The most dangerous element known to us, and which no Je'daii would dare to even attempt to capture or create."

"But if there's no hypergate—"

"Tales," Lha-Mi said again. "He chases a legend. But whether it exists or not is irrelevant. The threat is the dark matter he intends to use to try to initiate the supposed gateway. It could . . ." He trailed off and looked to his side.

"Exposing dark matter to normal matter would be cataclysmic. It would create a mini black hole," Dam-Powl said. "And Tython would be swallowed in a heartbeat. The rest of the system, too."

"So you see the dire threat we face," Lha-Mi said.

"Just one man? So arrest him."

"We don't know where he is. We don't even know which planet he's on."

"The intelligence is sound?" Lanoree asked, but she already knew the answer to that. Such a gathering of Je'daii Masters for this purpose would not have taken place otherwise.

"We have no reason to doubt it," Lha-Mi said, "and every reason to fear. If it does transpire that the threat is not as severe as it appears, then that's a good thing. All we waste is time."

"But the hypergate," Lanoree said. "Protect it. Guard it."

Lha-Mi leaned forward across the table. With a blink

he closed off the room—air-conditioning ceased, the door slammed shut and locked. "The hypergate is a tale," he said. "That is all."

Lanoree nodded. But she also knew that talking of a simple story would surely not require such care, and such an arrangement as this. *For later,* she thought, guarding her thoughts.

"And now to why it's you we've chosen for the mission," Xiang said. "The man is Dalien Brock, your brother."

Lanoree reeled. She never suffered from space sickness—the Force settled her, as it did all Je'daii—but she seemed to sway in her seat, though she did not move; dizziness swept through her, though the Peacemaker was as stable as the ground it rested upon.

"No," she said, frowning. "Dalien died nine years ago."

"You found no body," Xiang said.

"I found his clothing. Shredded. Bloodied."

"We have no reason to doubt our sources," Lha-Mi said.

"And I have no reason to believe them!" Lanoree said.

Silence in the room. A loaded hush.

"Your reason is that we order this," Lha-Mi said. "Your reason is any small element of doubt that exists over your brother's death. Your reason is that, if this is true, he might be a threat to Tython. Your brother might destroy everything you love."

He fled, I found his clothes, down, down deep in the . . . the Old City.

"You see?" Lha-Mi asked, as if reading her thoughts. For all Lanoree knew he had, and she did not question that. He was a Temple Master, after all, and she only a Ranger. Confused as she was, she could not help her thoughts betraying her.

"He always looked to the stars," Lanoree said softly.

"We hear whispers of an organization, a loose collection of cohorts, calling themselves Stargazers."

"Yes," Lanoree said, remembering her little brother, always looking outward to the depths of space as she looked inward.

"Find your brother," Lha-Mi said. "Bring him back to Tython. Stop his foolish schemes."

"He won't come back," Lanoree said. "If it really is him, he'll never return after so long. So young when he died, but even then he was growing to . . ."

"To hate the Je'daii," Xiang said. "All the more reason to bring him back to us."

"And if he refuses?"

"You are a Je'daii Ranger," Lha-Mi said. And in a way, Lanoree knew that was answer enough.

"I need everything you know."

"It's already being downloaded to your ship's computer."

Lanoree nodded, unsurprised at their forwardness. They'd known that she could not say no.

"This is a covert operation," Xiang said. "Rumors of the hypergate persist, but the knowledge that someone is trying to initiate it might cause panic. We could send a much larger force against Dalien, but that would be much more visible."

"And there's a deeper truth," Lha-Mi said.

"You don't want people supporting his cause," Lanoree said. "If news of what he plans spreads, many more might attempt to initiate the gate. More devices. More dark matter."

Lha-Mi smiled and nodded. "You are perceptive and wise, Lanoree. The threat is severe. We are relying on you."

"Flattery, Master?" Lanoree said, her voice lighter. A ripple of laughter passed around the assembled Je'daii Masters.

"Honesty," Lha-Mi said. He grew serious once again, and that was a shame. A smile suited him.

"As ever, I'll give everything I have," Lanoree said.

"May the Force go with you," Lha-Mi said.

Lanoree stood, bowed, and as she approached the closed door Lha-Mi opened it with a wave of his hand. She paused once before leaving, turned back.

"Master Xiang. Please relay my love to my mother and father. Tell them . . . I'll see them soon."

Xiang nodded, smiled.

As Lanoree left the room, she almost felt her little brother's hand in her own.

On her way back to her Peacemaker, a riot of emotions played across Lanoree's mind. Beneath them all was a realization that was little surprise to her—she was glad that Dal was still alive. And this was why she had been chosen for such a mission. There were her past achievements, true, and for one so young she had already served the Je'daii well. Her affinity with the Force and the Je'daii's purpose and outlook was pure. But her personal involvement might be her greatest asset.

Because she had failed to save her brother's life once, and she would not let him go again. She would do everything she could to save Dal—from danger, and from damnation—and that determination served the mission well.

But it might also compromise the assignment.

She breathed deeply and calmed herself, knowing that she would have to keep her emotions in check.

Two young Je'daii apprentices passed her by. A boy and a girl, they might well have been brother and sister, and for a fleeting moment they reminded Lanoree of her and Dal. They bowed respectfully and she nodded back, seeing the esteem in their eyes, and perhaps a touch of awe. She wore the traditional clothing of a Ranger—loose trousers and wrapped shirt, ink-silk jacket, leather boots and equipment belt—but as with her ship, she had also personalized her own appearance. The flowing red scarves were from one of the finest clothing stores on Kalimahr. The silver bangles on her left wrist bore precious stones from the deep mines of Ska Gora, a gift from the Wookiee family she'd grown close to during her time there. And her sword was carried in a leather sheath fashioned from the bright green skin of a screech lizard from one of Obri's three moons. Add these exotic adornments to her six-foot frame, startling gray eyes, and long, flowing auburn hair clasped in a dozen metal clips, and she knew she cut an imposing figure.

"Ranger," the young girl said. Lanoree paused and turned, and saw that the two children had also stopped. They were staring at her, but with a little more than fascination. They had purpose.

"Children," Lanoree said, raising an eyebrow.

The girl came forward, one hand in the pocket of her woven trousers. Lanoree sensed the Force flowing strong in them both, and there was an assuredness to their movement that made her sad. With her and Dal it had been so different. He had never understood the Force, and as they'd grown older together that confusion had turned into rejection, a growing hatred . . . and then something far worse.

"Master Dam-Powl asked that I give you this," the girl said. She held out a small message pod the size of her thumb. "She said it's for your eyes only."

A private message from Master Dam-Powl, beyond the ears and eyes of the rest of the Je'daii. This was intriguing.

Lanoree took the pod and pocketed it. "Thank you," she said. "What's your name?"

But the girl and boy hurried away toward the Peacemaker, a gentle breeze ruffling their hair. The ship's engines were already starting to cycle up.

Ironholgs stood at the base of her ship's ramp. It clicked and rattled as she approached.

"All good?" she asked absently. The droid confirmed that, yes, all was good.

Lanoree paused on the ramp and looked around. The Masters' Peacemaker and several smaller ships were being attended to, and farther afield there were only the hillsides and the ancient standing stones, placed millennia ago to honor long-forgotten gods.

The feeling of being watched came from elsewhere. The Je'daii Masters. They were waiting for her departure.

"Okay, then," Lanoree said, and she walked up the ramp into the comforting, familiar confines of her own ship.

But she was distracted. This short time on Tython, and hearing of Dal's mysterious survival, was waking troubled memories once again.